THE
ETERNAL
ONES

FORNA

THE
ETERNAL
ONES

THE GILDED ONES #3

DELACORTE PRESS

Text copyright © 2024 by Namina Forna
Jacket art copyright © 2024 by Elena Masci and Tarajosu
Map art copyright © 2020 by Robert Lazzaretti

Visit us on the Web! GetUnderlined.com

Educators and librarians, for a variety of teaching tools, visit us at RHTeachersLibrarians.com

Library of Congress Cataloging-in-Publication Data
Names: Forna, Namina, author.
Title: The eternal ones / Namina Forna.
Description: First edition. | New York : Delacorte Press, 2024. | Series: The gilded ones ; book 3 | Audience: Ages 12 and up. | Audience: Grades 10–12. | Summary: In her quest to confront the gods and save a crumbling empire, Deka must find the source of her divinity before her mortal body deteriorates, leading her and her friends to a new realm that unveils a heart-wrenching choice: become a god and lose her loved ones, or trigger the world's destruction.
Identifiers: LCCN 2023047081 (print) | LCCN 2023047082 (ebook) | ISBN 978-1-9848-4875-8 (hardcover) | ISBN 978-1-9848-4876-5 (ebook) | ISBN 978-0-593-80924-2 (int'l ed.)
Subjects: CYAC: Gods—Fiction. | Ability—Fiction. | End of the world—Fiction. | Fantasy. | LCGFT: Fantasy fiction. | Novels.
Classification: LCC PZ7.1.F6626 Et 2024 (print) | LCC PZ7.1.F6626 (ebook) | DDC [Fic]—dc23

The text of this book is set in 11-point Hoefler Txt.
Interior design by Kenneth Crossland

Printed in the United States of America
10 9 8 7 6 5 4 3 2 1
First Edition

For Suma, Sinka, Satu, and Baby Shekou.
I write so the world
is a better place for you.

◆ ◆ ◆

Golma

Northern
Provinces

Nagrabal

Gar Melanis

Irfut

Xibal

Hemaira

Western
Provinces

Southern Provinces

Hualpa

N'Oyo Mountains

Gar Monyani

Nibari Desert

OTERA

THE
ETERNAL
ONES

1

❖ ❖ ❖

The end of the world begins not with a scream but with a mist, spreading sinister tendrils on a dark, moonlit night.

Deep as I am inside Ixa's mind, I don't even notice. There's just too much to experience. I may be able to see only the faintest shades of color through my blue-scaled, feline-like companion's eyes, but even then, everything I glimpse is breathtaking. Groves of soaring silver trees sprout from pink stone hills. Scrubby purple grasses cling to their roots, tiny iridescent lizards darting across them. Glass flitters. They, like the silver trees and the purple grass, are native only to Gar Nasim, the haunting, remote island that is my current location.

Finally, after three months of running and hiding, pursuers constantly at our backs, I'm here on the island that Anok, the only goddess who's still our ally, told us to seek. The island where, she told me, I would find my way to Mother and, through her, the way to unlock my full power so I can defeat the gods.

Except there's no sign of Mother. Not even the faintest trace.

I sniff at a nearby tree, nose flaring with irritation when it immediately puffs a noxious odor in my direction. Trees and plants, they all have defenses invisible to the naked eye—after spending most of the last few weeks inside Ixa's mind, I understand that now. And these silver trees, in particular, are quick to express their displeasure.

The tree releases another puff of odor our way, and Ixa wrinkles our nose, the motion sending a tickling sensation down the rest of our body. *Stinky,* he says.

He's in here too, the shadow just behind my consciousness. I don't know how it works precisely, the way we share one body, one mind. Only that it does. And that while I'm here, I don't have to be in my own body. In the wounded, golden ruin that's all that's left of me after my confrontation with the Gilded Ones, the false goddesses I once thought were my mothers, all those weeks ago.

Britta calls it possession, what I do to Ixa. She says it's as if I'm one of the demons written about in the Infinite Wisdoms, the false holy scrolls whose corrupt teachings I once followed to the letter. But she doesn't understand. Ixa likes me here, welcomes me into his body. And I, for one, am grateful.

Whenever I'm in Ixa's body, I'm free. Free of pain. Free of the torment that plagues my every waking moment.

For the few moments or hours that I'm here, I can just be.

I lope to the next tree, nostrils already expanding to catch the scents in the air. Have to keep moving, have to keep going. This is the steepest hill in Gar Nasim, the site of the Old City. Around us rise the ruins of the long-abandoned city of rose-hued

2

stone, whose fallen buildings and the golden skeletons peeking underneath them tell a damning history. Of jatu, brothers to the immortal, gold-blooded alaki, slaughtering their sisters by the thousands in the very same city they once ruled. Of generations of deathshrieks, the monstrous-seeming creatures that are the resurrected forms of alaki, shrieking their songs of mourning to the wind.

No human would ever set foot here. No human would even dare.

But Mother has to be hiding somewhere close. Perhaps not in these ruins, precisely, but somewhere on this island nonetheless. Shadows, the onetime spies of the former emperor, Gezo, hide in abandoned places when they want to evade detection. That's what White Hands, my onetime mentor and now firmest ally, taught me.

I just have to keep—

"Deka?"

Heat sears my skin and I gasp back into my own body.

Now, Britta is crouched at eye level with me, her burly form blocking the door of the tiny house where my physical body's been hidden all day, her offending hand still on my shoulder.

"Don't touch me!" I hiss, jerking away, but that just sends my back slamming against the wall. The gold-crusted sores on my back tear open and pain explodes across my senses. I have to grit my teeth to keep from screaming.

I should be used to this by now.

In the months since my confrontation with the goddesses, when the sores first erupted across my skin, more and more of them have spread. They do so every time I use any of my abilities or move too vigorously, a constant reminder that my time is

3

limited. As White Hands has made clear to me, every moment that I don't reconnect with my kelai, which is the ancient name of the substance that gives gods their divinity, I'm closer to scattering into a thousand pieces, my body and consciousness lost forever to the universe. And once I'm gone, there'll be no one to stop the Gilded Ones or the Idugu, their male counterparts, from bleeding Otera dry in their ravenous competition for power.

When blood begins seeping down my spine along familiar trails, Britta scuttles back, blue eyes wide with horror. "Sorry, Deka!" she says. "I didn't mean to touch you. I swear I didn't."

"Of course you didn't." I can't help the bitterness that creeps into my voice.

I was away. For almost a day—one glorious, blissful day, I was away from this body. From this pain. I was free.

And now I'm back here, with Britta, who's standing there guiltily in her whole, unbroken body. Her body that heals within moments of any injury. Her body that's free of sores and wounds and scars.

Free of pain.

The anger inside me rumbles louder. I hurriedly stuff it back down. It's always there now—the anger as well as the pain. Monstrous twin serpents, slithering in the back of my mind. My new constant companions.

Even Ixa has never been so faithful.

Almost as if I summoned him, my shape-shifting companion rushes into the crumbling square surrounding the house. *Ixa here, Ixa coming,* he says, chest heaving with breathlessness, liquid black eyes wide with concern, as he threads over the broken stones and fallen statues.

4

He must have started back the moment I woke.

I place my hand on his brow, letting out a ragged sigh when I feel soothing relief flowing over me. Finally, I can breathe again.

I don't know why, but Ixa's presence is the only thing that ever makes the pain fade. When I touch him, it's as if I'm removed from my own body, even though I feel it there, dimly obeying my commands. The only thing better is when I'm in his mind, away from myself entirely. Only then am I completely free of pain, of the anger and accompanying emptiness that threatens to consume me.

I breathe again before looking down at him. *My thanks,* I say silently into his mind.

Deka welcome, Ixa replies, padding closer as I turn back to Britta.

I release another breath before I address her again. "What do you want? I was busy."

Hurt creeps into Britta's eyes, but she does her best to hide it as she announces, "White Hands has finally contacted us. She says we should search for any signals yer mother left us."

"And what do you think Ixa and I have been doing all day, running up and down the island?"

"Ye don't have to be rude, Deka." Disappointment, another expression I've seen often on Britta's face over the past few months, quickly overtakes her hurt.

Guilt swiftly rises in me at the sight.

Hard to imagine, but once upon a time, she was always smiling, always pleasant. If anyone could see the more favorable side of a situation, it was Britta. But now, her forehead is always furrowed and her blond hair hangs lankly around her face. It's as if the strain of running has sucked all the joy from her.

5

Or perhaps it's me and my anger, my continous lashing out.

I force myself to unclench my tensed muscles. "I'm not being rude. I'm merely stating facts."

"Then here's another one for ye: White Hands wants to guide us, help us be more effective."

"If she wanted us to be effective, she'd be here in person instead of merely projecting herself here," I scoff. "They all would."

Half our group left with White Hands about two months ago to travel to the Southern provinces in search of more allies for our cause. The twins Adwapa and Asha; Kweku, Adwapa's once slightly plump Southern uruni; Acalan, Belcalis's haughty and formerly pious uruni; our red-spiked deathshriek sister, Katya, and her betrothed, Rian; and even a few of the other deathshrieks still loyal to us all went. Now that all of Otera's deities—both the Gilded Ones and the Idugu—have shown their true faces, the One Kingdom is in chaos, one section of the population intent on sacrificing as many people as they can to appease the gods' hunger, the other trying their best to just survive these treacherous times.

Which is why White Hands is building an army.

While I'm here searching for Mother, the key to finding my kelai, my former mentor is halfway across the world gathering survivors. Gathering soldiers. If she can assemble enough forces, she can stop the gods, imprison them again before they consume enough sacrifices to regain their power. We can take back Otera without my ever having to need my kelai.

And given my current state, she needs to do it as quickly as possible.

Something is building in the One Kingdom, something

devastating. I can feel it in the air—a sense of foreboding—and I know I'm not the only one.

A tingle shoots down my spine. I turn to watch as White Hands coalesces in the square, her small, dark body a shimmering spectral image amid the half-broken statues that ring the center. She's using her gauntlets, the bone-white armored gloves that are the origin of her name, to project herself here.

The sight of her irritates me further. "Why even bother using the gauntlets when she can't do anything from wherever she is," I mutter sulkily. Just because I know the reason White Hands isn't here doesn't mean I have to be happy about it.

Then again, I'm rarely happy about anything these days.

"All right, stop." Britta's tone is stern now, and when I look up, her expression is laden with disapproval. "That's enough self-pity, Deka."

"I'm not—"

"Yer in pain, I know this. We all know this," she snaps. "But that doesn't mean ye get to turn into a surly bear every time someone so much as looks at ye. We're here. All of us—even Keita, who ye can barely speak to—"

She nods pointedly, and when I turn, my sweetheart's watching me from a nearby rooftop, that fire, as always, burning in his golden eyes. The moment he sees me looking, however, he turns away, a long, lean shadow in the darkness. He descends toward the rest of the group, who are now swiftly making their way toward White Hands.

Britta's not the only person I've been growly at these past few weeks.

"We're all here with ye, even if ye'd much rather snarl at us than just talk."

I sputter, "I don't—"

"No, Deka, ye let me finish." Britta steps closer, mouth set in a grim, determined line. "I know what is at stake here—we all do. More to the point, I know that yer not really angry."

I look up at her, startled, and her expression gentles. She heaves a deep sigh. "Yer sad, Deka. Yer stallin'."

I huff out a laugh. "Why? Why would I do that?"

"Because once we find yer mother, we find the way to yer kelai, an' once we do that, ye become a god. Ye leave us."

And there it is, the fear that's been haunting me all this while: Once I'm a god, I'll lose all my friends, the family I've painstakingly created over the past two years.

I'll be whole and free of pain, but I'll be alone again.

Suddenly, I can't think; I can't breathe. I have to clasp my hands to still their nervous trembling. "How did you—"

"I'm yer dearest friend, Deka. I know ye. We all do." She nudges her chin toward my friends, who are all waiting with the projected specter that is White Hands, the moon gleaming high above them.

Britta continues: "I know yer frightened, Deka, but we all are. Otera is fallin' to chaos around us—plagues, deluges, monstrosities at every turn. But that's why we have to keep movin'. Because if we, the strongest an' the fastest, are terrified, imagine wha it's like for the rest of Otera. Imagine wha it's like for the children, the girls.

"We have to keep goin', Deka, no matter the cost."

"But it's always *my* cost." The bitter words spill out of me before I can stop them. "Always, always. It's always me making sacrifices. Even now." I glare down at my wounded hands, at the golden sores crisscrossing them like lightning bolts.

"An' wha about me?" When I glance up again, hurt is shining in Britta's eyes. "Don't ye think I suffer?"

"How?" I scoff. "You're not the one in pain. You're healthy. You're still—"

"Whole?" Britta steps closer, eyes wide with pain. "How can I be whole when every step ye take makes ye flinch? When every movement makes ye gasp in agony? Do ye think I am without conscience, Deka? Do ye think I am without empathy?

"I can scarcely breathe, watching ye. All the time, I can't breathe. Ye may be the one in agony, but I am the one who watches. Have ye ever considered that—wha it feels like to be the one who can't do anythin' but watch an' hold their breath? Hope that they're there in case ye— In case ye—"

Britta stops there, unable to speak further. Her breathing is heavy now, ragged with the weight of all the things she's too devastated to say.

"My apologies," I whisper. "I didn't know."

"Of course ye didn't know. Because instead of leanin' on us, ye've turned away, become this rageful . . . shell."

"Because I *hurt,* Britta." The words rip out of me, a deep and painful admission. "I hurt all the time. Every single moment of every single day, and I don't know what to do. When I was in the cellar back in Irfut, there were moments of oblivion, at least, but this—it's unending. It's like my body is a prison, and I can't break free no matter how hard I try."

By now, Britta's eyes are welling up, and she looks horrified. "I'm so sorry, Deka. I wish I could share yer pain. I wish I could take it into myself, or better yet, heal it. But I can't. All I can do is support ye. An' push ye, because . . . yer deterioratin' . . . fast. So we have to keep pushing forward. And swiftly."

Her words are like a tremendous weight pressing down on my chest, sucking all the air out of my lungs. It's almost unbearable, their heaviness. I have no choice but to do the only thing I can to break the tension: push out my bottom lip and pout in an admirable imitation of a six-year-old about to dissolve into a tantrum. "But I don't want to," I whine.

"An' yet, ye have to." A twinkle, the first I've seen in weeks, lights Britta's eyes. She moves even closer to me—near enough to touch, but not so near that her skin accidentally brushes mine.

It's the closest we've come to embracing in nearly a month. The closest I've gotten to touching anyone that's not Ixa.

And it feels wonderful.

"Come along, ye," Britta sniffs. "We have a kelai to find."

"And a mother to reunite with." I glance at her, uncertain. "Think she'll be surprised by how I look?"

I'm still as lean and muscled as I've been the past few years, but now golden sores carve across my skin like lightning bolts.

Between them and the glowing reeds I've taken to braiding into my curly black hair, I look very different from the quiet, timid girl Mother left in Irfut.

"Well?" I prompt Britta when she doesn't reply.

"More like horrified." When I give an outraged gasp, Britta snorts. "Have ye taken a look in the river lately? Ye look like one of those broken potteries they piece back with gold."

"I always thought those were beautiful."

"Beauty is in the eye of the beholder, an' from where I'm beholdin' . . . " Britta makes a rude snorting sound.

My reply is an outraged huff. "You're supposed to be my friend."

"Friends are supposed to be truthful." Then she smiles. "An' truth is, yer actually prettier than ever . . . in a tragic, wounded sort of way. No wonder Keita's been moonin' all these days."

When I glance again at my uruni, he's reached the others, but his eyes are still burning longingly across the distance. It's all I can do not to shiver. Keita's hands may no longer be able to reach me, but his gaze very much does.

Britta humphs when she sees it. "Must want to take care of ye an' such," she mutters under her breath. "Boys tend to get like that, ye know."

"Do they now?" I ask wryly.

Britta only humphs in return.

Perhaps it's the joy of bantering with her again. Or perhaps it's that all the constant pain has dulled my senses. Either way, I don't notice the strange heat stealing across the clearing. Don't notice the unnerving stillness in the air.

Until I do. By then, it's already too late.

Not just for me but for everyone.

2

◆ ◆ ◆

The mist slithers over the broken rooftops like a silent preda-tor, ghostly tendrils slipping quietly from one building to the next. Britta and I are almost halfway across the square before I finally notice it, gathering at the very edge of the city. The only reason I do is that tingles come over me suddenly, rolling waves I feel deep in my arms and shoulders. I've felt them enough times before to know what they are: a warning. Something divine is at play. And wherever there is divinity, there is danger.

I take in the mist, my eyes narrowing. Its edges are tinged an eerie purple-black, and it seems to be . . . searching. There's a deliberateness to its movements, almost as if it's being directed toward a specific target.

My companions.

I whirl toward them only to blink, startled. Britta has nearly reached the rest of the group now, even though we were walking together just moments earlier.

How is that possible?

It's almost as if something has altered the distance between us. Propelled her closer to the others.

"Britta?" I call out, fear thumping in my chest.

There's no reply. Britta doesn't seem to notice me, much less the mist. It's like she doesn't see it at all, even though it's creeping ever closer, black tendrils growing increasingly bloated as they slither down the ancient streets.

Worse, she's not the only one who's oblivious. All my other friends are so deeply focused on whatever White Hands is saying, they don't even blink as the air slowly gets warmer and warmer, no doubt a consequence of the mist slowly rolling into the city.

Can't they see it approaching?

Can't they hear me calling to them?

"Britta!" I shout again, hurrying forward. "Keita!"

When there's still no reply, I break into a run, ignoring the pain that jolts through me with every footstep. Every nerve in my body is alive, every fiber of my being shrieking with fear. This is a divine attack. It has to be. We're here on this island, finally close to reaching Mother, and the gods, whichever group of them has sent the mist, want to stop us from doing so.

But how did they find me yet again? When I confronted the Gilded Ones, Ixa destroyed the ansetha necklace—the shackles they'd disguised as a gift, accidentally severing their hidden connection to my kelai. I also helped the others set fire to their mountain, giving the male deathshrieks who had been suffering underneath it the oblivion they'd so desperately called out for. Without their primary sources of food and power, the Gilded Ones' abilities should be limited now—as should those of the Idugu, who are tethered to them.

Given their newfound weakness, the gods shouldn't be able to see as easily across Otera as they once did, much less track me across it.

And yet, here the mist is.

"BRITTA!" I shout again, full-out sprinting now.

Sores rip open across my body, but I breathe past the pain. I have no other choice. If the gods take either Mother or my friends, Otera is lost. Because I would sacrifice anything for my family.

Anything.

A scaly shadow matches my footsteps. *Deka want ride Ixa?* Ixa asks, his eyes concerned.

Yes, I reply gratefully, hefting myself onto his back. The pain immediately fades—now a dull throbbing instead of the violent burning it just was.

Hurry, Ixa, I urge.

Ixa hurrying is my companion's grumbled reply as he runs faster and faster until we burst through the circle of statues.

The moment Ixa's claws scratch over a stone, whatever cocoon was muffling my friends' senses seems to unravel. Belcalis is the first to react, and she whips toward us, the moonlight casting a hawkish shadow over her sharp, angular face.

"Deka," she says, her usually coppery skin already grayish with worry. All the time spent running these past weeks has hollowed out Belcalis's once-proud features—carved shadows under her eyes and whittled her body to an almost feral leanness. "What is it?" she asks, running to me.

"The mist," I say, turning to the darkened city streets.

That's when I stop, alarm suddenly a deafening shriek in my mind. Between the time I last saw it and now, the mist has spread, its tendrils knitting into a web that's rapidly moving through the surrounding streets. Fear hitches my breath as I feel that strange heat rising, driving away the coolness of Gar Nasim's night air.

The mist is corralling us in. Herding my friends and I like cattle.

The gryphs—the winged desert cats my friends use as mounts—growl low in their throats and pace the edges of the square.

But when Belcalis looks in the direction I'm pointing to, a puzzled expression creeps across her face. "What mist? All I feel is this gods-blasted heat." She wipes her hands over the back of her neck, which is now glistening with sweat.

"It's there." I point, unnerved. "It's wrapping around us."

And yet, I notice, it's not moving any closer in. I squint and see that the mist has formed an almost perfect circle around the square, but it's not trying to approach us anymore.

Why?

"Wha's there? Wha's happened?" By now, Britta has noticed our discussion and is hurrying over, her blue eyes worried. Sweat drips down her forehead in little trails.

"There's some sort of mist surrounding us," Belcalis answers. "I can't see it, but Deka can."

"So it's divine—like the river of stars in the Chamber of the Goddesses." Britta immediately makes the connection, her eyes surveying the area.

"You can't see it either?" Belcalis frowns at Britta.

"No."

"You need to leave, now." This statement comes from White Hands, who has hurried over, the others behind her. There's a grim expression on her face, which, like the rest of her body, shimmers slightly at the edges—a subtle sign that she's not actually physically here.

Everything in me stills. "You know what it is."

White Hands nods.

"I've been hearing rumors of a new abomination of the gods: a shimmering mist that beguiles its victims, entices them before snatching them away."

"Let's be on our way, then," Britta says, tugging her gryph's reins, but a hand reaches out to stop her.

Lamin, the silent, gentle giant who's Asha's uruni.

He's walked over so quietly, none of us even noticed his arrival—not that we ever do. Despite his height, Lamin is the stealthiest member of the group. We suspect he was some sort of spy before he entered the Warthu Bera, the training ground where we all learned to be warriors, but no one is certain. Lamin never talks about his past.

Lamin never talks about much of anything, truth be told.

We didn't even know he was familiar with this region of the empire until he volunteered to come with us when the group was splitting into two.

"What about Deka's mother?" he asks, his reddish-brown form a towering silhouette against the darkness of the night.

My heart skips a beat as I remember: "She might be hiding somewhere near, or even inside, this city."

That's the conclusion I've reached after spending the entire day searching for her across the other end of the island. She wasn't there. Which means she must be somewhere close to here.

"But she can't see the mist!" Horror rises in me at the thought. Most people can't see the workings of the divine.

And if she blunders across its tentacles, it'll take her, and the only chance I have of finding my kelai, not to mention reuniting with my only remaining family.

I turn to regard the mist again, that fear coursing through me. It's remained exactly where it was, those tendrils gathering.

What is it waiting for?

I have no time to dwell on that. I turn to the others. "We have to signal to her. Warn her."

"But that might alert our pursuers." These grim words come from Li, Britta's usually buoyant sweetheart.

He's staring into the darkness, moonlight highlighting his pale skin and long black hair as he gives us this reminder: everywhere we go, the worshippers of both the Gilded Ones and the Idugu follow, both groups in a desperate race to capture us and hand us over to their respective gods.

I sigh. "At this point, we have no choice. It's either that or—"

"You could use your combat state," Li suggests, as if thinking out loud, but then Britta glares at him, another reminder: while I can still enter the combat state, I can't use it to do much without pain striking every part of my body, rendering it unmovable.

I'm nearly powerless now, and that's by design. One of the most horrible truths I've learned over these past few months is that my body is an arcane object that was created by the Gilded Ones for one purpose and one purpose only: to allow them to steal my power. My body was never truly mine to begin with.

By the time I fell from the cosmos to this world centuries ago in the form of the god known as the Singular, the Gilded Ones were already aware that their counterparts, the Idugu, were conspiring against them. Plotting to gain dominion over them.

So they schemed to find a way to finally and decisively win their never-ending war.

They did so by trapping a portion of my kelai in a golden seed, one that would eventually grow into a human-seeming body, given the right conditions and amount of time. One that would eventually form a small but powerful connection to the rest of my divine powers and give them a way to feed from it, take it for themselves.

But first, they needed the perfect vessel to bear their baby god, an alaki who could nurture such a creature in their womb without being destroyed by it.

They needed my mother.

Why she was that perfect alaki, I still don't know. White Hands tried planting the seed in several others over the centuries, but it never quite took.

But then Mother came around, and I was finally born. A girl who would seem human, and then alaki, so as not to arouse suspicion, all the while growing in power. All the while, reconnecting, slowly but surely, to the rest of my kelai. And all the while, allowing the Gilded Ones, my false mothers, to slowly but surely siphon off what much of it they could.

But then we had our confrontation, and Etzli forced my ansetha necklace to grow roots into my body—roots Ixa almost immediately ripped out. In doing so, he accidentally severed the tenuous thread between myself and my kelai.

As a result, this body is failing. And soon enough, it will be dead.

Without my kelai to give it power, any abilities I use outside the combat state speeds up its disintegration. Now I have mere months, perhaps even *a* month, left.

I can feel it already, the growing emptiness inside me. The emptiness that signals my diminishing life force.

Just the thought has that all-too-familiar panic surging inside my mind. Then Keita steps forward.

"What if I send fires to guide her?" he suggests.

My heart leaps. "Fires?"

"Small flames. Wisps, really." Keita sounds almost bashful. He's been training every day, and control over his ability has increased in the past few weeks—a very welcome development.

Keita's gift is related to his emotions—specifically, his anger. Any time he feels anything close to fury, heat pours out of him, so hot it sears his clothes and everything else in the vicinity. It's a massive inconvenience, given that we had to leave behind our infernal armor, the golden armor made from alaki blood we all used to wear. Although it slowed us down and was too distinctive to blend in, it was also heat proof, unlike the dark leather we wear now, which has singe marks all across it.

I watch as he gestures and flames appear in the air. One more gesture, and they're racing across the city.

"If she's anywhere nearby, this should draw her out," he says.

"Send them toward the hills. The mist isn't there," I urge, keeping my eyes on the flames as they arc through the darkness like shooting stars. Each one is a wish: *Please let them lead Mother to safety. Please let them—*

The flames sputter out.

I whirl to Keita, horrified, when they disappear completely. "What happened? Why did the flames die?"

He doesn't reply. Doesn't even seem to hear me anymore. His eyes are fixed off into the distance, a strange expression gleaming in them.

"Keita?" I ask when he remains silent. As I stare at him, confused, a pale shadow stumbles past us. Li. There's a look in his eyes, that same vacantness that Keita's have.

"Li?" It's Britta's turn to be worried.

She tries to grab him, but he wrenches his hand out of hers.

"I have to go. It's calling me." He continues walking leadenly past the broken pink statues toward the streets, where that heat is rising now. The mist is moving again, the tendrils gathering in on themselves.

I glance at Keita. Thankfully he's still standing where he was, staring off into the distance. Li, however, keeps moving.

"Li?" Britta calls. "LI!"

She tries to pull him back, but he shakes her off like she's nothing—an impressive feat, given how strong Britta is. "Li!" She turns back to me. "What's happening to him?"

The answer comes from White Hands. "It's the mist," she swiftly answers. "It's trying to take them!"

Determination grits Britta's face. "Not while I'm here!"

A tingle rushes through me as she gestures, and mounds of pink stone form over Li's feet. For a moment, I breathe, relieved: Britta has Li caught. She's used her abilities to encase his feet in stone. But then he absently gestures, and that stone crumbles into sand, allowing him to continue walking.

My eyes widen as yet more tingles rush through me. "Did he just—"

"I think it's safe to say Britta's no longer the only one who can manipulate the earth!" Belcalis shouts as she hurtles toward Li, arms outstretched.

She slams back, thrown by Li, who has shaken her off like she's a doll. My eyes round. There's only one explanation for this sudden burst of power and strength: Li is a full-fledged jatu now. A true jatu, one born of divine blood, with the strength and speed to match.

My divine blood.

I'd thought the process had stopped now that I'm severed from my kelai, but apparently, that's not the case. Or perhaps Li has had this power all along and never thought to use it.

"No, Li, we're trying to help you!" I shout, urging Ixa toward him.

He continues lurching straight for the mist, which is now pulsing rhythmically in response to his footsteps, the tendrils unfurling, with iridescent nubs stretching toward him. "I'm coming," he calls out to it, a dazed look in his eyes.

"Li, stop!" I shout, continuing onward, but the distance between us suddenly seems so far . . . so very far.

And then a dark, lean figure staggers past me.

Keita, his eyes just as dazed as Li's.

All the air rushes out of my body. "Keita, no . . . ," I whisper, but he doesn't hear me. Doesn't even see me as he stumbles for the siren call of the shimmering mist.

"So beautiful . . . ," he murmurs, golden eyes alight with flame.

And he's not alone.

Another, even taller figure shuffles after him: Lamin, his eyes just as entranced, his footsteps echoing in the darkness.

"No!" I shout again, spurring Ixa in their direction. But like before, we're too far away. Much too far. Once more, the mist is altering my perception of distance, using it to separate me from the others.

"Stop them!" I cry to Britta and Belcalis, who are much nearer. "Stop the boys!"

But it's already too late.

The moment the boys are in close proximity, the mist's tendrils lash out, each one so fast, there's no time to dodge— not that the boys would have even tried, given how enthralled they are.

"White Hands!" I shout, whirling to her. "What do I do?"

Except my former mentor suddenly seems leagues away too, her body disappearing into the darkness. By the time I turn back, the mist's tendrils are snapping again. Then they've wrapped around me, searing ropes radiating white-hot pain that I only dimly feel since I'm still firmly seated on Ixa. Within moments, my friends and I, and even the gryphs, which have remained close beside us all this while, are hurtled through the air into a sound-muffling, all-encompassing darkness, heat buffeting us from all directions, slicing through our black leather armor and skin.

"No!" I shout when Ixa is wrenched away from me by the wind.

The moment we're separated, all the pain he muted explodes across my senses. Tears burst from my eyes, but I can't feel them past the sheer, overwhelming agony. My entire body is on fire, lightning bolts sparking under my skin.

"Ixa!" I shout. "Britta! Someone! Anyone! Somebody help me!"

There's no reply, just that heat searing into me, that wind, hurling me around like a doll until, finally, there's a great whoosh-ing sound. Just like that, I'm slammed down with such force, all the air explodes from my chest, replaced instead by more agony, spreading like a wave across my body.

And then I open my eyes, and I see the twinkling of stars.

3

◆ ◆ ◆

It's still night where we are, but there are no longer any pink ruins, no longer any silver trees. Only the heat remains, pressing down on my chest like a hand, slicking my hair to my skin and my armor to my body. I look up at the stars, willing my breath to return. Every part of me is throbbing now, my body a mass so raw and inflamed, it's almost too much for me to turn my neck when I hear my friends and their gryphs falling beside me.

"Oh, me belly," Britta groans, but I still don't move to fully face her.

The pain—it rolls over me in waves. Agony, constricting me. And it's chased by another feeling, a nauseating certainty deep in my gut. There's something wrong about this place. A constant, eerie echo seems to vibrate every time I so much as breathe.

Something is lurking in the distance. Some sort of creature. But it's not ready to reveal itself yet. I have the awful feeling, however, that it will soon enough.

Then a cool, scaly body drapes over mine. Ixa's. *Ixa here,* he says reassuringly in my head as the pain recedes.

That feeling—that unnerving wrongness—remains, however.

This place is unnatural, but of course it is. It was created by gods drunk on desperation and power. I can only imagine what abominations we'll soon encounter.

Thank you, I reply quietly to Ixa before I sit up and take in my surroundings.

The first thing I see is sand, all of it as red as the blood that once proved girls' so-called purity in the ritual we all endured once we turned sixteen. Entire dunes, as far as I can see. Everywhere I look, sand, sand, and more red sand. And enclosing it all, that strange new sky, which, upon closer inspection, looks nothing like the one I just left behind. Here, the stars are nearer, nebulas spinning so close, I could reach out and touch them if I wanted. And at their edge is absolute darkness, giving the strange impression that this place is a lifeless bubble—just sand, sky, and nothing else.

Except there's life here. I still feel those creatures, their movements an ominous thrumming under my skin.

"Deka, are you all right?" Keita rushes over, only to stop just as quickly, an uncertain expression on his face.

He tentatively offers me a hand, the gesture hesitant. He knows, as well as I do, that even the slightest touch can be excruciating.

When I don't move, Keita swiftly retracts his hand and glances away, but not before I see the hurt flickering over his face. It's one thing to know that physical touch can hurt me, but another entirely to be confronted with the reality of that knowledge.

Awkwardness, that awful state I'm steadily becoming used to, sprouts its venomous thorns once more. Keita and I used to have a rhythm, a certainty in each other. Now we have lapsed silences and hands that don't touch.

I swiftly rise, trying not to wince when waves of pain roll over me. "We should scout our surroundings," I murmur, scanning the dunes, which ripple outward in an endless sea of red.

I squint, focusing on something protruding from the dune just beyond ours. It's an immediately identifiable skeleton: human from head to midsection; hands reaching out in a soundless, eternal plea; equine forelegs uplifted as if to defend their owner. Talons cap them instead of hooves. An equus, an intelligent hybrid that wanders the deserts of the Southern provinces. More skeletons like it litter the dune behind it, all of them half hidden by the sand.

Nausea churns my stomach.

"So this is where the enticed go," Britta says grimly as she comes to stand beside Keita and me. "How many otas ye wanna bet there are very few, if any, survivors of this place?"

"None," I reply. I wouldn't put any money on survivors. I turn to the others. "Feels like it's some sort of holding cell from which the gods harvest their food." Food, of course, being humans and other sentient beings.

"A hidden world dedicated to sacrifice . . ." Belcalis shakes her head, her lips curling in disgust as she mounts her white-striped gryph and rides over.

"Sacrifice is always the deepest desire and sustenance of the gods," I agree.

That's why the Idugu had those girls killed on that platform

26

in Zhúshān, the Eastern city where we first encountered the Idugu; why the Gilded Ones kept all those male deathshrieks hidden underneath their chamber.

The gods of Otera can proclaim all they want that they desire only worship, but their purest nourishment comes from the deaths of their followers.

"They're desperate now," Britta observes, shaking her head.

"Which is why they've given all what power they have to create this place," I reply, glancing around. This place—it's like being in the end times. Like experiencing what it will be to exist if my premonition about the destruction of Otera comes true.

I shudder. All I can do is hope there aren't more of these places . . .

"Not to mention all the proxies," Belcalis adds.

"Can't forget those monsters," Britta says with a sigh, referring to all the strange new creatures the gods have created to help them feed on the life force of humans. She turns to us. "I almost pity the gods, ye know. They used to be all-powerful, an' now killin' people is the only thing they can do to get their power back."

Unless, of course, they discover I'm here. That their greatest enemy, and the key to regaining their power, is already in their grasp.

Just the thought terrifies me.

When I die, my kelai will somehow seek me out once more—that's what Anok all but implied when last I spoke to her. And if there is a god or group of gods nearby, they can snatch that energy before it reaches me, steal enough raw power from it to rule Otera from now until infinity.

"All the more reason we have to get out of here," Belcalis says, urging her gryph onward. "We have to find the way back to Gar Nasim. Preferably before we're eaten by whatever monsters lurk in these sands."

"Wait, there's something here?" Britta looks startled as she surveys the area.

I sigh. Britta might be the physically strongest among us, but her senses have never been as sharply developed. They haven't needed to be. Britta hasn't experienced as much trauma, as much pain, as the rest of us. That's why she isn't as wary of her surroundings. It's both a blessing and a curse, this lack of awareness. She can't see threats coming the way Belcalis can, but she also doesn't immediately suspect that everything is a threat—a failing Belcalis and I are guilty of, as is Keita, who's held a sword since he was nine.

"Yes," I reply, glancing at her. "More proxies." Even now I can feel them, thrumming under the sand as they have been since the moment we arrived. "If they manage to eat any of us, it'll give whatever group of gods who made this little pit of monstrosities the ability to materialize."

"And capture you," Belcalis mutters.

"And capture me," I acknowledge.

"I mean, us they'll probably torture, but you . . ." Belcalis's eyes narrow as she considers the proposition.

"Best we get going, then," Li says hurriedly. He's finally shaken off his daze and made his way to Britta, as is his habit. Ever since they became sweethearts, the two can't stand to be apart for too long. "Probably in that direction."

When he points in the direction opposite of where I felt

the presence, Belcalis nods approvingly at him. "Your combat senses are expanding, I see."

"Combat senses?" Li frowns at her. "What combat senses?"

He looks bewildered, and I sigh. Perhaps he isn't as alert as I thought.

I close my eyes, already sinking into the combat state. What I'm about to try is risky, but I won't just wait helplessly and allow my companions and I to fall prey to the gods. I have to act. Holding on to this determination, I reach deep inside myself, trying to locate whatever remaining power I can. If I can just create a door out of here, we can be safe. We can find Mother, and then my kelai.

All I have to do is make a door and go through it, and though I've never done so successfully before, the knowledge is somewhere inside me.

If there's a time to unlock it, it's now. My abilities have always blossomed when I needed them most.

But even as I breathe in, the pain begins surging, an upwelling of agony that rises from the depths of my belly. It crashes over me, my entire body jolting under the force. Even Ixa's presence isn't enough to absorb it completely.

Deka all right? he asks, alarmed.

It takes me some time to reply, I'm so busy shaking.

Fine, I finally manage, my teeth clattering. *I'm fine.*

There are now three jagged lines of sores up and down my back, lightning bolts of pain digging their way deeper into my muscles. They'll join the rest of my wounds, become part of the broken pottery that is my skin.

I slump against Ixa, suddenly unable to remain upright.

"Deka!" Britta sounds horrified as she hurries closer. She stops just short of me to look me over. "Wha happened? I look away for one moment an' ye hurt yerself!"

"I was trying to find a way out of here," I reply, weariness already taking hold, "preferably before we all get killed."

And that's looking more and more likely than ever. Because I'm weak now. A burden. I can't do even the simplest things anymore.

The defeat must be apparent in my tone, because Britta stiffens. "Yer not gonna die, Deka," she says quietly.

"Aren't I?" I don't even bother with my usual evasions as I stare back at her.

I can already feel it, the emptiness growing in my stomach that is a direct result of my attempt to use just a small fraction of my abilities.

So much of my kelai is gone now. So much. And once it's completely finished . . .

Britta moves closer, forcing my attention back to her. She gazes into my eyes, her expression fierce. "I may not know wha we'll find here in this mockery of a prison, but I do know this: I refuse to let it defeat us. Just as I refuse to let ye sink into whatever dark place yer wantin' to sink into."

She turns back to me, her eyes determined. "We're gonna find our way out of here, Deka, an' the moment we do, we're gonna find yer mother, find yer kelai, an' make ye a god."

"But how?" My replying whisper is tinged with pain and frustration. "How do we find our way out? And even if we manage to do so, how do I become a god?" It's a question I still haven't answered, a problem I haven't even come close to solving yet.

"Do I just touch my kelai? Do I have to do a ritual? What are the basics of the process?"

"We'll figure it out, Deka."

"*How?* We're trapped, Britta. We're trapped here, and there's no way out. And I can't, I can't—" I lower my head, defeat weighing down my entire body.

"No!" Britta's sudden snarl forces my head back up. She rounds her gryph in front of me. "Ye will not fall to despair, Deka. I will not allow it!" As I stare at her, shocked, she continues, "I'm here with ye—we all are. So we're all going to find our way out of here, an' when we do, we take one step at a time, an' we figure out how to reunite ye with yer kelai an' then we make ye a god. Do ye understand, Deka? We will make ye a god!"

There's absolute belief in her eyes now, a sureness even all my uncertainties can't pierce. I let her words flow through me. Strengthen me. Finally, my spine straightens. "I understand."

"Good. Now ye remember this, Deka: No matter wha it takes, I'm not lettin' ye cross into infinity. I'm not lettin' ye die."

"I hear you," I say quietly.

"But do ye believe me?" Britta's eyes peer into mine as she waits for my answer.

I nod. "I believe you." I may not believe in myself, but I believe in her.

My words seem to satisfy her. "Good," she huffs. "Now let's find our way out of this gods-forsaken place."

She urges her gryph on, her face bright red with emotion.

I'm just about to breathe out the lump in my throat when another person falls in beside me: Keita, now on his hulking dark gray gryph.

31

I turn to him. Nod. "You heard everything."

He taps his ears. "Sharp hearing."

I'd almost forgotten about that. Almost forgotten that most of the boys now have senses as sharp as the girls'.

I keep my attention on Keita as he continues: "Also, Britta is very loud when she's emotional." He says this almost wistfully. "I'm the exact opposite."

Which, of course, is one of the main reasons for the awkwardness that's grown between us. It's not just the lack of touch; it's the lack of truths, of saying the things we need to say out loud.

Keita and I both know that sooner, rather than later, I'll be either gone completely—dead and dispersed back into the universe—if I fail at my mission or, if I succeed, transformed into a god, a being so out of reach, he and I will never be together again.

But neither of us has said it. Neither has even broached the topic.

So the silence just continues growing, a gulf we don't want to bridge.

"Except for now." I return my attention to Keita as he continues, those golden eyes shimmering in the low light. "Britta is right: We will overcome this, Deka. We will make our way out. And then you will end the gods. Of that, I have no doubt."

There's so much certainty in his eyes, my heart pounds. I'd forgotten that Keita could be like this—so firm in his convictions, he leaves no room for doubt. "My thanks," I reply.

But Keita shakes his head, the simple movement layered with a thousand meanings. "I'm always here for you, Deka. Always," he says.

Just like that, he's gone—riding to the front of the group, where Li and Belcalis are back to bickering again, as is their habit.

Ixa and I watch him go, Ixa considering, me trying to hold back the tears now stinging at the corners of my eyes.

Keita love Deka, my shape-shifting companion observes, glancing at me. *Friends all love too.*

They wouldn't be here if they didn't, I reply, thinking of how much my friends have sacrificed just to be with me. Safety. Family. The love—however conditional—of goddesses.

But I can't dwell on that, can't dwell on how much they've sacrificed—especially not now, with that thrumming growing ever louder.

I sigh. *I love them too . . . almost as much as I love you.* I pinch Ixa's scaly blue ears, attempting some small amount of levity, even in this dire situation.

I can almost feel him smiling—well, giving me the Ixa version of a smile, when he wriggles in pleasure. *Don't die, Deka,* he says simply.

I'll try not to, Ixa, I reply, and then we continue on, the thrumming rising ever more menacingly in the distance.

As it turns out, our new surroundings are even more desolate than I anticipated, those red dunes spreading out for leagues in every direction, the midnight sky pressing ominously down from above. The only things that break the monotony are the equus skeletons and the mountains jutting in the distance. Those mountains are not like any I've ever seen before. They're made of black stone, and each one curves so drastically, it resembles a crescent moon rising out of the sand. Wing flaps sound near them, the frantic flitter of thousands of tiny creatures moving in concert. I haven't yet seen any sign of them, but I know they're somewhere nearby and they must be at least partly responsible for some of the skeletons we've seen protruding from the dunes.

While most of the skeletons are halfway eaten, bones and all, many more remain whole except for missing strips of flesh.

It's those skeletons that worry me when I hear the wing flaps.

Whatever those flying creatures are, it's only a matter of

time before they make their way to us. We have to find a path out before that happens, only I have no idea where to look.

How precisely do we get out of this place?

As I survey our surroundings, tense, Britta does the same, her eyes squinted against the brightness of the stars. "There has to be an escape route," she mutters. "I mean, who would create a trap without one?"

"Literally everyone," Li replies dryly. "That is the meaning of the word *trap*."

"Speaking of which," Belcalis interjects, glancing at me, "any idea yet which group of gods is responsible for this abomination of a place?"

I shake my head. "Not the faintest."

I used to be able to distinguish which god made which creations, but that was before my body started breaking down, before any use of power led to such excruciating pain, I'd scream just thinking about it.

Britta's gaze wanders back to the sands. "There has to be a way out. There has to be."

"I'm with you there, heart of my hearts," Li agrees, using one of his annoying endearments for Britta. "I refuse to lose hope. We'll find our way out; we have to." On cue, he squeezes her shoulder reassuringly.

When she leans into it, smiling up at him, envy twinges through me. Keita and I used to be like that, always touching.

I force away the depressing thought. "I agree with you two as well," I say. "There has to be a way out. There's always a weak spot somewhere. We just have to find it."

"And fast." Keita's voice is low as he rides beside me, so I glance at him, immediately alert.

"What is it?"

"The light is fading," Lamin answers from the other side of me, his silhouette dark against the rapidly deepening twilight. "Has been ever since we got here."

Alarm trickles down my spine. It's been so bright here all this while, I forgot that it was the middle of the night. "But the stars—"

"Are growing dimmer. And there are more dark spots." Keita points upward. "Look."

I follow his finger, my alarm growing when I see he's right. The edge of the sky is dark, as before, but now there's also a tiny, almost imperceptible black spot in the middle, as if a shadow has swallowed all the stars. Those flapping sounds are concentrated at that spot. As is that thrumming. It vibrates through me—a warning.

"What happens when it gets fully dark?" I ask.

Lamin points at the next dune over, where large trails ripple across the red sand, equus skeletons in its wake. "I assume that's when whatever made those tracks emerges."

"That's what I thought." I urge Ixa on, rushing him toward the top of the dune, where Li waits. But as we approach, Li suddenly stops, his entire body stiffening.

"Uhh, everyone?" he calls. "Over there."

"Wha now?" Britta sounds irritated as she urges her gryph onward, but then she stops too, eyes focused on where Li's pointing.

The moment I catch up to them, I do the same.

A short distance from us is what looks like a plain, except it's made of the same glossy black material as the mountains. An obsidian floor almost, but one that covers leagues and leagues of sand. What's shocking, though, is the group of girls kneeling in the middle of it, robed and hooded priests at their side, all of them carrying daggers. Each of the girls is wearing a gold mask, the kind only the wives of village elders wear, except, judging from their awkwardness and the baby fat swathing their bodies, none of these girls is even old enough for the Ritual of Purity. None of these girls is even old enough to leave the children's corner of the temples.

"Those would be the sacrifices we've been expecting," Li says grimly, immediately recognizing the scene below, as we all do, from having seen it hundreds of times before.

Swords are unsheathed and war hammers hefted, my friends already preparing to do battle with the priests down on that obsidian floor. One thing we've always agreed upon is that we save any innocents along the way. Except when I peer closer, I notice what the priests are doing.

I hold up my hand. "Wait, something's strange."

I point to where the priests seem to be *handing* the girls the daggers and whispering encouraging last words to them before they themselves hurry, footsteps fumbling through the darkness, toward the series of black columns that stand, silent guardians, at the very edge of the black stone floor.

The priests are all human, I can tell that immediately. If any of them were jatu, their vision would be as sharp as ours in this low light, but every one of them stumbles about as if blind, their clumsiness exacerbated by the fact that they don't have any torches.

They don't want to disturb the creatures hiding in the sands either, that much is apparent.

The moment they reach the columns, they begin blindly

pressing the black stones, as if searching for a specific spot. It's almost amusing, watching them, except they're clearly villains: they left those girls out on that obsidian floor to die.

Britta squints. "Wha are they doin'? Why are they touchin' those things?"

My own eyes widen as I realize: "That's how they're getting out!" I hiss. "They're using those columns!"

Now Britta grins. "I knew there had to be an exit!"

As we both watch, rapt, one of the priests reaches the last column and presses something there. The moment he does so, his hand disappears, then his whole shoulder. My breath hitches. It truly is the exit.

I commit the exact location to memory as the priest then gestures to the others, who all follow him as he steps through the rift in the column, as silent as the tomb.

My group remains quiet as well—just as we have this entire time, but our efforts, as it turns out, have been in vain. I look back toward those strange mountains, where that thrumming sound is getting louder with every moment that passes. The creatures know we're here, likely felt our footsteps the moment we landed in this place. Their bodies are already uncoiling in the distance, readying themselves to hunt whatever unlucky prey has stumbled their way.

We have to hurry now.

I return my attention to the others. "I saw where they pressed the column," I say. "We take the girls, make our way out through there before those things come out of the mountains."

"Let's hurry, then." Britta grasps her war hammer as we all ride across the sand.

We've just finally crested the next dune over when the sky just to our right suddenly goes black. Terrified gasps rise from the obsidian floor, the girls swiftly huddling together, their eyes looking in the same direction that ours are. It's as if all the stars there were candles and someone just snuffed them out. The gryphs begin growling low in their throats.

I turn to my friends. "Hurry!" I urge.

Then we hear the cracking sound.

It's coming from the darkness, where one of those curved black mountains is shuddering. As I watch, unnerved, another crack sounds, this one even louder than the first. Then another sounds, and another, all in swift succession until—*boom!* A column of eerie blue light explodes into the air from the peak of the black mountain, releasing four towering black reptilian shapes, which fly in the direction of the obsidian floor and the girls waiting there in terror.

When an eerie scream splits the air, that horrible thrumming underneath it, I glance down at Ixa. *Go!* I command.

And Ixa begins running, headed straight for the girls.

As he moves, a familiar feeling slithers over me, oily yet suffocating. "The Idugu," I whisper, hoarse. If I wasn't certain before, I am now. I turn to the others. "Whatever those things are, they're connected to the Idugu."

"Which is why the mist snatched all of us boys first." Keita curses under his breath as he urges his gryph on.

The male gods have been dead set on vengeance since we escaped their temple three months ago, and Keita is the primary target of their wrath. After all, he's the one who burned their temple to dust.

"HURRY!" I shout, abandoning all pretense of quiet. "Get the girls through the columns."

Half have risen and are swiftly removing their masks, horror on their faces. But they're not what worries me. It's the other girls. They remain kneeling, lips moving in fervent prayer. One of them, in particular, a lanky adolescent with the same dusky skin and midnight-black hair as the others, seems to be intent on keeping her companions in place—even the ones who want to leave.

I sigh. There are always girls like that, girls who believe so desperately that they'll get the lives they've been promised if only they sacrifice everything that they are.

That's how those who have power retain it: by promising they'll share some of that power if a chosen few obey whatever commands they have been given.

I spur Ixa on. "We have to get them away from here!"

"Deka." This call comes from Lamin, whose eyes are busy surveying the area as he keeps pace with me. "We might not have time to rescue all of them—"

I cut him off by pointing. "Whatever those flying things are, they're proxies for the Idugu. And those girls are designated sacrifices. So if any of them die before we reach the gate—"

"The Idugu will be able to manifest here." Lamin nods his understanding, urging his gryph faster now.

I glance back at the beasts, trying to gauge how much time we have. They still haven't left the vicinity of that mountain, that strange blue light illuminating their massive leathery wings as they fly in aggressive circles around it.

"Why aren't they comin' for the girls yet?" Britta's puzzled question echoes my thoughts.

I squint at the creatures, trying to answer the question, until finally I spot the pattern. "The darkness—they're not moving past it!"

"But those stars over there are already dimming," Keita says, pointing to the area just next to the cracked-open mountain, where the stars flicker dully, as if holding on to the last of their power. It's the same with the patch of stars just in front of them.

The moment they turn black, the creatures fly toward them.

"A path!" I gasp out my horror. "The dimming stars are a path."

Even now, the creatures are winging closer and closer, slick black bodies gleaming in the darkness. That strange blue light pulses from what look like scales on their sides, as well as the single, gigantic circle that vibrates and thrums in the middle of their chests. Their hearts, no doubt. It's the only weakness I can discern. They have no eyes to gouge out, no mouths that I can see. But they must have mouths somewhere. How else to explain all those half-eaten skeletons littering the sands?

I keep my eyes trained on the creatures, marking their progress, as Ixa makes his way to the obsidian floor, where the girls are still arguing among themselves.

That is, until we emerge from the darkness.

As they stop to gape at us, I hurry Ixa over. "We have to leave. Now," I say brusquely.

But instead of rushing toward us in relief, the lanky girl I noticed earlier just looks up at me. Then she notices the boys riding beside me. She quickly lowers her gaze, her eyes fixed respectfully to the ground. I bristle with annoyance. One thing about Otera that hasn't changed: women are always desperately subservient to men, even ones they don't know.

41

No wonder so many of them are so easily taken advantage of. They've been primed their entire lives to not only tolerate abuse but to also expect it as their fate.

"Evening greetings, travelers," she says, her trembling voice the only indication of her fear. "Who might you be?"

It's ironic, actually. Even in a situation like this, she still retains her manners.

"It doesn't matter who I am," I say, urging Ixa forward once more. "What matters is we have to leave before those things come." I point at the creatures, which have now moved to the patch of darkness a few steps removed from the obsidian floor.

"What things?" another girl asks with a quiver. She appears to be the oldest—a plump, frightened little wisp of about thirteen or so.

Her large brown eyes worriedly search the distance, but it's clear they see nothing. Being human, she can't see the creatures from so far away, even though they're approaching ever nearer, that awful sound echoing from their chests.

A few minutes more and they'll reach the obsidian floor.

"Is it the wraiths?"

"Wraiths?" I echo, tension stringing my muscles tight as yet another patch of sky darkens, this one almost to the edge of the floor.

"Vale wraiths," the plump girl says. "They're the only things that live here in the shadow vales, but we haven't seen any."

"And yet you seem to be able to," says the lanky girl, her eyes narrowing. A hateful, considering expression fills them as she stares at me. "You can see the wraiths, can point them out in the darkness." She takes a step back. "And there's gold dripping from your body. . . . You're an alaki, one of those monsters." Then she looks at Ixa. Her eyes widen. "The Nuru!" she shrieks.

The word slices through me, as sharp as any blade. *Nuru.* That is the name the Gilded Ones gave me. The name they told me meant "beloved daughter." The entire time I was with them, they assured me I was their only full-blooded daughter, born when they cried tears of gold and vengeance.

But that was a lie. I was never their daughter; I was their slayer, a deity descended to this realm to end their wickedness. Except they captured me, lied to me, fed from my kelai, all the while using my power to amplify theirs. All the while pretending that they were the all-powerful gods when in fact they were leeches, sucking me dry. *Pawn.* That's what Nuru actually means.

"You're the Nuru," the girl continues accusingly. "I recognize your foul mount, the blue drakos."

Ixa sniffs, displeased by this characterization. *Rude, rude girl.*

When he bares his teeth at her, she takes an alarmed step back.

"I no longer answer to that insult," I say, fixing her with a cold glare. "I am the Angoro, slayer of the gods—that is the title I have chosen for myself."

"Angoro or Nuru, we will go nowhere with you." The lanky girl's jaw juts stubbornly, and she glares at the other girls. A stern reminder to them. "We are the chosen maidens of Gar Nasim. We will give our lives to the great god Oyomo to ensure that Otera is made whole again. We will heal what you broke, Deka

43

of Irfut, and ascend to the Blissful Lands, where we will be re-united with our families in the beyond."

She sounds so certain that she'll go to the portion of the Afterlands reserved for only the most faithful, it's like looking in a mirror at my old self. Once upon a time, I was like that: firmly sure of the infallibility of the gods.

"Oyomo is a lie," I say, abandoning all attempts at civility. "He is the creation of a vengeful group of gods called the Idugu, who aim to bleed humanity dry. The only thing you're doing by sacrificing yourself is giving those monsters your life so they can continue destroying Otera."

"You're the one who lies!" the girl spits. "You're just trying to tempt us from our path!"

The plump girl slides nervous eyes toward her. "But what if she's telling the truth, Palitz? You saw how frightened the priests were. . . ."

"You're too easily led, Nevra," the dark-haired girl hisses. "These demons will say anything."

"All right, we don't have time for this!"

As Palitz sputters, Belcalis scoops her up and plops her onto a gryph. She turns to my other friends. "Get the girls. Preferably before we all get eaten."

"Ye heard her!" Britta grabs two more girls as they run for Palitz, then holds them tight as they kick and scream against her before going for two more. "Careful now," she tuts. "Don't want me to accidentally crush ye." She gives them a warning squeeze.

That's enough to stop them from struggling any further, and just in time.

44

As my friends round up the protesting girls, the other girls hurriedly falling into line, a deep roar sounds, followed by darkness. The stars above us have died, snuffed out by an invisible hand. We all freeze where we are, glancing at each other.

And then the first vale wraith flies overhead.

5

◆ ◆ ◆

The vale wraith smells sickly sweet. It's the first thing I notice when it lands, its colossal body buckling the floor underneath it. That musky-sweet scent suffocates the air, a vile flower on the verge of rotting. It mixes with the acrid odor of Keita's flames. He's sent several floating into the air above us so everyone can see what's happening. Now that it's a combat situation, the girls have to be prepared to defend themselves too—even if it's just by running to safety. Nevertheless, the odor is unbearable. Just one whiff ties my stomach into knots, memories of my final night in the Chamber of the Goddesses rushing back.

The goddesses used to smell sweet like this too. Always so sickly sweet. But that was because they were using the flowers that Etzli, the deceptively innocent-seeming, motherlike goddess, created to feed on a very specific prey: the male death-shrieks they'd kept trapped underneath their chamber all those centuries. Perhaps that sweet smell is a marker for all proxies, a sign that the gods, wherever they may be right now, are readying themselves to feed.

I immediately slip into the combat state, the world falling away until all that's left is the gleaming white shadows of my friends, the girls, and the vale wraiths. I may not be able to fight like my friends. I may not even be able to fully use my abilities, like my voice. But the combat state is my truest, most natural state of being. The gods can take everything else from me, but not this.

I turn to regard the battlefield. Everyone's bodies now shimmer in front of me, their strengths and weaknesses laid bare under the power of my gaze. Especially the wraiths, the rest of which have now landed as well. I focus my eyes on them, trying to find any weaknesses, any hidden tricks. But all I see is their glowing hearts, beating in their chests.

"Any word, Deka?" Britta asks, calm as she hefts her war hammer.

She's used to my directing battles from a distance these days. And she's used to creatures like these, which is why all she feels now is anticipation. I can see it in the way her fingers thrum against the handle of her war hammer.

She's ready for battle.

She nudges the girls she was holding back toward me, and they quickly scurry over, as all the rest are doing. Given the chaos that's brewing, I'm the safest spot in the entire area.

Grow, Ixa, I silently command when they approach. He needs to be large enough to carry them all to safety.

When he obligingly kneels, his bones already lengthening, I turn back to Britta, who's still waiting. "Their hearts," I say,

47

pointing at the vale wraiths. "Aim for their hearts. And the glowing scales on their sides. That's where they're vulnerable. Just buy us time! I'll get the girls to the columns."

"Understood!" Britta says as she gestures to the others.

The floor beneath her immediately cracks, pieces of the obsidian crawling up her feet and over her armor to form a secondary skin. Britta's ability is controlling all forms of earth, and her newest trick, which she learned from Belcalis, is using what materials she can to make a secondary armor. Never again will she be caught unawares by a stray arrow to the gut, as she was when she first became an alaki. Belcalis too has covered herself in armor—hers made of her own golden blood, only, unlike infernal armor, it's still alive, still pulsing around her.

Britta and Belcalis are not the only ones shielding themselves. Li seems almost shocked as he gestures and sand swirls around him. He turns to Belcalis, exhilarated. "I'm doing it! I'm actually doing it!"

"Don't use too much energy and exhaust yourself," Belcalis cautions as she goes bounding forward. "Head in the game, Li!"

The only people who don't immediately cloak themselves in their gifts are Keita and Lamin. But Lamin doesn't seem to have a divine gift yet, and Keita's fire always simmers just under the surface, waiting to ignite. His eyes are already burning, little flickers of orange in the darkness.

Which means it's time for us to go. I call to the girls, who have not yet made their way onto Ixa. "Hurry!"

Everyone begins moving, except for Palitz, who's still staring at the wraith, despair written across her face. She may not be able to see the creature in its entirety, given the darkness, but she can see the glowing scales on its sides, the ominously slithering way they move in the gloom. Her friends have to drag her toward Ixa before she finally moves on her own. I nod, understanding: It's one thing to believe blindly in the gods. It's another to see them in the full, terrifying flesh.

As she mounts, a pair of small flames light Ixa's horns—a gift, courtesy of Keita. "My thanks!" I shout, nodding his way.

Keita nods back as he returns his attention to the nearest vale wraith, the one that's slowly muscling forward, as if it's stalking prey—which, of course, it is. Everyone here is prey to the colossal, lizard-like creature with its black skin gleaming in the darkness, that blue reverberating in its chest.

Keita beckons to it. "Come, then, wraith," he says. "Let's have at it."

But the wraith just stops where it is, and a grating sound filters into the air. I watch, puzzled, until the glowing blue in its chest suddenly snaps open, revealing a giant gaping maw of a mouth, row upon row of jagged teeth surrounding what look like . . . eyes? One pupil slides toward me and I stop, then stare back, caught. There's intelligence in that gaze. Calculation.

And then that suffocatingly oily feeling slithers over me.

"Idugu," I say, grim. "How kind of you to honor us with your presence."

"Deka of Irfut," the voices of the four male gods echo smoothly and eerily as one through that vile mouth.

Just like that, I'm back in their temple, learning how they and the Gilded Ones used to be the same entities—four gods who once descended to Otera to bring the fledgling human race peace and wisdom. That is, until they made the fateful decision to cleave themselves into two—the masculine Idugu and the feminine Gilded Ones.

Gods modeling themselves after lesser beings—especially using a flawed understanding of those beings—always ends in world-shattering consequences.

"How fortunate to find you here," the Idugu say, slithering closer, but I don't look at them as I glance down at Ixa, subtly digging my heels into his sides.

Go, I command silently, and Ixa bolts, racing across the obsidian floor.

Now that the vale wraiths are here, we have to take the long route to the monoliths, since they're blocking the direct path. I keep my attention on the wraiths the entire time, watching them for any sudden movement.

"It's almost like you wanted us to find you here in the nest of our beloved children," the Idugu sneer through the wraith's mouth.

"Children?" Disgust roils through me as I consider the vale wraiths. "These are your children?"

"The most useful of all the ones we have recently spawned," the Idugu reply with a cruel laugh. "Proxies, I believe you call them. They soothe our hunger in every province of Otera. And the moment they consume a single one of you, we will be able to materialize in this realm."

Their eyes slide toward the girls, who are holding on to Ixa for dear life behind me. "Won't you do that for us, children? Won't you sacrifice yourselves to us?"

I don't bother to glance back at the children. I can already predict their expressions: devastation, betrayal. It's not every day you see the face of your god in a monster.

I urge Ixa onward. "Faster!" I say.

This command enrages the Idugu. "Prepare, Deka of Irfut.

Your death is ours for the taking. As is your divinity." Then the wraith rears up, chest-mouth opening again.

A column of fire immediately blasts it away. Keita leads the others as they leap into the fray, swords and abilities at the ready. They've instinctively separated into pairs, two fighters to each wraith, except for Keita, who's alone. But he has his fire and is using it with abandon now, sending pillars of flame the wraith's way.

All the while, Ixa continues running, paws eating up the distance between the columns and us. One of the vale wraiths lunges at him, but he swiftly dodges, sliding sideways until he's out of reach of that snapping chest-mouth. This isn't the first time he's had to ferry a group through a deadly situation. It isn't even the first time this week. The next vale wraith that snaps at him is the one the Idugu spoke through, but Keita blasts its neck with fire before it can reach us.

"My thanks, Keita!" I shout, not that he can hear me.

He's concentrating on the battle now, all his thoughts focused and precise. All my friends are.

"Do not let them get away!" The Idugu's command ripples from vale wraith to vale wraith, but my friends are more than an even match for them.

Nevertheless, I can see the strain on Britta's body as she and Li struggle to take down a snapping vale wraith. The two may be formidable fighters, but they're starving and sleep deprived. Even the greatest champions could falter under such conditions.

"Just a few minutes more," I promise, turning to the columns.

They're just a short distance away now, but the stars are dimming ever more quickly around them. Now that the Idugu know that the vale wraiths won't defeat my friends, they're intent on awakening reinforcements: I can hear those flapping sounds growing louder in the distance.

I gesture for Nevra, the girl who seems older than the rest, to dismount the moment we stop. "The door is on that column," I say, pointing. "Take the oldest girls and find it!" Even as I tell her this, I hear a warning crack in one of the mountains and the loud flapping getting closer. "Hurry!" I shout. "There are more monstrosities on the horizon. Worse ones!"

"For Infinity's sake!" I don't know who's more shocked, me or Nevra, when she curses, then motions for the others to hurry.

Within moments, the girls have sprinted to the columns, and then a victorious shout rings out. One girl is waving her hand next to one of the columns, and it's disappearing and re-appearing. Thank Infinity for human children's sharper night-time eyesight. "The gate!" she says excitedly. "I found it!"

I immediately gesture to the other girls still on Ixa. "Go!" I tell them. To my friends, I shout, "OVER HERE! WE'VE FOUND THE GATE!"

"COMIN'!" shouts Britta.

She and Li disengage from their vale wraith, as do the others, then they all ride toward me as fast as they can.

Once I'm sure they're near enough, I urge Ixa onward. *Let's go,* I say.

Deka, Ixa replies, relieved. He doesn't like it here any more than I do.

Forward he goes, headed toward the girl, who has her hand stuck through the gate to mark its position. Suddenly a distant scream reaches me. I whirl, horrified to find Belcalis jumping from her gryph, which one of the vale wraiths has caught in its maw. Lamin effortlessly snatches her midair, and then his gryph flies toward us, as do the others.

Belcalis's gryph disappears down the vale wraith's throat, then moments later, an enraged roar sounds. Only creatures capable of worship, like humans, equus, alaki, and other such beings, can provide the sustenance the Idugu need to materialize. All others are merely meat. The vale wraith roars again, but I pay no attention to it as I turn back to the gate, through which most of the children have already fled. Only Nevra, Palitz, and the girl who found the gate remain. I motion for them to hurry just as Ixa and I near the shimmering circle of air.

"For Infinity's sake, move! We all have to get through!"

Nodding, Nevra runs through the gate, the others following her.

I turn to my friends, but Britta is already charging over on her gryph, waving me onward. "Go, Deka!" she shouts. "We're right behind ye!"

A glance confirms this before I slide through the gate with Ixa, the shimmering air adjusting effortlessly to absorb his bulk. But as the darkness wraps around us, surrounding us in muffled silence and extreme heat, Ixa turns toward me, his eyes suddenly panicked.

Deka, he says, *last girl! She didn't come through!*

I turn back, horrified, but the darkness has already swallowed me so completely, I have no visibility remaining. *What girl, Ixa?* I ask, terror piercing me. *What girl?*

Ixa doesn't reply, only lets out a long, miserable growl as the darkness spins us once more. And then I'm lost to the pain.

When I open my eyes again, I'm falling toward a grassy plain at the very edge of a cliff, a jungle stretched out below us. Ixa barely has time to grow wings before we're tumbling onto it, bodies slamming roughly against ankle-length grasses that slice my tender skin.

Nevra and the other children are scattered behind us in a wild tumble. Some are so close to the cliff that if they had landed just a few lengths to the right, they would have tumbled over the ledge.

"MOVE OUT OF THE WAY!"

I barely have time to urge Ixa aside before Britta and the others come falling through as well, the wings of their gryphs slowing their descent. The moment they land, I rush toward the children, dread rising as I swiftly count. All are accounted for. All except for one.

Groaning, Keita dismounts from his gryph and walks over to me. "It was the mouthy one," he says tiredly, shaking his head.

"The mouthy one?" Nevra glances around, panic settling into her eyes as she searches for her friend. "Palitz," she calls. "Palitz!"

Keita shakes his head. "She jumped away right before Ixa went through the gate."

"What?" Nevra blinks, her eyes devastated. "No . . . ," she whispers. "No, no, no . . ." Then she looks up at Keita, bewildered. "Why didn't you stop her? Why didn't you do anything?"

Keita wearily shakes his head again. "I'm sorry," he says softly. "Not everyone wants to be saved."

"But she was a child," I return, dismay rising inside me. How did I not notice? How did I not see her? I turn back to Keita. "Children don't know what they want."

"This one did," a voice says from behind me. Belcalis's. "You could see it in her eyes. . . ."

"Which is why we snatched her right before we went through the gate," Lamin says bluntly, tossing an enraged Palitz from his gryph.

Nevra is back on her feet in a heartbeat. "Palitz!" she gasps. "You're alive!" She runs over and embraces her friend so tightly, there's barely any air between them. Then she shakes her. "Why did you do that? Why did you do that?"

Palitz bursts into tears. "I just wanted to save everyone," she sobs. "I wanted to be of use. All I had to do was sacrifice myself." She pushes Nevra away and advances on the other girls, enraged. "That's all we had to do—sacrifice ourselves, and everyone else would be saved. Our entire village. The gods would grant us peace in the Blissful Lands, and everything would be healed. Otera would be whole again."

Nevra shakes her head at her. "You saw those things, Palitz. Those weren't gods; those were demons."

"But the priests promised." Her friend's reply is a broken whisper. "They promised me. They said if I was faithful, everyone would be safe."

Her words are almost identical to the lies I was fed once my blood ran gold. I turn to Britta, who's shaking her head sadly.

Beside her, Belcalis is grim. "It never ends," she says with a sigh. "Every time we try to beat them, they create a new lie."

"And they always tell the girls to sacrifice themselves for it," I say, saddened.

I'm so tired now, so overwhelmed, I don't even notice the tingles prickling across my shoulders. The tingles that mark the arrival of a descendant of the gods. By the time I turn in the direction they're coming from, a sinister flapping is sounding, as if some great winged creature is rising into the air.

"That is the way of the male gods," an unnervingly low voice says.

Everything inside me goes cold. There, just beyond the cliff, is a familiar winged figure—one I was certain I killed just three months ago.

"Melanis," I say, grim.

The last time I saw Melanis, she was falling into the abyss underneath the Temple of the Gilded Ones, her legendary glow overshadowed by the fires exploding around her, her gold-tipped wings broken and torn. She was defeated, utterly and completely.

That was then.

Now, Melanis is suddenly here, and she's changed so drastically, she barely looks like the glowing, beautiful alaki I once knew. Her wings, once lush with pure white feathers tipped with gold, are now leathery, bat-like monstrosities. Her skin has paled from a healthy golden brown to a sickly whitish-gray that evokes dark, musky places—places like caverns and tunnels and all the other hidden realms where light has lost its way. Most alarming of all are her eyes, once a warm, welcoming brown but now almost completely white, except for the tiny black pinpricks of her pupils.

Melanis the Light is gone, and in her place is a frightening creature I scarcely recognize, a monstrosity of the gods that's not quite an alaki and not quite a deathshriek but something squarely in between. It's the same with the twenty or so women following her, who surround the cliff completely, their wings flapping in unison in the warm, dark night. Once, I would have called them Firstborn alaki, the ancient daughters of the Gilded Ones, but they're all as wizened as Melanis now, their leathery, gaunt bodies bleached of color. Their eyes have turned white as well, and some of them have transformed even further: noses so completely flattened, they're barely slits; ears enlarged and pointed at the tips.

Hunters, I name them immediately.

High-pitched shrieks echo between them, a sound similar to those of deathshrieks, except it's higher, almost inaudible at times.

As the children scuttle together, trying to find safety in numbers, I remain where I am, mentally preparing for battle once again.

"Deka," Melanis calls out in that unnerving voice, which somehow manages to be both low and high-pitched at the same time. "How fortunate I am to find you here today."

"*Fortunate?*" I huff out a bitter laugh. "That's not a word I'd ever use with you. Especially not now. *Corrupted,* perhaps. *Evil?* Certainly. But *fortunate* . . . ?" I tsk, all the while glancing to my side, where both Belcalis and Keita remain, their eyes watchful.

Be ready to move, I tell them silently.

Neither makes an overt response, but I can see Keita's eyes, as well as Belcalis's, surveying the cliff, searching out any escape routes, any weaknesses. They're the other tacticians in our group, always searching for the best way to approach a battle. If I don't find something, they will. I just have to have faith in them. In us.

Melanis doesn't seem to notice our silent exchange, or perhaps she's just pretending not to. Either way, she flaps closer, seeming amused. "There's that spirit I so enjoyed from you, Nuru."

I stiffen. Twice in one day now, I've been assaulted by that word.

I heft my atikas, breathing when I feel the long swords' reassuring weight in my palms. "If you value your life, you will never again call me that."

"If I value my life?" Melanis laughs as she slowly lands on the grass. "How presumptuous you are, Bringer of Chaos." She leans conspiratorially closer. "Did you know that's what the humans are calling you now, the Bringer of Chaos? They blame you for everything that's happening. Well, they blame the gods as well, but mainly you."

When she nears me, her gait lurching and unsteady, my eyes dart to her legs, then back up. Melanis's legs are now strangely bowed, and her toes, which are now exposed since she no longer wears the golden sandals she once used to, are more like claws.

"You've changed," I observe dryly.

"This from the girl who looks like a poorly pieced-together mosaic."

"I'm told that's beautiful in some cultures."

"Deka," Britta whispers from beside me—a warning. Melanis is too close now. She'll be within striking distance soon.

The winged Firstborn's eyes snap toward her. "You will shut

your mouth, Britta of Golma, else I will slice your lips from your face and hand them to you while your skull still bleeds."

Britta takes a step back, intimidated despite herself. Even when Melanis was beautiful, she was frightening, but now, a strange, evil sort of frenzy animates her every movement.

I breathe, trying to still my racing thoughts, trying to get myself to a place of calm. *Think, Deka, think,* I command myself.

I glance at Belcalis and Keita, but both shake their heads: they have nothing yet. No way for us to escape this cliff, much less Melanis and her minions, who are all still circling.

"There's no way out, Deka," the Firstborn confirms, wagging a bony, claw-tipped finger at me when I glance back at her. "I know you're trying to find one, but there is none. My hunters are spread out all across the jungle. Listen." She opens her mouth as if to shriek, except no sound comes out.

A tingle rushes over me, one that's amplified when shrieks suddenly ring out from the trees behind us. The muscles in my body string even tighter: Melanis is now capable of making sounds inaudible to even alaki ears. I absorb this information swiftly as I return my attention to her.

"There are more of us hidden in the trees beneath this cliff," she explains. "You're surrounded, as are the humans." She smirks pointedly at the children, who hurriedly step back, frightened, at the sight of her new needle-sharp white teeth. "Delightful little sacrifices, all of you," she finishes.

The children shrink even closer together, huddling at the edge of the trees now.

Satisfied, Melanis turns back to me and my friends. "I'd rather not kill them just yet, but understand this, Deka: all you have to do is make one false move, and they all die. And as for you . . ." Her milky-white eyes gleam eerily in the moonlight as she says this.

I shudder.

One or more of the Gilded Ones is watching me through them. I can feel it, a frenetic energy in the air. Melanis has always been their preferred instrument for spying.

"You," the Firstborn continues, her voice layered with the power of the goddesses, "I will bring back to the mothers, so that they can drain your kelai one drop at a time."

By now my heart is pounding so hard, it's like a drum in my chest. I force myself to meet her gaze. "And how do they intend to do that?" I ask—a desperate attempt to buy more time. I'm completely out of escape ideas, but Belcalis and Keita are still there, still thinking. . . . "I'm not connected to my kelai anymore. I'm just a shell now, an empty vessel."

"Stalling for time, Deka?" The goddesses immediately see through my ruse. They tsk. "Must be the children's presence. Humans always do that—make you forget yourself."

"Is that what happened to you lot? Forgot everything you are as you transformed into hateful caricatures of yourselves?" I reply, my eyes surreptitiously sliding to the others. *Get ready,* I say silently. Then I turn back to Melanis and the goddesses, my body already slipping into the combat state. "Don't worry, I'll be sure to remind you of just who you are and where you belong."

"And how will you do that?"

My thighs squeeze Ixa's midsection in response. *All right, Ixa, let's go—*

All I hear is a flapping sound, then Melanis is on me, her clawed hands ripping brutally into my throat. Gold pours out— so much of it, it splashes all over me and Ixa, turning everything slick and liquid. I can't breathe now, can't even scream, there's so much of it. My throat is on fire, every movement I make searing the burning deeper into me.

The more desperately I try to pull away, the deeper Melanis's claws go. The aura of power has disappeared from her, the goddesses having retreated so she can fight me with all her raw ferocity. "You won't die from this, Deka," she snarls. "Not quite yet. There's life in you still."

Ixa wriggles out from under me to snap at her, his teeth biting through her arm, but she hurls him away with such force, he smashes into a nearby tree with an audible crack.

The moment he's gone, pain slams into me like a hammer, all the injuries I've acquired bearing down on me with full force. I'm in so much agony now, everything is a blur. Distantly, I hear screams, the sound of fighting, but I can't move, can't even so much as turn my neck, which is still bleeding profusely.

All the while, Melanis flaps over me, her face contorted in a mask of fury.

"Do not play games with me, Nuru," she hisses. "I know everything about you, pawn to the goddesses. Everything that the mothers know, I know. Even the fact that you and that beast are forever conniving with each other."

Her words no longer reach me.

I've passed to the other side of pain now, a place where everything is just instinct and sheer, desperate survival. Somehow, I manage to grasp one of my atikas, but when I stab up, Melanis is prepared, the clawed tips of her wings snapping together to protect her vulnerable belly. My sword clangs against them and she flaps them back open, sending it flying. More pain jolts through my arms. More wounds open, gold already welling there. I gurgle, trying to buck her off me, but she holds fast, claws digging in.

Until a massive blue body rams into her.

As she goes flying back, Ixa takes advantage of her momentary shock to roll himself in my blood, his wounds healing the moment it touches them. My blood heals Ixa's wounds the same way his touch makes my pain go away. It's part of how he and I are mystically intertwined, although I still don't know the true reason for it. All the explanations the Gilded Ones gave me were lies.

Melanis comes flying back, and I can only watch, body shuddering as she picks Ixa up and hurls him away from her before rushing me again.

She snatches me by the throat once more, those white eyes blazing with fury. "This is not the same match it was three months ago, Nuru," she roars as she launches into the air with me. The other hunters immediately join her, their bodies circling her like a malevolent cloud, their shrieks piercing into my ears.

Then a column of fire blasts through them. Keita is trying to clear the space around us, but it's too late now—much too late. . . . Melanis has me in her grasp, and we're so high up in the air, a blistering wind is rushing past my ears.

All the while, Melanis glares down at me, her eyes white with malice. "I'm stronger now," she says. "Invincible. And you are weaker. Broken." She pulls me up close, so close, we're almost nose to nose. "You threw me into the abyss once," she snarls. "Hurled me down but didn't finish me. Now I will return the favor."

"What about the mothers?" I manage to ask past the blood gurgling in my throat. "I thought you were bringing me to them."

"The mothers can wait. After all, it will take much more than this to kill you."

She unclasps her fingers.

I drop so abruptly, I can't even scream. All I can do is tense my body. Rage against the unfairness of it. After everything I've done, all the battles and trials I've endured, this is how I'm defeated? By being thrown to the ground by the ancient horror who once called herself my sister? Fury is the endless scream in the back of my torn-out throat. It carries on and on until finally, I land.

Only, I'm not shattered. My bones aren't broken by the ground. More to the point, I'm not even on it. I'm an inch above, floating on what appears to be a cushion of air.

Beneath me now are the remnants of a stone ruin similar to what we left behind in the abandoned city, except instead of pink, this stone is black, rainbow lights shimmering in its depths. As I weakly push off it, attempting to stand, a tingle races through me. A very familiar one. Divine energy.

Whatever caught me—prevented me from breaking . . . it was the work of the gods.

But it doesn't feel like the Gilded Ones or the Idugu. There's something strange about it, something . . . *new*.

And when I stagger up, still in a stupor, I'm startled to see more of that rainbow-tinted black stone is somehow rapidly growing, building itself around me, a temple rising from the ruins.

"Treachery!" Melanis shrieks as she descends, the temple taking shape around her as well. "There is treachery at work here!" She points down at me and my companions. "End them!" she commands her hunters.

They swoop down toward us, those white eyes gleaming malevolently in the dark.

But as they near, claws extended, another tingle races through me, this one almost immediately followed by a low whoosh. Out of the corner of my eye, I see the outline of a gigantic war hammer swinging; that's all I glimpse before Melanis's hunters are suddenly flying backward. I watch, awed, as their bodies crash into the trees and then past them to the forest beyond. Melanis herself is blasted so far into the darkness, I can't even sense her anymore, only hear the impact as she hurtles across the forest.

Yet my friends and I are strangely unscathed. Untouched by whatever it was that attacked Melanis and her hunters.

We all look at each other in shock. Then a voice booms through the air.

"Bow your heads, mortals!" it commands, shattering the stunned silence. "Bala arrives."

A massive person in a suit of armor made completely of that black rainbow stone plummets to the temple floor, their landing so powerful, the newly built temple floor shakes.

And yet, it does not give way.

Instead, the black stone reaches up to create a platform to hold them, the person contained in that strange suit of armor. The person who is a colossus. That's the first word that comes to mind when I see our new rescuer, who is at least twice as tall as Lamin, the tallest person here, and so burly, even Britta's muscles seem inferior by comparison. Even stranger, they almost seem like part of the temple that now encloses us. The rainbow-tinted black stone that makes up their armor is the same that adorns the sprawling, triangular structure that has somehow built itself around my entire group and the surrounding trees in the space of minutes.

I'm so stunned, I can only ask one question. "Who are you?"

That's all I manage before pain explodes all over my body, all my injuries returning to the forefront now that I'm no longer in active danger.

Deka! Ixa gasps, running over as I fall to my knees, my entire body trembling.

I've been so caught up in the shock of what just happened, I forgot how injured I was, how much blood I've lost. And now, I'm paying for it.

Ixa swiftly wraps his body around me, chasing the pain away, but it doesn't matter—I'm still growing colder, still gurgling for air. My extremities have all turned numb, a warning. If I lose any more blood, I will die.

I watch distantly as Britta and the others rush over, the armored stranger forgotten. "Wha do we do?" she gasps when she kneels beside me. "She's still bleedin'!"

"Move aside," Keita says, hurriedly wrapping a cloth around my neck. "Deka, hold on," he says, pressing down. "Just hold on!"

But I'm slipping away, the pain receding as a strange peacefulness pervades me. A stillness. The stars are so bright, so very bright. . . . And the night feels wonderful, everything in harmony, everything connected. I could just slip into it, just disappear forever.

But then a rhythmic thumping returns my attention to the present. Our rescuer is walking over to me.

"Deka of Irfut?" they ask in that booming yet strangely indeterminate voice. When I don't reply, they sigh in a distinctly impatient way. "Well, this is untenable." They extend an armored hand toward me and then close their eyes, mumbling a few words under their breath in a language I cannot understand. "May the blessings of Entimon fall upon you, child of Otera," they finish in Hemairan, the language of the capital, and then they gesture over me.

My entire body jolts as a strange warmth sears through it. Then my wounded skin begins knitting itself together—and not just my new wounds either. All my sores are swiftly stitching together as if they were never there. In mere moments, my body is completely smooth, as unblemished as it was before the first sore erupted on my skin.

Everything is as it was before, everything except the hollowness. That I still feel deep inside me, only it's muted now that my body's whole again.

It's like whatever timekeeper is in charge of my body has started again, added more time to the balance.

"Deka, you're healed!" When Keita kneels before me, his eyes round with shock, I immediately enfold him in my arms. For a moment, he's completely still. Then he embraces me as well. I gasp, tears stinging my eyes. His touch is warm . . . and painless.

"I can touch you," I whisper. "You can touch me!"

I squeeze tighter, trying to embrace him even more, but then the blood rushes from my head. I sway, lean against him to prevent myself from falling. As I do so, I catch a whiff of his scent, that wonderful tang of fire and steel.

Then a dry humph sounds across from me. "Healing doesn't reverse blood loss," my rescuer explains dryly when I look up at them, bright green eyes rolling from behind their helmet. The sight jolts me. Whoever my rescuer is, their eyes seem unnaturally large, as if they go on forever.

They're certainly not human, or anything close to it; if I wasn't certain of that before, I am now.

"You'll need to get some food in you, Angoro, preferably swiftly or you'll swoon again," they continue as I gape at them.

"Here." Britta all but shoves a piece of jerky into my hand.

I snatch hers, elated to feel its calloused roughness once more.

All the while, I continue embracing Keita with my other hand, while he squeezes me so hard, I feel slightly faint. "Careful, careful," I say. "This is temporary. I haven't reconnected to my kelai."

"Oh." Keita pulls back. But then he stares down at me, uncertainty shining in his eyes. The uncertainty that, I know, is a silent plea for permission.

But he should know better than to ask for permission right now. Not when I'm looking at him the way I am in this moment.

"Just hurry and kiss me," I urge, impatient.

He grins as he swiftly does so, the warmth of his lips so wonderful as they move over mine, my knees wobble from the sheer joy of it. I wrap my hands around his neck, squeezing him tighter against me.

"Deka," I hear him breathing against my lips. Not a protest, but a plea to continue.

"Ahem! AHEM!" Keita and I reluctantly separate as my rescuer clears their throat. "If you're quite done pawing each other . . ."

I sigh, reluctantly untangling myself from Keita. I'm not

concerned our rescuer will attack us. If they wanted to do that, they would have done so already. "We are," I say finally, glaring at our interrupter. "But who are you? You never said."

"More to the point, how do you have the power to heal her?" Keita subtly places his body in front of mine.

If there's one thing we've all learned, it's to be suspicious of anyone displaying new, terrifying abilities. And this person, whoever they are, has those in the multitudes.

"*I* don't have the power," my rescuer sniffs, their voice abruptly changing. Suddenly, it's not the thunderous boom of a mighty warrior but a more youthful high pitch, like that of the girls we just rescued, who are still huddled in a corner under Li's and Belcalis's watchful eyes.

"Entimon, god of healing, does," they continue. "They lent it to me, even though I am not their godsworn, but Bala's."

"Entimon, god of healing? Godsworn?" I echo. Every one of my senses is on the alert now. I've never heard of a god named Entimon, much less a godsworn, whatever that is. Who is this person, this . . . girl? And why is she speaking of a deity I've never heard of before? "Who are you?" I ask again. "Why did you heal me?"

"You are Deka of Irfut, correct?" When I warily nod, she walks closer, imperiously demands: "Present the key as proof."

"The key? What key?"

When I still don't move, she growls under her breath. "The key, Deka—the one your mother gave you."

My heart leaps into my throat. "My mother? You were sent by Mother?"

"Of course I was," the girl huffs, annoyed now. "I've been waiting for a month now. All you had to do was present the key and it would have summoned me. Thank the gods I heard your fighting, or I never would have found you in time. Then Umu would have had my head."

Umu. Everything in me stills. That's Mother's name, the name only her dearest friends and family know.

I swiftly fumble under my armor, taking out the necklace that's been hidden here all this while, the one Mother gave me all those years ago. It's a tiny gold chain, the orb dangling from it engraved with an eclipsed sun whose rays have been curved into wickedly sharp daggers. An umbra, the symbol of the Shadows, the secretive group of assassins to which both Mother and White Hands once belonged.

"You mean this?" I say, raising it. The moment it catches the moonlight, a beam of light erupts from it, one that swiftly splinters into a rainbow. Shock erupts from me in a gasp. "What is that?"

"The signal I've been waiting for," the girl says with a huff. "A month spent waiting in this uncivilized realm. An entire *month*, and all you had to do was expose it to the light!"

By now, my friends and I are all looking at each other. This was it? The way we summoned Mother? All this time spent looking and we could have just done this?

The irony is almost too much to bear, so I turn back to the girl. "Who are you?" I ask once more.

To my surprise, the armored girl kneels begrudgingly, then says: "Most honorable greetings, Angoro Deka of Otera. I am Myter, godsworn of Bala, deity of the pathways. The gods of Maiwuri humbly await your presence. As does your mother."

7

❖ ❖ ❖

"Deity?"

That's the only word I can somehow form after the girl's stunning announcement.

The entire cliff is silent now, everyone just staring at each other, bewildered, as am I. Myter just proclaimed herself a godsworn—whatever that is—of a god I've never heard of. And considering that Otera has only eight gods—four Gilded Ones and four Idugu—that's impossible. There are no other gods in the One Kingdom, no other creatures that would even dare to consider themselves deities. I would think Myter mad except for the things I've just seen—the way she easily defeated Melanis and her hunters, the temple now surrounding us, even the fact that she knew Mother's real name.

And then there was that strange tingling I felt, the one so very different from those I've felt before. Not to mention the fact that she healed me, that all my senses have returned, sharper than ever. In fact, except for the hollowness inside signaling my

71

diminished life force and the pounding headache that must be a side effect of all the blood I've lost, I'm whole and hardy again, something I didn't think possible.

As much as my entire being wants to discount what Myter said, I can't. She's unlike anyone I've encountered before. If there's one thing I've learned over the years, it's that creatures like her don't just appear out of the ether. There has to be at least a kernel of truth to what she's saying. Either that or she's a very convincing liar. After all, I have been fooled before. Many, many times before. Myter could very well have access to arcane objects powerful enough to heal my body and let her read my mind at the same time.

I glance suspiciously at her armor and hammer as I walk closer to her. "Did you say a *deity*? Of the *pathways*?" I ask. "And what exactly are pathways?"

"And Maiwuri?" Belcalis adds, her expression blank the way it always is when she's faced with an unknown enemy. "You did say something about the *gods* of a Maiwuri."

"Never heard of a Maiwuri," Britta mutters.

Of our entire group, only Lamin looks unsurprised, but then his expression is always stoic, never even a hint of emotion breaking through.

Myter glances from me to my friends, blithely unconcerned. At least, that's what I assume, since I can still only see her eyes. "Indeed," she says finally. "The entire pantheon awaits."

Just like that, Li has had enough. "All right, what is this?" he demands. "Is this some kind of trick? Are you a creature the Idugu sent?"

"If I was, do you think I would identify myself as such?"

Li blinks as he considers this. "Well, no, but it never hurts to ask," he mutters.

Myter just stares at him. Then she sighs. "This is infuriating. And pointless. Come, Deka." She turns to me. "Your mother waits."

"I just have a few more questions," I reply. "You said 'gods,' plural, of Maiwuri?"

"Indeed."

"Exactly how many gods are we talking about?"

Myter seems to think for a moment, then she shrugs. "The Maiwurian pantheon is vast compared to Otera's. Eighty gods, five new ones waiting to emerge."

"Eighty?" Keita repeats, stunned.

"Five more waiting to emerge, so eighty-five demons . . . ," Belcalis whispers, as if trying to reconcile herself to the thought.

Myter's head swivels in Belcalis's direction. "I can hear you, you know," she sniffs. Then she turns to me. "You may not believe me at this moment, but I vow to you, Deka, that Maiwuri and its gods are no threat to you and yours. In fact, we are your firmest allies against the Oteran scourge. Consider my defense of you against those . . . creatures," she says, referring to Melanis and her hunters. "That and my healing your wounds were peace offerings. A demonstration of goodwill from Maiwuri to you.

"Now then," she continues decisively, "will you come or not? I can't remain here much longer. My presence has upset the balance of things."

"But go with you where?" My eyebrows furrow. "And what balance?"

"Did you not hear me the first time?" Myter is distinctly

annoyed now. "To Maiwuri. To where the gods and your mother await. And as for the balance of which I spoke, it is the one that exists between the pantheon there and the ones here. There are rules to be observed, consequences if any are broken."

"But where is Maiwuri?" Keita insists, even as his hands tighten on his atikas. He's still deeply suspicious, as are Britta and Li. "I've never heard of it."

"Me neither," Belcalis seconds, her expression grim.

"Of course you wouldn't have." Myter huffs out a breath. "The Oteran gods, if you can still call them that, have intentionally rendered you all ignorant." She shakes her head as she turns to me. "I believe you still call it the Unknown Lands."

"The continents that lie south of the Southern provinces—those Unknown Lands?" Li's skepticism has returned. "The place where there's untold wealth and glory if only you can reach it? Those Unknown Lands?"

"Indeed." Myter inclines her head.

"No one who's gone there has ever returned," I say dryly, thinking of the hosts of stories devoted to the famous explorers who tried and were never seen again.

"And yet here I am, a creature who's certainly neither human nor alaki, responding to the key on the necklace your mother left you. Your mother, who is the very reason you're here on this island in the first place. Again," Myter prompts in a long-suffering tone, "shall we go, or do you want to die here on some unknown, abandoned cliff so that the so-called gods of Otera can feast like vultures on what remains of your kelai?"

As I remain quiet, still thinking, I hear a hesitant whisper: "What about us?"

To my surprise, Nevra, who's been huddled in a corner of

74

the temple this entire time, is now staring at Myter, as are all the other children. "What happens to us?" the girl asks in that small, uncertain voice.

Myter turns to her and sighs. "I'll give you two choices: I can take just you and your friends back to Maiwuri with us, or I can take all of you and your parents as well."

Beside Nevra, Palitz, eyes wide, asks, "So you mean we can't—"

"After what you've seen, I can't let you return to your villages," Myter says, shaking her head, "and even if I could, I doubt you'd be safe."

When I step forward, alarmed at this declaration, Myter lifts a hand before turning back to the children. "Don't worry, you'll be welcome in Maiwuri. More welcome than you are here."

"And you won't hurt them?" I slip into the combat state as I ask Myter this question, paying close attention to the sound of her heartbeat, since I somehow can't see any bit of her body under the armor she's wearing. Something about it interferes with the combat state, prevents me from seeing the full truth that is Myter. All I can do is listen.

"Of course not!" Myter's heart—well, *hearts*—don't skip a beat, much less hasten the way I've learned all liars' hearts do, as she says this.

"Why?" I ignore the fact that she has two hearts as I walk closer to her, head cocked in curiosity. "Why would you do that for children you don't know?"

Myter considers Nevra and the others before she turns back to me. "Because they are children," she says simply. "Children don't deserve to be caught in the wars of the gods. I certainly didn't."

75

There's a mournfulness in her voice now, a depth of emotion that tells me that no matter her appearance, no matter what her voice sounds like, Myter is certainly not a child, and likely hasn't been one for a very long time.

She turns back to Nevra: "Well, what is your choice?"

Nevra thinks. Finally, she says, "I don't know about the others, but I'd like my parents to go with you, please."

"Mine too." To my surprise, this response comes from Palitz, her voice small.

Then another girl: "Is there space for my family also?"

"And mine?"

Before long, the entire group is gathered behind Myter, who nods and kneels in front of the children. "Of course there is. All are welcome in Maiwuri. Lord Bala creates pathways for all." She turns and points.

My eyes widen.

A man has appeared in the very center of the temple, his body seeming to coalesce out of the shadows. It floats a little distance off the ground, his robes trailing beneath him. Almost immediately, I know he's a god. I can feel the power emanating from deep inside him, even though at first he looks very modest, perhaps even plain. His skin is as midnight dark as Anok's, but if you glance at him at just the right angle, rainbows seem to glisten just under it.

Pathways. The word emerges, unsolicited, deep inside my mind.

Those rainbows thread through his black hair, which is twisted into a thousand coils so long, they nearly brush the hems of his robes. They seem snakelike almost, those coils, especially the way they move and undulate, like separate appendages, fanning out behind Bala. I'm not frightened of them, just as I'm not frightened of Bala himself, whose brown eyes radiate a deep kindness from underneath his slight, almost mournful brows.

So this is the god of the pathways.

It's strange how easily I accept it, but I do. It's undeniable, the divinity that cloaks him. But the Gilded Ones and the Idugu were also cloaked in divinity. And they were all monsters.

Beside me, Britta gapes. "Deka, is that—"

"Yes," I say with a nod. That is undoubtedly a god.

Even if it weren't for the power coming off him, I can feel the infinity in the pathways that tangle through his hair, moving in tandem around him, speaking in a whispering language all their own.

We mean you no harm, the pathways seem to say. *Come with us and all will be well. We promise you will be safe.*

This message is, apparently, as much for Nevra and her friends as it is for me, because the children all begin slowly, reverently walking over to Bala, who opens his arms in welcome. As I watch, fascinated but uneasy, the god's coils reach out to touch Nevra. Just like that, she's sucked into thin air, her body disappearing as if she was never here.

I take a step forward, alarmed, but Myter swiftly shakes her head.

"My Lord Bala will personally take her to her destination," the towering girl intones, her voice sounding more respectful than it has since we've met her. "He will take them all to their destinations."

"And he would not harm them?" Suspicion tinges my voice.

"My Lord Bala would never harm a child! Never!" There's such conviction in Myter's voice, some of my tension disappears. "He will ensure they are all safe, this he vows to you."

When I nod, appeased, Bala holds out his arms again, and the children resume walking over to him. Once the last of them is gone, Myter turns to me. "Now it's your turn. Do you choose to go?"

An answer in the affirmative immediately surges inside me, but I hastily tamp it down. This all feels too easy. "Why?" I ask, my eyes squarely on Bala. "Why do you want me to go? What exactly do the gods of Maiwuri want with me?"

"They want to aid you, of course," Myter answers, as if her words are common sense. "You are the Angoro, the Singular, who descended to kill the Oteran gods. The gods of Maiwuri wish to aid you in this regard."

"Aid her?" This disdainful reply comes from Belcalis, echoing my thoughts. "They are gods, are they not? An entire pantheon of eighty or so, you just said. Why do they not just end the Gilded Ones and the Idugu themselves?"

"Because they do not know the true names of the Oterans." Myter is the one who speaks, but there is a reverberance to her voice now, one I can almost feel coming from Bala. It seems that he uses her to speak, just as the Gilded Ones did Melanis.

Which makes sense, of a sort. In the earlier days of Otera, the voices of the gods would drive their worshippers mad.

Perhaps Bala has so much power, he must do the same.

I turn to Myter as she continues, her voice normal again: "The gods need the true names of the Oterans to sing the songs of their unmaking. But they've hidden away that knowledge, and finding it would require that the gods of Maiwuri come into

78

contact with them, which they cannot do due to the corruption that has infected the Oteran pantheon.

"And even if that weren't the case, the divine covenants forbid direct interference by one group of gods with another."

"Didn't ye just interfere with Melanis?" Britta seems puzzled now.

"I am not a god, and neither is she. The rules are different for us immortals. But you'll learn more about that if you come with me." She glances squarely in my direction, her voice taking on that reverberance again. "Now then, Angoro Deka," she says, "what do you choose? Stay or go?"

The question rings in my ears as I turn to my friends, all of them tense as they wait for my answer—or for the command to attack. After all, Bala and Myter are still the unknown. Still potential threats. But as I look at Bala, my fear and distrust fades. This entire while, he hasn't tried to persuade or subtly influence me. And I've been influenced by gods so many times, I have a sixth sense for it now. I would feel it if he did, feel the subtle pull of divine energy. But I've felt none of that.

Most important, I have the feeling that he'd accept any answer I choose without trying to change it into the one he seeks.

That, more than anything else, is what convinces me. I sheathe my atikas, then turn to the others. "I want to go," I say. "But I don't want to make any decisions without the group."

After all, I'm not the one who'll do the bulk of the fighting should things go sour. I may be healed now, but that emptiness is still inside me, which means I will eventually develop more sores, more wounds. The healing I received was only a temporary reprieve.

But it's one I'll savor while I have it.

For a moment, there's only silence. Then Britta steps forward. Sighs. "If there's one thing I know, Deka," she says, "it's that the world is shit wherever we go. If there's a chance we can save ye, or even a chance we can see a paradise before it all ends, I'll take it."

Belcalis nods beside her. "This is what we came here for," she says, before continuing under her breath, "New gods. Why does it always have to be more gods?"

"I can still hear you," Myter reminds her.

As Belcalis rolls her eyes, Keita turns to me, his gaze intent. He's been touching me this entire time—a hold on my back, little wondering grazes of his fingers. I don't think he even notices how much he's doing it.

He nods at me. "No matter what, I'm here. You know that, Deka, right?"

All I can do is embrace him, put my forehead against his. "I do," I whisper.

Then I return my attention to Myter. "All right, then," I agree. "Let's go see my mother."

"Finally," Myter huffs. She turns to Bala and bows. "My Lord, the pathways."

Bala surges up into the air, darkness melding with a thousand rainbows. His coils explode across the temple, shimmering and shining, until a bright, fragmented light flashes.

And then we're in the pathways.

8

The pathways are thick with fog, and yet I see them perfectly: they appear as a black road, rainbow lights sparkling brilliantly inside its stones. There's a forest in the distance or, rather, the suggestion of one. The fog wreathes around the silhouettes of trees, which, like the road, sparkle with the light of a thousand rainbows—as does the fog itself. It's the oddest thing: even though it's dark here, everything is bright with light and color. This space itself is a contradiction. And that isn't even what I find strangest about the pathways: Except for the fog, everything seems to be made of strands of hair. Bala's hair. I peer more closely at a strand in one of the stones, but doing so hurts my head. The more I stare, the more those rainbow lights glitter and swirl. I reach out to hold tighter to Ixa and Keita, only to find they're no longer there.

They're both silhouettes in the distance, each standing on his own stone road, each one wreathed in fog. Alarm surges through me. "Keita? Ixa?" I call out.

"They walk their own paths." When I turn, Myter is walking beside me. Or, rather, she's standing and the path under her is moving. It's clear she's a part of it, as much a creature of this realm as the stones and the trees. "Every individual must take their own path the first time they walk the pathways," she says. "Even you, Angoro Deka."

Her tone rankles me. "Bring me back my friends!" I demand, angered.

"Why? Do you no longer know how to walk alone?" She seems genuinely curious, so I stop, breathe, remind myself:

Not everything is a threat, even things that sometimes seem like it.

"I know how to walk alone," I finally reply.

"I had begun to wonder," Myter says. She glances at me, those brilliant green eyes unblinking from behind her armor. "There are those persons who cling to companionship even to their last, binding their loved ones to them with desperation and all the force of the strongest manacles. Those, I find, tend to be the most insidious of villains, trapping their victims in chains they call love."

At this not-so-subtle accusation, my hackles rise. Every muscle tenses. "I'm not like that," I grind out. "I'm not like the Gilded Ones."

"That's good to know," Myter says, removing her helmet.

And all my other thoughts fall away.

Myter is massive. I had expected this, given the size of her armor, but expecting and experiencing are vastly different things. Her feline-green eyes are three times the size of mine, and the rest of her features are similarly immense, though at the same time relatively delicate and humanlike. Her skin is a gold-dusted brown, her nose an upturned button, and her eyes tilt up at the sides. While her curly hair is nearly as black as Belcalis's, each curl that bounces against her cheeks is the size of a priest's wristlet. Each of her hands is as big as my face, and her legs are almost as tall as my entire body.

"What are you?" I manage to ask past my slackened jaw.

"I am a godsworn, as I said before."

"A godsworn?"

The look Myter gives me is one of pure disdain. I was so in awe of her, I forgot she could be like this, snotty and condescending. "You do not know what a godsworn is?"

I shrug. "I don't know why you assume I would."

This reply seems to shock Myter. She glances pointedly to her left, where Lamin is suddenly visible, his path running parallel to mine. All my friends are visible now, all of them staring in wonder at Myter—all except for Lamin. He just gazes at her, and she back at him, silent messages seeming to fly between their eyes.

I frown, glancing from one to the other.

It's as if Myter knows Lamin. Or, rather, that she expects something from him. Except that can't be possible, because Lamin rarely speaks, and when he does, it's only ever to our group. Even if it weren't for that, he's certainly never been to the Unknown Lands, much less met a creature like Myter, whatever she is.

I turn to him. "Lamin?"

To my surprise, my friend glances away.

"Lamin, what's happening?"

When he doesn't answer, Myter turns back to me with an annoyed sigh. "Every time I think this day surely cannot grow any worse, it does," she says, almost as if she's speaking to herself. Then she nods. "All right, pay close attention, Deka. A godsworn is a mortal who bonds themself to a god—"

"In sacrifice?" Belcalis asks suspiciously.

"—in partnership, to ensure that the deities understand those in their care. The godsworn act as intermediaries, allowing their chosen gods to experience the breadth and brevity of mortality through them, while they, in return, can spend time in contemplation of the Greater Divinity."

Belcalis's upper lip curls into a sneer. "So they're the only path to understanding the gods. Wonder where I've heard that before."

"No," Myter says firmly. "There is no one path to the Greater Divinity, no one method that is better or more just. Becoming a godsworn is just one of countless possibilities. Every creature in every realm must find their own."

"The Greater Divinity?" I still don't understand exactly what the term means.

"The cosmos, which we all serve," Myter explains.

"It is the natural and divine order." To my surprise, this soft explanation comes from Lamin, who's now glancing back to me with that guilty expression.

What exactly is happening?

Myter's expression is downright exasperated now. "Do you know nothing, Deka?" she snaps.

"Well, no," I reply, unable to contain my irritation any longer. "I've spent the past eighteen years being deceived, leeched on, and taken advantage of by the Oteran gods. So no, I know nothing of this Greater Divinity or this natural and divine order or anything else you've just nattered on about."

Myter's mouth opens, no doubt to make another brisk reply, but then the ground suddenly rumbles, a low warning sound. Myter's eyes flash, as if she's seeing something far away from us. I still, immediately recognizing that look. Myter's speaking with Bala—even now, I can feel the peacefulness I associate with him radiating through the passageway's fog.

Once the two are done speaking, Myter swiftly turns back to me and bows, her expression chastened. "My apologies, Angoro Deka. I forgot the difficulty of your circumstances."

"Your apology will be accepted only if you tell me more about the godsworn," I reply stiffly.

Myter nods. "The godsworn are representatives of the gods. At times even their protectors, like the ebiki that follows you, for instance." She points at Ixa, who dutifully chirps, and my jaw drops.

"You know what Ixa is?" I ask, flabbergasted.

The Gilded Ones told me they'd created him as a gift for me, but that was another of their lies. They didn't make Ixa—they didn't even know where he came from, which is why he, unlike most beings, has been able to see through them from the very first moment.

"He's an ebiki," Myter replies. "They're plentiful in the capital this time of year."

A thousand questions are circling my mind, but I force myself to remain focused. "You said he was my godsworn? How is that possible? I'm not a god."

"Not right now," Myter corrects, "but you were once, and, Greater Divinity willing, you will be again. Now, Ixa—that is what you called him, yes?"

I nod.

"He is your primary at the moment, I assume."

"There can be more than one?" asks Britta, who by now is fascinated. When she turns to us, her path slides closer, as do the others'. I thought that my friends would be in that fog the entire journey, but it seems they can control their roads if they choose—just as I can control mine.

I turn back to Myter, and my path slides closer to hers.

"Countless," Myter assures us. "Godsworn can serve as living conduits for a god's power."

"How?" I ask.

"The more apt question is why," Myter corrects, her voice taking on that reverberance I've heard before. I can't help but wonder if it's actually been her or Bala who's been speaking to me all along. "It is harmful for all involved when the gods spend too much time on the physical plane, as you've no doubt seen with the Oterans. Which is why they bond with godsworn. Usually, each god starts with at least four bonded, but there can be hundreds, even thousands."

They both turn to Ixa, their beings so blended now, I can't tell where Myter stops and Bala begins. "As Ixa, however, seems to be your only current bonded," they rumble, "he cannot fully heal you the way you can him."

I blink, their words sinking in. "Wait, Ixa can heal me?"

I knew he could ease my pain, but this . . . this could change everything. I've been fearing the return of the sores, but if I can figure out how to get Ixa to heal me, perhaps I'll have more time, more strength, as I continue on my journey.

When they nod, I swiftly ascertain, "And the reason I can heal him with my blood is because he's my godsworn?"

They incline their head once more. "Indeed. But you need at

least four to heal you entirely, and I doubt you can manage that number of godsworn in your current state. Ixa can, however, take your pain, as you have seen. That is part of his function: all godsworn keep spaces inside them for their gods; each one is a living temple to their deity."

"Which is why ye can slip into his mind!" Britta gasps. "I knew it wasn't possession!" she says triumphantly.

"That's not what you said last time," Li mutters.

"Shut it, ye," Britta hisses, elbowing him.

As I stare at Ixa, Myter gestures with her chin, her voice losing Bala's reverberance as she says, "We're almost there. I know you're used to Otera, so do try to contain yourself when you gaze at the wonder that is our capital. It won't do to seem like too much of a bumpkin."

It's all I can do not to roll my eyes, but when I glance at Britta, she's already doing it for me. "I'll try," I reply dryly. "I know it'll be difficult, but I'll try."

The closer we get to the end of the pathways, the dimmer the rainbow lights glow. Where once they were brilliant things, they're now the barest suggestion of a shimmer. The power, or whatever it was, that guided us here is coming to an end. We're almost at our destination.

The mere thought raises my anxieties.

"So, Mother is expecting me?" I ask, fingers twisting together as my worries return.

The last time I spoke to Mother was on what I assumed was her deathbed. What will she think about the person I've become? The things I've done?

"I would assume so." Myter's unconcerned reply is like cold water dousing all my hopes.

87

"You don't know for certain?" This cold, almost accusing statement comes from Belcalis, who is now walking out of the fog toward me, as are my other friends.

Around us, the pathways are slowly disappearing, the fog and forests fading as brightness and the sound of waves crashing take their place.

The children are still absent, but that, I assume, is because they're with Bala, in different pathways all their own.

"No." Myter shrugs. "Bala and I are not involved in the inner workings of the pantheons. We just mind the pathways."

"And defend them when necessary?" Belcalis adds. When Myter blinks at her, she continues bluntly: "I've been thinking. No Oteran has ever been to the Unknown Lands and returned that I know of. We didn't even know they truly existed. I assume there's a reason for that."

"Indeed," Myter confirms, cheerfully twirling her hammer. "Bala and I are the reason. As long as the gods of Otera remain alive, no Oteran living can cross the pathways twice. Anyone who tries runs afoul of, well, me."

"So where does that leave us?" I ask, everything inside me tensing.

"Gods and godsworn are different," Myter says.

"We're not godsworn," Britta says.

"Yet," Myter replies meaningfully, glancing at me.

I stiffen as the suggestion rings in my mind. Could it be possible? If I regain my kelai and become a true god, could Britta and the others truly become my godsworn? More to the point, would they want that—to become my glorified helpers? My living temples?

I consider my relationship with Ixa, the way I can enter his mind so easily, and shudder. I don't think I could ever wish that for my friends. For Britta. For Keita.

But I'm getting ahead of myself. There's a much more important question at hand.

"If Mother is here, does that mean my kelai is here too?" I ask. I don't sense anything to that effect, but that doesn't mean it's not possible.

"I know nothing of it," Myter says impatiently. "And, more to the point, why are you bothering me with such questions? You have the godsworn of Sarla with you, a living avatar of the god of wisdom. Why don't you ask him?"

I frown. *The godsworn of Sarla?* What is she going on about?

As I peer across the darkness that marks the last of the pathway, a heavy sigh answers my question. I turn to find Lamin stepping forward, his hands grasping at something under his chin. As I watch, confused, he pulls what looks to be a thin, almost gelatinous membrane off his face, and just like that, the person I thought was Lamin is no more. In his place is a pale, inhumanly shimmering creature with all the same features as Lamin, except his loosely curled hair now glistens white, as do his eyes, which have barely more than a pupil in the center of them instead of the warm brown I'm so used to.

"What in the name of Infinity is this?" Li asks, jerking back as Lamin turns to us all hesitantly, his hands fidgeting the way they do on the rare occasion when he's nervous.

Suddenly my ears are ringing. It's all I can do to keep standing. I never suspected, never once. Two years in close companionship with him and this person—this *creature* standing in front of us—is the true Lamin. And I never once suspected. Never even dreamt it.

I'm at such a loss now, I just stand there, my thoughts racing.

Thankfully, I'm not the only one standing here, near the pathways' exit. Keita is here as well, and he knows just what to do. He walks closer to his friend, his face carefully blank even as his fists are clenched as tightly as I've ever seen them. "Explanations. Now," he demands.

Lamin sighs again, his unnervingly white eyes brimming with remorse. "I know this looks bad, but I want to say first that I am not now, nor have I ever been, your enemy."

"And just saying that makes it true," Belcalis grits out, hands on her daggers. She's infuriated as well, as is the rest of the group.

Lamin grimaces when he notices. "I had no choice but to keep the truth from you all. It was my pact. I was sent to Otera by Sarla."

"For what reason?" Keita demands, his eyes hooded now.

"To ensure that Deka was led down the path to discovery about the treachery of the Oteran gods."

When he turns pointedly toward me, the last two years flash past, memories of all the time I've spent with him. The friendship the others and I cultivated with him. The friendship that, it's now apparent, was based on lies. Every time I was with Keita and the other uruni, Lamin was there—always quiet, always watchful, perfectly unobtrusive. I just assumed, as did everyone else, that it was his nature. But now I know otherwise.

"So you were manipulating me?" I can't hide the hurt that forces its way into my voice. "All this time, you were manipulating me?"

Lamin hurriedly shakes his head. "I could not speak, could not even write, about my true purpose. It was forbidden, so I remained silent until I was finally able to do otherwise."

"Ensuring Deka learned the treachery of the Oteran gods? And what of your treachery?" Keita has a dark, foreboding look in his eye as he asks this question—that same quiet look he gets when he's deciding whether or not to end someone's life. Even now, embers are stirring in those golden depths, his gift rising up to meet his call.

Lamin must see it, because he hurriedly answers: "I never betrayed anyone! Mostly, I served as a witness, allowing the gods to see what was happening in Otera, especially where Deka and you all were concerned." By now, his voice has lowered to a mumble.

"So they were spying on us through your eyes," Belcalis clarifies.

"Yes." Lamin nods miserably.

"All of us, not just Deka," Belcalis clarifies again.

Another nod.

"Why?"

"The assumption was that, as Deka's closest companions, you would be the first to exhibit any gifts once she began growing in power. That was how they would know she was ready for the truth."

"But they didn't just ask you to watch," Belcalis continues, a disgusted expression on her face. "You insinuated yourself into our group."

"Pretended you were our friend." There's a look I've never seen before in Li's eyes as he says this, a quiet fury as he asks, "How precisely did you manage that?"

It's the exact question I have as well. Our uruni were chosen at random. The luck of the draw. And yet Lamin ended up in our group. And, now that I think about it, I wasn't even friends with the twins when he was bonded to Asha. I disliked Asha and Ad-wapa when I first met them, and they felt the same toward me, it seemed. But they were White Hands's spies, sent to watch over and protect me, which was how they and I were placed in that wagon together. . . .

My eyes widen as I realize: someone must have known who they were, known they would eventually be placed near me, which was why Lamin was assigned as Asha's uruni.

Someone knew they were spies and placed another spy close to them.

The realization has my thoughts twisting on themselves.

All this time, I'd found it strange that Lamin chose to come here with us rather than remain with Adwapa and Asha while they traveled with White Hands. But he's always managed to re-main close to me. Quietly, unobtrusively . . . My thoughts begin flying again as I continue examining every interaction I've ever had with him—every raid, every mission.

"How?" I ask, echoing Li's question, even though I now have a suspicion. "How did you manage it?"

"With the help of other godsworn loyal to the Maiwurian gods," Lamin says.

"So there were others?" Britta sounds shocked.

"All over Otera," Lamin confirms. "As there have been since time immemorial."

"Others like who?"

Lamin lowers his head. "I cannot say."

"Cannot or will not?" Keita wants to know.

Lamin doesn't answer. So I try a different approach. "Why now? After all that time spent with us, why are you speaking of this only now?"

"Because this is the only time he can speak." This interjection comes from Myter, who places a commiserating hand on Lamin's shoulder. "Except for myself and a few others who always remain with their god, the godsworn who leave Maiwuri are placed under covenants."

"Covenants?" I frown.

"They prevent you from speaking or writing or even hinting about the things that you should not."

Lamin nods. "I could not speak the truth of my origins or my mission, no matter how much I longed to do so."

"Reason number two thousand eight hundred I don't have dealings with the gods," Belcalis mutters. "Present company excluded." She nods at me.

I nod back before I turn to Lamin. "Then why now?" I ask. "What's different?"

"Now," he says, walking forward, where the pathways are wending their way toward a bright white light, "I am back in Maiwuri. The covenant doesn't apply here," he continues, as if relieved. "Which means I can show you the truth of the world in which Otera resides. Of Kamabai."

He gestures and I step past him through the light, into paradise.

9

The brilliant blue of water lies in front of me, glittering so fiercely, I have to shade my eyes against the glare. We're standing on a cliff overlooking a vast ocean, a warm breeze curling around us. The sky is a crystalline shade of azure, a rainbow sheen tinting it. Except it's not, in fact, a rainbow. When I squint at it, confused, it shimmers, almost like a bubble covering the entire sky. What exactly is that? I try to peer closer, but a sudden tingling stops me. I whirl to find that the pathways have completely disappeared—vanished the way they came—and in their place stands Bala, Myter at his side, with the children and a group of people I assume are their parents, all glancing around in open-mouthed awe. Bala's eyes, though, remain on mine, his presence as calm and gentle as ever.

"This is where we leave you, Angoro Deka," Myter says, her voice layered over once more. "We will continue on and take this group to their new homes."

It has been my greatest honor bringing you here, a deep, warm voice continues in my mind. I know, without the slightest doubt, that it belongs to Bala, that he is actively projecting his thoughts into mine. The god bows gently to me. *May we meet again on the pathways.*

I hope that as well, I reply, startled when I realize I actually mean it.

Despite my confused feelings about Lamin and his betrayal, I somehow hold no ill will against Bala, even though he is part of the very pantheon that sent Lamin. All the other gods I've met left me with a sense of awe. With the desire to worship and abase myself to them. But Bala only seems filled with gentleness and compassion. He doesn't seem to want me to worship or serve him. He doesn't even seem to have any true desires of his own. He just is. Like the sun or wind or any other element. He simply exists.

Ixa seems to feel the same way, because he nods as he ambles up to me. *Ixa too,* he adds cheerfully. *Ixa hope we meet again.*

As the god gives us another quiet bow, a thought occurs to me. "Wait, is this where we meet the other gods?"

"No," Myter says, pointing up. "Sarla's godsworn will take you the rest of the way."

I frown, glancing around. I see only the clear blue skies and the water sparkling around us. "I don't understand. Where are the—"

But Myter is already gone, as are Bala and the children. We're alone on the cliff now. Then Lamin points. "Look," he says. "Here they come."

I follow the direction of his finger, and my jaw drops. The sky is shimmering again. Or, rather, something is shimmering inside it. A city. The more I stare at it, the more my astonished mind confirms it. There, suspended in the sky, is a city—the most majestic I've ever seen. Gleaming buildings the color of gems rise from verdant mountains, the bases of which are wreathed by clouds. Waterfalls cascade into the ocean below, graceful birds with iridescent wings flittering through them. Trees the width of entire streets sprout up, elegant apartments carved into their crystalline trunks. It's as if everything is interconnected, all part of the same, massive organism.

"Is it the Blissful Lands?" Britta asks, awed, as she stares at the city.

Lamin shakes his head. "No," he replies, an eager smile easing the tension from his features. "That is Laba, the Seat of the Gods and the capital of Maiwuri. Come." He waves us closer to the edge of the cliff. "Sarla's riders will be here soon."

Even as he says this, a pair of glasslike gates I hadn't noticed opens underneath one of the waterfalls in the middle of the city and a group of gigantic gray creatures flies out, riders on their backs. Each creature is flat, with a sleek, triangular body dominated by glistening wings that undulate in the air currents. Tiny, almost unnoticeable gray eyes take up each side of the creature's snub-nosed faces, and as for their mouths, I can find no sign of any, although they all have curved silver horns protruding from their heads and spots or stripes on their skin. Except for a glimpse of similar creatures dancing in the waters surrounding Hemaira, I've never seen anything like them before.

I'm not surprised to see that the riders have the same pale, shimmering skin as Lamin. I turn to him. "This isn't over," I say. "Our conversation. You've deceived me since we first met, deceived all of us."

"It was never malicious," Lamin replies hurriedly, that worry returning to his features. "I never harmed any of you."

"That remains to be seen," says Keita, his expression forbidding. He hasn't forgiven Lamin yet either.

But we can't concentrate on that right now. "All right," I say. "Let's meet these new godsworn."

"Deka . . ." Lamin is hesitant when he turns to me. "They don't mean you any harm either."

I give him as frosty a look as I can summon. "That's what everyone always says."

Lamin nods, his expression decidedly miserable now, but when the creatures begin their descent toward us, their wings gliding lazily across the currents, he swiftly kneels, his frown melting into a relieved smile. He crosses his arms over his chest in greeting when the frontmost rider, a tall, severe-looking woman of sixty or so, hops off her creature and nears.

"High priestess," he says respectfully. "I have returned."

But the woman just humphs. "Lamin Chernor Bah. Is that how you greet your aunt after all this time?"

Aunt? Britta mouths this word when I glance at the others, shocked.

A smile twitches up the side of Lamin's face. He surges up and sweeps the woman into a tight embrace. "Aunt Kadeh," he declares. "I'm home."

The woman breaks out into a glowing smile, all traces of severity erased from her expression as she begins raining kisses over his forehead and cheeks. "Oh my boy, my beloved baby. You're finally back."

"That's Lamin's aunt?" Li's whisper is loud enough for everyone to hear.

Including the woman. She turns to us. "Only one he has. Raised him from the time he was an infant with my own brood." Then she looks back up at him, ruffles his hair. "So, you've finally returned."

Clearing his throat, Lamin nods, then glances pointedly at me. "And I brought the Angoro."

The woman immediately sinks into a deep kneel. "Your eminence," she says respectfully, "I am Nenneh Kadeh. I am honored to receive you. I hope my nephew has treated you well." She gives Lamin a pointed glare.

"That remains to be seen," Belcalis mutters, but I quickly step forward.

"To this point, he has been one of our closest companions," I reply, an answer that is both truthful and yet not. I still haven't decided what to do about Lamin.

I turn to the other riders. There are about ten of them, mostly women, all of them wearing flowing white robes with long silver hoods whose patterns match the patterns on the creatures they ride. "So," I say politely, "am I to assume you are our escort to Maiwuri?"

"Indeed," Nenneh Kadeh answers. "We were sent here by Sarla, deity of wisdom."

The words seem to be a signal, because the moment she utters them, it's as if something takes her over. She abruptly straightens, her gaze seeming far away. When she glances at me again, she suddenly seems like a different person, one whose movements are as fluid and graceful as their gaze is sharp.

A shiver rushes over me as I nod at the god staring through Nenneh Kadeh's eyes. "Afternoon greetings," I say calmly. "You must be Sarla."

It's almost surreal. Mere hours ago, I had only eight gods to worry about, and now there's an entire new pantheon with who knows what ambitions I must deal with.

"A pleasure, Angoro," Sarla says through Nenneh Kadeh's mouth, their voice low and melodious. "We are most grateful to see that you arrived here safely. Our bonded will see you safely to Maiwuri."

Nodding, I give them a quick bow. Deep enough to be respectful but not so deep it is obsequious. I will never prostrate myself before a god ever again. "My thanks."

Sarla nods again, then Nenneh Kadeh's body sags. The god is gone, and the woman has returned in their place.

Nenneh Kadeh turns to me, smiles. "Well, then, Angoro, shall we?" She points to her creature, massive silver stripes racing down its purple-gray back. "You can ride Maida with me."

"As long as Ixa can fly alongside," I automatically say.

Nenneh Kadeh inclines her head. "Your godsworn is, of course, welcome. As are your gryphs," she says, turning to the others. "They can use the currents behind the horn rays to glide. I assume they will welcome the respite."

"They will," I say, walking over. We're not the only ones exhausted after the events of the past few days. The gryphs and Ixa are as well. I glance up at Nenneh Kadeh, who is almost as tall as her nephew. "How do I get on?"

The priestess demonstrates by walking directly onto one of the creature's wings, which is flapping wetly across the grass. From their moisture and sheen, I get the sudden sense that it's as much an aquatic creature as it is an aerial one. "You just walk on. And don't worry: horn rays' wings aren't sensitive."

I squint at the horn ray, which ripples softly as it blinks its gentle black eyes at me. "All right, Maida," I whisper, "it's you and me."

But as I prepare to get on, a hand stops me. Britta's. Her eyes are grim as she pulls me to the side, well out of range of Lamin's aunt. At least, that's the hope. Given how little we know about the godsworn, we can't be sure yet what the nature and extent of their abilities are.

After all, we didn't realize, until Lamin pulled off his mask, that the types of godsworn for each god looked distinctly different.

"Deka," Britta begins, but I hold up a hand, to both her and Keita, who's also walked over.

I know it's possibly a trap, I acknowledge with battle language, the hand gestures we use to communicate with deathshrieks or in situations where speaking isn't an option. Over the years, it's expanded into a complete language. *That Mother may not be there. Or that we may still be stuck in the shadow vales and this is some sort of illusion. Either way, we'll figure it out. We always do. But Myter healed me, Britta. And she feels different—her, Bala—even this Sarla. They all feel different from the Oterans. I know it's painful to hope again, but let's at least try. If everything they're saying is the truth, then we're near to getting my kelai and ending the Gilded Ones and the Idugu once and for all.*

And if they're lying? It's Keita's turn to gesture now, and there's a look in his eyes. A determination.

It matches mine.

We put everything to the flame and burn that pretty floating city to the ground. I add an extra lyricism to my hand movements as I say this.

A smile ghosts over his lips. "You're so delightful when

you're frightening," he says out loud, fire gleaming in his eyes as he softly caresses my cheek.

Britta rolls her eyes. "And that right there is me sign to exit," she mutters, walking away as Keita kisses my cheek, leaving soft little trails of fire.

Warmth washes over me, and I look down, overwhelmed. It's been so long since I've been touched this much, so long since I've felt anyone's skin on mine other than Ixa's. And the fact that it's Keita's hands, Keita's touch . . .

It's all I can do to keep from folding myself into him. "I know," I manage to say past the heat rising in my body. "It's the same with you." I say this last bit with battle language. *You're so handsome when you're being devious.*

"That's because I'm always trying to match you." He kisses me one last time, then sighs and takes a step away, letting in the outside world again.

Once my pulse has steadied, I turn to Nenneh Kadeh with a bright if patently false smile. "Shall we?"

The elder just grins. "What are we waiting for, then? Onward, to Maiwuri!"

10

◆ ◆ ◆

The ride to Maiwuri is even smoother than I imagined, Maida's wings gently gliding over the wind currents as the ocean sprays mist softly over us. Nenneh Kadeh is clearly adept at guiding the horn ray, so I just lean back and savor the experience—the sun beaming gently on my face, the refreshing coolness of the blue water . . . It's so clear, I can see the fish dancing just under the surface. I watch, fascinated, as a school of tiny silver fish leap out of the water, the fins on their sides spreading into wings, which they use to flap away from the larger purple fish leaping behind them. I know I should be tense and on the defensive, that I should spend however much time it takes to get to the city strategizing contingency plans, but the combination of the warm sun and cool ocean spray lulls me into a dazed contentment I haven't felt in months—perhaps even years.

Later, I can panic. Later, I can be apprehensive. For now, I just want to be.

As my eyes slide closed, I become aware of something strange: a low, soothing thrumming that seems closer and closer with every passing moment. I would mistake it for the thrumming I heard in the vales, except it's deeper. Richer.

Welcoming.

Here! Ixa suddenly calls from beside me, where he's been flying in the form of a small blue bird, his nightflyer form. Except he's not speaking to me. *Deka and me here,* he says to his mysterious questioner.

When I open my eyes, alarmed, I see Ixa rapidly shrinking as he transforms into a new creature I've never seen before: a tiny scaled being that almost looks like his former kitten guise, only this one is scaled all over and has velvety, almost bat-like wings of a brilliant, jewellike blue.

"Ixa?" I ask as he flaps down toward the waves.

But he doesn't seem to notice me anymore.

Ixa here! he says happily, speaking to something beneath the waves, something that is so massive, the water around us darkens as it approaches, sending those purple fish fleeing for the depths.

I scramble over Maida's side to get a better look, and that's when the breath gasps from my body.

There, just beneath us, swims a group of creatures that are at once familiar and yet not: massive reptiles with gleaming blue scales edged with gold, and golden horns crowning their brows as well as jutting out all the way down their backs. They look something like sea drakos, those colossal swimming reptiles I once thought Ixa was descended from, except sea drakos don't have liquid black eyes that shine with intelligence and compassion.

But Ixa does.

I gasp: these must be the ebiki, Ixa's kind.

I hadn't imagined I'd get to see them here—much less so quickly.

Ixa swiftly flaps down to the single ebiki at the front of the group, a craggy leviathan whose scales are more gold than blue and whose head is considerably larger than all the others—so enormous, in fact, it seems almost like an island, a shimmering oasis under the water.

As I watch, Ixa lands on that immense head, which, when it crests the surface to look at me, causes waves to surge around us. Eyes filled with the same gentleness and intelligence as Ixa's peer into mine, their gaze so arresting, I gape, unable to look away. So this is a full-grown ebiki.

Even the horn rays stop advancing and instead settle for making low circles on the wind currents.

"Deka," Britta gasps, staring at the creature. "Is that—?"

Mother, Ixa happily informs me. *Deka, Ixa's mother here.*

I gape at Ixa. "*Your* mother?"

Just the sheer magnitude of her . . . it's almost more than I can comprehend.

Even Li is, for once, at a loss for words. "That's one big mother," he whispers.

As my friends and I remain where we are, mouths agape, Nenneh Kadeh and the rest of Sarla's godsworn rise from their perches atop the horn rays, the movement so fluid, I know they've done it countless times before. They bow deeply to Ixa's mother. "Queen Ayo," Nenneh Kadeh declares, "we are honored by your escort."

Those gigantic black eyes, each one the size of a single horn ray, don't move from my face. They just continue staring. And then finally, that colossal mouth opens.

The sound that emerges from it is a rumble that vibrates through my entire being. Even stranger, it's immediately understandable. "Deka," Queen Ayo says the single utterance so powerfully, my body suddenly feels light—lighter than it ever has before.

And then I hear it again, this time from another ebiki. "Deka."

And my body lightens again, that emptiness inside me, for a moment, almost seeming to disappear, erased by this feeling of lightness, of connection.

"Deka," another creature calls.

Then another. And another.

One by one, the creatures call out my name, each vocalization so filled with power, my body trembles with it.

"Deka!" Britta gasps, urging her horn ray over. "Look at yer skin!"

She points at my hand, where, slowly, surely, the gold that still stains it from Melanis's attack is retreating—or, rather, being absorbed back into me. And it's not the only thing that's changing. That emptiness in my belly, that hollowness that I've felt for so long, has been erased, replaced with a strange, content feeling—as if I'm whole again.

And it's all the ebikis' doing. I can see it in their eyes, their expressions. Every utterance of my name is a prayer, an invocation to the Greater Divinity Myter spoke about earlier, on my behalf. And it's healing me. Not just the few blemishes that remain on the outside, but all the damage on the inside as well, the damage that even Myter, using the full power of a Maiwurian god, could not undo.

Tears fall down my cheeks. All these weeks of pain, of sheer, unrelenting panic. Every day in struggle, in desperation. But now I'm here, and I'm bathed in light and wonder and everything that is good.

It's as though these creatures' vocalizations are striking straight to the core of me, purging me of all my pain, my worry. And all the while, Ixa's mother stares at me, that black gaze never blinking.

Not even when I begin to sob, heaving desperate tears.

"Thank you . . . thank you," I whisper to Queen Ayo.

I've been so frightened these past few hours. Frightened the sores would swiftly come back. Frightened that Mother would not be here, or, worse, that she would reject me and I would never find my divinity.

But now I'm here and the ebiki are here and I'm whole again. Truly whole, not just on the outside but on the inside as well.

I can feel everyone staring at me, puzzled, but I don't care. I just want to exist in this happiness for as long as I can. For however long I'm here on Maida, the ebiki surrounding me, I want to revel in this feeling of being perfectly safe.

And the ebiki seem to understand, because they circle around me, rumbling my name reverently to the wind until finally, I'm out of tears. Out of emotion. And there is just peace.

Just the ocean breeze wafting where sobs once did.

When their songs have quieted, Ixa flitters over to me, pleased. *Deka all better,* he says, flying back up to cuddle on my chest. He wraps those wings around me, which are just as velvety and warm as I imagined, if not more so. *Mother say Deka have two weeks now before get weak again, maybe more. Ixa happy.*

Two weeks . . . That's how much time I have before my life force begins depleting again, before the sores start opening again. I'm not even dismayed by the thought. It's much more time than I thought I'd have. I'll treasure every day, every moment that I can go without pain.

I look down at Ixa, this miraculous creature that's been so instrumental to my well-being, to almost every move I've made since my blood ran gold, and I squeeze him tight.

"Thank you, Ixa," I say. "Thank you for everything." Then I glance at the other ebiki, all of which are still waiting patiently underneath Maida, gentle eyes unblinking. "Thank you all."

The reply, when it comes, is a deep, reverberating sound. "Welcome," Queen Ayo says in that unending rumble, and then she starts moving again, the other creatures following behind her, waves surging in their wake.

The entire group watches them go, awed, as I am, to have been witness to what is almost certainly a scene out of the deepest, most hallowed mythology.

Only when the ebiki are a distance away does everyone regain their faculties.

Nenneh Kadeh turns to me, awe in her eyes. "You are most fortunate, Angoro," she remarks, "to earn the loyalty of the ebiki. Not every god is as fortunate, particularly not the fledgling ones. It is a deep honor."

I nod. "It is," I agree.

I hold on to this feeling as we continue on, letting it buoy me all the way to the city and whatever victories and treacheries wait there.

◆

If Maiwuri seemed beautiful from afar, it's stunning up close. Those jewellike buildings gleam in the warmth of the setting sun, making the entire island seem lit from within. Its cloud foundation, which I noted earlier, is just lowering to the ocean when we reach the city, those clouds scattering into sparkling white sand the moment they touch the water. Power tingles through my body as the island's colossal trees begin stretching even taller, their brilliantly hued leaves misted by the waterfalls that curve along the floating hills, each one dividing the city into distinct districts.

There, to the west, is a district filled with gardens—plants and mushrooms of all colors and shapes growing in voluptuous abandon while vines wreathe every building and monument, every statue and gate. To the east is a more austere district filled with forbidding white buildings that hold the intimidating aura common to institutions of law. It's flanked, almost ironically, by a pleasure district, immediately apparent by the hordes of drunken people spilling out of brightly colored houses, goblets and horns of wine in hand, their bodies in all the colors of the rainbow. Yet another district seems filled with libraries and bookish people in all manner of dress, most of whom have affixed strange glass contraptions to each eye, and who are all, to the very last person, pale-and-shimmery-skinned like Lamin and his aunt.

These must be the godsworn of Sarla, the god of wisdom. A

paler and more academic lot I've never seen in my life. I can't help thinking that Acalan, the most scholarly of our uruni, would feel at home there.

I can't wait to tell him about it the moment I see him.

Then I remember: I probably won't ever see Acalan again. Nor Adwapa and Asha, nor Katya and Rian. Nor any of my other friends. Not in this form, at least.

If what Anok and White Hands told me is true, once I meet Mother, she'll lead me to my kelai, and then I'll ascend to divinity and smite the gods, thus bringing Otera into an era of peace, free of divine meddling and celestial aggression.

The thought fills me with conflicted feelings; relief at being able to finally free Otera from its divine oppressors, sadness at leaving my friends . . . I reflect on this as Maida drifts to a landing in the waters just in front of the city. Once I'm a god, Otera will finally be peaceful. Everyone will lead the lives they want to. Except for me. Yes, I'll be happy the gods are gone, happy Otera is safe, but I'll be separated from everyone I love—my friends, Mother.

All this time, I just wanted to hold her again. To smell her scent. Hear her voice. But I'll only get to do that for a few moments, a few hours.

As tears sting my eyes, a shadow shifts beside me: Keita, hand extended to help me off Maida while Nenneh Kadeh unsaddles the massive horn ray.

The devastated expression on his face as I step off the glistening gray animal is an exact replica of mine, but he tries to hide it with a rueful smile. "Nervous, Deka?" he asks, glancing pointedly at the island, those jewel-hued trees rising in front of us.

"Terrified."

"Once you meet your mother, it's the first step to divinity. . . ."

"I know." I can't help the misery that creeps into my voice at the thought.

Keita hooks my arm in his and then squeezes it, the simple touch so overwhelming, it's some moments before I realize he's speaking again. "You know . . . you're healed and your body isn't in imminent danger of breaking again. Otera won't fall apart tomorrow if you wait a day or two to repair your bond with your kelai."

"Except it will." I sigh. "Every second I delay . . ."

"The One Kingdom worsens." Keita sighs as well, weariness seeming to weigh down his entire being. "Sometimes, I wonder what it would be like to not have the fate of an empire on your shoulders."

"Peaceful, I expect."

As we both consider this, Nenneh Kadeh walks over. I swiftly turn to her. "So, where do I find Mother?" I ask.

"In the Hall of the Gods," the older woman says. Then she shakes her head. "But meeting her is not possible at this very moment, I'm afraid."

I'm immediately on the alert. "What do you mean?"

"Your mother is godsworn not only to Sarla but also to Baduri, deity of hearth and home and keeper of Maiwuri's temples."

"But I thought ye could be godsworn to only one god." Britta's look of confusion as she walks closer mirrors my own. "I mean, it seemed that way from all the explanations."

Nenneh Kadeh inclines her head. "That is the usual case. There are, however, exceptions. . . ."

"Which occur only under the direst circumstances." Lamin's entire body is strained as he turns to Nenneh Kadeh. "Has something happened? Is something the matter with Deka's mother?"

A thousand worries rush through my mind. Then Nenneh Kadeh shakes her head. "To my knowledge, it was a precaution, given Umu's origins. Baduri can never leave the temple, which means their godsworn cannot either."

"So she is a prisoner." Rage fills me as I understand what she's saying.

"More like an honored guest," Nenneh Kadeh swiftly corrects. "One who chose her circumstances, as all godsworn do. So, as Umu cannot come to you, you must go to her."

"Let's go, then," I say, striding onward, even though I have no idea where the temple is.

Nenneh Kadeh shakes her head again. "Unfortunately, I cannot take you at this very moment. The path to the Hall of the Gods opens only at certain times. The earliest you can see her is this evening."

My rage builds. "Three months," I say, advancing toward her threateningly. "Three months I've spent, racing across Otera, fighting all sorts of monsters, all so I can see my mother, and now you tell me I have to wait till evening?"

Nenneh Kadeh looks so miserable now, it's as if she wants to melt away. She shakes her head. "My deepest apologies, Angoro Deka. I cannot control the pathways."

"Well, *you* might not be able to," I begin, "but I—"

"—find it perfectly understandable." Keita hurries in front of me before I can finish my sentence, then nods at Nenneh Kadeh. "As do the rest of us. We understand and we will adjust."

I whirl to him. "No, I—"

"Deka," Keita says, swiftly cutting me off. "You may be

healed, but you are hungry and exhausted and suffering from blood loss. And you are meeting new gods. Gods you have never seen before." He lowers his voice pointedly as he says this. "Better to meet them when you are at your peak."

"I *am* at my peak!"

"And what about the rest of us?"

When he glances at the others, I follow his gaze. That's when I notice: my friends all look haggard and weary. The same sort of weariness I felt before the ebiki called to me. Even though they're standing here, nodding me on, they all seem weighed down, by pure exhaustion.

Keita lowers his voice again. "We all need to be prepared for whatever we may find."

Like Mother in captivity . . . I silently fill in the words he's not saying out loud.

"Which means—"

"—we need rest." I finish Keita's sentence with a nod in the affirmative.

One of the very first principles we learned in the Warthu Bera: Take any opportunity you can to rest. You never know when you'll need it.

"And food," Li adds, ambling closer.

I have to clench my teeth. "I suppose a bite won't hurt," I say grudgingly.

"And a bath too?" Li seems hopeful.

"Don't push your luck," I growl.

Then I notice the way Belcalis subtly perks up at the suggestion. Yet more guilt rises inside me. I've been so focused on my own needs, I forgot I'm not the only person on this journey. Not the only person who has needs to tend to.

Thankfully, my friends have forgiven my selfishness.

I sigh. "And a bath too." Then I turn to Nenneh Kadeh. "Lead us on to dinner. And then I see Mother."

Nenneh Kadeh nods, pleased. "And then you see your mother."

11

❖ ❖ ❖

Once the horn rays have flown away, Nenneh Kadeh and the rest of the godsworn lead us and our gryphs to the scholarly-looking district I noticed earlier, where one of those jewellike buildings unfurls like an elegant flower in the middle of a grove of blue-leafed trees. It's relatively austere, compared to the grandiosity of the rest of the island, a muted yet cheerful yellow structure, but at its center is a courtyard with a small, fragrant garden. At one end, platters of food are piled on a bright yellow table that seems to emerge from the floor itself.

"For you, our honored guests," Nenneh Kadeh says, gesturing.

My friends and I don't have to be told twice.

We converge on the table faster than a nest of sting-flies on a rotting carcass. Within what feels like minutes, the entire table is wiped clean of the very last morsel, and we're all licking our lips and belching politely into the wet cloths we've been handed.

"My thanks," I say when we're done.

Nenneh Kadeh inclines her head. "It is our pleasure. And now, if you please, your chambers await."

Li lifts a finger. "With hot baths, I hope?" When we all whirl to frown at him, he wrinkles his nose. "Whaaat? I'm filthy."

"If you'll follow me." Nenneh Kadeh gestures at the group, leading us down a bright hallway with clear glass walls that peer into even prettier, tinier gardens.

That's not our final destination, however. The godsworn lead each of us to our own separate room, inside which are small but luxurious bathing chambers covered in the same yellow stones as the exterior.

Any lingering suspicions I have about Nenneh Kadeh, the godsworn, and this island in general flit away the moment I spot the sunken tub brimming with heated water. Li was right: a bath was exactly what we all need. All my worries can come later. For now, I will soak my weary body for the first time in a month and finally rid myself of the ever-present stink of gold and blood.

"Thank you. This is all I require," I say, swiftly waving the godsworn out the door. I would be more polite, but I'm too tired to manage it.

Once they're gone, I strip off my filthy leather armor and make proper and lengthy use of the tub. Afterward, I put on the white sleeping robes that have been laid out on the massive canopied bed, sink into the cloth mattress, which is so soft, it might as well be a cloud, and fall soundly asleep.

By the time I wake, attendants in diaphanous pink robes are waiting by the door, lengths of blue fabric in hand. I know immediately that they're godsworn, because even though they look mostly human, they're all pleasantly soft around the edges and have an airy way of moving, as if they'll float away if I take my eyes off them for just one moment.

"Have I been asleep for long?" I ask, yawning groggily.

"Only a day, Angoro," the foremost attendant, a short, plump man with gold paint dusting his eyes and cheekbones, says in a voice that manages to sound both high-pitched and melodious, as if he's singing every time he talks.

"A day?" I leap out of bed, headed for the farthest corner of the room, where I left my armor. But when I get there, Ixa is sprawled across it in his adolescent form, body lean and serpentine, tail stretched toward the door.

I poke him with my foot. *Move, Ixa!* I urge.

But Ixa sleeping, he whines as another attendant steps forward, one who looks so smoothly male and female, I know immediately that they're yandau—those who are neither one nor the other.

"Our deepest apologies. We were told not to disturb you, Angoro," they reply in that singsongy voice.

Like all the other attendants, they're wearing a golden half mask, which covers their nose and mouth just as golden nail extenders cover their fingertips.

"Well, you were told wrong," I say, rolling Ixa away as I search for my armor, only it's gone, as are all the rest of my old clothes. I whirl to the attendants. "Where are my things?" I ask, infuriated.

"Discarded," the foremost attendant says regretfully, shaking his head. "They were . . . unsalvageable, Angoro."

"They were mine!"

"We have brought replacements." He gestures and the other

attendants hurry forward with the blue fabric, which turns out to be an astonishingly long dress. "For you," he says respectfully. "I oversaw its creation myself. May I?" He looks at me so hopefully, my anger fades.

I glance down at the dress, which is so long, it requires at least four people to carry it, then back up at him and sigh. "Very well." I hold out my arms as the godsworn approach with the dress.

It takes nearly half an hour to get me into the dress, but once they're done securing me into it, I examine my reflection in the wall of cascading water that separates my room from the bathing chamber just beyond it. I've never seen anything like it. The collar is embroidered with gold and precious gems, and the rest of it molds and fits to my body as if it were a second skin. The fabric shimmers in the low evening light almost like scales, and some sort of insignia is embroidered on the cape that trails nearly to the room beyond. Only when I look at my reflection in the water wall again do I realize that the insignia is of an ebiki, one that looks very much like Queen Ayo.

The final touch is a crown of gold and blue coral that drapes over my forehead and threads through my hair. To my surprise, it begins to grow the moment the attendants affix it to my head, four golden horns sprouting above it.

They look so much like Ixa's, my reptilian companion chirps, pleased. *Deka pretty,* he says, staring up at me. *Deka pretty with horns.*

I nod. *You look wonderful too.*

Indeed he does. While I was being dressed, the attendants were hard at work on Ixa. His claws have been tipped in gold, as have his whiskers, and some intrepid soul even managed to do the same to the tip of his tail. All he's missing now is a crown, but as far as I'm concerned, he already looks like royalty.

"Oh, Deeeeka . . . ," Britta calls out cheerfully as she makes her way through the door, which the attendants have opened for her and Belcalis.

Then she sees my dress.

She rushes over to me, amazed. "Ye look like a queen! A queen of the ebiki," she exclaims, gaping at my horns.

"One who's been asleep for an entire day," I grumble.

"Same," Britta says, "although ye can't deny we needed it."

"True," I acknowledge grudgingly.

Much as I hate to admit it, this is the sharpest I've felt for months. My mind is clear, my body is relaxed, and I feel almost happy, if that's possible. I'm about to see Mother, about to reunite with her after two years apart.

I return my attention to Britta, who's now whirling for my benefit. "You look beautiful," I say when she's done, a compliment that is no exaggeration.

Britta is wearing a stunning red dress, little golden hearts at the neckline and hems. She has always loved the color red. How the attendants knew, I have no idea. A small circlet adorns her forehead, red gems sparkling there, while yet more gems adorn her ears and neck. She touches her new necklace shyly.

"I don't know how they knew I liked red an' hearts, but it's like they read my mind."

"They likely did," Belcalis humphs, walking closer.

In contrast to Britta, she's wearing a dark purple shirt and matching pantaloons, which mold so closely to her legs, it seems almost scandalous to gaze upon them. The fabric is as iridescent as my own, so it shimmers in the light, giving the appearance of scales. She wears no jewelry, only a thin golden circlet that high-lights her long black hair, which flows down her back.

When Britta turns to her, confused by her words, she explains: "They're godsworn to Nian, deity of love and beauty. They have a sixth sense when it comes to clothing and adornments."

Britta wrinkles her nose. "An' how do ye know that?"

"Because unlike the rest of you lot, I explored instead of sleeping the day away."

Of course she did. Belcalis is suspicious of everyone and everything. She'd never sleep in a place she hasn't thoroughly scouted. It's one of the things I admire most about her.

If I hadn't been so weary, body and soul, I would have done the same thing.

I glance in her direction. "So, what did you find?"

Belcalis shrugs. "Everything seems benign. For now." With that dire warning, she walks closer to me, her eyes taking in my new finery. "It truly is stunning," she says, soft just for a moment.

My cheeks warm. "Thank you," I reply, glancing shyly again at the water wall.

In all my years, I've never worn anything as fine as this, nor dreamt I ever would. Even when I was the Nuru, the goddesses' loyal pet, no one ever offered me such beautiful clothing. I was always in armor, always standing unobtrusively at the goddesses' side. An attendant instead of a companion. A subordinate instead of an equal. But this—this is not a dress that allows you to stand to the side. This is a dress that demands you be the center of attention.

Why the gods of Maiwuri would grant such a thing to me, I

don't know, but I'm grateful. At least when Mother finally sees me, she'll see a daughter who is whole and relatively healthy, instead of the wounded and scarred person I was mere hours ago.

The reminder has me turning toward the door, ready to head to the Hall of the Gods. As I begin to walk, however, Belcalis steps in front of me and taps her lips.

"There's only one touch missing," she muses.

My eyebrows furrow. "What do you mean?"

Instead of replying, she removes a dagger from her side, uses it to slice her palm. "Now that you like masks again—"

"You mean, now that I've *reclaimed* them," I correct, reminding her.

For much of Otera, masks are a symbol of oppression: women are required to wear them to show not only that they are the property of men but also that they are pious and obedient. But I like to wear war masks whenever I go on a mission, as the ultimate symbol of my status as a warrior. For me, war masks are a symbol of self-expression, signaling that I can not only protect myself; I can protect others.

Belcalis nods, holding out her bleeding palm. "Now that you've reclaimed them," she repeats dryly, "I have a gift for you." As I watch, awed, her blood rises into the air and spins like threads to form a delicate, almost invisible golden mask that allows my skin to show through, giving the illusion that my face is covered by golden scales the same way my dress is. More like a shimmer than a mask.

"Belcalis . . . ," I breathe, astonished.

I'd forgotten about this, that my friends' divine gifts can be used not only to protect themselves but also to entertain, to amuse, and even to create.

And create she has. In all the years I've worn masks, *seen* masks, I've never seen anything like this.

"It's beautiful," Britta says. "How did ye learn to do that?"

"I didn't." Belcalis shrugs. "I just thought I could make it, and so I did." She returns her attention to me, her dark eyes peering into mine. "No matter what happens at the meeting, no matter what we encounter, I just want you to know that you carry my love and strength with you."

"That ye carry all our love and strength," Britta affirms.

I glance from her back to Belcalis, tears pricking at my eyes. "Oh, you two," I say, sobbing now. I gather Britta close, then gesture to Belcalis, waiting until she steps forward to put my arms around her.

Belcalis has endured so much, suffered such atrocity, she rarely allows herself to touch or be touched. You have to ask her for permission, have to wait for her to be comfortable.

So I do just that, breathing in tandem a few seconds with her until her body relaxes. "Thank you," I whisper to her. "Thank you."

Belcalis nods, hooking her arm in mine. "Now we can go."

Britta swiftly does the same to my other arm, and just like that, we're out the door and into the light-filled hallway, where Keita, Lamin, and Li are waiting.

They've all been given new clothes as well.

Lamin is now dressed like all the other godsworn of Sarla, in sedate white robes with a cloak whose hood he only partly allows to conceal his face. "Evening greetings, Deka," he says, ducking his head shyly.

I manage a swift nod despite the fury I still feel over the revelations of his misdeeds. "Evening greetings, Lamin," I reply coldly.

Then I turn my attention to Keita and Li, who are both wearing vaguely similar robes, that fury still simmering deep inside me. I still haven't decided how I should address Lamin's betrayal. At least with Adwapa and Asha, they were sent to the Warthu Bera, the training ground where we all learned to become warriors, specifically to ensure my safety. They were always on my side. Lamin, however . . . The mere thought of it upsets me, so I focus my gaze on Keita. His new robes are dark blue, his favorite color, so he and I look like a matching set, although his clothing has none of the accents that mine does. Keita has always been a simple dresser.

The most decoration he allows is a simple circlet, but like mine, his has blue coral threaded through the gold.

Li, on the other hand, is at his most flamboyant. His robes are iridescent green and purple, like the brightly colored glimmerbirds that display their tails on Otera's amarul trees when greeting the sunrise. Gold embroiders his neckline and hems, and yet more gold drips from the golden circlet around his brow into his long black hair, which has been brushed to silken brilliance.

Li preens when we approach, showing off the long gold earrings affixed to both ears.

"Don't they suit me so perfectly?"

"Of course they do, ye bloody glimmerbird," Britta sniffs, even though there's appreciation in her eyes, and another, more primal feeling I'm not certain I want to see.

It feels too private, too intimate to intrude upon.

Li gathers her close. "You know you like it," he whispers in her ear.

I ignore them and keep my eyes fixed on Keita, who hasn't quite noticed me yet, he's so busy surveying the room for threats. Just watching him stops my breath. I've never seen him so elegantly dressed, so handsome. The attendants have even paid special attention to his hairline, fading away the hair there while allowing the little coils that have grown over the past few months to flourish at the top.

The whole effect emphasizes his eyes, which glow in the low evening light.

Suddenly, I'm warm and flushed all over.

I venture a hesitant little wave, my heart pounding harder than it was just seconds ago. "Evening greetings, Keita," I say softly, drawing his attention to me.

He doesn't reply, but his eyes flicker over me, a slightly dazed look in them, as if he's just been hit over the head with Britta's war hammer.

"Deka," he breathes, his voice suddenly hoarse. "You look . . ." He walks closer, takes my hands in his. He clears his throat as if trying to take control of his voice. "You look like a goddess. Like *my* goddess."

My cheeks heat, and I glance up into his eyes. The fire there is burning brightly. It ignites a similar feeling in my body, and suddenly, I have to fight to keep from squirming. His hands are warm . . . oh, so warm. . . .

"Thank you," I finally manage to say. "You look amazing too. Like a prince. *My* prince," I add.

"I will always be yours. You know that, Deka."

I do. I've known it ever since he carried me in pieces to that lake two years ago so White Hands and the other Firstborn could heal me after the former emperor ordered me dismembered.

Before then, I'd never known a man, much less a boy, who

would put a woman before his own safety. But Keita did that. He aided me when no one else dared. He defended me when no other man was willing.

He presses his forehead to mine, and I sink against him, savoring the feeling. The warmth. Ever since Keita received his fire, he's become like a furnace, always boiling. It unnerves the others, but not me. Never me.

I like the heat.

"Angoro Deka . . ." It's some moments before a hesitant voice interrupts the spell. I reluctantly pull back from Keita, then turn to find Nenneh Kadeh standing by the door in what appears to be her finest regalia, the white robes so sleek, they almost seem like a stream of fabric flowing over her.

"It is time," she says quietly.

I nod, then look at Keita. He smiles at me, squeezes my hand. "No matter what happens, I'm here."

"We all are," Britta says, a sentiment that is repeated by the rest of my friends, who nod encouragingly at me.

I glance at them, gratitude shining in my eyes.

Then I nod back at Nenneh Kadeh. "I'm ready now."

"Wonderful." She gestures to the open door. "It is time to meet the gods of Maiwuri."

12

◆ ◆ ◆

I expected to meet Mother in a temple somewhere in the administrative district, but Nenneh Kadeh and Lamin escort me toward the mountains that loom in the center of the island. Lamin has recovered from our earlier awkwardness and is becoming more authoritative as we go, as if he's remembering his time here, remembering the person he used to be before he was sent to Otera and forced to become a member of my group. I watch, disgruntled, as he taps the side of a jewel-green tree trunk and a staircase appears out of thin air, the clear, glasslike steps appearing one by one to spiral off into the evening sky.

Britta wrinkles her nose doubtfully. "Ye want us to get onto that?"

"Yes." Lamin nods. "It's the only way up."

"That thing?" Britta is clearly still skeptical. "The one with no handrails that goes up an' up an' up?"

"It won't allow you to fall. Watch." Lamin demonstrates by walking up a few steps into the air and then intentionally stumbling sideways. Magically, more steps appear, and this continues no matter how erratically he walks. "See?" he finally says, satisfied.

"More demonstrations of power from the gods of Maiwuri. Wonderful," Belcalis says with a weary sigh, taking a few steps up.

Keita, meanwhile, just turns to me and extends his hand. "Deka?"

"My thanks," I say as I accept it, again marveling at the warmth of his fingers against mine.

No matter how much I resent these new gods who have imposed themselves on my life, I remain grateful to them for this body, which can, for the moment, walk and move without pain and accept the touch of others without fear of damage or agony.

I remain hand in hand with Keita as we ascend, leaving behind the streets far below, the rushing waterfalls, and the quiet, shadow-filled gardens whose flowers glow under the dim light. By now, it's nearly night, and the moon swells on the horizon, a glowing yellow orb. Lanterns spark into flame, the glowing insects lighting them chirping a soothing melody. Ixa, who has already changed into his nightflyer form, trills along with their melody, bewildering more than one insect into silence. It's all so magical, I'm momentarily distracted from the panic, the apprehension, building inside me.

I'm going to meet the gods of Maiwuri. I'm going to meet Mother. My journey may finally, finally, be at an end.

A thousand conflicting emotions stir inside me until the continued ascension of the stairs begins slowing. Then, finally, unexpectedly, we're at water's edge again—only this isn't the beach we landed on; it's a beach somewhere deep *inside* the sky. A work of divinity I would have never reached had the stairs not taken us there. No wonder Nenneh Kadeh told me that it was unreachable yesterday when I wanted to go. Even with Ixa and the gryphs, neither I nor my friends have found our way here.

Once our feet land on sand, Nenneh Kadeh and Lamin suddenly stop, as do the retinue of godsworn trailing them like white-robed ducklings following their parents.

"This is where all of us must leave you, Angoro Deka," Nenneh Kadeh says. "You must walk the rest of your path alone."

As I sigh, Belcalis humphs beside me. "Now, doesn't that sound familiar . . ."

Britta, meanwhile, turns abruptly to her, eyes narrowed in suspicion. "Wha do ye mean, 'all of us'? We're goin' with her."

Nenneh Kadeh shakes her head. "While I greatly admire your loyalty, young alaki, there are places even you cannot go. You must leave Deka's side, as must we all."

"Must we?" Keita rumbles, flames sparking at the sides of his eyes. He's ready to fight, as he has been from the moment we entered Maiwuri. "Because that's certainly not happening."

Nenneh Kadeh sighs. "I don't think I'm explaining properly. Perhaps it's better if I show you." She gestures toward the water.

A low roar sounds as the sea suddenly parts, the waters in front of us splitting into two to reveal a sandy floor covered in glistening coral, bedraggled sponges, swiftly moving crabs, and, strangest of all, what appears to be a gleaming mother-of-pearl path, which wends its way from the sandy shore to the steep incline below.

Britta gapes at it. "Is that—"

"The path to the Hall of the Gods," Nenneh Kadeh says softly. "Sarla has opened it for you, Deka. But once you enter, it will close around you."

I whirl to her. "Wait, so you mean the water will—"

"Fall in around you? Yes," Nenneh Kadeh confirms.

"But that will kill her!" Britta sputters. "Ye know that will kill her!"

At these words, Nenneh Kadeh turns to her, looking stern. "She is the Angoro. This path is made precisely for her. She will be safe, as will her godsworn." She looks pointedly at Ixa as she says this. "We, however, will not. And that is why we cannot walk the path with her."

I turn from the water back to her, mulling over this information. "You can guarantee my safety?"

At my question, Nenneh Kadeh blinks, her eyes suddenly far away. Finally, she answers. "Sarla informs me that this will not be the first time you've had a meeting with the gods underwater."

I shiver, remembering the time nearly half a year ago now, when I met underwater with Anok, the wisest of the Oteran goddesses and my only ally among them. That meeting sent me down the path to uncovering the truth about the Oteran gods and their depravity.

And it was one that only Anok and I were privy to.

I frown at Nenneh Kadeh. "How did you know that?" No one else should have been able to see through the spell Anok cast, but then, everyone else there was a citizen of Otera.

The Maiwurians, apparently, are different.

She taps the side of her nose, back to being herself again. "As I said, we have watchers everywhere."

When she glances pointedly at Lamin, he flushes and looks

away. So it was him. Of course it was him. How much more has he seen over the years and shown Sarla? How much more has he been privy to?

"Once a spy, always a spy," Li sniffs dismissively, causing Lamin's flush to spread. No matter how he protests, he knows exactly what he's done.

Nenneh Kadeh glances between the two and then back to me. "Perhaps while you have your meeting, the others will have one of their own. It seems they have things to sort out."

As Li and Belcalis continue glaring at Lamin, Britta and Keita walk over to me.

"What do you want to do?" Keita asks in a low voice, glancing at the path, which is still open, waiting for me to enter.

"Ye don't have to go if ye don't want to," Britta adds. "I know we're on a mythical floating island surrounded by eerie people with the power of unknown gods—"

"That's quite the scene you've laid out," Keita mutters.

"I'm just tryin' to paint an accurate representation of wha we're up against," Britta huffs before turning back to me. "I know we're basically surrounded, but we've faced worse. We faced worse just yesterday. We can do it again."

Keita nods as he reaches out, squeezes my hands. "I think what Britta is trying to say is that all you have to do is say the word. We'll topple all those pretty little buildings if we have to—destroy the entire place, if it's what you wish."

I look at them both, so supportive, always there for me, no matter the odds. Then I pat both their shoulders. "It's all right," I say. "I can handle this. It's just a few gods, right?"

Britta smiles wanly. "Just a smallish pantheon of eighty or so."

I nod. "I'll speak to them, see my mother, get my kelai. Everything will be all right."

They both nod, but uncertainty lies in their eyes, fear flickering just behind them. So I lean in closer. "And if anything goes wrong, you begin razing, understood?"

A grim smile slices Britta's lips. "Perfectly."

"And with pleasure," Keita says.

I take a step back.

"All right," I say out loud. "See you all soon."

As Britta and Keita nod, Lamin suddenly approaches, his eyes hesitant. "Deka?"

"Yes?" My response is as cold now as it was when I first saw him this evening.

"I know you must be doubtful and mistrustful, but just remember, they're your allies . . . and so am I."

"I'll try not to forget that when you're once again spying on me."

Lamin looks down, chastened. "I don't know how I can ever begin to apologize for that."

"I do." I look up at him, my expression firm. "You can remain here when we leave."

When Lamin's eyes flit to mine, stunned, I continue with the speech I've practiced since I first began climbing those floating steps this evening. "I can't trust you; you've proven that. Your loyalty was never to me and the others; it was to them, the people we didn't even know existed. To the gods we didn't even know were watching us. All of whom you sold our confidences to. *My* confidences to. So when we leave, I don't want you to come with us. I want you to stay here, with your family. You're not part of our group—you never were."

Lamin steps forward, his eyes wide. "But, Deka, I—"

"No," I say, turning away. "That is what I have decided."

He tries to walk closer, but Keita steps in front of him, his eyes firm. "Consider yourself lucky that's all she asks of you," he says quietly. "If it were White Hands, she would have already taken your head."

Tears fill Lamin's eyes, those strange yet unnervingly familiar white eyes. "Deka," he says, pleading now as he turns to me, "I never meant to betray you."

I stare straight into his eyes so he can see the determination in mine. "And yet that's exactly what you did."

As Lamin hangs his head, I turn to the others. "I'll see you all soon. Until then."

"Until then," my friends reply.

Then I gesture to Ixa, who swiftly flitters to the ground, already transforming from a nightflyer into his adolescent form, only there's a difference now. Instead of seeming more feline, the way he usually does, he now seems more reptilian, perhaps in preparation for this aquatic adventure. Once he has fully transformed, we head down onto the path, walking slowly and surely onward until, moments later, the water comes crashing down around us, only it doesn't inundate us the way I expect. Instead, it surges around me in a swirling pattern, creating a pocket of air that grows smaller and smaller until finally, it dissipates, leaving me several leagues beneath the surface with nothing but the ocean currents billowing around me.

For a moment, all is silent except for the thunder of the waves crashing far above. I hold my breath, almost frightened to inhale. But then I remind myself: I've walked underwater before, survived being inundated before.

And more to the point, this water doesn't feel anything like all the water I've encountered before. It's so light, my body moves effortlessly through it, my dress seeming to repel the water rather than take it in. Could it be that the Maiwurian gods have intervened to allow me to move about easily in this new environment?

I take a cautious breath. Water immediately rushes up my nose, only it's not alone. Something accompanies it: air. *I can breathe!*

I take another breath, this one less water-filled. Then another, and another, and another, until finally, I'm breathing. And that's not the only thing I'm doing. I dart through the water, my body moving so swiftly, it's as if the currents are air. I blink, shocked, when my eyes begin to adjust, the darkness of the water lightening until suddenly, I can see everything around me with perfect clarity.

I'm on what appears to be a ledge, the surface some leagues above me, deeper water looming in the distance. Oceanic plants sprout all around me, some of them long and stringy, others short and squat, with glowing leaves in all the colors of the rainbow. It's like each plant is its own little light in the gloom of the deep water, attracting fish and crustaceans and all sorts of other creatures I could never even have conceived.

A jellylike mass moves so fluidly in the currents, lights shimmering up and down its sides, that it takes me some time to realize that it's not the currents that are moving it but the creature itself. It's swimming toward a small school of shimmering silver fish and—

My jaw drops when the creature suddenly expands to three times its size and envelops half the school.

So land isn't the only place that's brutal. Water is as well.

I'm so fascinated by this observation, I almost don't notice when the first low rumbles build in the water. Then one sounds near me. I whirl, jaw slackening, when a massive blue-and-gold reptilian body surges past me, three more joining it. Ebiki. The colossal creatures are floating in front of me, an honor guard of sorts. That comforting rumble I associate with them reverberates through the currents, and I turn, grateful to see, far in the oceanic darkness, a pair of gigantic black eyes. Queen Ayo. She's there, a silent witness, although I have the sense that she can't come any closer due to her size. This part of the shore isn't deep enough to carry her. The golden scales on her sides gleam underwater, a soft, subtle glow that is replicated on the sides of the other ebiki, whose scales gleam and pulse as well.

As does Ixa's. To my surprise, my companion is also glowing as he stares eagerly at the others of his kind, each one so gigantic, he may as well be a speck in comparison.

Look, Deka, Ixa says, excited. *Mother here.*

But he doesn't dart in her direction. Instead, a deep, soothing rumbling passes between the two, so low, I feel it more as a vibration in my bones than anything else. They're speaking, communicating with each other.

Once they're done, Ixa turns to me, eyes earnest. *Mother says I carry,* he says, his body lengthening, until soon, he's the size of a full-grown horse. He looks up at me expectantly. *Deka ride,* he instructs. *Ixa carry.*

Nodding, I sling my legs over his back, then brace myself as he bolts into the currents, his fins cutting through the water as easily as a knife through butter. His movement is a signal to the other ebiki, who arrange themselves on either side of us as Ixa and I follow the mother-of-pearl path deeper and deeper into the water, heading toward the end of the ledge and the abyss looming just beyond it.

A cool blue glow is rising from it, one whose origin I'm not certain of until we swim over the ledge and the ground drops out below, revealing the massive structure floating in the middle of the darkness.

The Hall of the Gods.

13

◆ ◆ ◆

I've seen hundreds of temples since the day my blood ran gold and I discovered the truth of what I was. The one floating in front of me, however, is a thing not of this world. The walls seem to be made of light, not stone, and the water swirls around it in a radiant, shimmering glow, its power palpable even from this distance. There's something behind it, something dark and almost ominous, but I can't concentrate on it. Not that I even want to try. All I see is that light, that temple, and all I feel is awe.

I turn to Queen Ayo, who has accompanied me the entire way, melodic rumblings sounding from inside her colossal chest.

Pray I have good fortune, I say to her as I inhale for courage. I'm finally here. The place where all my questions will be answered.

A deep, vibrating rumble is her reply. Her eyes blink slowly, as if to say, *I'll be right here waiting.*

My thanks, I answer as I swiftly float off Ixa.

I turn to him. *Come on,* I say. *It's time to meet the gods.*

Deka, he chirps, and then we swim through the water and into the light.

The Hall of the Gods seems to be made purely out of beams of light—not stone or any other tangible material. Glowing walls soar up to a ceiling that extends far past the limits of my gaze. Columns shimmer in all colors of the rainbow, a slow, deliberate pulsing that reminds me of the glowing plants I saw on the ride to the temple. The floor itself is blue, only it's not any single shade I've ever encountered before; instead, a thousand undiscovered hues weave and alternate before my astonished eyes.

Then there are the thrones. Ten float at the center of the floor, with two godsworn kneeling in contemplation on either side of each. Power ripples from every throne, a reflection of the god sitting there. I shiver just looking at them, even though I don't see the gods themselves yet. As with the emperor's throne back in Hemaira, the thrones here are veiled. But unlike there, however, here each veil varies according to, I suppose, whatever function the god fulfills. One throne is wreathed with bouquets of perfumed flowers and vines that undulate and whisper to each other; I assume it's the seat of the same god the plant district belongs to. After my experience with Etzli, the underhanded goddess who used her blood-eater vines to feed from her unsuspecting victims, I am immediately repulsed by it.

The throne just next to it, thankfully, is a much more welcome sight. It's covered by heartfelt sighs and lovelorn flutters. Having never before encountered sounds and feelings being utilized like this, it's some time before I can pull my eyes away.

Yet another throne is covered by thunder and lightning; another, the happiness of a mother holding her babe in her arms for the first time.

There are so many thrones, so many veils, it's some moments before I finally find the one I'm looking for, the throne veiled by the scent of old scrolls, the flapping of paper, and the fervency of intellectual discovery. One glance is all it takes for me to know, without a shadow of a doubt, that this throne belongs to Sarla, the deity of wisdom. Which means . . .

My heart pounds in my chest as I see the lone godsworn kneeling beside it, a slight figure clothed and hooded in the same heavy white robes that distinguish Sarla's godsworn, though her hems are embroidered with little red flames that flash and dance as if alive.

Even from this distance, I recognize those delicate hands, that graceful, almost dancer-like posture.

Tears flood my eyes. "Mother!" I rush over, heart pounding.

"Deka?" Mother flings back her hood, revealing her face in all its familiar glory.

And my heart nearly leaps from my chest.

The last time I saw Mother, she was lying on her deathbed, face pale and haggard, body nearly wasted away. Her dark brown skin had turned to ash, blood the color of rubies dripped from her nose, and deep sores cracked the sides of her mouth. Later, I would learn this was all a ruse: Mother was an alaki, a descendant of the Gilded Ones; she couldn't die from, or even contract, human illnesses. But she needed to keep the village elders and jatu off her trail as she tried to find a way to keep me from being discovered, so she faked her death and fled Irfut, hoping to get to White Hands so they could formulate a way to rescue me.

Except somewhere along the way, she discovered the truth of the Gilded Ones, the truth of the fate they wished for me. And she tried to save me. She suffered horrifically as a result.

The knowledge that she put herself in such danger, sacrificed herself for the sake of my safety, has kept me moving forward these past few months as we fled both the Gilded Ones and the Idugu. If Mother did all those things on my behalf, surely I could keep going, no matter what the odds. But now she's here, right in front of me. I'm filled with so much joy, I might explode.

"Mother! Mother!" I gasp again, squeezing her tight. Kissing her cheeks and nuzzling my chin across her tightly coiled, short-cropped brown hair.

Thankfully, her skin hasn't changed into that shimmering white of Sarla's other godsworn, and her eyes are still the soft, welcoming black I know. But those are the only things that have remained constant.

When I was growing up, Mother always seemed voluptuous, with the exaggerated curves that distinguish many tribesmen from the deep Southern provinces. But now I can feel that she's become wiry, having lost much of her pleasing plumpness. And in a surprising twist of fate, I've grown taller than her—me, Deka, the one all my friends mocked for never achieving the towering height that distinguishes most Northerners.

Of all the things I expected when my blood first ran gold, this was the farthest from my mind: that one day, my own mother would look up at me instead of my looking up at her. That Umu, the woman who was once a Shadow, a deadly assassin and spy, would one day have to tilt up her chin to gaze into my eyes, tears of joy dripping from hers.

"Oh, Deka." She sniffles. "It's you, it's really you. Sarla told me you'd be coming, but I couldn't believe it, couldn't allow myself to—" She abruptly takes a step back, examines me, astonished. "Just look at you; you've become strong. And what is this dress?" Then she notices Ixa. She kneels down in front of him. "And who is this charming little ebiki?"

Ixa lets out a long, contented purr as she strokes him under his chin. *Ixa like,* he says happily to me. *Deka do more this.*

But all my attention is on Mother, who has stood once again and is now looking me over as if her eyes cannot get enough of me. "You look like . . ." Her eyes widen, as if the thought awes her. "You look like one of them," she says, nodding toward the thrones. "You look like a god."

A familiar expression shines in her eyes, one I've seen all too often in the past few months—especially when I was Nuru, supposed daughter to the gods.

Reverence.

The sight of it turns my stomach.

I can tolerate it from strangers, even acquaintances, but I can't take it from her. Never her.

I embrace her again, if only to remind her that I'm flesh and blood. "I look like your daughter," I say firmly, gazing into her eyes. "No matter what, I'm your daughter."

I may have once been a seed, a golden spark of divinity, but she was the one who carried me for eleven months—much longer than is usual for a human pregnancy. She was the one who nurtured and protected me when I thought I was nothing more than a human girl.

In all the ways that count, I'm her daughter.

Mother nods. "I know, Deka," she whispers. "Of course I know. I'm just—" She sniffles once more and wipes away a tear. "I'm just so happy!"

I embrace her again. "I've missed you so much, Mother. So much."

"And I you," she replies. Then she bursts into tears, her eyes filled with misery. "And I'm so sorry, Deka. Sorry I couldn't save you, sorry for all you had to go through, and your father—"

"He's dead." I cut her off before she goes any further, the words a vise squeezing all the air out of my chest.

Talking about Father is like opening a raw, painful wound and then digging the knife deeper into it. Yes, he apologized as he died, and yes, I forgave him. But I didn't forget. I will never forget. How can you forget the man who beheaded you instead of protecting you? Father not only gave me to the village elders when my blood first ran gold, he beheaded me himself when I resurrected the first time. Left me in that temple cellar to experience many more deaths until White Hands intervened and took me with her to the Warthu Bera. How can you forget such a betrayal? How can you forget the man who would rather obey the lies of an ancient book than the tug of his own conscience?

I might have let go of my anger over his actions, but never again will I allow anyone to treat me so poorly, to manipulate me so. I will never again mistake abuse for love and cherish it the way I once did with the man I used to call Father.

Mother looks down, nods. "I know he is. I felt it when it happened. When you live with someone for so long . . . sometimes you just know." She looks up at me, her eyes brimming with a thousand emotions, a thousand words left unsaid. "My deepest apologies, my daughter. I heard what he did to you. I heard all the things he—"

Her voice abruptly quakes, and she bends slightly, struggling to breathe, struggling to regain her composure. "I heard about the Ritual of Purity and the temple and the cellar and the beheading—"

When she turns away, her breath coming in strangled gasps, I hurry to embrace her. "I survived it," I swiftly say. "I overcame it."

"But you shouldn't have had to do that. You shouldn't have had to. I trusted that man. Trusted him to keep you safe and he—"

I squeeze tighter. "What's done is done. And it's not your fault, Mother. You didn't put that sword in his hand or force him to betray me." Mother nods again, but I can almost feel the guilt radiating from her, the guilt that no doubt looks very much like my own.

Is this where I got it from, this habit of blaming myself for anything and everything?

But no, Otera is the reason, the culprit. Its culture is. The Infinite Wisdoms—the false holy books on which I was raised—conditions women to take on the sins of everyone else. No matter the situation, no matter the person, if something happens, it's always the woman's fault. And barring that, it is the fault of the men who love other men, or the yandau, or the maimed and injured, the infirm—anyone who isn't a typical Oteran man.

It is always the fault of those on the periphery.

We are the ones Otera sees as inherently weak, shameful. We are the ones who must always shoulder the blame.

The reminder is sobering. Joyous as I am to reunite with Mother, I need to focus on what I came here for: taking back my kelai. Using it to kill the Gilded Ones and the Idugu and get Otera back to peace. And even more important than that, creating a world where everyone is equal. Where people are seen and loved for themselves instead of castigated for their differences. Which, again, is why I need to speak to the gods of Maiwuri.

But before that, I have an important question. "My kelai," I say, turning back to Mother. "Do you know where it is? Is it here?"

Mother stills. "It's best you speak to the gods first. And then we can talk."

My muscles immediately tense. There's something important she isn't telling me.

Suddenly, that premonition, the one I've had before about how Otera's fate and mine are intertwined, surfaces, as do a thousand other horrible suspicions.

I immediately suppress them. There's no point in falling apart now, not when I'm finally here, at the place where all my questions will hopefully be answered.

So I kiss the back of Mother's head, letting her familiar scent of spice blossoms and anatari peppers wash over me. "We will continue this later," I say softly.

And then I walk toward the center of the temple.

14

◆ ◆ ◆

The temple has changed while I wasn't looking. More thrones have appeared, floating in orderly, concentric tiers behind the ten more massive ones at the center. Enough, I'm guessing, that all eighty Maiwurian gods must now be present behind the veils of their thrones.

The very thought unnerves me. I no longer like it when I can't see the actions of the gods.

Thankfully, their godsworn are all there, and they're standing now, instead of kneeling, silent witnesses to the proceedings.

"Well, then," I say aloud once I take full stock of the changes. "Do any of you plan to reveal yourselves, or are you going to remain hidden this entire meeting?"

"We did not wish to disturb you, Angoro Deka. . . ." The answer arrives almost as a wave, rippling from one throne to the other. "We have been waiting for you. We have always been waiting for you."

Power crackles as the veils slide back from the thrones and

143

the gods finally reveal themselves. I glance from one to the other, unimpressed. There they are, those divine white gazes I know so well, only this time, they're set in skin of all different colors, from the usual human shades of brown, yellow, and pink to the shimmer of rainbows or even distant stars. Robes sewn from molten lava and ice sparkle alongside those made of petals, or rainbows, or even wind. There's so much variety, so much to look at, I don't know where to turn next.

When the gods speak again, it comes as a single, clearly vocalized thought. "Angoro Deka, we are honored to have you with us here today. Come forward, that we may receive you."

I turn to Mother and she nods. "Go to them, Deka," she says softly. "Speak with them. In them, you will find the allies you need for your upcoming task."

At her words, a thousand questions rise up inside me, horrible suspicions as well. But I suppress them and do as Mother advised. Once I'm near the thrones, I stand as proudly as I can. I spent nearly a year bowing and scraping before the Oteran gods, and they used that subservience to take as much from me as they could. I refuse to do so here.

"I would like to speak to Sarla," I say, turning back to the wisdom throne, which has somehow appeared center to my gaze.

Mother is once again kneeling beside it, those flames on her hems dancing until they become real flames—a furnace surrounding her. That furnace is a symbol. While Mother may kneel next to the throne of wisdom, the flames surrounding her show that she is also godsworn to Baduri, the small, plump red goddess of hearth and home who I'm certain I see in flashes from the corner of my eye. Unlike the other gods, Baduri seems to be content fading into the background, as much a part of the scenery as the walls made of light and the thrones floating inside them.

But she's not my concern; Sarla is.

I return the full force of my attention to the wisdom throne.

The god who emerges from behind its veil is neither male nor female, nor any type of gender I can discern. They're almost like a void, so austere compared to the other gods, it would be easy to overlook them. Their skin is the same pale shimmer as their godsworn, and their eyes gleam as white as the midwinter snow. I carefully avoid looking into them, knowing that some gods enjoy trapping others with their gaze, Etzli being a prime example.

"We are Sarla," the god says, their words replicated by every other god in the room. It's somehow both a whisper and a roar, and the sound rattles my bones.

I glance around, unnerved. "You all speak as one?"

"We are one," Sarla insists—alone this time. "Merely different facets—"

"—of the same—" another god continues.

"—being," all the gods finish as one.

"So you have not separated yourselves from each other like the Gilded Ones and the Idugu," I say. "You did not sever into two."

Sarla shakes their head.

"There is no true difference between severed and unsevered," they reply. "There is only balance. The natural and divine order."

I frown. "What do you mean?"

"The gods of Otera thought themselves above humans, above equus and ebiki, above the beasts in the field, the plants, above dust, above all sentient beings—even above this world itself. They forgot that we are all one, and each of us is all." These words are a declaration, an earthquake shattering through my bones. I can feel it rumbling through me, penetrating to the very core of me.

It's all I can do to remain upright under the power.

And yet, my thoughts whirl. Everything the gods just said contradicts what I know. At least, what I thought I knew. "So you mean that the severing of the Oteran gods was not what caused them to fall?"

The gods shake their heads in tandem. "Male, female, yandau—all the other iterations. There is no difference, all merely countless expressions of the same thing. God and mortal. Immortal and man. Person and planet. All part of the Greater Divinity. The natural order. This is the understanding the gods of Otera forgot. And when we tried to remind them, they attempted to war against us and to prey on those we serve."

I frown. *Serve.* No god I've ever met in Otera has used that word. Even the utterance of it is unthinkable. But the gods of Maiwuri, it seems, use it purposefully. They believe they serve. Not lead, not protect, not oversee. Serve.

I let this knowledge sit with me.

The gods continue. "It is also the reason we created the Great Barrier."

I blink. "The Great Barrier?"

"A veil, protecting Maiwuri from Otera, shielding it so Otera's gods would never again turn their gazes here."

I remember that rainbow shimmer I saw coating the sky. The one I just glanced at and then immediately forgot about.

But perhaps that is by design.

I snort, my awe dissipating as I understand. "So instead of stopping them, you ran like cowards and put up a barrier leaving the rest of the world to suffer?"

There is a pause as the gods process this insult. Then Sarla speaks again. "Corruption," they say. "It spread from the gods to their children to the humans, to Otera itself. Had we remained, it would have infected us, driven us to treat those we serve the way our Oteran kin treated everyone around them. So we chose to protect Maiwuri, for the sake of the entirety of Kamabai."

"Kamabai?" I've heard the word before, but I'm not certain what it means.

"This world. The twelve continents. Four in Otera, eight in Maiwuri. All together, they make up Kamabai."

Suddenly, I feel weak. "Twelve continents . . ."

My legs—my entire body—is boneless from the revelation.

The world is so much bigger than I'd imagined. So much bigger . . . And the Gilded Ones knew. All the while, they knew. How much more about the world have they kept from me? From everyone around them?

I have to breathe deeply to return my attention to the present.

I glance at Sarla again, careful not to meet their gaze. "All right, so you created a barrier. What's changed? Why bring me here now?" The Maiwurian gods can say all the pretty things they like, but they want something from me.

Whether I will give it to them, however, remains to be seen.

A small thunderstorm wreathes Sarla's head, visible manifestation of their anguish.

Gods don't feel the way we do and, as a result, don't display their emotions in the same way. When a mortal is sad, they cry. When a god is sad, hurricanes drown entire villages.

The deity of wisdom continues: "The corruption of the Oterans has infected the world itself. Those shadow vales—they are only a taste of what is to come. And they're encroaching ever closer on Maiwuri. There are many more than you saw, created by both Oteran pantheons."

"Countless," the other gods echo.

"Countless?" I repeat, my mouth suddenly dry.

All this time, I've been thinking there were only one or two. And that they were all created by the Idugu. But if there are countless shadow vales being created by both sets of gods, that means those gods are consuming sacrifice on an unimaginable scale. One even White Hands's army won't be able to affect, much less end.

I've been so naive, thinking the Oteran gods were enfeebled enough that White Hands and a few allied forces could stop them in the event that I became too weak to fight. But if there are that many vales . . .

Suddenly, I think of the darkness lurking behind this temple. The darkness that is now very obviously a shadow vale. Doubtless, the Maiwurian gods wanted to show me the consequences for the people here if I refuse their requests.

The consequences for people all across the world, across Kamabai.

"The vales are a sign," Sarla says, nodding their head as if they're reading my mind. "A foreshadowing of things to come."

Something about their words strikes deep inside me. That

premonition, the one I've had again and again. For the first time, I don't look away from Sarla's endless gaze as they explain, "The very fabric of this realm is coming apart. This world, as we know it, will soon cease to exist. A few years, perhaps even a few months. The actions of the Oterans endanger not only their empire but the entirety of Kamabai as well."

After Sarla finishes speaking, I remain as I am, letting their words wash over me, sink into me. So it is true. The inkling I've had, the thing that I've feared all this time—it's a reality. The world truly is ending.

And yet, somehow, I'm not panicked by this fact.

I suppose I've suspected it for so long, I've had time to get used to the eventuality. Which is why I turn back to Sarla, anger now erupting. "So let me see if I understand correctly. You want me to risk my life by killing the gods of Otera so you don't risk your own. These are the very same gods you allowed to brutalize Otera for centuries while you hid behind your little barrier. The very same gods you didn't stop when they strayed from the path—that's what you're telling me?"

I give a short, bitter laugh, amazed at the gall of these pious, ethereal-seeming creatures. For a moment there, I almost thought they were different. That they were better than the gods I knew. But deities, it seems, are similar everywhere—only ever concerned with their own survival and petty rivalries.

To their credit, the gods of Maiwuri don't even bother denying it. When they reply, they do so as a collective. "Untold millions—billions of souls—depend on us, even those in Otera. As the pantheons there have abandoned their duties in their quest for more and more power and sacrifice, we are the ones who step into the void, who fulfill their duties—a feat that requires the birth of ever more fledgling gods to compensate.

"For now, all we can do is power the Great Barrier and keep the entirety of Kamabai, our world, from imminent collapse. But if we enter into a fight with the Oterans, all these efforts will be for naught. We will be corrupted, as will everything else. The world will end, and us with it."

"But gods don't die," I retort. "At least, as long as someone like me doesn't end them."

"We, do, however, disperse," Sarla corrects. "Only to form again. As does every living thing eventually. But that takes centuries across light and time. And by then the existence that we call Kamabai will be lost. . . . This lifetime may be fleeting, but it is precious nonetheless, and we would like to preserve it. And that is why we ask your aid, Angoro."

Sarla rises now. Then they do something startling—they sink to their knees. A rustling sounds in the chamber as all the other gods do the same.

I watch them all, mouth agape, as they say in unison, "We beseech you, Angoro Deka—fulfill your purpose. End the Oterans. Save Kamabai. Save us all."

"Save us all . . ." The words repeat around the hall, a reverberant plea that sinks deep into my bones.

I'm in such a state of shock now, it takes me moments before I can gather my thoughts again. "But I need my kelai," I say, returning to the question that drove me all the way here, to this strange, floating place in a strange ocean leagues upon leagues away from my own. "Where is it? Do you have it here?"

Sarla shakes their head. "We do not." But as I stiffen, panic already rising, they turn to my mother, who has been watching the scene, agitated, and gesture. "Umu, however, knows where to find it. Umu?" they beckon. "You should explain to Deka how you came to join us. And how you came to be as you are."

"As she is?"

I watch, confused, as Mother walks over to me, then slowly begins unfastening her hood and cloak. "Now, Deka," she says, "I want you to remember one thing: I'm here. That's all you need to know, is that I'm here. I'm still me."

"What?" I frown, confused by her words. "What are you talking about—"

And then she removes her outer garments, showing what I didn't realize she was concealing all this while.

And I begin screaming.

15

◆ ◆ ◆

Mother has no body. Or, rather, she has only the barest outline of her body from the neck down. Her face is as it always was. Her wrists and hands. Even her feet, which are covered in delicate leather sandals. But the rest of her seems to have faded away, become translucent like those gelatinous creatures I passed on the way here. A map of blood vessels is all that remains inside, all of them emanating from her beating golden heart. But her skin, her muscles, her bones—they're all gone. I've seen all sorts of awful things over the years, a thousand abominations frightening enough to haunt my nightmares to eternity. But to see my own mother like this, more a specter than a person . . . I clutch my stomach, all the food I ate earlier rushing to my throat.

Mother hurries over, embraces me. "It's all right, Deka, it's all right. I'm here. It's as I told you, I'm here."

But that's not true. While she *feels* like she's here—her body feels as solid as it did when I touched her earlier—

"You're not," I whimper, unable to hold back my emotions

now. "I can feel you, and you're solid, but you're not here. Why are you not here?"

"Umu is a wraith." The answer comes from all the gods, who stare at me implacably, as if they cannot possibly understand my agitation.

I turn away from them, inhaling in quick one-two-three breaths to get my emotions under control. I cannot allow them to take me over like they used to. I vowed I never would again. And yet here I am, weeping and carrying on like a neophyte entering her first battle. *One two three,* I count swiftly in my mind. *One two three. And when you reach four, you will stop. Four.*

Stop.

Inhaling again, I hold on to that word. Then I straighten, releasing my emotions and all my other doubts into the currents. I take a few more breaths before I turn back to the gods. "A wraith? I saw vale wraiths in the shadow vale. Mother is nothing like those creatures."

"We speak of wraiths in the traditional sense," Sarla replies.

At their words, everything inside me shrivels. "But wraiths are—"

Sarla inclines their head. "Restless spirits that have some amount of corporeality, just not enough to maintain their form permanently."

By now, my body is shaking so hard, I'm almost afraid it'll come apart. I whirl to Mother, desperate again. "But you're here. You're alive. Please tell me you're alive." My emotions are surging again, a hateful panic sending a lump to my throat. I squeeze her tighter. "You have to be alive, after everything I did to find you. You have to be."

Mother squeezes me back, places her forehead against

mine. "Breathe, Deka, breathe. I'm here, just as I told you. I'm here."

"But?" I prompt, waiting for the end of the sentence.

I know Mother like the back of my hand. I know her smell, the way her hair springs back if you pull it just so. I know exactly how she shivers after she walks in after seeing the first snow of the season. That's how I know the moment she's being evasive. As she is now.

When Mother doesn't answer, I turn to Sarla, who nods sadly. "Umu is only partly alive. What you see before you is her spirit, which is why she can never leave this place."

"We could not bring her back in her entirety," another voice says. This one sounds like the crackling of flames over fresh kindling, like the warmth that envelops you when you first enter your home after a long day.

I turn to find Baduri stirring in the hearth that makes up her throne. "Doing so would disturb the balance. Thus, she is bound to this temple, bound to its hearth. Were she to step one foot out, she would return to the natural order and have to take her rightful place within it."

A hot-cold sensation washes over me.

The natural order.

"You mean death." When Baduri doesn't reply, I turn to Mother. "That's what they're saying, isn't it?" My voice is high-pitched with hysteria.

This is the dire circumstance Lamin warned about, the reason Mother is bound to two gods. She's already dead. All this time searching for her, and she's already dead.

My ears are ringing now, my body slick with sweat. I can't breathe, can't think.

Mother takes my hand, squeezes it gently. One squeeze, then two, then patterns of two and three, just like when I was a child and needed comforting. "I almost reached Fatu," she begins quietly, her eyes sad.

"White Hands," I automatically correct. "She prefers to be called White Hands now."

"White Hands." Mother accepts my correction. "I nearly reached her. Myter had come to me a few days after your fifteenth birthday, you see. They and Bala"—distantly, I note that she has called Myter *they* instead of *she,* marking them as yandau rather than female, as I have been assuming—"are among the few who can interact with others outside Maiwuri. The few who are allowed to."

Like Lamin, I acknowledge silently, waving for her to continue.

"They told me the truth of what you were: not alaki, not Nuru, but Angoro—god killer. I knew I couldn't do anything to help you by myself, so I tried—oh, how I tried—to get to Fatu. White Hands. But I was discovered at the gates of Hemaira. Can you imagine—me, a Shadow, recognized? One of my old sisters remembered my voice. Remembered I had run away from the Warthu Bera years earlier. That was that." Mother shrugs eloquently.

"Once the high priests discovered I was your mother, they took me to the place where they had hidden your kelai, chained me near it so they could see if and how it reacted to me."

"That's where I found her." Myter's voice rings across the temple as they float down to stand beside Mother.

They do it so swiftly, I barely have time to swallow the fact that my kelai is in the hands of the Idugu's priests, and, by extension, the Idugu themselves. No wonder the Gilded Ones had to enact such stealthy methods to consume the bits of it they could.

"But I couldn't free her," Myter continues. "She was bound by celestial gold, which I couldn't break, and because she was in the capital at the time, Bala couldn't emerge so close to where the Idugu rested and risk corruption."

I hear none of Myter's explanations. The only thing I hear is "So she was alive when you found her."

I level my gaze at Myter, who, to their credit, does not falter. Instead, they raise their chin.

"Yes," they answer.

"But after you left with her, she became like this."

"Yes." Myter has the good sense to be concerned now. They take a cautious step back.

"What did you do?" I ask, rage simmering inside me. I feel it rising, an audible crackle over my skin. "Tell me exactly what you did to Mother."

Myter lifts their chin again. "I took her spirit—"

"With my blessings," Mother quickly interjects, sensing my rising anger.

"And brought it here and bound it to the temple."

"And her body?"

"I left it where I found it. I knew the Oterans would never destroy it," they quickly add. "It was too valuable. It had served as your vessel for nearly a year. It had to have something special, something different."

My head is spinning. Round and round it goes. And my ears are ringing. When my voice comes, it's as if from far away. "So you just left her. You just left my mother there, among those

156

monsters." I turn to Mother, accusing. "And you allowed them to. You allowed Myter to kill you!"

"No, I allowed them to take my spirit so I could find a way to contact you. I couldn't do anything imprisoned in that chamber, but here, I could slip into your father's dreams and I could speak to Anok when she discovered me doing so."

I still, brow furrowing. "So that's how she knew?"

I'd wondered how Anok knew where Mother was without the other goddesses knowing. Usually, they all seemed to share knowledge, as if they were different facets of the same brain.

"Yes. She was almost too far gone to the corruption when we first met, but I was able to communicate with her. It was she who warned me to no longer travel through dreams. If she could find me, so could the others."

"And that's why you never visited me?"

Mother nods. "At first, the ansetha necklace prevented me from doing so. Then, Anok's warning did." She brightened. "But that's the beauty of all this, Deka, don't you see? You can follow my body."

I blink. "Follow it? To where?"

"Your kelai." Mother is almost gleeful now. "Your kelai is back in Otera. Exactly where, I'm not certain. The priests keep it hidden under all sorts of arcane objects and divine power. And they move it frequently, to keep the Gilded Ones from finding it. But they don't do the same to my body—they don't hide it with arcane objects, because they think no one will seek it.

"You can use that to your advantage, Deka: find my body, and you'll find your way there, to your kelai."

"And once you do," Sarla adds, "all you have to do is reclaim it, then surrender yourself to the natural order—"

"Wait." I hold up my hands to slow the god down. This is all moving too fast for me. "So all I truly have to do is die? That's all?"

I'd already known this, but it seems too simple, somehow. It seems too easy.

My suspicion is confirmed when Sarla shakes their head. "Much more than that," the god says. "You have to *choose* death of your own accord. Without coercion, without fear. Sacrifice," they intone. "All becoming requires sacrifice."

"Of course it does," I mutter. It's always sacrifice with the gods.

"Choose death, Deka," Sarla finishes, "and you will be reborn to your true self. A god. A conduit for the Greater Divinity."

"One that will destroy the Oteran gods and restore the balance to this world," the gods all intone with a devastating finality.

I glance across the temple, the weight of the demand sinking into me. I can save Otera—the entire world, even. All I have to do is die a mortal death. *Choose* a mortal death.

It's ironic, actually. All this time, I've known I would die one way or the other. But I did not know I had to choose it willingly. But apparently, I have no choice. Because no matter my objections, no matter how much I want to remain as I am, in this body, with my friends, who have all become family, becoming requires sacrifice—the sacrifice of Deka for the Singular, the sacrifice of this life for that of a divine one.

And once I do all that, give up everything that I am, I'll be reborn a god. A creature I despise. A plague on this world. One that may bring it peace or, perhaps, succumb to corruption and finally end it all.

16

◆ ◆ ◆

The dining chamber Keita, Britta, and my other companions are waiting in when I return is on the topmost branch of the tallest tree in Maiwuri—a sprawling, vine-covered behemoth that more closely resembles the highest tower of a palace than it does a tree. I have to use Ixa's winged form to reach it. It's an enchanting space. The tables and chairs are formed from twisting purple vines, and each one is adorned by the same glowing insects we saw as we made our way to the beach earlier, which hum and vibrate in the foliage. Softly shimmering night birds fly past the clear glass walls that protect the chamber from the wind currents outside, their ethereal glow and melodious songs lending a magical cast to the entire affair. It does nothing to calm my tension as I descend from Ixa, who flaps off into the night, to commune with the rest of his kind, no doubt.

"Deka!" Keita says when he spots me. "How was it?"

"Devastating," I say as I exhaustedly walk over, doing my

best not to meet his eyes. After everything I've learned, my entire body is heavy, as is my spirit.

I knew, of course, after I battled the goddesses, that ascending to the ranks of the divine would mean giving up my old life—not just my mortal body but my friends, Keita, everyone I've ever known and loved. That's why my friends and I have remained so intently focused on finding Mother and overcoming every obstacle we met along the journey. If we stopped, there was not only the looming threat of torture and death but also that of the truth: gods and mortals don't mix. Gods are too remote, too unpredictable. And mortals are too easily killed.

Sooner or later, our journey would come to an end. And with it, our years of companionship. We all knew this fact, which is why we tried to avoid it as long as we could.

What none of us knew, however, was that the end of my journey would entail my accepting death—giving in to it. And now that I have this knowledge, I'm not certain I want to share it with the others. It's bad enough saying goodbye, but saying goodbye in such a manner? I don't think I could bear it.

And more to the point, I don't want to.

Despite everything I know, I don't want to surrender my life. I don't want to leave my friends, my chosen family, behind. I don't want to be alone for an eternity.

The Gilded Ones and the Idugu, at least, had each other when they arrived on this plane. When I ascend, I'll have no one. I'll be alone, a singular god surrounded by the ashes of the pantheon she decimated.

Keita glances back at me, his eyes worried. "Deka?" he prompts.

He's clearly waiting for me to explain my pronouncement. But I'm not ready to just yet.

I try to buy time by glancing at the table, which is overflowing with all sorts of food—the choicest of grains, the best cuts of meat and fish. "After I eat," I insist. "I'll tell you after I eat. For now, I'm starving."

"Of course." I can see in his eyes Keita knows I'm stalling, but he doesn't push. Instead, he just places his hand on my cheek and strokes the skin there. "At your own pace, Deka," he says quietly. "I'll be here when you're ready."

Then he leads me to the table, where the vine chairs curl back of their own accord to accommodate us, only to curl forward again, holding us securely in place.

The meal the godsworn have prepared this evening is much more opulent than the one we received when we first arrived. Where yesterday we satiated our hunger with hearty grains and simmering stews, whole roasted fish and meats now lay in front of us, artistically arranged on gigantic leaves sprinkled with bright, crystal-dusted flowers. Little sweet cakes shaped like animals line a tower of desserts, which include rice pastries, banana puffs, and other such delicacies. To top it all off, glittering streams of fruit juices flow like little waterfalls from both sides of the tree trunk surrounding us.

If I wasn't hungry before, I certainly am now, so I hurriedly gulp down the food the leafy, plant-covered attendants offer me, barely even noticing the elegant little gold-tipped fern plates they're using to serve us.

It takes at least half a plate of food before I'm ready to talk, and by that time, my friends are all tapping their feet with impatience.

That includes Lamin, who, to my surprise, is now sitting quietly next to Britta, his eerily pale skin shimmering in the moonlight. After my pronouncement to him earlier this evening, he must have determined to make what amends he could, which is the only explanation I can think of for why the pair is sitting cheek by jowl, as if they weren't just at loggerheads earlier this evening.

When he sees me looking, he inclines his head but doesn't say anything—not that I expected him to. One thing that remains constant about Lamin, godsworn or not, is his dedication to stoic silence.

"Well?" Britta urges when I still don't speak. "Wha happened? Details, Deka, details!"

"You can't just say things are devastating and then leave us in suspense," Li agrees.

I sigh, then glance at the attendants serving us. Their leader, a tall, willowy green woman that very much resembles a newly sprouted sapling, nods to her companions the moment she notices my gaze. They all swiftly fade back into the tree like shadows, the leaves rustling to herald their departure.

Once I'm certain they're gone, I begin. "What happened is that I saw Mother and she was a wraith."

"Ye mean like the ones in the vale?" Britta seems confused, as do the rest of my friends.

"No, I mean like a spirit—one bound to the temple of the gods."

Britta takes a moment to absorb this information. "So she's . . ."

"Dead. All this time."

"Oh, Deka." Britta rushes to enfold me in her arms.

As I sit there, allowing myself to be comforted, a hesitant

cough draws my attention. Li's. "So . . . not to be insensitive . . . ," he begins, a statement that all but ensures he's about to be precisely that, "but how does that relate to your kelai? Was it there? Do you have it?"

I shake my head as I quickly tell them the story Mother told me, including about tracking down her body. "The priests, apparently, cloak my kelai with all sorts of arcane objects, but they don't do the same for Mother's body."

"But how do we find it?" Keita rubs his forehead wearily. "It's not like any of us can sniff out her scent on the wind."

"We can if we have her things." When everyone turns to me, I shrug. "All we have to do is get a sample of her clothing, and then Ixa will—"

"Wha? Sniff out your mother's scent across Otera? Now how does that make sense, Deka?" Britta seems outraged by the suggestion.

I deflate. "It was an idea. I got so overwhelmed after everything the gods told me, I never thought to ask exactly how I—"

"You'll use your combat state," says Lamin. I turn to him, startled. "Your combat state is more enhanced than any other person's as a result of your true nature as a divine being. It not only helps you see the truth of things; it also allows you to sense all sorts of things we can't even imagine. And that should include other people's purest essences, their primordial selves."

I blink. "I don't quite understand what you're saying, but I feel like you have something there."

Lamin eagerly moves closer. "You were correct when you said you needed your mother's things. Specifically, you'll need something that carries her scent, since scent is what spurs the most powerful memories."

"Can't we get that from here?" Li asks.

"Wha part of 'she's a wraith, only her spirit is on this island' do ye not understand?" Britta retorts.

Li holds up his hands. "It was just a suggestion."

Lamin ignores the pair as he continues: "Once you have something with her scent on it, all you have to do is expand your senses to search for her essence. You should be able to follow its traces to her body."

Britta glowers at him. "An' when were ye planning to mention this? After we'd scoured the entirety of Otera?"

Lamin has the good sense to seem chastened. "It just occurred to me," he says sheepishly. "I've become so used to being a warrior, I've forgotten to use my training as a godsworn." When I frown at him, he expands: "All godsworn are trained to understand the workings of their deities and all the gods in general. I spent most of my childhood learning. That's why I know so much about your combat state."

"An' ye never saw fit to tell us any of this before?" Britta sputters. "Give us the benefit of yer understanding of the gods?"

"Divine covenant," he reminds her calmly.

"Covenant, my arse." Britta sniffs. "Ye just wanted to remain loyal to yer keepers here."

As she glares at him, Keita turns to me again. "And what about the actual death of the Oteran gods? Will the Maiwurians aid you in killing them?"

I shake my head. "Apparently they cannot. Interacting with their kin would expose them to corruption and hasten the ending of the world."

"The ending of the world." Keita blinks. "Did I mishear or did you just say 'the ending of the world'?"

I still. There it is, the truth I didn't want to share. I sigh. "The shadow vales are, apparently, just a herald. The world is tearing at its seams. If the Oteran gods are not destroyed soon, their corruption will spread across the world and end all life as we know it."

"Ye mean eventually, right?" Britta moves closer, her eyes desperate. "Tell me ye mean eventually, as in hundreds of thousands of years."

I shake my head, those horrible feelings surging again. "I can't," I whisper, tears pricking my eyes. "The gods back home may not be able to acknowledge the truth, or even see it, but what they're doing, their war with each other, is killing not only Otera but Maiwuri as well. The entire world is suffering because of their folly, and soon—perhaps in years, perhaps even in months—everything will come to an end because of them."

A low whistle cuts the silence as Belcalis leans heavily back in her chair. "And the gods of Maiwuri want you to just ride back to Otera and fix it all for them."

"Yes." I don't even bother to try to prettify my answer.

"You, Deka of Irfut."

"Yes."

"Ye, Deka, who only a few years ago thought ye were human." Britta reenters the conversation, her eyes blinking fast now, as if she's trying to understand, trying to comprehend.

But there is no comprehending this—only trying to survive it.

"Yes," I say, "I'm the one they want to fix this. Me, you—all of us."

Britta seems to sit with this for a moment, then tears glaze her eyes—tears not so much of sadness but of frustration. I know this because of how red she gets, how tightly her hands clench into fists. "After everything we've done. Everything. I can't . . . I just . . ." She pounds the table, the single blow so hard, she breaks a chunk off the side.

"Britta," I begin, but she's already rushing off, then hiding behind a cluster of leaves, her gasping sobs audible even from a distance.

When I begin to stand, Li shakes his head. "I'll go get her," he says quietly.

As he rushes to her side, worry in his eyes, I watch, thankful: I'm no longer Britta's only person. Li is here as well. It's his job to hold her now, his job to comfort her. And it's a relief. Given how I'm feeling, I don't have it in me to comfort anyone else.

Once they've disappeared, Belcalis gulps down the rest of her drink. "Well," she says dryly, "that's one way to react to news of the world ending."

"Is there any other?" Lamin seems genuinely curious. But that might be because he's digesting things too. What I've said is a lot for anyone to absorb, much less comprehend.

I'm still attempting to.

"Yes," Belcalis says, picking up her drink horn and walking over to the tiny stream of palm wine flowing down the side of the tree trunk. She fills it until it's overflowing. "There's this." She downs the wine in one gulp, then thrusts her horn under the stream again.

Once it's full, she nods at us. "A good night to you all," she says. "I'm going to get myself some much-needed rest if we're all likely to die soon."

Lamin rises, walks slowly after her. "I'm going with you."

When he reaches the edge of the branch, he turns to Keita and me, uncertain. "I imagine you'll be leaving soon?"

"Tomorrow," I say, since there's no point in holding grudges anymore. Any which way we go, this is probably one of the last times I'll see Lamin.

I don't want the memory to be laced with animosity.

He nods, thinking. "I know it's not my place any longer, but please, don't leave without saying goodbye."

I nod. "We won't."

He nods. And then he's gone too.

Now Keita and I are alone, the vastness of the night enveloping us like a cloak. I'm grateful when he immediately moves over and enfolds me in his arms. He buries his nose in my hair, as if trying to douse himself in the scent, the memory.

I do the same, closing my eyes so that his warmth completely surrounds me, protects me. For minutes, perhaps even an hour, we're content just to remain there, wrapped in each other.

Who knows when next we'll get the chance.

Finally, Keita stretches, moves my legs over so I'm sitting sideways on his lap. "So," he begins, his eyes glowing in the darkness, "the world may truly end?"

"Seems possible—well, probable, given all that we have to face." After my conversation with the gods, I'm suddenly not the Deka I was a mere day ago, confident that everything would work out.

If there's anything I've learned, it's that the universe conspires against me, that it throws out every obstacle it can to muddy my path.

Keita nods as he looks up at the stars. Then he sighs. "Hard to believe that."

"And yet it is what will come to pass if we fail. I saw a shadow vale in the water, Keita. It was there, this ominous, awful thing, and it was right beside the Hall of the Gods. We can't escape what's happening, no matter how hard we try."

"We can only fight." Keita nods once more, his eyes weary. "Then again, that's always our only option, fighting. Is that all life is—fighting, struggle?"

I shrug. "I don't know. That's all I've ever experienced, especially these past two years."

"Me too." Then he sighs. "I wonder what life is like for other people, the lucky ones."

"I don't think there are any." When Keita looks down at me, I shrug. "Once upon a time, I thought you were one of the lucky ones. Then I learned your story."

Like the stories of most of my other companions, Keita's is horrific. Deathshrieks slaughtered his family when he was a child, killed them as they slept in the summer house they'd built near the Temple of the Goddesses. The temple their cousin, Gezo, the former emperor of Otera, had neglected to mention was there.

Only later did Keita learn of Gezo's treachery. The former emperor had sent his family there on purpose, to ensure that they all died before their branch of the royal line became too popular and threatened his reign.

Keita glances at me, then nods. "Perhaps you're correct. Everyone has their pain. Some just have more than others."

"Indeed," I agree.

And then I lapse into silence, allowing the insect calls and nocturnal birdsong to swell and fill the space where our words should be. And there are so many words now, so many things to say, except I don't want to say them, because voicing them makes them real. Makes them final.

The silence continues, lingering longer and longer until I can't bear it anymore. I look up at Keita, my entire being suddenly desperate as I place my hand on his cheek. "Keita," I begin, not surprised when he looks away from me, unable to meet my eyes.

He knows what is coming.

After all, we've been avoiding it for the better part of a month. For an eternity, it seems, given how desperate everything is all the time. "If I become a god—"

"*When* you become a god."

"*When* I become a god, what will become of us?"

Keita continues looking pointedly away, now leaning his head back so his eyes can search the night sky. "I expect we'll continue as we are."

"Sweethearts?" I scoff. "A boy and a god?"

Keita's eyes flick to mine. "A worshipper and his goddess. Or perhaps even a godsworn and his goddess."

I stiffen. "That's not funny, Keita. I would never wish that for you. *Never.*"

"But I do worship you, Deka. Now, then, always. And if bonding myself to you will keep me by your side forever, I would gladly do it."

"But I wouldn't want you to."

"It's not up to you." Keita's reply is swift, and it is firm. He looks down at me, his eyes burning now as they peer into mine. "You heard Myter: I have a choice. And I choose you. Wherever you are, that is where I wish to be."

The devotion in his eyes is so raw, I look away. "And what about family? Children? All that is possible for you."

"If I survive this."

"*When* you survive this," I rebut stubbornly, despite the lump building in my throat.

Keita shrugs. "You're the only one I've ever envisioned having them with," he says quietly.

"*Why?*" The question rips out of my throat. "Why me? Why has it always been me?"

"Because you're the only one who saw me after my family—" Keita clears his throat as if it's suddenly clogged. Then he tries again. "After my family died, you were the only person who saw me—the real me, the person I was inside. Not Keita the warrior. Not Keita the jatu, or Keita the recruit. Or even Keita the noble. You saw Keita the boy. The one with feelings. The one who was real."

He laughs, a sad little sound. "Oh, it was out of fear, at first, all that attention you paid to me. Perhaps even hatred. You thought I was out to destroy you. So you tried to maneuver around me. But you had to understand me to do so. And then, once you saw who I truly was, you tried to befriend me. The Keita inside, not the automaton they'd made me."

He shrugs again. "My friends, everyone in the Warthu Bera, they only wanted my darkness, my thirst for violence. But you wanted my softness, my smiles. My heart. And you wanted all the other parts of me too—even the more sinister ones. You were the first person to want that in years. The first person since my family . . ."

He sighs. "That's why it's always been you. That's why it'll only ever be you."

By now, a sob is rising from deep inside my chest. This declaration is all I've ever wanted to hear. Except now I know how much it'll cost him. A life. A family. Children. I myself have never truly wanted any, but I can see how, with him, perhaps I would have. And now there's no longer that option. But I don't want to bring that up anymore, so I do the only thing I can do.

I kiss him.

Keita blinks, as if surprised, but then he swiftly accepts the kiss, his lips searing against mine. Sweet little flames, burning into my soul. His mouth tastes like fruits, like the cakes he's been eating.

It tastes like home.

But then Keita *is* home. That's what he's been for me ever since that first moment we started regarding each other as allies instead of enemies.

"If this is one of our last few moments, I want to savor it," I say between kisses. "I want to remember it forever."

"Me too," he says, lips pressing down on mine so firmly, I almost forget I haven't told him the other thing I needed to tell him—the truth of the condition I need to fulfill in order to take back my kelai and ascend to divinity.

But that can come later. For now, there's only this.

"Kiss me, Keita," I urge against his lips. "Kiss me until I forget everything."

"Just as long as you do the same," he replies.

So I do just that.

17

◆ ◆ ◆

By the time the sun rises in the sky the next day, my friends and I are already saddling the new gryphs the Maiwurians have given us. Nenneh Kadeh tried to persuade us to rest, build up our strength, but given the urgency of our task, our group has agreed that we need to move on as quickly as possible. Time is short, not just for us but for the whole world. We need to prepare for the arduous journey ahead. After all, we're going to the one place I hoped never to return to—the place where everything began for me.

"Irfut." Britta shakes her head as she considers the unpleasant proposition. She's saddling the gryph closest to me, a pale silver cat with paler wings. It'll blend in perfectly with the snow in my former home village. It's sure to be the cold season there now.

We're leaving the gryphs we brought with us behind. They're exhausted from the journey and still half starving. The new ones are fresh, especially important since we need them to carry all the gifts the Maiwurians have loaded us up with—not just food supplies and the like but new armor, each piece suited to our particular gifts, like heat-resistant material for Keita. What's more, the new gryphs are used to ebiki, so Ixa's presence won't alarm them as it did our old gryphs when we first started out.

"Why did it have to be Irfut?" Britta groans, shaking her head.

I sigh. "Because that's where all Mother's things are, the ones that still smell like her."

"And smells spur memory, which helps in the combat state," Britta says, parroting Lamin's words. "Can't believe we didn't think of that earlier."

"Sometimes, the most practical solutions are the ones most easily missed." The words spill out of my mouth before I even think them, a testament to how deeply ingrained they are.

Britta snorts. "That sounds like something White Hands would say."

"It's precisely something White Hands would say, which is why she said it—repeatedly," I remind her.

Britta blinks, a fine display of confusion. "An' where was I when she did?"

"Complaining of your menses."

Britta taps her lips. "Haven't had them this month yet." When I turn to her, alarmed, she swiftly tsks. "An' this is wha starvation an' stress will do to ye! They bother everythin' in yer body!"

As she grumbles under her breath, I clear my throat, unsure of how to continue. "And you're certain it's just that, starvation and stress?" I begin delicately.

"Of course it is, Deka, why would ye—" Britta gasps. "Ye don't think me an' Li—"

"No, I was just—"

"Just because ye an' Keita have been carryin' on doesn't mean me an' Li have been—"

"We haven't!" I'm quick to deny. "We didn't last night! We just kissed and . . ."

"An' . . . ?" Britta quirks an eyebrow.

"And *you know.*"

"No, I don't." Britta is so delighted now, every trace of her prior horror is gone. "Yer going to have to spell it out for me. With pictures even, so ye can set the scene."

I shake my head. "I'm not going to set the scene, you—you pervert!"

"How am *I* the pervert for askin' questions about a topic *ye* raised, an'—" Britta stops, frowning as she realizes. "Yer tryin' to distract me!" Then she grins, delighted. "So wha really did happen last night, Deka? Did ye hold each other tightly an' kiss an' caress an'—"

"No!" I say hurriedly. "No to all that and whatever else it is you're thinking in that twisted little mind of yours." I humph sanctimoniously. "Get ahold of yourself. We have a mission to complete."

"Ye mean like ye did last night?"

I grin. "We did embrace and kiss and so forth."

"Really?" Britta seems delighted. "How forth is so forth? Because Li and I also so forthed a little last night." When I glare at her, she laughs. "All right, all right, I'll stop. I'll focus." She clears her throat. "So, have ye told White Hands we're goin' to Irfut yet?"

I shake my head. "Couldn't figure out a way. Her gauntlets can't pierce the Great Barrier, and the gods refuse to communicate with the outside. Nothing goes anywhere except via Bala and Myter, and they already grumbled yesterday about how much they've upset the balance, whatever that is. Oh, and they're yandau, by the way—Myter, that is."

"Good to know," Britta says with a nod, her eyes filled with concern now. "All jokes aside, are ye certain ye'll be all right, Deka? Goin' back to Irfut?"

Back to the place where I was locked in that cellar and murdered nine times because my blood ran gold instead of red. . . .

I nod. "I'll be fine. Truly," I insist. And for once, I actually believe it. I'm not the girl I was there anymore. I smile as I look up at her. "Don't worry, I have myself well in hand. Even if the wounds return, I'll still be able to defend myself. They won't see me coming."

But Britta is suddenly stuck on my last few words. "Wha do ye mean, 'if the wounds return'?" She glances at me, her gaze sharp now. "The ebiki cured them. I saw them do it."

"For now," I reply, my jaw suddenly tight. "But when we leave here, we leave the ebiki behind. It'll take time, but the wounds will appear again."

"Oh, Deka." Britta hurries toward me, her eyes wide. "Why didn't ye tell me?"

"There wasn't time, what with everything happening so fast." I ball up my fists as fear suddenly rises, a heavy, suffocating emotion. "I keep telling myself I can endure it," I whisper. "If it comes again, I can endure it. But I don't know if I can. I don't know if I want to. . . . I'm so tired, Britta. So very tired."

Soft arms engulf me, holding me tight. Offering me comfort,

understanding. "Me too," Britta whispers, leaning her head on my shoulder. "I'm tired too. Tired of being strong, tired of fighting. But we have to endure it."

I nod. "We have no choice."

"Oh, I'm not so certain of that." Lamin enters the stables, and Britta and I turn, startled to hear his voice.

I haven't seen him all morning, so it's something of a shock to see how he's transformed between last night and today. He's wearing formal robes, but not the ones I'm now accustomed to seeing Sarla's godsworn wear. While his are the usual white, they have trailing sleeves and a cape that falls ever so elegantly on the grass.

If he notices my examination, he doesn't comment. Instead, he just says, "Queen Ayo sent me. She wishes to speak with you. She and her children have prepared a gift."

Britta and I glance at each other.

"A gift?" I ask.

"One even Ixa contributed to," he continues, mysterious.

"So wha is it, or are ye goin' to keep bein' vague in yer new getup?" Britta humphs.

"Oh, this?" Lamin looks down as if startled. Then he smiles ruefully. "Spent the better part of the last decade in armor, so I wanted you to see me in something different before you go." He sighs, steps forward. "Deka, I want to say—"

I stop him with a hand to his arm. "I'll be seeing you," I say quickly. "Not goodbye, but I'll be seeing you."

It's as much as I can give him—acknowledgment that we may one day meet again on better terms.

It's not likely, but it is possible.

Anything is possible.

Lamin nods, then looks at me again. "Do you think you can ever forgive me?"

I nod. "I already have." When he brightens, I add, "But that doesn't mean I'll forget."

He sighs, nods. "That's a good strategy, I suppose."

"Practical," I say, heading out of the stables. "And also merciful, considering that if you did come back with us, White Hands would have your head."

If it's possible for Lamin to go any paler, he does, that unnerving white skin glistening in the bright sunlight. "There is that."

"Indeed," I say, continuing on. "Lead the way."

◆

To my surprise, Lamin skirts the shoreline entirely once we reach the beach. I thought Queen Ayo would be waiting somewhere in open water, but Lamin leads us instead toward what looks to be a small temple on a grassy hill. It's a quiet, understated affair, a red stone building surrounded by an arbor of sweet-swelling fruit trees that overlooks the glistening blue ocean. Once we round the top of the hill, he leads us down a path through the center of the arbor to the entrance to the temple, which lies just beyond a small stream. We have to walk over a tiny curved stone bridge to get to the door. It's more of a footpath, really, but Britta and I both slow the moment we approach it, our footsteps hesitant and uncomfortable.

That bridge looks familiar. Too familiar.

Suddenly, I'm back in Abeya, standing in front of the water bridge into the city of the goddesses, the one that refused to form for my companions and me when we went to confront them.

Britta notices my hesitance and smiles ruefully. "Memories, am I right?"

"Unfortunately so," I say, shuddering. I reach out my hand. "Together?"

Smiling, Britta swiftly takes it. "Together."

Hand in hand, we dash down the bridge to the safety of the solid ground beyond it. Lamin follows at a more leisurely pace, his white robes trailing behind him.

Once we reach the entrance to the temple, a small circular structure that arches high above us, he stops and waves me on. "This is where I leave you," he says quietly. "You will find Queen Ayo at the bottom of the stairs."

Britta sends him an arch look. Unlike me, she neither forgives nor forgets. "I'll lead the way," she sniffs, walking ahead.

I swiftly follow behind her.

The moment I approach the entrance, I stiffen. It's quiet. Too quiet.

Suddenly, every one of my alarms are raised.

From the moment we arrived, this island has been a constant hum of activity. The footsteps of the godsworn as they go about their daily tasks, the calls of the monkeybirds and the insects flitting around the trees. The island is always alive with sound and movement.

Here, however, there is nothing. No noises, no movements I can discern. Just the rushing of waves and the bubbling of the stream. And a low, echoing hum from somewhere deep inside the structure—a sound I can't quite make out.

If this is a temple, where are all the priests? Where are all the worshippers?

Britta must have the same concerns, because she turns to Lamin, a thin, insincere smile suddenly slicing her face. "Ye know, I'd rather you go first, if it's all the same to you," she says.

Lamin steps back, hurt on his face. "You think I'd betray you?"

"Again?" I remind him dryly, stepping closer. "You've done it once before, which is why I'd also like you to go into that dark, strangely quiet temple first." I smile insincerely as well. "Fool me once and all that."

Lamin sighs, that hurt blossoming across his entire face. For a moment, I'm almost swayed by it. Swayed by my former companion's visible pain.

Then he looks up. "Unfortunately, I cannot obey that request. Queen Ayo allows only an honored few to see her in her current form."

I shrug. "Then I suppose this means you are now one of those few."

Lamin sighs again. "I don't think you understand, Deka, I—"

Deka? A familiar chirping call sounds in my mind. When I turn toward the entrance, a blue snout is poking through it. Ixa's back in his adolescent form, and he prances out to nudge at my legs. *Deka, Mother waiting. You come! Come!*

As I blink at Ixa, stunned that I never even felt his presence, Lamin smiles sadly at me. "As I said, all is well. The queen is waiting for you."

"Then I suppose we have to get going. We'll see ye back at the stables," Britta says, waving him off.

Lamin just looks at us, pain in his eyes, then sets off across the bridge, his robes once again trailing behind him. Britta and I watch until he disappears down the hill.

The moment he's gone, I glance at Britta. "Think I was too harsh?"

She shakes her head. "Not harsh enough. If this was the Warthu Bera, he'd have been flayed to death for what he did. Spying is one of the worst betrayals, no matter how pretty the excuse." She squeezes my hand. "Stay the course, Deka."

I nod. "I know," I say, then I cross the threshold into the temple.

The moment I enter, my brows gather. This temple is not at all what I expected. But then, it was never a temple in the first place. I just assumed it was from its exterior. What it actually is, is a dark, circular library, its walls filled with shelves of scrolls and adorned with giant mosaic-tile murals of the ebiki. Floating orbs shine a wafting blue light on those murals, giving the illusion that the ebiki are underwater, their blue scales gleaming in the near darkness. I want to take a moment to just admire them, but then Ixa bounds to the center of the room, where a staircase beckons, its steps descending into the darkness below. He glances at me excitedly.

Deka come, Mother wait for us below!

Nodding, I make my way carefully to the staircase. That strange hum I heard is echoing up from it. As is the sound of water.

"Looks to be a cavern," Britta announces as she marches down after Ixa.

I follow behind, my eyes swiftly adjusting to the darkness, which increases as we descend until it's almost all-encompassing.

"I still don't understand how Queen Ayo can be here, though," I muse, watching as a shimmering blue light begins playing on the walls. "If it's a cavern, the water will be too shallow."

Britta shrugs. "Maybe we're meant to take a boat out?" Then she brightens. "Or maybe the gift *is* the boat—but no, that would be inconvenient. I'd rather Bala take us straight to Irfut." Then she glances at me. "How are ye doin' on creatin' doors again?"

I sigh. "Poorly? Nonexistently?"

Britta frowns. "*Nonexistently?* Is that even a word?"

I don't answer Britta. I can't. Whatever I was about to say is forgotten, my next few words erased as I see what waits for us at the bottom of the cavern.

18

◆ ◆ ◆

The bottom of the cavern is as I expected—a small beach of crystalline white sand surrounded by the soaring cavern walls. But that's not what holds my attention. The water—or rather, what's inside it—does.

There, coiled around one of the small boulders that jut from the water's depths, like a serpent clutching an egg, is Queen Ayo. But the Queen Ayo I know is a reptile of mind-bogglingly gargantuan proportions, a creature who would seem practically out of myth if she weren't so very, very real.

The person sitting in front of me, however, is one of the most beautiful women I've ever seen: a face to rival that of Melanis in her prime and a figure almost as voluptuous as the statues you find in old temple ruins. In fact, almost every portion of the ebiki queen is perfection to look upon, except for that tail, which lazily strokes the water, the gleaming spikes on the back of it a visible warning despite all her beauty. *I am dangerous,* that tail says. *Do not approach.* It's a message shared by the rest of Queen Ayo's features, which seem more in keeping with her reptilian nature. Her skin is a shimmering, gleaming gold-edged blue, just like the scales she had in her ebiki form, and the strands of her hair are like gathered tentacles, which shift and slither softly around her as she turns to face me.

Her eyes, though, are still the same gentle black, that gray pupil a crescent moon in their center.

Britta edges closer to me, awed. "Is that who I think it—"

"Deka . . ." The cavern's stone walls echo Queen Ayo's voice, which somehow seems just as powerful now as it did in her ebiki form.

I walk closer to the shore, kneel in front of her. "Queen Ayo," I acknowledge respectfully. "You are a shape-shifter?"

I had considered it before but had never given it any real thought. I suppose I was so awestruck by her size, I could not imagine she could be anything else, even though Ixa's primary characteristic has always been his shape-shifting.

"We . . . all are." The queen gestures an elegantly clawed hand, and now I see the other ebiki swimming silently in the water, their forms just as humanlike as their monarch's. Except, strangely, they're all male—like Ixa, who I never thought could achieve a humanlike form.

And yet, all the rest of his species seem very at home in one. Even the males. But if they can, perhaps he can as well.

I turn to my blue companion, who is now happily paddling in the water, his fur having easily given way to scales and fins.

"Will Ixa—"

"What?" When Queen Ayo suddenly appears in front of me,

water dripping from her scaled body, *my* heart jolts. She moved so fast, it was less than a moment between my turning my gaze from Ixa and her arrival by my side.

I hurriedly kneel, putting all the respect I can into the gesture. The gods I will not kneel to, but Queen Ayo . . . she's a different matter altogether.

She glances at me curiously, head tilting to one side. "Will Ixa . . . ?" she prompts.

"Change into a form like this?" I ask, clearing my throat to calm myself. "Like you are right now?"

Her black gaze flicks to Ixa, and she gives her offspring a considering stare. "One . . . day," she says in that stilted way, her eyes sliding back to me.

Her voice is filled with strange pauses, almost as if she has to seek out the words before speaking them. I suppose when you're used to communicating mentally, it takes time to translate your thoughts into words spoken aloud.

"Usually . . . it takes us . . . hundreds of years to achieve a skin that can . . . communicate with . . . ground-walkers. But our progeny . . . Ixa . . . progresses swiftly. He is . . . only an infant, and yet see how he . . . maneuvers."

I turn to find Ixa playfully snapping at the other ebiki, who gamely flee from him in what appears to be a game of chase.

"You . . . must stand." When I turn back to Queen Ayo, she is offering me a hand, a disconcerted look in those gentle eyes. "It is not . . . proper for a . . . deity . . . to kneel before their . . . godsworn."

Nodding, I take her hand, which I'm surprised to find is warm and smooth, and rise. Even then, I have to look up at her. I feel like a small child compared to her towering height, and

I'm doubtlessly not the only one. Britta, who's standing just next to me, comes nowhere close to being shoulder to shoulder with the monarch.

"Why did you choose me to be your god?" I ask, curious.

The gods do not choose their godsworn; their godsworn choose them—that's one of the most important things I learned during my time in the Hall of the Gods and on the walk back afterward. Myter, I am told, pestered Bala, who was then a solitary god, for almost an entire lifetime until the deity of the pathways relented.

Queen Ayo's shoulders roll into an elegant shrug. "Why do the . . . waves choose the . . . moon, why does . . . the grass choose . . . the sun? You were . . . there, we felt you, we felt your . . . call, and so we . . . answered." Her black eyes peer into mine, that crescent gray pulling me into their center. "We ebiki are . . . fierce creatures . . . solitary warriors, the . . . terror of all oceans. For us . . . might is what . . . determines . . . leadership. The . . . strongest . . . male . . . transforms . . . becomes . . . queen. When you . . . called us, when you . . . explained to us your task, we agreed. We bound . . . ourselves to you. We sent you our . . . most precious . . . progeny, the first . . . offspring born to us in a millennium. All this . . . we have done for you."

"But why? And what task did I ask of you?" My head is swirling with questions now.

"War." The queen's mouth spreads into a terrifying grin, teeth the size of daggers seeming to split that beautiful, lush mouth. "You called us to . . . devour, to destroy, to wreak . . . havoc on the Oteran gods. As . . . queen . . . as the . . . mightiest . . . I could . . . not refuse . . . such honor . . . The . . . time will soon come . . . our goddess." I watch, shocked and slightly horrified, as the monstrous and beautiful queen of the ebiki sinks to her knees, that terrifying light shining in her eyes.

"Call upon . . . us, and we will come. And we . . . will destroy all your . . . enemies and any that . . . stand in your way. When the . . . barrier falls and the world . . . begins to collapse, call . . . on us, and we will . . . come to your side."

I'm so unnerved now, all I can manage is a small, tense nod. "My thanks," I say hoarsely.

"A deity does . . . not need to thank their godsworn," the queen replies, as if she did not offer an entire celestial genocide on my behalf. "Not for . . . fulfilling our purpose, and certainly not for this."

She gestures and a group of ebiki suddenly emerge from the water, their humanlike male bodies graceful even as their tails carve undulating tracks in the sand. They're carrying something behind them, what looks to be a chest carved out of mother-of-pearl.

Britta squints at it, intrigued. "Wha's that?"

"A gift for . . . our . . . honored deity," Queen Ayo replies, gesturing to the nearest ebiki, large with bright silver edging the blue of his scales.

He bows solemnly to her before leaning down to open the chest, whose interior is so bright, it takes my eyes a moment to adjust. The moment they do, my eyebrows rise. There's a piece of clothing inside. It looks somewhat similar to the dress the godsworn gave me, with its scale-like blue cloth that shimmers with gold, except there's much less fabric, and the garment ends in pantaloons instead of a skirt. What's more, it seems like it's meant to mold to the body like a second skin.

"It's armor . . . made from our . . . flesh," Queen Ayo explains when I turn to her, puzzled.

My eyes widen. "Wait, you mean you—"

"Our last . . . molt," the queen continues, allowing me to breathe.

For a moment there, I thought the armor might be made of dried ebiki flesh, but thankfully, no, it's just scales. The thinnest flakes of ebiki scales, given how thick and tough the ones I've seen on them are.

"It contains our . . . essence," Queen Ayo continues. "Wear it always and it will keep your body . . . whole, prevent you from falling into . . . disrepair. Protect you from harm."

I frown. "Do you mean these scales will keep the wounds from reappearing?"

She shakes her head. "Only . . . as long as . . . you do not use . . . too much . . . power. As long as . . . you . . . wear . . . it, this . . . will keep . . . your body from . . . disintegrating . . . until you reconnect . . . with your kelai. It contains . . . our prayers . . . and our . . . power."

She gestures, and the ebiki obligingly lifts the garment up, wraps it around his arm, then points it away from himself. He nods at her. With a speed so fast, I nearly don't catch it, Queen Ayo *moves,* slicing at the material with the dagger-sharp tip of her barbed tail. The ground splits where her tail lands, but the armor on the ebiki's hand doesn't move. Doesn't even budge.

I gasp. "So that is—"

"The most . . . durable . . . armor known to all . . . Kama-bai. Not even the blood of the . . . Oteran gods can cut through it." Retrieving it with her sharply clawed hand, she extends it toward me, head bowed. "This . . . we offer to you, our . . . deity. Our flesh to . . . protect you on your journey. Such that you will . . . ascend when and only when . . . you are prepared."

I slowly take the armor, marveling at the almost buttery softness of it. For some reason, I expected it to be hard—immovable, even. "My tha—" I stop myself before the words come, remembering the queen's earlier correction about thanks. Instead, I just nod at her. "It is much appreciated," I finish.

She inclines her head, turning back to the water. "We are . . . glad."

She pauses to pick up Ixa, who has now emerged from the water and is glancing up with curious eyes. Holding him to her cheek, she carefully nuzzles him, that strange purring sound I heard earlier now emanating from them both. It's as if they're communicating, saying a last goodbye. Once she's done, she puts him down again and slithers into the water, where all the male ebiki are waiting. Seeing her there, floating among them, I finally understand her words: the ebiki are one of those groups of creatures that are all born male. The strongest turns female and becomes queen. There are no female ebiki other than Queen Ayo, just as there are no baby ebiki other than Ixa. I glance at him, finally comprehending, for the first time, how truly precious he is.

I've always known he meant the world to me, but now I understand he means much more than that to the world itself: The first ebiki born in a millennium. The last of a race of creatures powerful enough to rival the gods.

And he is my companion.

Queen Ayo smiles dotingly at him, those alarming teeth gleaming. Then she turns to me. "Take care of our . . . offspring,

Angoro Deka," she instructs. "He is the . . . last we will ever have before we . . . continue on to the deep waters and another queen . . . ascends."

I kneel to gather up Ixa, who's transformed to his usual adolescent form, then nod at the queen. "I will," I say. "Ixa is more to me than a companion. He is my dearest friend."

The queen blinks, what appears to be a glassy second eyelid swiftly closing across her eye. "For . . . this . . . we are . . . glad," she replies. Then, just like that, she's gone.

And now Britta is looking at me, tears in her eyes. Relief so strong, she's nearly shaking with it.

"What?" I ask, confused. "Is something the matter?"

Britta points at the armor, which doesn't look like armor. "Oh, Deka," she gasps excitedly. "It's a cure. The queen gave ye a cure! Just seconds ago, ye were worryin' about it, an' now this."

I shake my head as I glance down at it. "It's not a cure, precisely," I begin carefully. "But it is a reprieve. I can keep my body safe for now—"

"An' even more brilliantly, ye have an army for when ye need it," she adds.

And given everything the Maiwurian gods told you, you most likely will. Britta doesn't have to say this part out loud for me to know it's true.

The mere thought of it exhausts me, so I sigh as I add, "All I need now is to find my kelai. And fast. Very fast." If there are as many shadow vales as the Maiwurian gods say—which, of course, there are—the Gilded Ones and the Idugu are getting more powerful by the minute.

Britta grins. "So wha' are we waiting for, then? Lead the way!"

19

◆ ◆ ◆

When we exit the temple, my body now securely covered in Queen Ayo's armor, we find Keita, Li, and Belcalis rushing toward us, panic on their faces.

"Deka!" Keita says, running over the bridge and embracing me. "We returned to the stables and you were gone. And then Lamin told us he sent you here."

After I return his embrace, I nod, glancing from him to the others. "If he did, why are you so panicked?"

"It was me," Belcalis says, uncomfortable. She glances around, surveying the area. "Something's wrong."

"What is it?" I ask, immediately alert.

"I don't know." She shakes her head in frustration. "All I know is that it's something. There's something I'm missing."

And Belcalis is rarely if ever wrong when it comes to these things.

I whirl to Keita and Li. "Everything's packed?"

"Already in the saddlebags," Li answers.

"And the gryphs are primed and ready to go," Keita adds.

"So let's say our goodbyes, then," I say, marching forward.

"And then what? Fly swiftly away without informing me?" My entire group whirls around, gasping, as a familiar voice suddenly reaches our ears. White Hands. She's floating just over the tiny stone bridge—or rather, the specter of her is. Light filters through it, giving the impression that it's a reflection and nothing more. Which, in many ways, it is.

I gasp, shocked to see her. "White Hands, how are you here?" Nothing is supposed to penetrate the barrier between Otera and Maiwuri, not even White Hands's gauntlets.

"Same way I always am, using these," she says, raising her hands to display the armored white gloves. "The more pertinent question is, where are you? All this time, I've been trying to speak with you—"

"Us too!" Cheerful calls ring out as Adwapa and Asha jostle to be seen behind her.

They appear to be in some sort of ancient grove, purple-trunked ganib trees towering above them, their glossy green leaves rustling in the wind. Where that grove is, I can't tell, but I don't dwell on that, given I'm still caught by the impossibility of the situation.

"How did you do it?" I gasp, rushing closer to White Hands. "How did you make your gauntlets pierce the Great Barrier?"

White Hands seems perplexed by my question. "The Great Barrier? What are you going on about? And where are you? You disappeared completely from Gar Nasim. We were concerned."

"Concerned?" A word so close to *worried*, I glance at White

Hands, wondering if she's all right. Then I remember her question. "We're in Maiwuri—the Unknown Lands," I quickly explain.

White Hands's eyebrows furrow. "The Unknown Lands? But how did you—" Then she stops herself. "This is like the last time, isn't it? When I visited you after you got stranded in Hemaira. You fell afoul of some godly device."

I nod in return, grateful she's such a quick study.

I swiftly fill her in on everything that's happened, starting with when I met Bala and Myter, then I finish by saying, "I will begin my search in Irfut using some of Mother's effects."

By now, the stables are in sight, so I hurry toward them, relieved. Belcalis is still casting suspicious looks about. Whatever threat it is that has her on edge hasn't abated, although White Hands's presence seems to have made her feel slightly better.

"And what about you?" I ask her. "Where are you now?"

White Hands doesn't reply. Instead, she looks up, distracted by something in the jungle behind her. I follow her gaze to the group of strange creatures suddenly flying down from the treetops to meet her, their images slightly blurred due to their distance from the gauntlets.

I squint at them, then gasp. Aviax!

I can tell because, while their shape is almost human, they have wings where their arms should be and fingers that end in delicate but sharp claws. Like the birds they so resemble, their bodies are covered in brilliantly colored feathers that shimmer in the sunlight. I've never seen aviax so close before. Unlike their horselike cousins, the equus, they do not tend to associate with alaki or, indeed, any of the other humanlike races. They rarely leave their mountaintop cities, the majority of which are securely hidden in the great jungles of the Southern provinces, and when they do, they remain so high above the clouds, they're usually just specks on the horizon.

I've only seen them in passing once or twice before, but now, apparently, White Hands is with them.

"General White Hands," the one in the front says stiffly. It's a large male with bright green plumage.

She turns to me apologetically. "I must go, Deka. I'll call upon you in two days' time. Do be ready to receive me."

I nod. "I'll be waiting," I say, waving her off.

As I do so, the sound of harried footsteps reaches my ear. "What's this?" Nenneh Kadeh gasps. "You must end this now!" When I turn fully toward her, the older godsworn is pointing at White Hands's image while running toward me with a group of the yellow-robed, warlike godsworn and Lamin by her side.

She shakes her head at White Hands. "Please, whoever you are, you must flee before you are followed. Communications such as these can be tracked, and if another senses a disruption in the barrier—"

"Understood." White Hands nods swiftly, snapping her fingers. Just like that, she is gone.

And Nenneh Kadeh is once more rushing toward me, her eyes alarmed, her voice panicked. "Why did you do that, Angoro Deka? You were warned repeatedly!"

I frown. "Warned about what?"

"The barrier!" Nenneh Kadeh says, exasperated. "You were warned not to disrupt it!"

"And I heeded that warning," I snap. "The barrier is intact."

"But she was here! That woman was here! Which means others will come. The balance has been much too disrupted, which is why the vale has grown."

She points and I follow her gaze toward the ocean. My stomach immediately plunges. There's an ominously dark area just past the shallows. The shadow vale I saw when I went to the Hall of the Gods—it's massive now, writhing as it sucks in more and more water.

That wrong feeling pours from it, as does something else: a familiar tingling.

"We have to go," I say to the others, hurrying onward, but even as I do, I hear it: the high-pitched shrieking emerging from the vale. The shrieking that sounds like deathshrieks but isn't.

"Oh, gods above, is that—" Before Britta can even finish her question, a dark shape explodes out of the shadow vale: Melanis, a victorious smirk on her face. Five of her hunters follow her, their pale, emaciated bodies seeming wizened by the bright sunlight.

The warrior godsworn unsheathe their swords, alarmed. "What in the name of all the gods is that thing?" one asks.

"Melanis, an ancient alaki!" I reply, reaching for my atikas as Keita and Britta immediately flank me, preparing for battle. "Stay clear of her wingtips. They're as sharp as knives."

"Understood!" the warrior godsworn say, positioning themselves around me.

Suddenly I notice Nenneh Kadeh standing at the edge of the grove, her body frozen in place. For all her calm assurance, she's a scholar, not a warrior. This is no place for her.

"Take her to the caverns," I command Ixa, who obligingly

grows to accommodate her and the two warrior godsworn now making their way over.

When Nenneh Kadeh notices, she shakes her head. "But honored Angoro, I—"

"You'll only slow us down!" This statement comes from Lamin, who swiftly loads her onto Ixa's back, then urges the two warrior godsworn to mount behind her. Once they do, he slaps Ixa's rump. "Go!" he says, and my companion takes off running, headed for the caverns Britta and I just emerged from.

Then they're gone, and it's just the remaining three warrior godsworn and us, all weapons raised aloft as we wait for Melanis and her hunters to arrive in the grove.

She does so within moments, she and her hunters flapping lower as she sneers, "Morning greetings, Deka. I would say it was a surprise to find you here, but that would be a lie."

"Melanis," I return coldly. "And just how did you find this place?"

"Same way I always find everything—using the trail of Fatu's gauntlets." She smirks evilly. "I know so intimately the smell of their power, I could recognize it anywhere. All I had to do was follow the odor, and obligingly, it led me through one of the mothers' shadow vales." Her smirk widens, lips splitting into a cruel mockery of a smile.

"Now that we're finally together again," she says companionably, "let's take your body for my goddesses to feast upon, shall we?"

I raise my atikas higher, my chin lifted in defiance. "You can try, but I'm not as weak as I was before, and now I have more allies."

As if confirming my words, horns sound in the distance, groups of armed godsworn spilling from Maiwuri's buildings, ready to join those here. There's no sign of the ebiki, but they may be too far out in the water to hear the sounds of battle. No matter, my friends and I are enough to handle Melanis now. I subtly lower myself into a more grounded stance.

This action, for some reason, amuses Melanis, who flies lower. "Allies. Is that so?" she purrs. "Because I brought allies too."

She smirks again, and suddenly, power begins emanating from her, so much more power than she herself could ever create. Vines slither down her torso. Sinister green vines, moist-petaled black flowers sprouting from them. Blood-eaters, the monstrous creations of Etzli, the goddess who feeds on behalf of the Gilded Ones.

Horror washes over me.

If Melanis is here, covered in vines and power, that means only one thing: she's brought Etzli with her, and perhaps other Gilded Ones as well.

I whirl to the others. "It's Etzli!" I shout. "She's using Melanis as a vessel!"

"Perceptive as always, Nuru," the goddess rumbles, her voice causing Melanis's eyes to turn white as she flaps within fighting distance. "But all the perception in the world will not save you." She gestures to the ground. "Rise!"

Blood-eaters immediately erupt from the soil, the vines swiftly wrapping themselves around my body. A few of the black flowers immediately begin snapping, moist petals seeking purchase through my skin to burrow their way inside me, just as the ansetha necklace once did.

Thankfully, I'm wearing Ayo's armor, so their carnivorous mouths have nowhere to burrow. And I'm still filled with the ebiki's power, which means . . . "Down," I command, drawing on every last bit of power Queen Ayo and the ebiki sang into me just two days ago.

Etzli, who's trapped in the fleshy cage that is her own daughter's body, immediately plummets to the ground, along with all the hunters around her.

As I stand there savoring the return of my power, however little of it remains, Etzli writhes on the ground, wings flapping uselessly as she attempts to fight against the effects of my command. "What is this?" she shrieks. "What did you do to me?"

I smirk. "Used a little of the power you tried to steal. Now then." I lift my hand as I slip deeper into the combat state, summoning all the power I can.

It's surging to the surface to obey my command when a sharp twinge jolts through me. My fingers are suddenly tingling, little sparks at the tips. I don't have to look down to know what they are. Sores, forming in response to how much power I used. They don't hurt, not yet, but I know that's coming soon. Pain is always the shadow that follows the sores.

I grit my teeth. "No," I hiss. *No, no, no!* Not now. I thought it would take more power—way more power than this to drive my body to the brink again—but that, it seems, is not the case.

Etzli laughs. "What's this, already reached your limit, Deka?" She flaps again, trying to pull herself from the ground, but thankfully, my power holds.

I stretch out my hand again.

"Deka?" Britta asks beside me. Then she sees my fingertips. Sees the gold stripes forming there. "Oh no. Stop, stop it now!"

she commands, then she whirls to Keita. "What are ye waitin' for, Keita? Help her! Burn them! Burn them all!"

"On it!" Keita shouts, eyes turning red as he whirls in the direction of Etzli and her hunters. He gestures and their bodies immediately burst into flames, as do all the plants Etzli has summoned, everything writhing and snapping as his power reduces the grove to dust.

But it's not enough. Even before the flames die, Etzli and the others are already back up, their wings flapping against the heat.

"How dare you, son of man!" Etzli shrieks, her body blackened to charcoal as she barrels into him. It's clear she has completely taken over Melanis now; the winged Firstborn's body has taken on an eerily distinct glow, and her eyes are the same milky white I'm so familiar with from spending time in the goddess's presence.

Keita sends another pillar of flame toward her face, but she smashes straight through it to snatch him up and toss him into the stream just in front of Queen Ayo's library.

"Know your place!" she hisses, enraged. Then she turns to me, eyes burning with fury, the charcoal flaking off her body. She's already healing again, the way all alaki do. "No more running, Deka. No more hiding, no more power. I'll bury you in the obsidian grave where I buried Anok."

I stumble. "You buried her?"

"Oh, you didn't know?" Etzli slows, a cruel smile spreading across her face. "I imprisoned her in the obsidian pit your Fatu left behind when she turned our food supply to ash."

The pit where all those male deathshrieks had been.

My body goes cold at the reminder.

One of the most horrific things I learned during my confrontation with the Gilded Ones was the fate of their sons. I'd

198

always wondered why there were no male deathshrieks. Then I discovered the truth: the goddesses trapped the resurrected bodies of their sons in the cavern underneath their chamber. They fed from them, devoured their bodies to grow stronger.

For the Gilded Ones, every male deathshriek was born a sacrifice.

Etzli shrugs. "If she loved our sons so much, she can be with them. For eternity. And you can join them."

As I stand there, unable to absorb the thought of Anok imprisoned in the darkness below the Chamber of the Goddesses, unable to bear the thought of yet more sores traveling over my body, a shout reaches my ears.

"Funny ye should say 'bury,'" Britta calls out, Li by her side. They gesture together, and the ground immediately rises, earth exploding up and over Etzli before swiftly slamming her down into its depths.

Once it's done, Britta triumphantly wipes her hands while Li staggers, obviously weakened by using so much energy. "Take that!" Britta crows, staggering as well.

I grin at her. "My thanks, Br—"

My friend jerks backward, thrown clear across the grove by three hunters, who advance on her the moment she lands, a cloud of swift winged beings.

"Britta!" I shout, panicked, as I run for her. I can't let the hunters get near her.

Strong though she may be, Britta falters against opponents who are faster. That's her weakness: speed. And these hunters clearly know that, which is why the moment they near, they snatch her up and toss her between them like one of those leather balls the children in my village used to play with.

"BRITTA!" I'm almost to the edge of the grove when a powerful tug sends me flying backward. Etzli. She's flapping into the air, eyes blazing with fury.

"No more running, Deka," she roars.

She gestures at the space in front of us, concentrating until the air there begins to gather, growing and forming. Horror slams through me. She's summoning a door, and not just any door: one that leads back to Abeya, the city of the goddesses.

I can see it now, the once-gleaming peaks shining through the rift that appears in the air. The temples, now broken and damaged, but still gleaming, nevertheless, atop them. I scream, struggling against her grip. If I go through that door, the goddesses will kill me and then snatch my kelai before it reunites with me.

They'll use me to become all-powerful once more.

"Keita!" I shout desperately. Etzli's grip is too strong for me to break, and she's pulling me closer and closer to that door, closer and closer to my doom. "KEITA, HELP ME!" I shout again, but he's too far away, as is everyone else—even Britta, who's still where I left her, pinned down by the hunters.

Etzli is smirking now, victory in her gaze. "He can't help you, Deka," she says. "He'll never make it to you in time."

And my heart sinks as I realize she's right. This was her plan all along, to use Britta to lure me far enough away from the others that she could send me through the door.

Etzli must have noticed the comprehension in my eyes. She smirks. "At last, you understand. There's nowhere to run, Deka. Nowhere to hide. From here, it's Abeya, and then it's time for you to die. You can't escape it."

"Can't I?" I growl, already imagining Queen Ayo. In my panic, I'd almost forgotten she was there—that the ebiki were there, just beyond the shoreline.

I project my thoughts as loudly as I can. *QUEEN AYO!* I shout with my mind. *I NEED YOU!*

Far off into the waters, a massive shape immediately breaches from the waves. Queen Ayo, the other ebiki surrounding her. They're a distance away from shore, but they're rushing in at full speed. In five, perhaps ten, minutes, they'll be here. All I have to do is stall, wait Etzli out.

I glare up at the goddess. "I'll fight," I say menacingly. "I'll fight you the entire way there, or I'll change the direction of the door, the way I've done so many times before."

Etzli's smirk only widens. "Before?" She arches an eyebrow. "Before, you were whole, filled with power. Now you are only a fraction of yourself. Foolish child. How can you fashion yourself a god killer when you don't even have enough power to fight against one small door? How can you hope to beat us when you can't even heal your own wounds?" She glances contemptuously down at the sores marring my fingertips, the sores that are tingling even fiercer now, a prelude to the burning that accompanies the pain.

I take a breath before I look up at her. Look up at that hated, contemptible face. "I may not have that much power," I say, stiffening myself against the pull of the door, which is opening wider now, wind sucking me toward it, "but neither do you. You're a false god, Etzli, a demon masquerading as divinity."

"Then isn't it wonderful," Etzli says, "that you're here to deliver us true power? Because once we have it, we'll devour our

201

counterparts, then we will come for Maiwuri and the rest of Kamabai. We will remake the world in our image, and you, *Nuru,* will give us the power to do so."

She gestures, and the door explodes open, that hateful lake and the water bridge atop it, crystallizing into view.

A cold sweat breaks over me. I can't go back there. I won't go back there. I won't ever step foot in that place again. I can't—

"ENOUGH!" The word is accompanied by a flash as eighty shimmering figures suddenly appear around us, each tall enough to reach the sky.

The gods of Maiwuri. They're all around us now, watching. Blocking the door, which shrinks back to nothing.

Etzli falls to the ground, dropping me as she does so.

She swiftly picks herself up, our struggle forgotten as she points a gnarled finger at the celestial figures in the sky. "You dare! You dare lay hands on me! You who broke the covenant. You who stole her from our grasp!"

The gods sigh, a rumble that sends quakes through the ocean behind them, turning it dark and choppy where mere seconds ago it was placid. "It took Bala two minutes, two thousand chronomeres, to take her. You have spent much more time than that in our domain, Etzli of the Oterans. Our part of the covenant is fulfilled. It is now you who are breaking the covenant. Be gone from here, kindred."

"Be gone?" Etzli sputters. "The Nuru yet remains. She belongs to our side of the barrier."

"Then we will send her back, so that you have no more excuse to linger."

"*I* will take her." Etzli is so firm in this reply that my heart sinks as I wait for the gods to answer.

Then they shake their heads as one. "We took her; thus, we will return her."

"TREACHERY!" Etzli spits. "You conspire with our counterparts."

"No, we seek to restore the balance, as is our duty. You would do well to remember yours."

As I breathe out a relieved sigh, eighty heads turn as one toward me. "Come, Deka," they say, and I blink, startled, as Bala and Myter suddenly appear, all my friends as well as the fully packed gryphs beside them.

All that time I spent hurrying back to the stables and I'd forgotten he could do that, gather my companions in the blink of an eye.

Myter turns to me. "It's time to go now, Angoro. We will take you."

Behind them, Etzli is in a fury. She turns to the Maiwurian gods, eyes blazing. "Take her where?"

"That is your answer to discern," the gods reply. "Consider our covenant honored. We bid you farewell, Oterans."

There's another flash, and everything falls away.

20

◆ ◆ ◆

The pathways have changed since the last time I saw them. Instead of a misty road, I'm now in the middle of a forest—but not the one I saw before. This forest is made of what appears to be crystal, the trees surrounding me like ethereal figurines whose graceful trunks arch high into the night sky, as if to touch the shimmering, glass-like moon. Water rushes in the distance, a stream wending its way through the grove surrounding me. The rocks guiding it are the same sparkling crystal as the trees, a thousand rainbows shimmering inside them. I have no doubt that all of it—the trees, the rocks, even the water itself—is an extension of Bala's power. But there's something wrong. I feel it thrumming inside me, this wrongness I can't quite put my finger on. And I know it has to do with the pathways. Pretty though it all is, the trees are too sparse, the water's too thin. I don't know how to explain it, precisely, but it's as if everything around me is suddenly faded—a softer, lesser version of itself.

And where is Bala? When I whirl around, alarm growing,

there's no sign of the kind, quiet god, and he's not the only one missing. All my friends are gone, as is everyone I was just in the grove with. Where are they? Did Bala leave them back in Maiwuri? Are they all right?

As my panic starts to surge, a familiar exuberant chirp sounds in my head. *Deka!* Ixa says, and I whirl just in time for him to launch into me.

I fall to the ground with a startled "oof." "Ixa!" I gasp, embracing him. "You're here!"

Deka, my companion says simply, giving me a lazy lick before he rolls off me to lick himself in the privates, his most unpleasant habit.

I shudder, but then the trees suddenly begin rustling around me. Their leaves tinkle like glass, as if something is moving past their lower branches. When I tense, preparing for battle, a familiar burly silhouette barrels toward me.

"Oh, Deka, thank creation!" Britta cries as she enters the grove, the others and their gryphs following her.

"We're all together," Keita says, taking in our new surroundings.

"Keita!" I gasp, yet more relief surging through me as I rush over to embrace him.

I was so worried about my companions. About everyone in that grove with me. To think, Etzli made it all the way into Maiwuri. I can only hope that the gods there ejected her and Melanis's hunters the moment Bala brought me here and that all the godsworn in Maiwuri did not have to suffer any losses because of me.

I cling tighter to Keita, not even minding when the pressure causes the sores on my fingertips to sting. I may be injured again, but at least I can hold him now, touch him and all my other friends whenever I'm upset. And as long as I'm careful and don't use my abilities as freely as I did back in Maiwuri, it'll remain that way.

I understand now what Queen Ayo meant when she said not to use too much power. Attempting to use any power outside of my combat state, as I did back in that grove, will trigger the sores. As long as I don't do what I did back then, I'll be fine. Whole until I can reunite with my kelai.

"You've made your way to each other—wonderful." We all whirl, startled, when Myter appears in the middle of the pathways.

How they managed to sneak up on us so silently, I can't begin to understand. They're the largest thing in the pathways, aside from the trees. By all rights, they should be crashing through the foliage, and yet they move with such delicacy. Or, rather, everything else moves out of their way. I watch, eyes narrowing, as a branch twists away from the godsworn's path, the movement so smooth, it's almost unnoticeable.

"But you had help, of course," they continue. "My divine lord is nothing if not a considerate being."

"And where is your divine lord?" I ask, glancing around. There's no sign of Bala, but he's supposed to be taking us to Irfut.

Myter's eyes go white. "We are recovering," the god says in that layered, gentle voice. "The corruption, it touched us when we sent our kindred back to their home."

I incline my head. "Bala. My deepest thanks for bringing us here." When Bala nods, calm as ever, I continue, apprehensive, "Will you and the others be all right?"

"As soon as we mend the rifts the Oteran's presence has caused. Etzli's appearance has destabilized pathways all across the realm. I must attend to them immediately or her corruption will infect us even more deeply.

"Thus, it is with deepest regret that I must leave you. Until we meet again." The god gives me a small, polite bow of farewell.

Just seeing it sends me into a panic. "Wait!" I shout. "You're still taking us to Irfut, right? We need to get there so we can find my mother's body as soon as possible." But Bala is already gone.

I know this because when Myter opens their eyes again, they're the only one glancing back at me. They nod at my crestfallen expression. "My lord has returned to Maiwuri, but he commands me to tell you that this is a task you must complete on your own."

"Complete on my own?" I echo, flabbergasted. "I don't know how to create doors, and even if I did, I don't have the power." I hold up my hands, showing Myter the sores. "Pinning Etzli down for just a few moments did this to me."

"And even if it weren't for all that," Belcalis adds, rushing over to Myter, "there's the small matter of time. We don't have any."

"That is not entirely true," Myter replies. When we stare at them, uncomprehending, they explain: "Time moves differently in the pathways. And being Lord Bala's godsworn, I can hold or lengthen it as I like. Observe." They snap their fingers, and suddenly, everything freezes. The wind, the leaves rustling in the trees, the water from the stream—everything just stops.

"Now, *that's* a trick!" Li says with an admiring whistle.

But I don't have the luxury of being amazed. "It's all well and good that you can hold time here, but what does that have to do with my inability to make doors?" There's a ring of hysteria in my voice now.

"What are doors but pathways by another name? I can teach you how to make them." Myter sounds surprisingly certain as they place their helmet on the ground. It slowly sinks down, absorbed by the soil underneath it. "The question is, do you wish to learn?"

I blink. "Do I wish to learn? Of course I do, but I don't have—"

Myter points to the perfect stillness around us. "Time? In here, you have plenty, for as long as I wish it. I can lengthen the moments into hours—days, if necessary."

I glance down at my fingertips, at the sores there, then sigh. "I would like to learn, I'd give anything to, but I don't have enough power anymore. I'd just injure myself."

"And yet you want to run out into the world with no plan, no foresight."

"The best-laid plans are the ones ye haven't discovered yet," Britta helpfully inserts.

"I assumed we'd create one along the way," I explain with a sigh.

"Well, now you don't have to," Myter says. "I know how you can harness power without injury. I'll teach you, if you're willing to learn. All you have to do is say the word."

I look at them, look at the certainty shining in those green eyes. Then I sigh. I could rush out there, or I could stay here, learn the one skill I've been trying to master for months now. "Yes," I say. "I'd very much like to learn."

Myter nods. "Then observe closely." They lift both their hands, then slowly open one palm. As if summoned, a single leaf drops from the tree above them. It stops in midair, its crystalline edges shimmering in the moonlight.

My eyes round. It's as if an invisible net has caught it. Like the one that caught me when Melanis dropped me when we were on that cliff on Gar Nasim.

Myter keeps their eyes on the leaf, which is still suspended. "In order to create miniature pathways or, as you call them, doors, you must first understand time and space. Both are malleable things, especially to the gods and those who serve them. If you can learn how to manipulate them"—they gesture and the leaf disappears—"you can control any pathway you wish."

Another gesture and the leaf reappears, this time, above the other palm.

My heart leaps as I watch it shimmering there. "How did you do that?" I've seen sleight of hand before, but this isn't a cheap trick done by a charlatan in a busy marketplace; this is a wonder performed by a being of near-divine stature. I know because I can feel the power they used as little sparks of lightning running up and down my body.

"Make the leaf move?" Myter closes both fists, and the leaf disappears. "It's up to you to work that out. I'll do it one more time. Observe."

"Wait," I say, hurrying to enter the combat state.

The world fades away as everyone becomes a glowing white shadow being. Their purest essence laid bare. And that includes Myter's. Strangely, I can finally see it now, despite the armor they're using. But perhaps that's because they want me to see it.

I'm starting to realize that Myter is much more powerful than I thought.

"You can proceed now," I announce, staring at them.

Myter nods, gestures with both hands. The air above their hands suddenly contracts. No, not the air. I squint closer, mouth slackening when I realize there are little pockets of stillness between the thousand shimmering strands of air flowing around me. They're what contracts and what, once Myter opens their hands, releases.

Space.

So that's what the colossal godsworn was talking about. It's the space that moves. The space between things.

"I see it!" I gasp, excited. "I see the space." Then I frown. "Why can I see it now but not before?" I've been in the combat state a thousand times prior to this and never seen what I just saw.

Myter smirks. "You're in the pathways," they say, gesturing grandly. "Everything here is purified to its simplest, deepest essence. Observe." They pull a glasslike piece of bark from the tree beside them and extend it to me. It shimmers with all the lights of the rainbow, but, as with everything else in the pathways, there's that strange, faded feeling to it.

"Outside, this would be a thousand things."

"Like real wood, for instance," Belcalis snorts.

Myter throws them a glance. "Not just wood but the mites that live on it, the smaller organisms that live on them, and so on. Here, it is simply bark—well, crystalline bark but bark nonetheless—as re-created by Lord Bala. This is the nature of the pathways. It is the essence of things purified, distilled, and re-created in Bala's image."

They raise their hand again and their body begins glowing once more. I watch through the combat state as energy seems to abruptly coalesce inside their stomach. Where it came from,

I'm not certain—I didn't see them drawing it from anywhere else inside their body. Before I can ask them about it, they gesture again. Just like that, the energy explodes, forcing the bark into the air in front of me. It's a scramble to grasp it quickly before it falls, but I manage, and then the bark is in my hand, a thing of strange lightness. So light as to be nonexistent.

As I turn it over again, marveling at this fact, Myter nods at me. "It lacks matter."

I frown. *"Matter?"* Another word I'm unfamiliar with.

"Matter is, roughly speaking, substance. Space is a where, but matter is a what. The piece of bark before you has only the slightest amount of matter. Which is why I can move it so easily. But you can move it too. Just as I moved it to the space in front of you, you can move it to the space in front of me. That is what it means to create a pathway. Just a little push of energy, just as I demonstrated."

I nod, keeping the image of the gesture Myter used to move the bark in my mind as I gather energy deep inside me. Then I breathe out a small, slow breath. "Space is a where . . . ," I remind myself as I reach out and pinch a tiny bit of the stillness between air currents. Then I try to imagine squeezing it enough that it narrows the space between myself and Myter. "Just a pinch," I say to myself, breathing energy into the movement. "Just a pinch. . . ."

And then I contract the air.

An outraged gasp is my only warning before Myter suddenly comes barreling straight toward me.

"I said move the bark, not me!" they snap, irritated, when they stop just in front of me.

I can barely hear them.

Welts are rising all across my body, a response to the power I just used. There's so much pain now, it's as if my skin is on fire, as if the very blood is boiling in my veins. Gold drips down my nose. I try to wipe it, but my hands are suddenly heavy, so very heavy.

"I thought you said you could stop the pain," I say, stunned.

Then I slump to the ground, unconscious.

"Is she quite serious?" Myter's voice is disdainful as their enormous booted toe nudges into my side.

I tense, readying myself for pain to explode, but the only thing I feel is a mild discomfort.

"Yer the one who promised her you could make it so she wouldn't injure herself." Britta's voice is loud in my ear as I blink groggily, trying to force my eyes open.

It's a failing effort. My body feels heavy as a woolen cloak soaked with water. But that's all I feel. Where's the pain? Where's all the bleeding? And where are the welts on my skin?

I stretch, searching for sores, for any remnants of the injuries I just incurred, but there's nothing there, nothing but that boot, nudging me awake.

"I said I *knew* how to do it, didn't mean I'd teach her immediately."

"So you just wanted to be pointlessly cruel," Keita says, his hand pushing the boot away. "Good to know."

"No, I wanted to teach her the difference so she knows. Up, Deka." When Myter nudges me with their boot again, I hear the scrape of a sword being unsheathed.

"Godsworn or no, you do that one more time and you will lose that leg, understood?" Keita's voice is cold with conviction.

Myter humphs. "Understood, if you'll tell Deka to stop pretending to sleep."

I sigh. "I'm up, I'm up," I say, rising blearily. When I open my eyes, it's to find my friends huddled in a circle around me, their expressions worried. Even Ixa is perched on the tree roots beside me, his body pressed to mine. He licks me with a rough pink tongue. I push it away.

"Why are you all staring at me? It's not like you've never seen me faint before."

"I haven't," Myter sniffs. "It was quite instructive. Now then, let's try again—"

"Again?" I interject, all sarcasm. "When I just finished healing from the injuries you promised wouldn't happen?"

"I promised you wouldn't *remain* injured. And look at you. You're completely healed."

Which is the truth, I'm aggravated to acknowledge. My eyes squint. "Even so, why would I trust you again?"

"Because this time, I'll show you how to harness the Greater Divinity."

"The Greater Divinity," I sniff dismissively. "The natural order you Maiwurians keep harping on about. If there even is such—"

"Shut your mouth and listen for once, Deka!" Myter's roar is as sudden as it is unexpected, and it shakes every tree in the vicinity. As I stop, startled, they continue in a lower, very tired voice. "Whatever doubts you may have, I am here. And I am here because the fate of my existence lies in you. You—a child with no understanding of her power, much less that of the

Greater Divinity. A girl who stumbles through every obstacle with very little awareness and even less common sense.

"Look around." They point to the trees, which now seem even fainter than they were when I last saw them, their crystalline edges dim, as if they're fading into the twilight. "Does this look like the pathways you first entered?"

"No." My eyebrows gather as I examine the grove around me. "They look . . . faint."

"That's because Lord Bala is fading. His power is being drained by everything he now has to manage. Shadow vales are *everywhere,* not to mention an Oteran god actually breached the Great Barrier, bringing with her corruption." Suddenly, Myter seems very much the world-weary, immortal godsworn they are, massive shoulders hunched over, eyes hooded with exhaustion, as they continue: "I should be at his side, helping him, but you and your friends are the only thing standing between this world and disaster. Between him and dispersal. So I will hold time for as long as I can here, and I will teach you until you have at least a rudimentary knowledge of the pathways and the Greater Divinity, so you have enough power inside yourself to fight the Oteran gods."

They walk closer to me, eyes determined. "So I ask you again, do you wish to learn?"

"Yes, I do," I reply, firm.

I thought Myter was toying with me before, so I didn't understand. They're under just as much pressure as I am, and my doubt and resentfulness has only added to their burden.

"Very well." Myter must see the sincerity in my eyes, because they walk closer, brusquely point to my hands. "When you pulled me to you earlier, your energy was concentrated in your fingertips. That's why your sores always start there—because that's where you concentrate your power. It's also the reason you got so exhausted. Instead of absorbing power from the Greater Divinity, you used your own energy."

They glance at the others. "I hope you haven't all been doing that."

"And what if we have?" Keita steps forward, arms folded.

"Then you have been hindering yourselves. Stifling your growth instead of enhancing it." Myter makes their way to the center of the grove. "I don't know what they tell you in Otera, but in Maiwuri, they tell us that the Greater Divinity is like water, or the air. It is all around us."

They gesture and suddenly, the forest appears to be underwater. Only, the sea around us is a sea of stars. It looks so similar to the river of stars in the Gilded Ones' chamber, nostalgia pangs my heart—but only for the briefest moment. I'm no longer that girl who is seduced by the reassuring chains of familiarity, I remind myself. I am the girl who breaks the chains and doesn't look back.

Myter continues: "Most mortals are only barely aware of the Greater Divinity. But that is why there are gods. Gods are the physical manifestation of the natural order. Since the Greater Divinity is too vast, too all-encompassing, to comprehend, we give each facet of it a name. A face. We breathe life into it."

The air punches out of my lungs. "Wait," I gasp, trying to understand what they're saying. I may be mistaken, but I don't think I am. "Are you saying *we* create the gods? Us, the lesser beings?"

"Indeed. Gods are the dreams of the sentient. It is our longing, our desire, that brings them forth into this realm."

"But they came before us," sputters Keita, who's just as flabbergasted as I am. "They were here before we were."

"Is that what they tell you in Otera?" Myter tsks. "Lies, all lies. Deities exist because we need them. That is why we are not lesser to them, why we do not serve them. We are all of us dependent on each other. All parts of one whole."

Suddenly, I remember how solicitous of Myter Bala is. How he is always calm and loving with them—a doting and supportive presence, not just to them, but to everyone. Could it be because he needs Myter as much as they need him? That all the gods need us as much as we need them?

I try to remember Anok's memories, the ones I experienced when I touched a sample of her blood. Did she remember a time before humans? It's hard to say. The gods have such a strange understanding of time.

"But what about before? Before mortals were created?" Keita's brow is furrowed as he asks this insistent question.

"Before, after, now," Myter says. "It's all the same thing, really. To the gods, time is a circle, never-ending. And they have the gift to understand how it all fits together. That's another reason they exist. To caretake. To shepherd mortals. That is what the Greater Divinity seeks."

"And how does it all relate to us here? Now?" Belcalis asks, impatient.

Trust her to bring the conversation back to the practical.

"You and others from Otera have been taught that you are beneath the gods, and you were never even taught about the Greater Divinity. That is why you approach your abilities as clumsily as you do. Because you think you have to rely on your own power. But the Greater Divinity is a part of you as much as you are a part of it. Think of it this way: If the Divinity is like air, you can breathe it. You can imbue yourself with it." Suddenly, I remember how energy coalesced inside Myter, almost as if they'd breathed it in instead of creating it themselves.

Myter seems to notice my realization, because they nod. "Next time you use your gifts, instead of reaching for the energy inside yourself, breathe in the Divinity. Connect with that which is already a part of you. And then use that to power your gifts. You are not alone in this world; you never were. And the sooner you understand that, the more powerful you will be.

"Now then, Deka, try to create a pathway."

Nodding, I close my eyes. And almost immediately, the combat state surges, allowing me to take in the streams of air moving around me. If I concentrate, I can imagine them as currents. Currents of power through which the Greater Divinity, presumably, travels.

I inhale, eyes flying open when I feel the power flowing into me. It doesn't feel that much different from mine, truth be told. In fact, it feels like it's a part of me, like it's always been there, an old friend waiting to welcome me. And that's precisely why it's so insidious.

Anything this simple, this easy, comes with a cost. I know this very well, which is why I stop. I let the breath settle just enough to fill my belly but not so much that it takes me over. I can feel it inside me now, a power suffusing the emptiness there, pushing back at it.

I cling to that feeling, let it build as I concentrate on one of the trees across the grove, an elegant silver sapling whose crystalline leaves are slowly fading around the edges.

"All right," I say, readying myself. "Let's do this."

I pinch the space between the air. Even before I can blink, I'm there, and I have to hold my hand out to keep from crashing into the trunk.

"Deka!" Britta's excited gasp fills the air. "Deka, ye did it!"

Heart pounding, I pivot to face my friends, who are still on the other side of the grove. Even stranger, my head doesn't hurt from the movement, and neither does my body. Nothing hurts at all, not even my muscles, which were exhausted just moments ago.

It's like I'm filled now, my entire body calm with the feeling that came after I breathed in that air. *The Greater Divinity* . . . So that's what it feels like, the force the Maiwurian gods spoke of. It's not harsh, or demanding, the way I expected it to be. It just is.

And yet, I still don't trust it.

I turn as Myter makes their way to me. "I did it," I say to them. "I created a pathway."

"And yet?" The godsworn seems to sense my hesitance.

"It felt . . . too easy." I struggle to put my feelings into words. "Every time I've used a new ability before, I've had to struggle for it, bleed for it. But this . . ."

Myter steps forward, placing their hands on my shoulders. Their green eyes bore into mine as they say, "Remember always, Deka, the Greater Divinity is as much a part of you as you are a part of it. That's why it's so easy for you to use. Because it's always been there with you."

"But that can't be right," I rebut, skeptical.

"Why not?"

"Because if this has always been a part of me, why haven't

I ever been able to use it before? Why have I struggled doing every other thing?"

Myter smiles. "Because you weren't taught to. No one in Otera was. And when you've been led down the wrong path, when you're focused on it, you fail to see what's in front of your very eyes. Don't continue resisting the Greater Divinity, Deka. It'll only be to your detriment if you do."

With those unnerving last few words, the massive godsworn walks off, beckoning to my friends. "You four—with me. Deka needs to train. As do you."

Li frowns. "But we don't—"

"Go with them," I interject. "And do as they say. All of you."

Sighing, Li follows Myter, as do the rest of my friends. And I turn my focus back to what Myter just taught me. After all, we have only a short amount of time before we return to Otera—back to our enemies and near-constant danger.

Until then, my friends and I will train, get our abilities as powerful as we can. Because if we don't, it'll mean the ascension of the Oteran gods and the end of us all.

21

❖ ❖ ❖

The Irfut I remember was a small, simple village: rows of brightly painted wooden cottages with straw roofs, a temple on the hill in the center, and, just beyond it, the forest, yet more cottages scattered around its edges. The one I grew up in stood a little way from the rest, a humble wooden building with a small stable next to it. It should be dusted in snow now, as should the entire village and the wall surrounding it, the wall that was built just last year by the jatu, supposedly to protect the villagers from the dastardly forces of the Gilded Ones.

When I add its shoddily built ramparts to the memory of Irfut I'm building in my mind, I grimace. It's just another of the thousand things I hate about the village of my birth, and yet I have to put that hatred aside now. I have a door to open.

"That's it," Myter encourages behind me as I slowly, steadily inhale, attempting to breathe in enough of the Greater Divinity's power to fill the remaining bits of emptiness inside me left by my now-depleted kelai.

A tear in the space in front of us immediately appears, a thin line, barely visible against the crystalline trees and foliage. A door.

After what's felt like days of training, I've finally mastered opening the pathways, which is why it's now time to return to Irfut and search for the location of my kelai.

"Go on, Deka," Britta whispers encouragingly from beside me when the tear stalls, reacting to my uncertainty about once again entering the village of my birth. "Ye can do it."

I nod, concentrating on bending the edges of space farther and farther apart. I will not let my awful memories of Irfut stand in the way of finding my kelai. I continue pushing. Then, finally, the door is fully open. And there it is: Irfut.

Or, rather, the remains of it.

I stare, stunned to silence, as I take in the charred husks of cottages, the misshapen ruin of what was once the wall. Bright red gleams in the corner—not blood but a broken door. It's the only spot of brightness in the village, which is now uniformly gray from the ash that covers everything. Wind whistles in the distance. Its sharp refrain echoes around the temple, the only structure that remains relatively upright, although its once-proud rooftop is collapsed and the statues that once lined its facade have been worn away, as if a sandstorm blistered over them.

As I stare at it, the temple seems to jolt. The door I opened has moved closer to it in response to my curiosity. That's the tricky thing about doors: they're easily influenced, especially by emotions. And mine are extremely heightened now. My stomach is in knots, as I think of my time in Irfut's cellar. Elder Durkas, the village priest, and the other village leaders spent weeks attempting to kill me for the sin of being an alaki. Nine times they tried. By nine different methods. And the entire while, I wished for death to come—prayed for it—because I believed I was wicked, inherently sinful.

Only later did I understand how deeply false this assumption was.

"Deka . . ." A warm hand massages my shoulder. Keita, worry in his eyes.

I put my hand over his. "It's all right," I say. "I'm all right."

I will no longer fall into despair when old memories rise inside me. I have power over them now. Power over myself.

To prove this, I step through the door, which has finally reached its full size. The acrid smell of ash and flame assaults my nostrils. The fire that consumed the village must have been recent. But not so recent it left any embers or warmth behind. I shiver as wind gusts over me. Ayo's armor may be sturdy, but it certainly isn't warm.

As I take in the full force of the devastation, Britta steps through the door after me. "Wha happened here?" she asks, eyes wide.

I glance around, searching for the answer. Before, this place would be ablaze with lights and music.

Now, there is nothing.

Then I take a step forward, and ash crunches under my feet. Another shiver rolls over me. There's a wrongness to it, a wrongness I've felt only twice before.

"Vale sand," Keita says as he kneels down and rubs a sampling between his fingers. "A vale opened here."

Britta frowns. "I thought vale sand was red."

Keita shrugs. "Maybe each vale is different. But the sand feels the same."

"How is it here?" I ask, unnerved. "Across the entire village?"

"It's as Lord Bala warned. The vales are no longer contained in their own realms; they are bleeding into this one." We all turn when Myter explains this from inside the pathways. "Soon there'll be no difference between the two. If you do not hurry, all of Otera will become a vale."

Suddenly, I can scarcely breathe, scarcely think. *All of Otera will become a vale.*

Beside me, Britta seems equally devastated. "But we've only been gone a few seconds, right?"

Myter promised to arrange it so that my friends and I would enter Irfut almost immediately after leaving Maiwuri.

They nod in affirmation. "But a few seconds is all the Oterans needed. There are more vales now. More wraiths. The deities here will try their best to gain as much power as they can."

Just as the Maiwurian gods warned.

Myter stares at me, the implication clear. I nod. "I understand," I say. "Thank you for all your help."

"Let us hope it will bring you success," the godsworn replies, bowing to me.

And then they're gone, leaving us alone at the door of the village temple. A familiar voice sounds from inside it: Elder Durkas.

"And so Oyomo in his divine wisdom wrought punishment on the land of Otera. For its wayward women had forgotten their place. They had demanded knowledge forbidden to them, defied their helpmeets and the natural order. Chaos did

Oyomo rain upon the One Kingdom. Chaos for the arrogance of women. For their refusal to submit."

The words filter through the door, each one a bitter but familiar poison. All my life, I heard words such as these. Listened to them, obeyed them, believed them to the point of hating myself. Hating everything that I was.

Emotion overcomes me, a familiar deluge. Fear, agitation, horror. And underneath all that, another feeling: *rage.* Sheer and overwhelming rage. All those years I sat there, listening to that filth. Letting it shape me, poison me. And now who knows how many other people are doing the same. How many girls . . .

I listen as Elder Durkas continues in that deep, authoritative voice. "But you, the chosen of Otera, can redeem yourselves, redeem your mothers. . . . Cast yourself into the vale. Give yourself to the Infinite Father, and you and yours shall be honored for this Infinity and the next."

Cast yourself into the vale. . . . My fists clench so tightly, I'm surprised they don't split once more. Already, he's sacrificing more girls, leading them to their deaths.

Britta turns to me, her expression grim. "Is that him? That rat-snibbler, Elder Durkas?"

"The very same," I reply past gritted teeth.

"Am I hearing right what he's saying?" Li says. "Telling the girls to sacrifice themselves?"

"That is what priests do," Belcalis reminds.

"And this priest enjoys it. Sacrificing girls," I say. No doubt he treasures the name of every girl he's caused to lose her life.

Keita turns to me. "What do you want to do?"

"What we always do," I return. "Intervene." I turn to Britta. "The door, if you please."

Britta's reply is a grim smile. "Me pleasure," she says. She gives the door a fierce kick.

It goes flying straight down the aisle.

I don't know who's more surprised, Elder Durkas or Ionas, the faithless blond boy I once loved, when my friends and I enter the temple. Elder Durkas is, as usual, at the altar, but Ionas is sitting in the front row, reserved for elders of the temple. I see no sign of his mother or father or, indeed, most of the other people I once knew. Half the temple's congregants are gone, especially the older women. Only the youngest girls and men just past marrying age remain.

It makes sense. If what happened here is anything like what happened on Gar Nasim, the elders likely tried sacrificing the older women to the shadow vales first. But that would not have been enough to satisfy the gods.

It never is.

Elder Durkas's mouth is so busy gasping open and shut like a fish, it takes him some moments to gather himself. "Deka?" he sputters, shocked. But only for a few moments.

He swiftly pulls himself up to his full height, which, I am amused to see, is not half as imposing as I once thought it was. But then, he himself is not half as imposing as I thought he was, his gaunt features now wizened by age and stress, what remains of his hair in straggles around his head.

"Vile demon, you've brought this calamity upon us!" he snarls. He whirls to the villagers. "See, it's as I warned! The demon, the cause of all our strife, has returned to—"

Before he can finish his words, both Britta and Belcalis rush down the aisle with inhuman speed. They grab him at the same time and force him to his knees.

Keita and Li remain where they are, glowering at the crowd. Daring anyone to move. Ionas, I'm amused to see, shrinks back into his seat, as if he'll become invisible if he makes himself small enough.

"Want me to shut his mouth permanently for ye, Deka?" Britta offers, her hand gripping Elder Durkas's gaunt shoulders.

I shake my head. "No, I have better plans for him." I walk slowly down the gray stone floor, so intent on the aged priest, his eyes now bulging in rage and fear, that I barely notice the villagers hurrying from their seats to flee the temple.

A few of the more foolish ones rush at me, but they're batted aside by Ixa, who's in his ox-sized adolescent form.

Then Ionas finally regains his courage. "Foul demon!" he cries, barreling toward me.

He hasn't taken even a few steps before Ixa slams into him. I smirk when I hear the familiar crunch of breaking bones.

Those would be Ionas's legs shattering against the stone floor. Barely adequate punishment, given that he ran me through the belly on this very temple's front steps two years ago. Still, it'll have to do. I have more important things to attend to.

I stop just in front of Elder Durkas. The elderly priest is now glaring at me, defiance in his rheumy gray eyes.

"Do what you will, foul demon," he hisses. "I will never bend to you. You and your kind have brought destruction upon Otera and—"

"Shh." I put a hand to his mouth.

I've had enough of his ramblings to last a lifetime. So has everyone else, I imagine. As he struggles against my grasp, I picture the lake that lies at the edge of the village. The one where he drowned me all those years ago. I can never forget the smirk on his face when he did so, the look of sheer victory in his eyes.

He has always liked control, but much more than that, he always liked eliciting terror from others, while pretending that he was helping them. I wonder how he'll react when the sandal is on the other foot.

When I turn, a door has appeared in the air behind me, the lake's waters gleaming prominently behind it. I glance back at Elder Durkas. "You told me once that water was purifying to the soul. Do you still believe that to be the case?"

The elder glances at the lake, at the water now rapidly spilling through the door. When he looks back at me, his eyes are so wide now, the whites gleam in the temple's gloom. "Surely you don't mean to—"

"Throw you into the lake? Indeed. I assume you'd prefer that to the vale you want to send these children to." I glance at the girls, still huddled behind the altar, fear shining in their eyes. "And wait, didn't you drown me in this lake before? Was it my third death or fourth, I can't remember. Those days in the cellar, they all blended together."

The elder nervously licks his lips. "I was trying to save you. To purify you."

I turn back to the girls. They still haven't moved, but they're listening to our conversation with the intensity only those scheduled for execution can maintain. Looking at them more closely, I realize that the oldest can't be more than six years old. Children. Babies, truth be told.

"And what about them?" I ask Elder Durkas, grim. "What wrongs did they need to purify?"

"They are female. It's their existence that created all this. Your existence." He snarls, spittle flecking his lips. "I should have ended you when I had the chance. I should have buried you so deeply—"

I toss him through the door.

"Swim," I say, turning my back to him as he flails in the water. "And perhaps if the Infinite Father favors you the way you so often proclaim, he'll intervene and save your life."

I close the door without another thought, a strange feeling washing over me. Not quite happiness, not quite relief. All those years I spent fearing that man, believing his every word. And he was nothing more than a charlatan.

But he'll never again use his voice to oppress others, never again use his power to kill.

Finally, Elder Durkas is gone. The demon that wreaked havoc on so much of my life has finally been defeated.

Britta walks over to me. "Think he'll make it back to shore?"

"Doubtful. If his robes don't do him in, the cold will. And that's assuming he can even swim." I shrug. "He always did say it was an unnatural act."

Britta puts her hands on my shoulder. "Feel better?" she asks, grinning.

"Like I could save the world."

22

◆ ◆ ◆

All that remains of the cottage I once called home is a shell.

Oh, most of the thatched roof and the walls, though blackened and crumbled, are still standing. But the entire back of the cottage is missing. Not consumed, as the rest of the village presumably was, by the vales, but broken by a fallen tree, whose bare branches protrude through the tiny quarters like grotesquely skeletal arms. I see them clearly from my position at what was once the front door. It has been chopped down to kindling, axe marks stark against the splintered wood. It's the same with most of the furnishings—the ones that remain, that is. Most have been carted away, or are now in pieces on the floor. I ignore the debris as I step inside, keeping my eyes firmly focused on that tree, on those skeletal branches, which are still growing despite the fact that the tree they sprang from is broken and dying.

It's a metaphor, surely. But one I choose not to unravel. I choose not to think anything at all. Instead, I will focus on those branches. Perhaps, if I stare at them long enough, I can ignore the missing furniture, the fact that every decoration, every item of value we ever had in this house, is gone.

And that, likely, includes Mother's things. Especially the ones that carry her scent.

"Wha happened here?" Britta walks in after me, eyes wide. "It doesn't look like the vales swept through this place."

"It wasn't the vales." Keita picks a broken plate off the floor and sighs. "The entire place has been ransacked."

"It was Elder Durkas," I say, suddenly wishing I still had my hands on him so I could throw him in the lake all over again. "Whenever someone brings disgrace on the village, he leads the villagers in casting them out. Destroying their memory. No doubt the moment the jatu came to take Father, everything here was fair game." Including the items we came looking for.

Britta must understand the implication of what I'm saying, because she looks at me again, worried. "So how do we find your mother's things?"

"We don't," Belcalis says grimly. "Look around you. It's winter. The village has been almost completely destroyed. If the survivors haven't already stolen all the things that would have had her scent on them, the cold and damp will have."

"Maybe we don't need her scent." When I turn to Britta, confused, her worry has gone, replaced by excitement. She rushes to explain. "Lamin said ye just need something that provokes a strong enough memory. An' anything here can do that. The whole reason we came to Irfut is because of how deeply yer tied to this place. All the strongest emotions ye have around yer mother are here.

"So maybe, ye don't need her scent; ye just need to remember her presence. An' this place is the best place for ye to do so. Ye just have to try, Deka."

Try. . . . I nod.

But when I look around—take in the devastation surrounding me, I'm suddenly so heavy, I can't remain standing a moment longer. I walk leadenly over to the hearth, where a single bench remains, its legs rickety and half broken. Mother used to place me on that bench when she was working. And then, as I grew older, I used to stand on it so I could help her in the kitchen.

Now it's all that's left. All that's left of Mother. All that's left of home. The place that I lived in for sixteen years of my life. It's an empty shell now. Just like everything else around me.

Tears slide down my cheeks and I wipe them away.

A hand presses on my shoulder. Belcalis's.

There's sympathy in her gaze. "I'm sorry, Deka. I know this must be distressing for you."

Distressing. No word has ever felt so inadequate.

Distressing is when you stub your toe, or stumble in weapons practice and fall on your arse. This, what I'm experiencing, is devastation.

My entire family is gone. As is my home. And now there's no going back, ever.

Not that there ever was.

I think of everything I've learned about myself over the past few years—my abilities, the truth of my origins. No wonder the villagers destroyed this place the moment they could. I never belonged here. I was always an outsider, a pretender. That's why I can't reconstruct the memory of Mother's scent even here, in the cottage where she birthed me. Why I can't even picture her face, hear her voice.

Because I never was hers to begin with. I never was her true daughter.

If I was, I would at least know her scent. Recreate it from memory. I wouldn't need things like clothes or this awful place to remember it. To find her body.

I brush away my tears, then shrug Belcalis's hand off my shoulder. "I'm fine," I whisper, looking down. "Everything is fine."

"Except that's not true, is it?" she says, not letting go of me. She comes closer, kneels at my feet, her midnight eyes burning into mine. "You may not be human, Deka. You may not even be alaki. But you can still feel pain. You can still feel anger. And it's all right—both emotions are appropriate, given the circumstances. This was your home, and they tainted it."

"Was it really?" I turn from her with a bitter laugh. "Was it ever truly my home, or was I just there, this *thing* that insinuated itself into their lives?"

I can see it now, the life my parents would have had if I had never been born. They would have remained as they were, happy. They could have perhaps even had more children—the son Father actually wanted.

But they never got those things, because I came along, and now they're both dead and their home is destroyed. Elder Durkas was right: this *was* my fault. It's always been my fault.

More bitter laughter wrenches from my throat. I swallow it down, then return my gaze to Belcalis. "I must seem in a dire mood indeed if you're the one talking to me about feelings."

"I feel."

When my eyebrows lift at this proclamation, Belcalis gives me a wry smile. "Sometimes I feel all sorts of emotions. And

232

sometimes"—she beckons to me and I lean in closer—"I even feel joy. Imagine that."

I laugh despite myself. "A shocking notion."

"Indeed," Belcalis says loftily. "But the point is, it's all right to feel. And it's all right to be overwhelmed when you finally give your biggest tormentor his comeuppance, only to find your home destroyed by him."

I blink, startled by this concise assessment. Trust Belcalis to cut to the heart of the matter. But I don't want to give her credit so easily. I sniff. "I'll take your word for it," I say. Then I glance around at my other companions, who are huddled around me, as if to protect me from the barrage of my own emotions.

Except they can't do that. No one can—or should—do that, not even me. If there's one thing I know from bitter experience, it's that if I hoard my feelings, if I let them circle and circle in the back of my mind, they will eventually consume me.

"It's strange," I admit finally, rising. "This was my home. And now it's not. And I don't have anywhere else to go. And that makes me angry. And it makes me sad. And it makes me a thousand other things. I have no home to return to."

I say the words out loud again, as if testing them.

"Neither do I." To my surprise, Belcalis shrugs in agreement.

"Me neither," Keita says.

Li glances away when I turn, waiting for his reply. But then he shrugs. "Well, don't look at me. I'm certain my family would take me back."

"Of course they would," I snort. Of our little group, Li is the most spoiled.

"But alone," he warns direly. "And . . . eventually. If I begged and pleaded enough."

"An' that's assuming they don't behead ye first," Britta sniffs.

"There is that," Li acknowledges with another easy shrug.

Britta humphs. "Well, I'm certain yer all welcome back to Golma with me. It'll be cold, but yer all welcome. Me family's very inviting. Salt of the soil, through and through."

"I'd rather cast myself on a pyre," Li mutters under his breath. When Britta glares at him, he shrugs again. "What, I hate the cold. Do you not feel how miserable it is right now?"

As the pair continue glaring at each other, Keita walks over, puts his arm around my shoulder. I sink into his touch, burrowing my head into his neck. "Home is where you are, Deka," he says. "It's where all of you are, even you"—he directs this last comment at Li, who grunts, pretending to be offended.

Then Keita returns his attention to me. "I know you're sad, but once this is done, we'll find a home—a much better place, where we can all live together peacefully."

He and all my friends, that is.

The thought is a sobering reminder. If this ends in our victory, I'll be a god, and gods do not reside with mortals. At least, not truly.

I don't say this out loud, and Keita doesn't acknowledge it, but we both know it is the eventuality. If we succeed, we'll soon part ways for different planes entirely. And if we don't, we'll still part ways, albeit in a different manner.

"That sounds like a dream," I say, nodding. Then I wait a few more moments, savoring Keita's touch, before finally, I pull back. "All right, that's enough sentimentality. Time to do what we came here for. We need to search the entire house for traces of Mother. Anything that might be sentimental enough to spur a strong response."

Belcalis nods. "There's sure to be something," she says in what almost seems like a hopeful tone. "Look at the way they ransacked this place—it's shoddy, shoddy work. They're sure to have missed something."

"That's precisely what I'm hoping," I say as I walk into the kitchen, where Mother, like most Oteran women, spent most of her time. If there's any bit of her remaining in this house, it'll be either there or in the room she and Father shared. But I don't have the strength to go up there just at this moment—not given how emotionally vulnerable I am.

The moment I fully enter the kitchen, however, I notice it, the strangeness. It's been niggling at me all this time, but I couldn't put my finger on it before.

"I can't remember her," I say, puzzled.

"Wha's that?" Britta has followed me, and she seems confused by my words.

"Mother, I can't picture her." I frown. "I'm here, I should be having memories of her—and I am, but it's strange. It's like I—"

I stop, suddenly chilled to my bones.

The air has shifted. "The Idugu," I gasp, immediately recognizing the heavy oiliness settling over my skin. "They're here."

"Get us out, Deka!" Keita rushes toward me. "Create a door!"

But when I try to sink into the combat state, a strange force clamps over my body, an invisible vise I can't see, even though it's taken firm grasp of me.

"No, no, Deka," a familiar voice says, tsking. When I turn my head slowly but painfully to the door, a shadowy figure is flickering there.

Okot. I recognize Anok's counterpart immediately.

Of the four Idugu, the male gods that are the Gilded Ones'

counterparts, only he has Anok's midnight-dark skin, as well as those deceptively kind eyes. *Deceptively,* because unlike the goddess I considered my only ally among the Gilded Ones, Okot is not kind. Not even near it. He is a monster that shapes itself as a deity. One that uses others to do his bidding and feeds off the pain and blood of innocents. The Merciless One, he calls himself.

"Do not struggle," the god continues, floating into the room like he's the essence of a being rather than an actual person. "It will do you no good."

The farther he drifts in, the more my friends back away, their slow but horrified movements telling me that he's chosen to make himself visible to them, a first for any of the Idugu. Unlike the Gilded Ones, the male gods thrive on secrecy and deception, a side effect of their years of being imprisoned by their counterparts. They rarely allow themselves to be seen and for centuries even convinced most of the jatu, their own sons, that they were a singular god called Oyomo instead of the four complements to the Gilded Ones.

The nearer Okot approaches, the larger he becomes, although the edges of his silhouette are strangely faded, tatters rather than a firm outline. He seems downright haggard, his body faded like the crystal trees back in the pathways.

He must be even more starved than he was when last I met him. But then, creating shadow vales takes power. Perhaps much more power than the gods have recovered from all the sacrifices the priests have thrown into the vales for them.

"I may be diminished," Okot says, as if catching my thoughts, "but I still have enough strength to hold you, to keep you here forever." His eyes glitter with the force of a thousand dying stars, a testament to his power.

I swiftly look away, unnerved. "It was you, wasn't it?" I hiss. "You took Mother's memories!"

"Indeed. I took every trace of her from this house. You won't find what you're looking for here."

His words send a chill through me. So he knows exactly why we're here.

"Why?" I ask. "Why are you doing this? What do you want?"

If it was my death, he'd have already sent me back to his temple via a door.

Okot moves closer so suddenly, we're face to face before I can even blink. I glance away again as a small thunderstorm suddenly lashes against me, a thunderstorm that I know his anger has unconsciously created. Like all gods, Okot manifests his emotions in all sorts of strange and unpredictable ways.

"Anok has been imprisoned by our sisters," he announces, his voice reverberating through my body. "They're draining her. Siphoning away all the sustenance from her being. It's only a matter of time now before she dissipates."

"As do you as well." Now I understand.

Like all the Oteran god pairs, Anok and Okot are connected. Two sides of one coin. What happens to one will eventually happen to the other. If Anok is being drained by her imprisonment, Okot is as well, which means it's only a matter of time before the other Idugu turn on him.

The Oteran gods are like birds of prey: the slightest sign of weakness and they strike, even against their own.

Okot inclines his head, agreeing with my assessment.

"Indeed. If the gods fall, Anok and I will be the first to do so. And even if they do not, we're both still vulnerable. Which is why I've come to offer you a deal."

"An' why would we ever believe anythin' ye say?" Britta hisses, braving a step forward.

One glance from Okot and she's frozen in place. "We?" he repeats softly. "There is no we, Britta of Golma. Any offer I make is for Deka and Deka alone. It does not include you."

"Then it is not an offer I would ever consider," I reply, my will turning to iron.

Every time I'm tempted to forget that the gods view mortals—even semi-immortals—as less than insects, I'm swiftly reminded of the fact.

Okot can threaten me all he wants, even try to manipulate me the way all the other gods do. But I will not allow him to touch Britta, nor any of my other companions. I close my eyes, sinking deeper into the combat state. If I can just connect to the Greater Divinity . . . If I can just enhance my power a little . . .

When I try to inhale the primal force, Okot abruptly glides back, a cloud forming around his brow. Whatever emotion it's expressing is not one I can readily identify. Not that I care to. Now that I'm deeper in the combat state, I can see that the vise Okot wrapped around me is loosening, perhaps due to his inattention.

"It seems I have erred," the god says, almost to himself. "Your bonds to these . . . mortals are much stronger than I knew."

"Stronger than you can ever imagine," I snap, still stealthily inhaling. I'm not yet able to connect to the Greater Divinity, but if I keep trying, it's only a matter of time. The vise is loosening every second. All I need is a few moments more . . .

"But then, your kind don't understand what it is to love," I snarl, trying to keep him talking.

"And yet I love Anok." As I still, startled by this sudden confession, Okot cocks his head, a strangely human gesture. "I despise her in equal measure, given how she betrayed me, but I love her still. I love her even though she betrayed me."

When the Gilded Ones locked the Idugu behind the veil that became their prison, Okot, the only of his brothers who had not played with human lives, begged Anok to free him. I saw that moment when I used the blood on my knife to peer into the gods' memories. I also saw how she declined and left him in that prison, believing, as her sisters did, that he was too volatile to be trusted.

That's why Okot is always so angry. Of all the Idugu, he's the only one who, initially, did not deserve the fate that befell him.

That has, of course, long changed. Okot is now just as guilty as his brothers, if not more so.

His eyes try to pierce mine, but I steadfastly look away. "The emotions," he says, sounding almost confused. "I cannot untangle them, and I do not know why."

I humph. "Because she's you," I reply bluntly. "What greater narcissism is there than in loving and hating your own self?"

"And yet, because she is also herself," Okot replies, almost wonderingly. "Together or apart, Anok and I . . . we are . . ."

"I'm not here to hear about you and Anok," I snap, pushing steadily against the vise. It's nearly loose enough to break free of now. If I can just get a little bit freer, touch that thread of divinity that's just out of reach . . .

"Indeed."

I gasp as Okot suddenly reappears in front of me. So close

now, our noses are almost touching. I can see the white of his eyes out of the corner of mine.

"You're here for your kelai. But, as I told you, I've erased every true memory of your mother, wiped it all from existence, so you cannot use it to your advantage."

As despair roils through me, Okot continues with a sly, almost calculating tone, "I could, however, just tell you where your kelai is, so you don't have to go sniffing across the continents. In fact, I could take you there, show you for yourself. That is what you want, is it not?"

I look up at him. "And if it is?"

"Then all you have to do is say the word and I'll take you there."

"But why?" The question rises again.

Why is Okot offering to take me to my kelai? Why hasn't he just killed me and taken it himself? I'm here, he has me, and yet . . .

My eyes widen. "You can't just take it, can you?" When Okot stills, blinking for just one second, I know I'm correct. The Gilded Ones were willing to kill me so they would force my kelai to emerge, but Okot, for some reason, is not, which means: "This is a proximity thing, isn't it?" I gasp. "If you kill me, my kelai will attempt to rush back to me. But you don't want that to happen, which means it must be in an undesirable location, perhaps one closer to the Gilded Ones. And you don't want them snatching it before you do."

Okot turns away, and I know I have him. I laugh. "Wait, am I correct? The place you last stored my kelai truly was near the Gilded Ones?" Mother told me the Idugu moved it periodically, but never in a million years did I think they'd be stupid enough to leave it in a place where their counterparts could access it.

And yet, that very much seems to be the case.

If Okot were human, muscles would be grinding in his jaw. Instead, thunderclouds smash across his brow as he dourly inclines his head. "I will admit, your kelai is in an undesirable place. But I can help you get to it. For a price."

"And what price is that?" I'd almost forgotten we were haggling.

"Amnesty."

When I frown at him, he continues: "My brothers and Anok's sisters will soon turn on us both. Have already turned on us, as you've seen with Anok. Now that we are weaker, we are prey to our siblings. But if you assume your divinity and become a deity once more, you can spare us when you end the others. Allow us to live. And in return, we will bring your mother back. We will give you back everything you have lost."

As Okot speaks, the cottage suddenly changes around us, the back wall repairing, the furnishings returning to their original places. Color seeps into the leached wood as Mother walks out of the kitchen, a plate in hand and a smile on her face. She's talking to someone, and when I focus on the image, shocked, it's me, only it's not me as I am now. This me wears the flowing robes of an adult woman, a half mask to hide the top portion of her face. She is smiling as she rushes to embrace Mother.

"Mother," Other Me says, "how happy I am to see you."

"And you," Mother replies, her voice so loving, my heart pangs just hearing it.

"Mother," I whisper, everything in me yearning for her,

stretching toward her. If I move just a step closer, I can breathe in her scent, fall into her arms the way I used to when I was a child.

Blue lights flash in the distance, a yawning darkness around them, but I don't pay any attention, just as I don't truly feel the accompanying wrongness. All I see is Mother.

"It's not real, Deka!" Keita's voice suddenly sounds far away, and when I turn, he's no longer there. None of my friends are. The only thing around me now is the house as it once was, with Other Me and Mother.

And yet I hear Keita's voice. "He's trying to trick you, Deka. Don't fall for it."

Fall for what? It seems so real. . . . Except for those blue lights, that wrongness, everything feels real, the house, Mother, Other Me . . .

I turn once more to the scene unfolding before my eyes. Once upon a time, it would have been my fondest wish, this cozy domesticity. To be the woman embracing Mother, all the while cloaked in the robes and mask of a proper Oteran woman, a husband at home, no doubt, waiting for her.

Except that's not my dream any longer. It hasn't been in a long, long time.

This house, this version of me, they're nightmares. Specters of a world I never wish to return to.

A cold rage fills me as I glance back at Okot. He's there just in front of me, his body becoming more and more solid the more I look at it. "It's a strange thing, seeing what others think you want," I say quietly. "Most times, it says much more about them than it does about you.

"You, for instance, think I want to be that girl, the one in the mask and robes of a wife. Except I tired of ornamental masks long ago. And I prefer armor to robes now."

"And what of your mother?" Okot sounds almost desperate as I stare up at him.

He's realized now that his cheap little illusion isn't working, that I'm not going to fall for the web he's spun.

"Reanimation is against the natural order," I say simply. And even if it weren't, I doubt Mother would want to return to the life Okot has prescribed for her.

"I am a god," Okot snaps. "I *am* the natural order."

There it is. The arrogance he's only barely managed to hold back. He truly believes I should want the things he's offering me. Except I've had a taste of other gods. I've seen that true deities serve the natural order instead of themselves. What Okot is proposing to me is an abomination, and I want no part of that.

So I return my attention to him. "I will be as well when I become the Singular once more. So no, I don't need you to bring my mother back. And even if I wished for that, she doesn't, and I would never force such perversion on her."

"You are assuming you have the choice." Okot's voice is suddenly the rumble of an awakening volcano, and those clouds flash so fiercely over his brow, they almost obscure it. Darkness wavers behind him, that abyss I've only seen glimpses of.

I look him dead in the eye, too far gone to fear his threats any longer. "I'm not the one who came begging to be saved," I snarl back, wriggling against his vise, which has somehow become tighter again. "I hope that when the others discover your treachery, they devour you to the very last drop."

Glaciers form around Okot's head, a crown of icy determination. "You will not bargain with me?" he asks, suddenly every inch the remote, unfathomable deity he presents himself to be.

"Not even if you were the last god in all of Otera."

"Then you leave me no choice."

Okot gestures, and the cottage vanishes. Darkness descends, the one I've been glimpsing all this while.

And inside that darkness, lights.

23

◆ ◆ ◆

"Keita? Britta?" I call out. There's no answer.

It's like my friends aren't here, and yet I feel them nearby, sense them somewhere in the darkness that crowds closer and closer.

My extremities are freezing cold now, as if all the blood has gone out of them. But something warm surrounds me, a moist, fleshy softness. It's accompanied by a strange scent, a calming, almost intoxicating aroma that reminds me of the flowers that once bloomed in the fields just above Irfut. A fluorescent blue-green mist wafts past my gaze. My eyelids grow heavier and heavier. It's as if that scent—that mist—is curling around me, lulling me to sleep.

I try to struggle, try to keep my eyes open, but the scent, it's too powerful.

Deka! Ixa's voice jolts through my brain the same moment his head butts against mine. *Deka wake!* he growls.

I'm trying, I reply groggily, struggling up.

But that softness just tightens further, keeping me in place. Squeezing my armor into me. If I were wearing anything other than ebiki armor, it would have no doubt broken under the pressure by now. I recognize this dimly, even though I'm still half asleep.

What is that thing? I ask sleepily. *What's around me?*

Monster, Ixa growls, snapping at something I can't see. *Monster trying to eat you!*

The horror of what he's saying shatters through my daze. I gasp up, push against the softness. As if in response to my efforts, the lights brighten and I finally see my captor.

A vale wraith.

I know immediately what it is—because how else to explain this coiling, writhing monstrosity of a creature? Its head is a colossal, shapeless mass that seems to melt into the slimy black tentacles slithering around me. Black grains powder them— black sand, which exudes the same sort of wrongness I felt back in Irfut and in the first vale. It covers the creature so completely, moments pass before I finally spot my friends, also wrapped in those writhing tentacles, their bodies limp as that scent wafts around them in a cloud of fluorescent blue-green, no doubt drugging them the same way it did me.

"Britta?" I shout, heart pounding with fear. "KEITA? BELCALIS? LI?"

None of them answer. They're all fast asleep as the wraith slowly, inexorably pulls them closer to its gargantuan head, its tiny blue eye slits narrowing as its gaping, rounded maw of a mouth opens to display row upon row of jagged teeth.

For a creature with no meaningful delineation between its

head and the rest of its body, it certainly has a lot of mouth. Mouth enough to swallow each one of my friends whole, as it clearly intends to do.

"BRITTA! KEITA! LI! WAKE UP!" I shout, but none of them so much as moves a muscle. They're too deeply drugged, too caught in the dreams that the creature is weaving using that hypnotic scent.

Panicked now, I try to wrench myself from the creature's grasp, but it's like fighting against water. The creature's skin is too soft. All my strikes just glide off it—as do Ixa's bites. Even when he grows to a larger size to fight, his mouth can't quite find purchase. The wraith easily slaps him away when he lunges in for another bite, sending him barreling into a far-off dune.

"IXA!" I shout, horrified, as he disappears into the darkness.

I fumble for my atikas, only barely managing to slide one out of its sheath.

As I do so, Okot appears, wafting across the creature's tentacles toward me.

"You!" I snarl. "Was this your plan all along?"

The god shakes his head in what I assume is an approximation of sadness. "It could have been different," he says mournfully. "We could have been allies, but you left me no choice, Deka. My brothers intend to relocate your kelai a few days from now.

"While you and yours remain here, I will oversee the relocation, and then I will steal your kelai out from under their noses."

"So what did you need me for?" I snarl.

Okot shrugs. "I wanted to be your ally. To create a new world with you. It is lonely, you see, to be a god without a pantheon."

He manages to seem almost remorseful as he continues: "It truly is a pity we could not be friends. I can see why my counterpart favored you."

"And I can see why she hated you!" I spit back.

Okot only shrugs, a rippling of his entire body. "If I possessed the capacity for human emotions, I would undoubtedly be hurt. Let us stop now. I will give you one last small mercy." He wafts closer, his eyes gleaming white as they peer into mine.

He's trying to hypnotize me, trying to take control of my mind. But I won't let him. Since the vale wraith is holding me in place, I can't look away. So I do the only thing I can—I grasp my atika by the blade, letting its sharpness bite into my palm. Letting the pain center me in the present. Keep me from being ensorcelled by the power in Okot's eyes.

Gold begins sliding down the hilt, my blood, dripping from the cut I've made.

Okot, thankfully, does not notice. "Sleep now, Deka," the god intones. "And never again wake."

I immediately flicker my eyes closed, pretending to sleep, but to my surprise, Okot doesn't disappear that very moment. Instead, he says one last thing, a sentiment so low, I almost don't hear it. An unexpected yearning, coming from a god like him.

"I truly wish we could have been allies," he whispers. "Together, we three could have changed the world."

With that, he's gone.

And I'm left in the darkness, the vale wraith's tentacles writhing around me. When I flick my eyes open again, it's to a sight from my deepest nightmares. The vale wraith has Li almost to that colossal mouth now. One more slither of a tentacle, and my friend will be consumed.

"LI!" I shout, fully unsheathing my atika.

I twist in the wraith's grasp with a strength and swiftness I did not know I possessed, slicing off the tentacle around me with one smooth movement. Then I'm running across that moist, soft body toward Li, who's in a deep sleep, his face peaceful despite the enraged screams the vale wraith is now making.

Even wounded as it is, the creature keeps trying to feed. Its tentacle pulls Li higher and higher, that mouth gaping wider, the teeth gleaming sharper.

"LI!" I shout. "LI! WAKE UP!"

But there's still no answer, not even when Ixa lunges out of the darkness to throw himself against Li's unconscious body. That blue-green scent cloud is wrapping ever tighter around Li, dousing him in a veritable mist of pheromones. He's lost to the world now.

Unless . . .

I sink into the combat state, suddenly grateful my friends aren't wearing the infernal armor that used to be their daily uniform. Each one contained a small portion of my blood, which kept me from using my abilities on them.

Now, however, they're completely unprotected.

"Li," I say, putting every bit of power and compulsion I can behind my voice. "WAKE UP!"

My friend immediately gasps upright, his eyes disoriented. "Wha? Huh?" he asks, glancing around. Then he sees the vale wraith. "What in the name of—"

"EXTRICATE YOURSELF!" I shout, another command.

Li obeys my command with alacrity, immediately twisting to wrest himself from the vale wraith's grasp. When the wraith lashes more tentacles at him, he slices through them automatically, his body fueled by pure instinct now.

But even that isn't enough. Yet more tentacles hurtle Li's way.

"IXA!" I shout, but I shouldn't have even bothered. My blue-scaled companion is already darting across the writhing appendages, nimbly avoiding their ever more desperate movements, as he makes his way toward Li, who's stabbing at yet another tentacle with his dagger. He twists it so that it embeds deeply in the slimy mass of muscle and skin.

The vale wraith screams again, a shatteringly high-pitched sound, but it's nothing compared to a deathshriek's cries, so I ignore it as I turn to my other friends, breathing to connect to the Greater Divinity's power once more.

"WAKE UP, EVERYONE!" I shout, putting as much compulsion as I can behind my voice. "FIGHT AGAINST THE WRAITH!"

The effect of the command is immediate. My friends gasp awake.

"Wha is this, Deka?" Britta cries, horrified as she glances around herself.

"Don't ask questions—stab!" Belcalis snaps, already doing as she advised.

Britta nods, ripping apart the vale wraith's tentacles with her bare hands. She doesn't even bother with her atikas. Beside her, Keita begins singeing tentacles with his fire. More shrieks echo into the darkness—terrified ones. It seems vale wraiths are frightened of fire.

The realization widens the smirk slicing across my face.

That is, until newer, fainter shrieks reply from the distance.

This wraith, it seems, is not alone. There are others.

"HURRY!" I shout to my friends, slicing off an incoming tentacle. I understand the method now—stab, then twist, to gain a hold despite the slickness.

Li stops hacking and sawing long enough to turn to me with horrified eyes. "There can't be more of those things out there."

Another shriek answers his question.

"We need to leave!" Belcalis shouts. "Can you open a door from here?"

"To where?" I ask, overwhelmed.

This vale connects to Irfut, but there's no point going back there. Okot destroyed every trace of Mother that remained. And the Warthu Bera is out of the question; I doubt that any part of our former training ground even remains standing after the battle that took place there three months ago.

There's nowhere I can think of that's safe.

"White Hands!" Belcalis replies. "Take us to White Hands!"

"But I don't know where she is—" I stop as I remember the place I last saw her in. That grove.

Despite what it feels like, we've been gone only a few hours since we saw her. She's probably still near that grove somewhere, and if we can make our way to her, we can regroup, perhaps even get to Mother's body before Okot does, even though I have no idea how.

But that's not my concern right now. Survival is.

I build the image of the grove in my mind, remembering the towering ganib trees, their canopies like domes, leathery vines dripping down from their purple branches. As I sink deeper and deeper into the combat state, I breathe in the Greater Divinity, letting the power rise inside me until I feel it, the answering tug deep in my body. The tug Myter taught me to watch for when I must travel to a place I've never been.

Once I have it, I pinch the air in front of me. Immediately, I see it—the tiny, shimmering line in the darkness. The line that is the sunlight coming in from the other side. It must still be day where the grove is. I pull, forcing the door wider, and sunlight floods in. The wraith screeches, its tentacles scuttling backward as the light burns through them, obliterating their protective layer of slime. So fire isn't the only thing they fear.

"Open the door wider, Deka!" Belcalis calls out, slicing through the tentacle that is still trying to hold on to her. "Massacre the beast!"

"With pleasure!" I call back, steadfastly prying the door wider until—

"Deka? Deka, is that you?"

There's so much sunlight flooding into the vale now, it blinds me. I can't see what's beyond the door. Even then, I recognize that voice, that accompanying blast of wind that is the divine gift of the twins Adwapa and Asha. "Adwapa?" I shout, relief flooding over me. "Is that you?"

"Help us!" Britta calls out. "There's wraiths in here!"

She doesn't have to ask twice. A familiar dark figure darts through the door, wind seeming to lift her footsteps: Adwapa in all her bald glory, looking even stronger than the last time I saw her. By her side is Asha, the luminous ferns interwoven in her black braids glowing like a bright green beacon in the darkness. She sends a spear hurtling straight into one of the vale wraith's eyes, the wind pushing it along with deadly accuracy.

The screech the creature releases is deafening. All its

tentacles shoot up at once, writhing horrifically as it tries to pull the projectile out of its eye. Unfortunately, the wind has driven it so deep, it's likely a fatal blow. My friends stumble to the sand, released at the same time from the tentacles the wraith has once more managed to wrap around them.

"Everyone, through the door!" I shout.

I don't have to speak twice. A mad stampede to the door ensues, Britta leading the way, Keita at the back.

I take one last look at the vale wraith, its eyes bleeding an angry fluorescent blue, its tentacles flailing all around it. Less than an hour ago, it was a monarch in the darkness, a squat toad sucking the life out of its unwitting victims so it could feed their essence to the Idugu. Now it is a roaring, shrieking mass of pain. As its makers will be when I'm done with them.

Okot will suffer for what he tried to do. I will ensure it.

"I hope you die a slow and painful death," I say to the monster shrieking in the darkness. Then I step out of the shadows into the light.

◆

The grove looks exactly as it did when I first saw it via White Hands's gauntlets: groups of ancient ganib trees intertwined with each other, each one a miniature forest in its own right. Velvety yellow flowers and dark red fungi sprout from the colossal purple trunks; bright-winged birds flit through the glossy green leaves and the masses of leathery vines that connect each tree to the next, making the entire grove seem like a single gigantic, interconnected plant. Except it's so much more than that. I glance around, mouth agape with awe as I realize that what I thought was just a grove of trees is actually the edge of some sort of monument—a sprawling, expansive network of stone steps that lead down to what appears to be a deep forest spring.

"Deka!" a familiar voice calls.

I turn, and there, running toward me, is Katya, the towering deathshriek who was my bloodsister back at the Warthu Bera before being reborn into this form. Her much shorter betrothed, Rian, struggles to keep up with her, his human legs no match for Katya's gigantic ones.

"Deka!" Katya shouts again, overjoyed. Then she skids to a stop a few steps in front of me, her green eyes suddenly unsure. The last time we saw each other, I was still very much injured, and easy to anger as a result.

I hold out my arms, tears dripping down my cheeks. "It's all right, you can embrace me."

"Truly? White Hands said you were healed but—"

"Come here, you!"

Katya squeals with delight as I clasp my arms around her, squeezing her tight. Well, squeezing her legs, that is.

Like most deathshrieks, Katya is inhumanly gaunt and tall, her body stretching nearly half the length of a ganib tree, her claw-tipped fingers nearly reaching past her knees. I have to crane my neck to look up at her.

"I'm fine now," I continue swiftly. "I learned how to keep myself from being injured."

"Oh, Deka!" Katya flings me up, the quill-like red spikes down her back rustling as she swings me round and round. "You're all right, you're all right!"

"I won't remain that way if you don't put me down soon," I grunt as I feel the bile rise inside me. It's one thing to be embraced but quite another to be spun about like a drunken whirligig.

"Oh, my apologies!" Katya swiftly releases me, then turns to the others in the grove, who have been walking cautiously closer. "It's all right, everyone, it's Deka! It's really her!"

That's all it takes to open the floodgates. Masses of people suddenly come rushing from beyond the ganibs, all of them calling out greetings to me and my other friends. There, hurrying over, is Mehrut, the plump, butter-brown alaki who is Adwapa's sweetheart. Acalan and Kweku, Belcalis's and Adwapa's uruni, follow Mehrut, burly, jokey Kweku already grinning while studious, quiet Acalan seems almost nervous in his excitement to see us. Behind them are more groups of alaki and jatu, and even deathshrieks, many of whom I've never seen before. It seems White Hands truly has been successful in her attempts to acquire more allies to resist the gods.

Then a pair of familiar white forms appear, relief in their eyes as they canter unhurriedly toward me. "Quiet One," the equus twins, Braima and Masaima, say together as one, "it's truly you."

"Couldn't be certain you weren't those tricky goddesses," Masaima continues, his pure white mane glistening in the late afternoon sun. The equus looks almost human from the waist up, except for his inhumanly large eyes and flattened nose that resembles a muzzle; the rest of him is horse, except for the iron-tipped, raptorlike talons that stand in for hooves. His coat is a velvety white that covers nearly his entire body.

"Their worshippers are always lurking about," adds Braima,

who looks identical to his brother except for the black stripe in his mane, which travels all the way down his back to his carefully manicured tail.

"Precisely, which is why one can never be too cautious." This comment comes from White Hands, who is now striding forward, footsteps as unhurried yet businesslike as ever. "And the Deka I knew didn't know how to open doors, especially not ones to places she'd never been."

"White Hands!" I hurry over and embrace my former mentor. To my relief, she embraces me back, her arms as strong and capable as ever. "The Deka you knew is much changed from when you last saw her. She's a bit more accomplished now. Much less wounded, certainly."

White Hands glances down at the ebiki armor covering my body. "So, it yet holds—the ebiki armor?"

I nod. "As does the power inside it."

And I'm not speaking of the ebiki's power either.

It's the Greater Divinity's power that's kept me going so far, the one thing that's kept the emptiness inside from growing. Even though I only call upon the amount sufficient to power my abilities, it's enough that I never need to draw from my own well. As long as I continue in this manner, the ebiki armor should hold, as should the time I have left.

I'll still die if I don't connect to my kelai, but it'll be at least months yet, instead of the mere weeks I had when I first crossed into Maiwuri.

"It seems you've had a time of it, Deka," White Hands says, looking me up and down.

"Like you cannot even imagine," I say with a sigh.

I nod meaningfully toward the edge of the monument, where the sound of rushing water obscures all else.

I head in its direction, White Hands immediately following behind, all business once more. Braima and Masaima follow us as well, their massive white forms keeping everyone else at bay.

Once we're out of hearing distance from the rest of the group, I turn to White Hands. "How has it been going, your quest for allies?"

"Not very well." She sighs. "The aviax remain as intractable as ever."

And yet she remains here. But I understand why.

Aviax are the only humanlike race with the ability to fly—an ability indispensable in long-distance combat, not to mention scouting, bolstering supply chains, and any number of other integral tasks. And now that the gods have opened more vales, we need them more than ever, since we have to move up the timeline of the offensive White Hands has been planning. If we're to stop the gods from feeding, we need to cut them off from their priests and followers once and for all. And we need to do so in a matter of weeks—perhaps even days now.

But it seems the aviax are as unapproachable as their reputations suggest.

That they're even allowing so many strangers near Ilarong, their capital city, speaks to the persuasiveness of White Hands.

I refocus my attention on her as she sighs again. "Now that you're here, however, perhaps I can build some momentum. They do love anything shiny and new, and you are the Angoro, a god trapped by flesh. You'll be irresistible to them." When I reluctantly nod, unsure how I feel about that statement, she continues: "And you—I assume you were not able to locate your kelai?"

I shake my head. "We went back to Irfut as Mother encouraged, but Okot was there. He locked me and the others in the shadow vale you just saw."

White Hands grinds her jaw. "So we're back to where we started."

"Not quite." When she glances at me, curious, I inform her of everything Okot revealed about my kelai.

"Fascinating . . ." White Hands stares down at me. "So why haven't they moved it yet?"

"I think it must be somewhere dangerous, somewhere where the Gilded Ones would notice any unusual movements. The Idugu must have placed it there at least some time ago, not giving any thought to its security, since they controlled Otera."

"But then you woke the Gilded Ones," White Hands says, putting two and two together.

"And everything changed," I say, nodding. "The goddesses would notice any strange movements in their territory—especially from priests or the Idugu—and they would act."

"Which means your kelai must be somewhere close to Abeya."

"More than that," I say, finally voicing the suspicion I've had since talking with Okot. "If the Idugu are reluctant to move it now, when the Gilded Ones are so weakened, that means it must be somewhere directly in the goddesses' territory, either near or in the Bloom." That massive expanse of greenery is the truest measure of the Gilded Ones' power, and every inch of territory it covers is linked directly to them.

"It's feasible." White Hands nods, tapping her bottom lip. "Only gods would be arrogant enough to forget something of such importance near their enemy's territory."

"But even if that's true," I say, slumping, "it won't be there for long. Okot said they would move it a few days from now."

"Which means we must move swiftly." White Hands nods decisively. "I'll have my spies in the region monitor any strange movements—"

I gape. "You already have spies in the region?" White Hands was with us when we fled Abeya just over three months ago—how has she already reestablished her network?

"I have spies everywhere," White Hands returns primly. "And the moment they notice anything strange, they'll inform me."

Familiar panic swells inside me. "But I should be out there, searching."

"To what end? Given everything you've told me, I doubt you'd find the Idugu's followers before my spies do. Besides, they'll be on the lookout for you. No, it's best you remain here and help me finalize battle plans as well as woo the aviax to our side. And there's more—something else I need from you."

I glance at her. "What?"

White Hands glances around, as if just now noticing all the people waiting to greet me. "We'll discuss it later," she says airily. "This is a reunion, after all. But, Deka?" She leans closer to me. "How much time?"

When she glances meaningfully down at my hands, I sigh, understanding what she's asking. *How much time before the emptiness caused by my depleting kelai consumes me and I scatter like dust on the wind?* "Much more than I hoped for," I reply truthfully. "I think I've bought myself a little extra time—a few more months if I keep the armor on and use the Greater Divinity to power my abilities. But all that won't matter, given the state of Otera."

"The end of the world?" White Hands asks.

"The end of the world." I nod.

"Plenty of time to discuss that after," she says, tugging me forward.

I frown up at her. "You're not frightened of the world ending?"

"I'm the oldest living alaki in history." White Hands shrugs. "If you think this is the first apocalypse I've encountered, you're sorely mistaken. Come along, Deka, we have places to be."

24

◆ ◆ ◆

The first of the places White Hands is referring to turns out to be a massive plain that's hidden deep inside the jungle, well beyond the grove of ganib trees. There, a river of wildflowers awaits, their blue petals undulating so softly, they almost appear to be swells of water. The thicket of trees surrounding them is in such a perfect circle, it makes my eyes narrow.

"Is this a farm of some sort?" I ask, glancing at Adwapa, who's walking along with me, Asha, as always, by her side.

"More like a landing area," Adwapa replies, looking pointedly up. The moment I follow her gaze, my eyes widen.

There, rising above us, is the mountain I saw when White Hands appeared to us in Maiwuri, although now that I'm nearer, I realize it's not just any mountain. This one has a series of peaks that soar high above the clouds, a city carved into them. So that is Ilarong, the capital of all aviax cities. Buildings arise from the delicate stone, so precariously perched, they seem like they're on the verge of tumbling into the abyss below. Flocks of aviax flit around them, either on their own or atop zerizards, the feathered, birdlike lizards commonly used as transport in Hemaira.

I watch the zerizards, stunned by how different they are here. Not in looks, perhaps, but in utilization. Back in Hemaira, zerizards were used as glorified horses to pull carriages. They very rarely left the ground. In fact, most had their wings clipped so they could never truly fly. Here, they're in their natural element, soaring through the clouds, pulling what look like delicate glass palanquins, their highly polished sides gleaming in the late afternoon sun.

I gape up at them. "Are those—"

"Zerizards, such as you have never seen before?" a cheerful voice says. "Why, yes, yes they are." A familiar whirring sounds as Lord Kamanda, the slight, gregarious aristocrat I met not so long ago, glides out of what seems like thin air on his golden chair, a pair of elaborately plumaged aviax at his side. Tall, bright red males, their necks and talon-like fingers are bedecked in heavy gold jewelry. They coo to each other as they stare at me, seemingly fascinated by my presence. It's the same with the other aviax now landing, all of them males who tower over even the tallest human. They glance around at the people now gathered in the glade before their eyes slowly, inexorably find their way to me.

The moment each one spots me, he cocks his head, cooing to his comrades in the birdlike aviax language.

"Beautiful, are they not, Deka?" Lord Kamanda asks, emerging from the conveyance that I now see has brought him here.

It's one of those palanquins, only this one is constructed of glass that reflects its surroundings, rendering it nearly invisible. The same glass armors the zerizards pulling the palanquin, obscuring them so completely, only their eyes are visible.

My jaw drops. No wonder aviax are so rarely spotted outside their cities. If they've been traveling in glass palanquins like this, they're able to render themselves practically invisible.

Lord Kamanda takes the startled gasps of the crowd in stride as he makes his way over to me in his chair, which glides just as easily over the flowers as it did the polished stone floor of his mansion back in Hemaira.

Once again, I wonder if that chair isn't some sort of arcane object, but no, I sense no divine power coming from it, only clever mechanics. Money truly does buy the finest things.

"Lord Kamanda," I say, grinning. "What an unexpected pleasure it is to see you again."

"And you, Deka," the nobleman replies with his usual pleased smile. Becoming an enemy of the empire by helping young alaki escape the Warthu Bera doesn't seem to have affected his optimistic nature in the least. He's still his same exuberant self as he adds, "And under such auspicious circumstances too."

"And what are those?" I can't help but ask.

Adwapa turns to me, a long-suffering expression on her face as she says, "Lord Kamanda has been working with us as the official ambassador to the aviax."

"A most colorful people," the nobleman confirms admiringly.

Adwapa rolls her eyes, no longer able to hold back the expression, apparently. One thing she can't abide is overly cheerful people. She and Belcalis are alike in that respect, and Lord Kamanda truly is one of the most genial people I've ever met.

I return my attention to him. "And your wife?" When last I saw Lady Kamanda, she was as enormous as a house, ready to pop twins at any moment.

A fond look enters the noble's eyes. "It is my deepest joy to tell you that she has just birthed the twins. They're up there." He nods up at the city, where a host of those delicate palanquins is now descending. "As is Thandiwe, of course."

"Of course," I echo, nodding.

Karmoko Thandiwe, head instructor and my battle-strategy teacher at the Warthu Bera, is Lady Kamanda's partner, her lover of at least a year. The pair met when Karmoko Thandiwe was searching for allies to rescue the girls who had been imprisoned in the Warthu Bera after I rebelled against the former Oteran emperor. That Lady Kamanda was married to Lord Kamanda was no obstacle either. Both nobles freely admitted that they were in a marriage of convenience.

I return my attention to Lord Kamanda as he adds, "Also, it is my deepest joy to tell you that Lady Kamanda and I have severed our marital bonds. As we can no longer reside in Hemaira, it is no longer necessary for us to uphold our union. And while we remain the deepest of friends and mates of the soul, as well as, of course, joint parents to our children, it's high time I venture off and find a person of my own, perhaps a nice older gentleman. Preferably someone of some heft." The exuberant noble sketches a plump figure with his hands.

I bite back a smile. "Then it seems I must offer you my deepest congratulations, Lord Kamanda," I say. "I am happy for all the wonderful developments in your life, and I wish you well in finding the gentleman of your dreams."

"My thanks," he says, then he nods. "And now, for my official purpose. As ambassador of the Armies of the Angoro—"

"That's what we're calling them?" I ask, frowning.

"Terribly clever, isn't it?" he replies with obvious pride. "I came up with it myself."

"Did you now?" I manage to reply faintly while the twins titter beside me. Then I pause. "And are we certain we want to keep that title?"

"Of course we do!" Lord Kamanda is so emphatic, all I can do is nod. "Now then," he says, clearing his throat, "I am pleased to welcome you officially, honored Angoro, to Ilarong, the capital of all the aviax aeries."

"My thanks," I say, nodding.

Then he beckons me. "This way. Your palanquin is here." He points toward a large palanquin in the center covered in the same sort of glass as his. "It should be large enough for you and all your friends," he says, nodding at my group, who are catching up to us now.

"Again my thanks," I reply as I enter it, the others following swiftly behind me, Ixa in his nightflyer form behind them.

The minute the door locks, everyone turns to me. "Well," Asha says, nudging me, "what did we miss?"

◆

My group is not the only one that's had adventures since the moment we split. That's what Adwapa, Asha, Kweku, Acalan, Rian, Mehrut, and Katya relay to me during the half-hour journey up the mountain to Ilarong. From evading groups of enemy alaki and jatu to narrowly escaping proxies to battling the Forsworn, the purple-skinned male deathshrieks that are loyal to the Idugu, White Hands's group has had a time of it, making their way across the Southern continent.

"We haven't blundered into shadow vales, though," Kweku says, shaking his head.

"And we certainly haven't seen hide nor hair of Melanis," Adwapa adds, leaning her head on Mehrut's shoulder. "Can't believe she's alive."

"And *hideous*," Britta adds. "Looks like a bat, smooshed nose and everything."

"No!" Katya gasps, shocked. If there's one thing she loves, it's gossip.

"Think she's still out there?" Adwapa queries, her eyes curious.

"Without a doubt," I say, gazing out the window. Ilarong is nearing now, its peaks stark against the rapidly setting sun. "If she survived having an entire mountain collapse on her, she can survive being hurled halfway across a forest."

"By a godsworn!" Acalan sounds excited. "Can't believe that there are actually such beings."

"Or that Lamin was one of them," Asha says, sadness rising in her eyes. Lamin was her uruni, and even though they weren't close the way the rest of us are, they still had a bond.

When she looks down, I put my hand on her knee. "I'm sorry, Asha. I know what he meant to you."

"And yet I never suspected. Me, one of White Hands's spies." She sighs sadly. "There's surely some irony in that."

"At least he never stabbed us in the back," Adwapa says

brightly. Then she frowns. "Literally, that is. Figuratively is another matter . . ."

"He betrayed us, hid his true loyalties." Asha sighs. "Deka was right to leave him behind in Maiwuri. Maybe one day, he'll atone for his actions."

"But until then," Britta says brightly, trying to lift the mood, "we'll be explorin' an actual aviax aerie. Look at Ilarong! We're here!"

She flings the door open, then gestures. As I exit the palanquin, I follow the path of her hands, intrigued. Ilarong is certainly not what I expected. The city's streets are paved with stone, and there are benches under the multitudes of leafy trees lining them. Given that this is a place populated by bird folk, I assumed that there would be neither—that the aviax would simply flit from one space to another, occasionally stopping to rest on the branches of one of the small, wind-twisted trees that sprout all across the mountain, or even the stone perches artfully carved into the buildings. But no. When I squint at one of the benches, Acalan, who is also just now stretching his legs, turns to me and shrugs.

"Humans," he says, a statement so matter-of-fact, I can almost imagine him adjusting a pair of those glass eye contraptions Sarla's godsworn were always wearing.

"What?" I ask.

"Once upon a time, the aviax coexisted with humans and equus. That's why the streets look the way they do—to accommodate the other races. It's fascinating, really, to think that so many types of creatures once lived here."

I nod, not even bothering to ask how he knows—if there's

one thing Acalan loves, it's acquiring information. Of our entire group, he's the most studious, although Lamin might actually have him matched, given he's an actual godsworn of the deity of wisdom.

I push all thoughts of Lamin out of my mind as I ask, "So what happened?"

"Oyomo did," a pair of voices answer as one behind me. Braima and Masaima canter leisurely over to me, their clawed talons tapping lightly against the stone streets.

"When the jatu took over Otera and made everyone worship Oyomo, they declared all the semi-human races bestial—nearer to animals than humans—and said that they should no longer mix, to prevent contamination," Masaima explains. "Evening greetings, Angoro, by the by."

He and his brother trot closer to me, and both lean in, as if about to take an exploratory nibble at my hair, as is their habit. But then both their noses wrinkle, disgust evident in their expressions.

Braima, with the black-striped mane, is the first to speak, and he sounds disgusted. "Angoro, you smell like—"

"Death?"

"Unpleasantness," he corrects. "Unpleasantness such as I have never before had the displeasure of smelling."

"Indeed," his brother agrees, backing away. "It is most foul."

I blink. It seems the equus aren't affected by the vale wraith's pheromones the way my friends were. I store the information away in case it should come in handy.

I maintain my amused expression as both say, "We recommend you take a bath. Immediately."

I nod. "I'll take that under advisement."

"See that you do," they reply sternly, and just like that, they're on their way.

Once they're gone, Keita separates from the other boys and walks closer, only to lean in as if to take a whiff.

"Try it and die," I say through clenched teeth, but Keita just shrugs.

"I hear there are hot springs on this mountain."

"Truly?"

There's an almost shy look on his face as he nods.

I look away, a blush heating my cheeks, when he quickly adds, "We could try one together if you wish."

I think about the prospect, Keita and I relaxing in a hot spring together. Except there's no time for that; there's so much we need to do to find my kelai. But no, White Hands has her spies searching the Bloom, on the lookout for the Idugu's minions.

There's nothing I can contribute to that search in this moment, so I glance up at Keita, not directly meeting his eyes as I ask, "Is that permissible here? Me and you in the same hot spring? Together?"

"This isn't the empire, Deka," Keita says, nodding up to the sky. "This is Ilarong."

I follow his gaze to the pairs of aviax flying past, tails intertwined.

Most are female-male pairs. I can tell because the males are much larger with much more brilliant plumage than the females, who, for the most part, come in shades of plain, grayish green. There are, however, some male-male and female-female pairs. Then there are the few aviax who are somewhat in the middle—grayish-green coloring with brightly feathered tails or the reverse. Those aviax, I suspect, are the ones who occupy the varied third genders.

As before, they all stare curiously at us when they pass, paying special attention to me with their birdlike yellow eyes. I can't help but wonder whether White Hands has disseminated a scroll or some such with my likeness on it.

Keita gestures at a pair flying past, a trio of downy chicks beside them. "Here, we can be whatever we wish. Do whatever we wish"—I bristle at what he's implying, and he quickly corrects—"within reason, that is."

Keita knows that I don't want to be rushed by what's happening around us. Since we met, there have been a thousand crises, a thousand battles, which is why I've always ensured that we've kept our courtship slow. We can live in fear and in the moment in all the ways that warriors do, but as lovers, I want more for myself. I want the perfect time—even though that might be an unwise sentiment, given that the world is fated for extinction.

But, as White Hands says, the world is always fated for extinction.

Keeping that in mind, I nod, shyly reaching out my hand to enfold Keita's. "Very well, let's go to the hot spring together."

"*After* ye eat." This demand comes from Britta, who's standing behind us, arms folded, Li beside her. "An' really, Deka," she sniffs, disapproval apparent, "ye'd think ye'd do more practical things with yer time than flittin' about to hot springs an' such, given the crisis we're in."

"But that's precisely why we *should* go to the hot springs," Li says, pulling her closer to him. He rubs a hand up and down her back. "If the world ends tomorrow, wouldn't you like to die knowing you'd had a few hours of bliss with me?"

"I'd rather I live, thank ye very much, an' that means plannin' for wha comes next, not flitterin' about to romantic places."

I nod. "True. But in this case, I think Li is right." When Britta turns to me, startled, I sigh. "We *never* have time. Ever since our blood ran gold, we've run from one place to another, always trying to stay one step ahead of death. And honestly, I'm tired, Britta." I look plaintively up at her. "Aren't you tired too?"

As Britta stands there, quiet, Belcalis places a hand on her shoulder. "I'm with Deka on this one. We're all exhausted, and we haven't seen each other in weeks. The gods will continue to do their worst, and the battles will always be there, but perhaps today we can enjoy our time together." She inhales as if preparing herself. Then she looks pointedly at the group. "For tomorrow may never come."

"For tomorrow may never come," everyone else repeats solemnly.

And then we begin embracing each other, tighter even than we did when we first reunited. After all, Belcalis's words are a reminder of exactly what we stand to lose if the world falls apart.

Each other.

◆

Dinner in Ilarong is a simple, hurried affair: braised meats heaped on top of a greenish but surprisingly delicious sprouted grain, the odd fruit or two. Since the aviax are bird folk, their tastes only barely overlap with ours and the equus'. This fare is the best they can provide to suit our palates, although I suspect that dinner in the grand hall, where White Hands, Lord Kamanda, and all the aviax dignitaries are in attendance, is a much more stately affair. But neither I nor my friends accept that invitation when it comes. It's bad enough we're stale-smelling and unwashed, but we refuse to be so in a place where most everyone is clothed in feathers all the colors of the rainbow and so much jewelry, we have to shield our eyes whenever they pass. Not to mention we want to avoid the stares. Most aviax stare so pointedly, it's as if they've never seen anyone not of their kind before, which is likely the case. From what I understand, only emissaries and other special designations ever leave aviax aeries; the rest remain close to their mountain cities.

I'm only grateful that they, like many species of birds, don't seem to have a particularly strong sense of smell, or all that staring would have another meaning entirely.

After dinner, my friends and I follow Adwapa and Asha to the hot springs, which, as it turns out, sit on one of the mountain peaks overlooking the city.

"Ahhh," Adwapa says blissfully the moment she sinks into the heated water. "This is the life." She closes her eyes, settling in.

Like all the other girls, she's wearing a thin loincloth and a chest covering for modesty, but given that we've all seen each other in various states of undress over the years, it's mostly a formality.

Mehrut swiftly curls up by her side, snuggling as close as she can get, then she closes her eyes too. I do the same with Keita, who lifts his arm so I can lay my head on his chest.

"You are very correct," Li says, making himself comfortable beside us. "This is how we *should* be living."

Deka... Ixa agrees, though only I can hear him. He's already fully submerged in the hot water, only his nostrils poking out above it. He makes a happy gurgling sound. Turns out he enjoys hot water just as much as he enjoys cold.

Who knew?

Britta rests her head on Li's shoulder. "You know, for once, I agree completely with you and Adwapa. This is perfection," she says happily, grinning up at him.

I glance at her. "Are you telling me you're actually happy with this heat?" I ask, my eyebrows raising almost to my hairline.

Britta is the most heat-sensitive person I know. The least bit of sunlight and she starts complaining; woe betide everyone if she's on her menses as well. You'll never hear the end of it.

But to my surprise, she gives me an arch look. "We have hot springs in Golma," she sniffs. "The heat from them even comes up under our huts. Just how do ye think we stay warm in the brutal cold?"

I shrug. "I don't know. I just assumed you put on more furs or something."

Adwapa squints at me. "And what about you, aren't you boiling in that thing?"

She's referring to Ayo's armor, which I'm still wearing even now, since I know that if I take it off for even seconds, I risk depleting what remains of my kelai should any danger arise.

I shake my head. "It's not that bad," I say. "Feels like a second skin almost. Besides, ebiki are aquatic animals. This is meant to be in the water."

"But wha about the dirt?" Britta wrinkles her nose.

I glance down. "Seems to be self-cleaning."

That's the strange thing I've noticed: while my face, hair,

hands, and feet may have been dirtied by our travels, the rest of me has remained clean ever since I put on the armor. I can only assume that is because the armor does such a wonderful job of keeping everything out.

I'll take it off eventually. But after everything that's happening is over. And I've killed the gods of Otera and danced on their metaphorical skulls.

"Convenient, that," Belcalis says. Then she glances at the rest of the group. "So, any hope about these negotiations? Not much seems to be happening outside talking in circles, from what I've seen."

Trust Belcalis to be in a place less than half a day and already have the measure of things.

"I'm meant to join White Hands in negotiations starting tomorrow," I say. Earlier, I explained this to the group, as well as White Hands's determination that we remain here while her spies watch the Idugu's followers' movements, but Belcalis was clearly too busy observing the comings and goings around us to take note.

"Here's hoping they're willing to listen to you," she says. "These bird folk don't seem very welcoming to outsiders."

Katya shrugs from her corner of the hot spring, which she dominates entirely by herself. "I don't know, the aviax have seemed very hospitable since yesterday."

"But that's due to all the gold Lord and Lady Kamanda brought to smooth the talks," Adwapa says.

"And to protect his children," Asha adds.

When I glance at them, confused, Adwapa replies: "Lord Kamanda was adamant about being the ambassador here, because this is one of the highest peaks in Otera. After all, if fighting breaks out soon—"

"Which it will," I remind quietly.

"—his children will be safe here."

"Wily," Acalan says, nodding his approval. "Everything about that man is wily, even though he doesn't overtly seem that way. It's astounding, honestly. I mean, you should have seen the way he charmed them with the gold. Brought almost his entire fortune to woo them. Birds and money, who would have thought." Acalan has a faraway look in his eyes now, one I've seen in my friends several times before.

Keita and I share a look. Acalan has finally found a passion for something other than old scrolls. It's just unfortunate that what Lord Kamanda is looking for is the exact opposite of a slim young man with an intellectual air.

Li stares at Acalan for a moment, then raises his eyebrows dramatically. "Astounding," he coos suggestively. "Oh, Lord Kamanda, you're so astounding. Will you be my commander and tell me what to do? Oh, Lord Kamaaandaaa . . ."

Acalan turns bright red. "That's not what I was—I mean, I don't—"

But Li is enraptured with his new game. He pretends to swoon against Britta. "Oh, Lord Kamanda, hold me, touch me."

And now Britta's in on the game as well. "I'll hold ye, I'll touch ye." She giggles, the sound so loud, Adwapa turns from her to Li.

"It's finally come." Adwapa sighs, shaking her head. "The day we've all feared."

"An' which day is that?" Britta asks, straightening.

But Adwapa turns to the rest of the group. "They're together so often, they're actually turning into each other. They've become—*the same person!*"

As she shakes her head again, I nod sagely. "It's dire, but we knew it had to happen."

Britta scowls. "Not ye too, Deka."

But I continue, unbothered. "Li's personality is so strong—too strong. His contagion cannot be denied."

Rolling her eyes, Britta turns to Li, and then they promptly fall over each other, giggling like fools. "Hold me, touch me," they coo as Acalan's blush turns deeper and deeper red.

A hand pulls me closer. Keita's. He grins down at me, his expression so similar to my own, my heart nearly bursts. "See, Deka," he whispers into my ear. "Home."

And to think that once I was a lonely girl who had no one. Now I have all these wonderful people. This wonderful family. I could fall into my worries, my fears, about what's happening with my kelai and the battles that are about to come, but I choose instead to remain in the present.

I nod at Keita, placing a small, quiet kiss on his chest. "Yes," I whisper. "It's nice to be home."

25

◆ ◆ ◆

The hall where the aviax host the official meeting to determine whether or not they will become our allies is shaped like an open flower. The first rays of the sun are just now spilling over its gleaming gold-and-green walls, which curve up and outward into a honeycomb of interconnected, hive-like glass perches. These perches are where the aviax nobles roost, their feathers preened to diamond brilliance, their ears and necks adorned with so many jewels, they glitter like stars. At least it seems that way from my vantage point on the floor, where I'm standing with my companions, as well as White Hands, Lord Kamanda, and a few human and equus commanders, whom I only briefly met the previous night.

We're all gazing up at the two aviax monarchs perched on a pair of delicate crystal thrones that rise so high into the air, they nearly extend past the reach of the towering glass walls.

I stare at the pair, fascinated. The king is an imposing male figure. He's so tall, he approaches Myter's height, and has such brilliantly colored plumage, he nearly obscures his much smaller, plainer queen. Where his feathers are shimmering shades of purple and green, hers are a plain, unremarkable gray, although her tail is a bright, iridescent purple, indicating that she may be yandau instead of female. I'm not certain, however, given how little I know of the aviax.

It would be easy to dismiss her as a silent observer of the proceedings, except for the intelligence that gleams in her eyes, sharper and more ferocious than that which inhabits the king's. I keep a wary focus on her as their vizier—a tall, distinguished-looking fellow with cerulean plumage that matches the splendid feathers that make up his mustache and beard—speaks. His disdain for our presence is clear in the way he grandly preens and flaps about.

As he sneers down his beak at Lord Kamanda, who is, for today, wearing exquisite purple robes and holding his ceremonial golden fly whisk—the symbol of Hemaira's highest-ranked nobility—I glance at White Hands, as I've been doing since we arrived. She's remained silent, seeming for all the world like a quiet observer, except she's wearing what I've termed her ambush armor, a suit of white bone so similar to her ceremonial armor, you could mistake the two, except this suit has more flexible joints, making it easier for her to move.

She's planning something—that much she hinted to me yesterday when she said she'd be asking me for something later, only now I regret not seeking her out earlier to ask what it is. But I slept later than usual this morning, thanks to my feather-soft mattress and leftover relaxation from the hot springs.

I needed the rest—we all did—so I'll just keep up my guard

as everyone else is doing until White Hands finally reveals her plan.

The vizier continues speaking: "While we understand the urgency of your request," he says self-importantly in the melodic, high-pitched voice I've come to discover is common to most aviax, "we the citizens of Ilarong have long held a policy of noninterference with all the other sentient races. This is the same for all aviax across the Southern provinces, whose representatives, as you know, are also in attendance. It is the decision of our combined councils that this is not our battle to partake in. Especially given that you now wish to change the timeline so precipitously."

He glances pointedly at White Hands as he says this.

After what I informed her about the shadow vales, she now wants to move the first offensive up to weeks from now, instead of the months we were planning.

"So everythin' he just said adds up to a no, doesn't it?" Britta, standing beside me, quietly queries.

"Basically," says Adwapa, who's flanking my other side. She tsks. "Too busy polishing their jewels to take their heads out of their arses."

Her sentiment matches mine precisely. It's clear the aviax have no true understanding of what's happening in the world around them, nor do they want to gain one.

Lord Kamanda, to his credit, betrays none of the annoyance gleaming in his eyes as he calmly smooths his robes. "With all due respect, honored personages, while you may not wish to engage in the coming war, the war will, eventually, come to you. It is only a matter of time. According to the Angoro, we have only a matter of months—perhaps even mere weeks—before the shadow vales bleed permanently into this realm and set the stage for its ultimate destruction. We need to act now, mount an offensive. We already have troops all across Otera waiting to begin the first wave of skirmishes."

Somehow, I'm not surprised when the vizier waves away Lord Kamanda's words with an annoyed *pfft*. "Hidden continents, shadow vales, a new pantheon of gods—meaningless fluff," he sniffs dismissively. He turns to White Hands. "Your war with your goddesses has altered your comprehension of reality, War Queen Fatu of Hemaira."

White Hands responds to this insult with a mild smile. "I prefer White Hands."

The vizier dismisses her words with a wave. "Very well—White Hands—not that your name should matter, given how far you have fallen." The vizier looks up at the monarchs, visibly seeking permission before he continues: "Once, you were the right hand of the emperor. Now you are a traitor twice over—not only to the Oterans, who were once your allies, but to the goddesses you called mothers. And now you wish to bring us into your madness."

"Ufff," Britta whispers, shaking her head. "He's really stepped in it now."

That he has. I can see the expression on White Hands's face, so bland it's as if she's not even bothered at all. But then White Hands doesn't get angry. She gets even.

"I would say we leave," Asha whispers, "see how these idiots deal with the vales on their own. But I want to see how this ends."

"Badly," Belcalis says. "This will end badly. For them."

White Hands does not seem to hear our whispered comments as she graciously inclines her head, as calm as ever. She ignores the vizier and looks up at the monarchs. "I understand your reasoning, honored majesties. You are the caretakers of your flock. You must protect them, especially against those who might not see the world in a way that is . . . how do we say, logical? That being said, I humbly ask that you allow me one last consideration."

The vizier harrumphs, annoyed at being ignored. He truly does have an incurable case of self-importance. "As if we would—"

"We're listening," the queen interrupts, holding up a delicate, feathered hand. The entire hall falls silent, including the vizier, who swiftly snaps his mouth shut.

White Hands puts a hand to her chest and bows in gratitude. "My thanks, honored Majesty." Then she turns to where I'm standing with my friends and nods at me.

I immediately tense. Here comes the favor she spoke of.

"I would like to introduce you all to someone important: Deka, the Angoro, slayer of the gods." She beckons to me. "Step forward, Deka."

Nodding, I slowly walk over, trying to project as much confidence as I can, given that the aviax are very literally looking down on me, including that odious vizier.

Once I stand beside White Hands, the king squints at me. "Rather small for a killer of the gods, don't you think," he murmurs thoughtfully, although that's easy for him to say, considering he's quite literally a giant.

The queen shrugs, an elaborate fluffing of the feathers. "Perhaps," she says, "but stranger things have occurred."

"Indeed," White Hands agrees. "Please do hold on to that sentiment. Now then, I've told you of Deka's recent adventures. Of the shadow vales . . ."

A tingle of foreboding goes through me, but the vizier, as always, doesn't notice the danger. For a being related to predatory birds, he doesn't seem to have much in the way of survival instinct. "All mindless fluff," he repeats disparagingly. "All mindless fluff."

White Hands ignores him. "There is one thing, however, I failed to tell you. Deka learned a new ability during her travels. One I wish to share with you. I suspect it might prove illuminating."

She turns meaningfully to me, and now I notice the mist that's creeping into the throne room, mist that's making everything darker, blotting out the sun. It's accompanied by the tingling that signals the arrival of other children of the goddesses.

I shudder quietly, knowing exactly what's about to happen.

"I want you to open a door to the last place you were, Deka," White Hands says. "I want you to show them what they're risking."

"But—" I glance at Lord Kamanda, sitting there unwittingly in his chair. At the vizier, perched on his roost just a few lengths above him.

Neither has experienced a shadow vale before. More to the point, neither seems prepared, should the worst happen. And the chamber has become dark now. Oh, so very dark. . . .

Almost as dark as the vales.

A worried chirping begins among the aviax, but White Hands ignores it as she slowly, deliberately places herself in front of Lord Kamanda. "Open the door to the vale, Deka," she commands. "I'm here."

I will protect him.

I nod. "I'll open it now," I say, already picturing that horrific darkness as I sink into the combat state. The Greater Divinity flows into me so easily, I almost don't notice when it does.

Then I pull the space in front of me apart.

Darkness immediately looms. Silence, deep and all-encompassing. And then those lights emerge, dim blue shimmers . . .

On the perch above me, the vizier cocks his head, intrigued. "Fascinating," he says, inching forward, a captivated look in his eyes.

It seems aviax are just as enamored of lights as they are of jewels.

"I wouldn't do that if I were you," White Hands says mildly.

"Do what?" the vizier asks, hopping toward the light.

Then a horrific roar sounds.

As the vizier darts back, terrified, a gigantic tentacle comes hurtling out of the darkness. Before it can connect with the vizier, a massive dark shape launches itself out of the shadows. A distinctive rattling sounds as it rends the tentacle in two.

Pandemonium ensues, panicked squawks and wing flaps rising as the aviax in the rows above us take flight, trying to get away from the reach of those tentacles, which are emerging swiftly from the darkness now.

I keep my eyes on that dark shape. "Sayuri!"

The gigantic Firstborn I once knew as the deathshriek

Rattle is suddenly here, as are a host of other deathshrieks, the mist rising farther into the air as they battle the other tentacles, which are now shooting across the room with abandon.

"Close the door, Deka!" Sayuri commands as she whirls, slashing one tentacle after another, the spikes on her back rattling together with each movement.

"Doing so now!" I reply, already picturing the door sealing shut.

A pained roar resounds as the door complies with my wish, slicing through tentacles in the process. Within seconds, the vale is completely gone, leaving only the blood-spattered floor and masses of still-twitching tentacles in its wake.

As the mist recedes and sunlight shines again, a horrified silence descends. It only lasts moments. There's a determined tone to the aviax's chirping as they fly back down to their perches.

In fact, the only one who's still silent now is the vizier. White Hands slowly, deliberately wipes a drop of the vale wraith's blue blood from his feathers before she turns to the monarchs, who are squawking furiously between themselves.

She points to where the door was as she says, "That dark place you just saw was a shadow vale, and the thing that attacked was a vale wraith, a monstrosity the gods use to grow their power. If you do not help us in our quest, the entirety of Otera will become like that vale in a matter of weeks, and that includes your precious Ilarong, as well as all the other aeries. Everyone here, even you, your feathered majesties, will be food for the gods. And, as you have seen, they have no aversion to eating aviax. In fact, they might even prefer you."

She smiles thinly at the monarchs. "Now then, do you still wish to send us on our way, or do you wish to become allies?"

The king blinks, then looks at the queen, silent messages passing between the two. Finally, he clears his throat and turns back to White Hands. "How many aviax do you need?"

"Every single one that you can spare."

26

◆ ◆ ◆

Sayuri is standing at the edge of one of Ilarong's many peaks when I find her later, her eyes closed as if she's listening to a song only she can hear. It's midafternoon now, and an ominous chill has settled over the mountain city—the mist exuded by her deathshrieks. How so many managed to infiltrate the city so stealthily I don't know, but I see White Hands in it all—my former mentor undoubtedly planned for the fact that the aviax would refuse to become our allies. Both the arrival of the death-shrieks and the opening of the vale are warnings to the bird folk: war is already here, whether you like it or not.

"Deka," Sayuri murmurs, her eyes slowly opening when I approach. She looks me up and down before musing, "Or should I be calling you the Angoro now?"

"Deka will do," I reply, my eyes fixed on the deathshrieks who move swiftly across the city, dark shadows compared with the aviax flitting to and fro as they gather supplies to pack their zerizard-pulled chariots.

I can only hope that a few of them have already been diverted to spy on Abeya and the Bloom surrounding it, but White Hands has repeatedly assured me that she has spies carefully watching the area. If so much as one follower of the Idugu steps foot in the mountains near the city of the goddesses, she'll know and send me and my friends out to apprehend them so we can reach my kelai first.

In the meantime, we will remain here to aid in preparations for our first offensive against the gods.

I return my attention to Sayuri as she nods. "Hmm . . . ," she says, stepping closer. The movement is so swift and fluid, she's in front of me before I notice she's taken a step.

I hastily retreat, unnerved to be so close to the deathshriek. Her claws seem even sharper than they were back at the Warthu Bera, and now they have been edged with gold, as have the spike-like quills on her back that cause her signature rattling sound.

Even more than before, Sayuri seems an intimidating shadow. But that might just be my guilt talking. There's so much I owe her, so much I have to atone for.

She stares down at me, unblinking, and I stare back, a fly caught in the gaze of a particularly large, particularly deadly spider. That is, until I realize.

Sayuri's eye contact is direct, unbroken. And she isn't peering off into thin air like she's seeing things that aren't there. I noticed this before, but for some reason, I didn't understand what it meant until now. "You're fully lucid," I conclude.

Could this be because she's no longer under the influence of blueblossom, the sweet-smelling flower the matrons at the Warthu Bera used to drug her into submission?

A bitter smile slices her lips as she repeats, "*Lucid.* . . . Such a fascinating word. So much judgment hidden in so few syllables. Tell me, Angoro, do you believe that you must remain attached to this world to comprehend everything that is around you?"

I blink up at her. "I—I don't know." I don't even understand what she's asking, truth be told.

Sayuri's smile spreads wider, now a baring of teeth. She gestures up with arms as long and gaunt as a conid tree's branches in midwinter. "This world, this physical realm upon which you and I stand now," she continues. "Do you believe you must remain attached to it, to what you see, what you smell, what you hear, to understand it?"

As if prompted, my mind immediately races back to Myter and what they taught me. The Greater Divinity. Space and matter. All things I still don't truly understand. But I know they're there, know that they're all forces that affect me for better or worse.

The Greater Divinity especially. Even now, I can't fully connect to it—or rather, don't *want* to fully connect to it, given my misgivings. What if there's some malevolent force behind it, some god that'll take me over the moment I truly let it in? I'm not certain I still believe that, but I hold off just in case.

"No," I finally say, sighing. "I don't believe that. There are a great many things I cannot see that still exist despite my inability to perceive them."

Sayuri's smile slices wider. "And you were so blind before."

Sayuri doesn't have to explain what she's referring to. The last time we spoke, right before she disappeared over the burning walls of the Warthu Bera, she hinted to me that the Gilded Ones weren't what they seemed.

"I wanted to live in a dream," I say, recalling that time. "A fantasy of what this world could be, rather than what it truly was. So I chose not to see what the mothers were. What they were doing."

"You still call them the mothers." There's no judgment in this, only a statement of fact.

"A slip of the tongue," I admit ruefully. "It's only been a few months since I believed—"

"That they loved you. That they cared."

There's a sorrowful understanding in Sayuri's tone. But then, she was one of the first four alaki born to them, a war queen—one of their primary generals. She was one of the chosen. One of the beloved.

Only, the Gilded Ones' love always comes at a cost. All the gods' love does. Sayuri and I both know that.

I nod before looking up at her again. "How did you find out about them?" I ask. "Initially, I mean. It must have been difficult."

I know from our prior conversations that Sayuri discovered what the goddesses were when they were at the height of their power. During that era, their pretense at doting motherhood was exquisitely calibrated, and their ability to erase the memories of anyone who went against them was flawless.

That Sayuri even suspected them then says a great deal about the strength of her mind, no matter how fractured it may seem now.

She shrugs, the movement rattling up and down her quills. "I went mad," she says simply. "And do you know, madness is illuminating. Because when you no longer think like others, you're forced to think like yourself. To see things in ways you might not have seen before. To see the truth. And that brings understanding, painful though it may be."

"So now you're here."

"Now I'm here."

"With White Hands, your eldest sister. . . . Who you promised to kill the next time you saw her."

"And I made good on that vow." Sayuri gives this reply so casually, it's moments before its meaning sinks in: *She made good on her vow to kill White Hands the next time she saw her.*

"You did?" I ask, surprised, though I really shouldn't be.

Alaki in general are a brutal race, and the Firstborn are even more so. Worse, White Hands, Melanis, and Sayuri are the three remaining war queens, the first daughters born to the Gilded Ones. Given how long most of them have lived, things like life and death are trivial matters to them.

"Indeed." White Hands, who has made her way up the path, Braima and Masaima at her side, answers. She nods to Sayuri in a companionable greeting as she expands: "Gutted me like a fish the first death, then broke my back the second—a most painful death, I assure you. We made peace after the third—a strangling, I believe it was."

Sayuri barely blinks at this mention of her savagery. "I decided she'd paid enough for her crimes to warrant a truce. For now."

"For now?" I gape. You'd think three almost-deaths would be enough punishment.

"Fifty years," says Sayuri. "That's how long I was caged in the Warthu Bera."

"A death for every year, quite a fair price for my betrayal." White Hands nods sagely. "If we win this war—"

"When we win this war," I manage to correct through my astonishment.

White Hands inclines her head. "*When* we win this war, Sayuri will take what is her due. Meaning, the other forty-seven deaths," she explains, when it's apparent I don't understand what she's saying.

I glance between the pair. "You two are the strangest sisters I've ever met."

White Hands humphs. "Have you met Melanis?"

"Recently, as it happens," I retort. "She was strange too."

"All Firstborn are like this. Half of us are always wanting to kill the other half," Sayuri says with a wise nod. She taps her lower lip. "Family: it is a complicated matter, is it not?"

Suddenly, my head is hurting.

"Don't worry, Quiet One," Masaima whispers in my ear as his brother nods, "this is how it always is when they're together."

I return my attention to White Hands. "So what now? What's our next move?"

It's not the Bloom, that much is certain. White Hands would have told me immediately if the spies there had noticed anything.

My old mentor smiles thinly. "Now we plan. The aviax, human, and equus generals, Sayuri, Thandiwe, and I will combine battle strategies so we can disseminate them across Otera. Even if you were to take your kelai back today, we'd still have to deal with all the priests and followers and such for both pantheons."

"'Today?'" I frown at this strange bit of phrasing. Usually, White Hands would say "in the next day or two," or something to that effect.

My old mentor continues as if she didn't hear me. "Peace won't come just because you end the gods. And we have to prepare for what happens if you fail. Besides, you have something else to do or, rather, somewhere else to go."

My eyes widen, nervousness rushing through me. "My kelai? Your spies have already located it?"

"Sayuri's spies have," White Hands corrects dourly, which of course explains why she didn't give me the news immediately. She does have her petty moments. "Turns out, they're even faster than mine, unbelievable as it may seem." As Sayuri sniffs, offended by this assessment, White Hands nods down to me. "Gather the others. You have to get moving now. I'll brief you before you leave."

I nod, a thousand emotions churning inside me as I turn away. Fear, doubt—hope. What if my kelai isn't where the spies say it is? Worse, what if it is? That would mean today could be the day I leave my friends, my family.

Today could be the day everything changes. No wonder White Hands used that specific word.

But again, what if it isn't? What if this is some sort of trap? My worries are circling now—round and round they go.

"Deka, enough." When I turn, White Hands has walked up to me, her head shaking in disapproval. "I can hear your thoughts scurrying."

"I just . . . ," I begin. "I know I must do my duty, but . . ."

White Hands nods. "Peace is never easy, Deka. Especially not for the ones who broker it."

I nod. Then I still, gathering my courage. "White Hands . . . ," I begin slowly, finally saying the words I've been holding back all this while. The words I didn't want to say until this very moment, when I have to. "The goddesses have imprisoned Anok. Trapped her in the mountain under Abeya. Okot feared they would consume her, which is why he tried to make a deal with me."

When I glance up at her, her gaze is as stoic as ever. I frown. "You knew."

She nods. "Even when she was imprisoned all those centuries, Mother spoke to me. She whispered in my dreams, in the wind. . . . But now she is silent."

White Hands's eyes are troubled. The Gilded Ones may have all contributed to her birth, but it is Anok she considers her mother—a sentiment the goddess shares.

"What do I do?" I ask, a simple question layered with a thousand meanings.

White Hands turns back to me. "The same thing you've always intended: take back your divinity and end the gods."

"Even Anok?" The question creeps out. Doubt.

If the time truly has arrived, I need to at least voice this one doubt.

White Hands's eyes are filled with pain, but her reply is firm. "Especially Anok," she insists. "It's what she wants, and we will honor my divine mother's wishes, just as we honor your purpose. We will ensure the end of the gods or die trying.

"Oh, and, Deka, one more thing." When I glance up, confused, she continues: "The place where your kelai is, it's Gar Fatu."

"Gar Fatu?" An awful feeling rises in the pit of my stomach.

This will be more difficult than I thought, in many more ways than one.

27

◆ ◆ ◆

Gar Fatu . . .

The words circle through my mind as I arrive back at the
tower, where my friends are already dressed in the leathery
black armor we use when we go on raids. Katya's even covered
herself in a dark brown paint, which, I assume, is camouflage.
Gar Fatu is one of Otera's most important strongholds, the last
stop at the southern border. It's also deep in the Gilded Ones'
territory, so stealth and speed are important—especially given
that we're likely to meet the Idugu's forces on the way. Okot has
wasted no time making good on his promise to retrieve my kelai
from its hiding place, and he's sent multiple groups so as to con-
fuse pursuers.

That's not the only thing, though, that makes this so difficult.

Gar Fatu is Keita's former summer home, the place where
his family was massacred. We'll be going back to the site of his
deepest nightmares, the origin of all his pains and fears.

My eyes flit to him the minute I enter the tower. He's standing by the door to the balcony, looking grim. My stomach sinks. I'd already suspected it when I saw the others in their armor, and Katya in her camouflage, but his expression confirms it—White Hands must have had Braima and Masaima inform my friends about our new task while I was speaking with her. They already know what we're about to do, and worse, where we have to go to get it done.

When I approach Keita, Britta nods to the others. "Come on then, you lot, let's give them their space."

Like everyone else in the group, she knows Keita's history—how his family was deceived by Emperor Gezo into moving into an area filled with deathshrieks. How they were all slaughtered one night, leaving him the sole survivor. We still haven't gotten all the details yet—Keita keeps them close to his chest—but we know enough to understand how that night haunts him, so much so that he began training to become a jatu at the tender age of nine in order to get his revenge on the deathshrieks he believed killed his family.

She quickly herds all my friends out, shutting the door firmly behind them.

And then Keita and I are alone.

I take a step toward him. "Keita, I—"

"It's ironic, isn't it," he says, turning to me, a feverish brightness in his eyes. "All that time we said we'd visit Gar Fatu, pay our respects to my family. We never went, and your kelai was there this whole time." He laughs, the sound layered with a distinctly hysterical edge. "This whole time, it was there."

"*Might* be there," I correct, swiftly walking over to him. I've never seen Keita this way before, so on edge, so brittle. "Okot's worshippers could have taken it by now."

Even though I don't want to admit it, it's a possibility. The first group that Sayuri's spies spotted isn't the only one in the region. Even as we spoke, White Hands got reports of other groups. No matter how fast we move, the Idugu's minions might be faster. But I can't think of that now, can't panic.

White Hands has made contingency plans in case that happens. Created all sorts of backups to ensure that I get my hands on my kelai and sing out the true names of the gods, causing their deaths.

Keita shakes his head. "But we still have to ascertain that's the case. . . ."

When he looks away, I place one hand on his shoulder, the other across his body. Keita's muscles are so taut, he's like a string vibrating with tension. "You don't have to come with us," I say comfortingly. "I understand if you wish to remain behind. You can—"

"Stay here?" Keita cuts me off before I can say anything more. "And what if your kelai truly is there? What if today is the day you ascend, and I refused to go? What if you left and I never saw you again?" There's a plaintive note in his voice now.

I move my hand to his chest. "I'd make sure to visit. I'd never leave without saying goodbye." Even as a remote and unfathomable god, I'd do that much. I'm certain of it.

Keita takes my hand, kisses it, his lips warm, oh so very warm. His eyes are determined. "You are my heart, Deka. Ever since the Warthu Bera, that's what you've been—my heart. Of course I'm going with you. If we're going to Gar Fatu, I'm leading the way."

Which of course he is. That's what jatu are trained to do.

And even if it weren't, that's what Keita does—puts himself in the path of danger, even if it means his own pain, his own suffering . . .

And mine as well.

Because somewhere deep inside me—in a hidden corner of my heart I'm ashamed to acknowledge—I don't want Keita to go. I don't want to have to say goodbye if this truly is the end of our journey together.

Keita seems to understand this, because he takes a step closer, wraps me in his arms. "I don't want to go either," he whispers, burying his face in my hair. "Not truly."

I squeeze him with all my might. "It's not fair. None of it. The gods, this situation, the fact that we might—" I stop halfway, choked by the sob that rises out of me.

"I know." He squeezes me tighter, plastering little kisses across my face and neck.

"We never got our time together," I whisper plaintively. "We never got to be alone, just you and me." I bury my head in his chest, listening to his heartbeat, that familiar sound I know so well. "I never even got to dance with you—truly dance with you."

"You mean like you Northerners do?" I can almost feel Keita cocking his head above me.

I nod, face still muffled in his chest to hide my embarrassment.

It was one of the things I most looked forward to when I still thought I would one day marry in the Northern way. Unlike Southern dances, the most popular Northern dances are for couples, and husbands and wives hold each other as they dance.

To my surprise, Keita nods. "Then why don't we dance now?"

I glance up at him in confusion. "But there's no music."

"And what would you call the wind whistling around the mountain?"

Keita's eyes are sparkling as the wildness there is replaced with a sly mischief.

I decide to play along. "And what about the lights?" I pout. "And the other dancers?"

"You mean those dancers?" Keita snaps his fingers, and a host of flames in the shape of tiny humans suddenly dance in the air around us. When I gape at them, astounded, he smiles down at me. "There you are, lights and dancers." He extends a hand. "Well then, Deka, shall we?"

I look up at him, tears pricking my eyes. I know what it's taken for him to put aside his own pain and create this festival of lights, but perhaps Keita needs it. And I need it too. So I nod, taking his hand, then I press my body to his and move slowly along to the sound of the wind whistling across the mountain.

The dance isn't seamless—neither of us truly knows what we're doing, since this is the first time we've ever danced. Still, it's the best thing I've ever felt: Keita's heated body pressed to mine, both of us moving in a slow, almost instinctual rhythm.

It's like time has suspended, like we're both surrounded in a bubble of our own making.

I'm so caught up in the dance, I'm disappointed when, after a few minutes, Keita slowly brings us to a halt, then removes his hands from my waist.

I sigh, glance up at him. "Time to go?"

He nods. Then he looks down at me. "So, how was our first dance?"

"Perfection," I say. And I truly mean it.

No matter what happens at Gar Fatu, no matter what obstacles or horrors we encounter from now on, we'll always have this—our one perfect dance.

I walk toward the door, but as I move to open it, a hand stops me. Keita's. All the mischief has disappeared from his eyes as he says, "Just one thing. We shouldn't take any of the deathshrieks with us." When I turn to him fully, he sighs, shaking his head. "I hate to admit it, but I don't know what I would do if I saw them there again, in that place. I don't know what I would do. . . ."

What violence I could commit.

The implication hangs in the air, a heavy warning. Keita is a jatu; he's used to killing deathshrieks, has been doing so since he was nine. He only stopped after we realized that not only were deathshrieks intelligent beings, they were the souls of resurrected alaki.

Now he harms deathshrieks only if they pose a threat to us. He may still be a killer, but he's not an indiscriminate one.

I nod. "All right. I'll let White Hands know."

But when I pull the door fully open, it's to the sight of Katya and Rian sitting in the chair just outside, Rian curled up in Katya's lap, since there's no way she, as a deathshriek, can sit in his. She's looking straight at us, hurt shining in her eyes.

"Does that include me?" she asks quietly, signing in battle language so Keita can understand her as well. "The no-deathshrieks mandate, I mean."

His eyes widen. "You? No," he says, shaking his head vigorously. "Not you. Never you."

"Why? I thought you said no deathshrieks."

Keita blinks, as if gathering his thoughts. "You wouldn't startle me the way the others would," he finally responds.

"A bright red deathshriek wouldn't startle you?"

Keita shrugs. "You're the only bright red deathshriek there is. Besides, you're brown now?"

"Forest-colored," Katya corrects. Then she nods. "All right," she says, still signing in battle language. "Because I fully intend to go with you." She turns to me. "I won't let you go to what may be your last day as a . . . well, whatever it is you are, without saying goodbye."

"I'll remain here, thank you," Rian says, "but if you hurt her, I will stab you," he warns, signing in battle language as well.

It's only been a little over a month since he reunited with Katya, and he's already almost fluent. Determination is a frightening thing, especially in a lover.

A snort sounds from beside him. "With wha knife?" Britta asks.

"I can find one," Rian mutters, the distinctive white streak in his hair flopping as he nods.

We all just smile. Rian is about as likely to stab someone as he is to grow wings and fly away. In a group full of warriors, he's the only one who's never truly held a dagger or a sword, and yet we love him still.

The atmosphere now ever-so-slightly eased, I turn back to Keita. "I will ensure that the other deathshrieks keep their distance," I promise. "But only if you promise that after we find my kelai, we'll stop and pay our respects to the resting place of your parents."

"And then we say a true goodbye." Keita's voice is so low when he says this, I almost don't hear him.

Or perhaps it's that I don't want to.

I turn and nod quietly, tears pricking at my eyes again. "And then we say a true goodbye."

◆

A small group has gathered when my friends and I make our way to the stables some minutes later to receive our last briefing from White Hands and Sayuri. At the front stands Karmoko Thandiwe, who, just a few months ago, explained to us that *she* was in fact a *they*. Their lover, Lady Kamanda, is, as always, by their side. Both are opulently dressed in cloaks of iridescent feathers—gifts, no doubt, from the aviax, a pair of whom flitter in the background, chasing two little boys who bear a striking resemblance to Lady Kamanda: her first pair of twins. The noble is what Mother used to call a miracle of fertility. In fact, when I first met her, her heavily pregnant belly preceded her like the bow of a ship. I blink as I continue watching her and my former teacher, who seems to be carrying something under that splendid cloak, something that wriggles.

When I hear a distinctive gurgling coming from it, my eyes widen. "Is that a baby?" I gasp, excitement rising.

I love babies. Not having them, mind you—which was the fate Elder Durkas and all the other elders in Irfut and beyond wanted for me and every other Oteran woman. Playing with them, however, is another matter entirely.

As I rush over, excited, I nearly miss the correction that comes my way. *"Babies,"* Lord Kamanda—who has been waiting behind his former wife and her lover—says, whirring forward. "Babies, plural." He nods at Lady Kamanda, who is now triumphantly unwrapping her cloak, presenting her own wriggling bundle, a round little ball of a baby who seems mostly made of big brown eyes and chubby little hands and feet.

It looks identical to the baby under Karmoko Thandiwe's cloak when they present it as well. "Girls," they say smugly. "More twins, just like that alaki in the camp said."

A month ago, an alaki in the war camp outside Hemaira's walls predicted that Lady Kamanda would bear twin girls. It seems she was very much correct.

A happy warmth suffuses me as the twin in Karmoko Thandiwe's arms gurgles again. It dissipates some of the panic and fear that's dogged my every step here. The fear of whether Okot has already taken back my kelai, or whether it was never in Gar Fatu in the first place and we're just going on a fool's errand, one that will hurt the group much more than it helps, given Keita's continuing distress.

To push back these thoughts, I stroke the baby's soft little hand, glorying when her smile breaks wider. "She's so beautiful," I say, glancing up at the karmoko, who has a proud expression on their face, their brown eyes beaming with contentment.

"Isn't she?" they agree smugly. They may not have birthed the twins, but it's clear they're still every bit a parent. My intuition is further confirmed when their face suddenly twists into a worried frown. "Assuming she's a she, that is. You never know with these things." An apt observation, given that Karmoko Thandiwe didn't reveal their identity as a yandau to us until recently.

"No," I agree. "You don't." I glance up at them again, smiling when I see the contentment in their eyes. "It's good to see you, Karmoko," I say.

"And you as well, Deka," they return. "Although I wish we were reuniting under better circumstances." They glance pointedly behind me, where a group of aviax are just finishing preparing our gryphs for the journey.

I force away the pang in my chest with a smile. "It does seem to be a pattern for us, does it not, always meeting with each other in dire circumstances."

"Such is life," they say with a sigh.

They tut down at me. "Becoming a god . . . You never did make things easy, did you, Deka?"

I shake my head. "My essential nature is complication, as it turns out."

I must have said these words more bitterly than I intended, because the karmoko's eyes gentle. "You are who and what you are, Deka, no more, no less. Always remember that."

I sigh. "I will, although . . . I imagine a god would be much more. That a god would *have* to be much more." I don't know what I'm saying, or even truly why I'm saying all this. All I know is that I feel a heaviness again, the same heaviness I felt all the way here, as if every step is leading me closer and closer to my doom.

"If you choose it to be."

When I glance up at them, confused, the karmoko explains: "I don't know much about gods—in fact, I'd be hard pressed to think of all the times I've truly prayed over the years. But what I do know is that gods have choices, just like we mortals. They can choose to become whomever they want.

"So if you're uncertain about what type of god you will be, perhaps you should take time to contemplate it—preferably before you retrieve your divinity."

The karmoko looks into my eyes, their gaze unwavering. "You choose who you want to be, Deka. This child will one day," they say, fondly stroking their daughter's fluff of hair, "and the only reason they'll be able to do that is because of all the sacrifices you and your companions have made.

"Why, then, should you, one of the main engineers of our new world, not do the same?"

"But what if I fail?" I whisper, frightened. I glance around to make sure no one else is listening before I add in an even lower voice, "What if I'm unable to stop the gods and the world ends? Or, worse, I do stop them, and I become even more corrupt than they were?"

Karmoko Thandiwe must hear the hysteria in my voice, because they just look at me. Then they sigh, juggle their baby onto one arm, and reach out with the other to pat me on the shoulder. "You won't fail, Deka," they say plainly. "It's not in your nature, and it's never been. That's why I'm not worried, despite everything that's going on. Because I believe in you. And more to the point, I know you. No matter what happens, you'll make the correct choice. I know you will."

My eyes are awash with tears now. I look up at the karmoko, humbled beyond measure. That they would say such words, express such faith . . .

I hold on to the feeling as White Hands finally arrives to brief us, confirming that the jatu are still searching the area around Keita's summer house, and then as I say my goodbyes and mount Ixa, my determination building all the while: *I won't fail.* Not just for my sake, but for these precious baby girls. For every person who's never had the chance to live their life in the manner in which they desired.

Holding on to this determination, I summon the door. Then I turn to Keita, who's walking beside me, as the others all are, his eyes still uneasy.

"Ready?" I ask.

"As I'll ever be."

I nod, squeeze his hand. Now I turn one last time to the others—to White Hands and the equus twins, to the aviax sovereigns, who have just arrived, to the Kamandas and Karmoko Thandiwe, as well as everyone else who came here to see me off. "Farewell," I say. "Hopefully, when we meet again, it'll be with joyous news."

"I look forward to it," White Hands replies.

Then I mount Ixa and ride through the door.

28

◆ ◆ ◆

Even before my friends and I exit the door, I can hear wings flapping faintly in the distance: Melanis's. Their rhythm is distinct, even mixed, as it is, with the sounds of the other hunters. No doubt she's here for the same reason we are: following the jatu. According to Sayuri's spies, Melanis's hunters have destroyed all but one group of them and they haven't left the region yet. If we move fast, we can overtake them. Or, better yet, Melanis and her hunters can, leaving us space to hunt for my kelai at our leisure. After all, the Gilded Ones still don't know that it might be here, or that I'm coming to look for it. If they did, this entire area would be crawling with every alaki and deathshriek at their disposal. As Melanis and her hunters are the only ones here, we still have time, although we have to be swift. If the ancient Firstborn is in contact with the goddesses, as I assume she is, it's only a matter of time before they inform her that a door has been opened here. The moment she hears this, she'll come searching for the group who opened it.

I give the signal to move out, ears cocked for any sign of Melanis's group. Thankfully, she and the hunters have all but disappeared. They're too busy pursuing the jatu to notice us.

"This way." Keita brusquely motions us toward the thick copse of trees that marks the entrance to the jungle surrounding what remains of his family's summer house. He's been tense ever since we entered the door, as if he's bottled up all his emotions so tightly his entire body has turned rigid. "If we use this path, we can overtake them."

I quickly follow his directions, breathing out a sigh of relief when I see no trace of blood-eaters sprouting among the bushes; the throbbing, black-petaled flowers are the first telltale signs of the Bloom, the expanse of greenery that displays the extent of the Gilded Ones' recovered power. Even better, I don't hear any strange sounds coming from this jungle that might accompany one of the proxies the goddesses have created. The Bloom hasn't stretched to here, visible confirmation that the goddesses' power hasn't recovered substantially since our confrontation despite, or perhaps because of, all the vales they're opening. If there's one thing I learned from my confrontation with Okot, it's that opening vales requires vast amounts of power. It'll take the gods time and numerous sacrifices to recover what they've lost.

But once they do . . .

I push the thought away as Keita beckons us over to a particularly thick stand of bushes. "The cave should be just around this corner," he says, making his way through the foliage.

Before we left Ilarong, he explained that a system of caves lies under this area. He used them to flee to safety after his family was massacred. Today, we'll use them to enter his summer house without being detected.

It would have been so much easier if I could open a door, but I can't create doors to places I've never been. Now, more than ever, I regret not visiting with him when I had the chance.

"Are you certain the caves are this way?" I turn my attention to Adwapa as she examines the area, scowling.

As does her sister.

"Everything looks like overgrowth to me," Asha says.

Keita turns to them, his eyes grim. "I'll never forget this place. Never. Even if they razed everything to the ground and built a thousand palaces over it, I would still know where to go."

"Well, that's reassurin'," Britta muses, glancing at me pointedly. She's also worried about his state of mind.

I just shake my head. "Let's get a move on."

"I second that," Belcalis adds. Then she suddenly stiffens, points up.

Wing flaps are sounding. Melanis is returning. Which means the Gilded Ones must have told her about the door.

What are we waiting for? Kweku motions using battle language. *Move!*

Into the jungle! Acalan urges us on, slipping so quietly into the bushes, only the leaves rustle.

Just that sound is enough to attract Melanis's attention. "Intruders!" she shrieks, her voice so shrill, it bounces across the trees. "Where are you hiding?"

Prickles run down my spine at the sound. Melanis's voice is harsher now, less human than when I last saw her. She's becoming less the alaki I knew and more like one of the Gilded Ones' many proxies, a creature of pure vengeance and fury, driven only to serve the gods.

"This is the territory of the mothers, Idugu scum," she calls out, her hunters also screaming around her. "When we find you, we will rip you limb from limb, and then we will feed your entrails to the beasts."

"Creative," Britta mutters as we rush onward. "Ye have to give her that."

"But did you hear what she said? Idugu scum!" Adwapa seems almost gleeful with triumph as she turns to me and very softly says, "The goddesses can't distinguish who opens a door! They don't know it's you who came through."

"And let's keep it that way," I whisper back, ducking beside a tree when a familiar winged figure passes overhead, a few others with her.

Katya swiftly does the same, the brown she's painted on her bright red skin blending her against the tree trunks. Melanis's hunters don't even notice her as they fly past, but then, I should have expected that. Deathshrieks are naturally stealthy despite their massive size.

Once the hunters have passed, Keita beckons us over to what appears to be a huge cluster of vines. "It's here!" he proclaims, wrenching aside the mass to reveal what looks to be the mouth of a cave.

It's small and low to the ground. Child-sized.

Keita blinks. "A bit smaller than I remember. But it's much bigger inside, I promise," he says as he continues pulling at the vines.

Within moments, he's fully uncovered the entrance, which is barely more than a cramped hole in the ground. A look of dismay flashes over Katya's face when she sees it, but she quickly hides her unease.

309

"I'm sure we can make it bigger," she whispers, as if convincing herself. "We just have to dig a little."

Britta steps forward, cracking her knuckles. "Allow me," she says and breathes in deeply.

The hairs rise on the back of my neck as I feel her power rising to the occasion, the Greater Divinity's swirling around it. All my friends—the ones who were with me in the pathways, that is—have been practicing using it to amplify their power.

Li moves to stand beside her. "Let's do this together?" he asks.

Britta grins. "Together."

They gesture at the same time, and slowly, quietly, the dirt at the base of the cave's opening moves aside, heeding the call of their combined power.

Ixa help too! A scaly body muscles past the pair. Ixa begins quietly but enthusiastically digging, dirt and stones moving under the force of his claws. In less than a minute, there's a hole big enough for me to crawl through.

Not that Britta and Li needed the help, but Ixa is too pleased with himself for anyone to mention it.

See, Ixa help, he says with a happy little wriggle.

Thank you, Ixa, I reply as I crawl my way in.

To my surprise, the cave is massive.

I expected a cramped, dark space, but no, rays of sunlight stream down from the ceiling, which soars so high into the air I can only glimpse portions of it from where I'm standing. Ferns and vines of all sorts fill the cavernous expanse, which is at least the size of a small field, and there's even a tree or two in the center.

"Would you look at that. . . ." Kweku whistles as he crawls in after me. "It really is huge."

I don't reply, too busy craning my neck around to take in my surroundings. No wonder Keita assured us the cave was sizeable.

I turn back to the entrance, where the others are now wriggling in one by one, aided by the mounds of dirt Britta continues slowly and stealthily to move, Li and Ixa by her side. "Will we have any problems entering any other parts of the cave system?" I ask, gesturing to the still relatively small opening, which Katya is just now struggling through. "For her especially?"

Keita shakes his head. "She'll be fine," he replies when she finally makes it through. "That should be the smallest space we encounter."

"I hope so," Katya grumbles, signing so Keita can understand her.

You'll be fine, he signs back swiftly. *Promise.*

Katya nods, but her eyes are still doubtful. Not just about what Keita said but about him as well.

There's a strange air around Keita now, a brittleness almost. And it's coupled with heat that pours off him as if from a furnace.

He grunts. "We'll be safe here. The caves look like hills from above, so no one suspects they're here, and even if they did, no one would ever come here—at least, no human would."

I nod. This portion of Gar Fatu was once a common route for deathshrieks journeying to the N'Oyo Mountains to worship the imprisoned goddesses. That's the very reason Gezo sent Keita's family here: to put them in the deathshrieks' path.

That said, Keita heads for the back of the cave. He doesn't even check to see if the rest of the group has made it through safely.

I follow worriedly after him. "Keita, wait," I call, concerned. "Britta and Li have to seal the entrance."

The pair are just now extracting themselves from the entrance, which has flattened back to its previous state, obeying the call of their gift. They also manually rearranged the vines outside as best they could before they entered. "There," Britta announces, dusting off her hands. "It's not perfect, but it should fool all but the keenest eyes."

"Well, here's to hoping Melanis's hunters have much worse eyesight than they do hearing," I sigh, turning back to Keita.

I'm not surprised to find he's already made it to the other end of the cavern. "Everyone get moving," he says brusquely to the group as he bursts into a run. "We have half a day to get there, and the jatu are already in the lead."

Nodding, I follow behind him, picking up speed. From here, it's a race all the way to the summer house.

After all, we have a kelai to find.

❖

The rest of the cave system remains as bright as that first cave, even when we travel deeper into it, crossing over an underground river using a long-abandoned bridge whose stones are so stylistically carved, there's no way it was made by nature. Between the sunlight streaming in from those tiny holes in the ceiling and our ability to see almost as well in the dark as we do in the light, it's easy for my friends and I to navigate even the darker, gloomier areas of the cave. The entire time, we maintain a swift run, an easy feat for us. Back in the Warthu Bera, we used to do it for hours every morning.

"Think some ancient civilization lived here?" Adwapa asks, not the slightest bit out of breath, as she peers at the soaring walls around us, which have what look like cleverly hidden windows embedded in them all the way up to the ceiling.

"Without a doubt," Acalan says, his voice loud and excited now that we're in so deep, there's no chance Melanis can hear us. "There's those sun-holes in the ceiling and then the windows as well. But none of it seems human made," he muses, squinting. "I don't see any stairs, so how did they get up there?"

"They flew," Keita says curtly. When we all turn to him, he continues: "Aviax used to live here. Some other creatures too. I would look at the carvings they left on the walls when I got frightened." Then he falls quiet. "I looked at them a lot. Especially when the deathshrieks searched the mountain."

My stomach twists as I realize what he's saying. The horror he experienced. "Oh, Keita," I whisper, hurrying toward him. I can't imagine what it must have felt like to be only nine years old, parents just slaughtered, and to have to hide in these caves as groups of deathshrieks mad with bloodlust searched the area above him, their shrieks splitting the skies.

Worse, it sounds like he was here for quite some time, much more than the day or so he initially told me. I can't tell if it's that he doesn't truly recall, or that he doesn't want to let on—not just to me and the others but to himself—how terrifying the experience truly was.

One of the things Keita hasn't been able to change, even after all our time together, is his need to always be the protector—even if it's just himself he's protecting.

He runs faster, a deliberate attempt to evade my touch. "We have to keep moving," he says brusquely, doubling his pace. "Can't dawdle and risk the goddesses sending more pursuers."

"Or worse, losing Deka's kelai," Acalan adds, following after him.

As I sigh, keeping pace with them, a soft footstep falls beside mine: Belcalis's. "Think he's going to be all right?" she asks quietly, her eyes on his back.

Somehow, I'm not surprised she's the one who's asking. Belcalis may be solitary by nature, but she and Keita have become close in the past few months. More so than anyone else in the group, the two are brutally practical—sometimes, even to the point of being callous, like White Hands so often is.

I shrug. "I don't know. This place, it's filled with all his worst memories."

Belcalis nods. "Losing his family, and in such a brutal way."

I nod. "I can't imagine how devastating it must be." I lost my parents more recently, so I can only begin to guess what it felt like for Keita at nine years old, the disorientation and loss.

"That why he's emitting so much heat?" This question comes from Adwapa, who's now beside us, her brow slick with sweat. "He's like a gods-damned furnace, that one."

I sigh. "I'll talk to him," I say.

But Belcalis shakes her head. "Let me." When I slow to glance at her, she explains: "I know he's your sweetheart, Deka, but he's also my friend. Perhaps the truest male friend I'll ever have." She seems almost pained to admit: "I . . . care about him."

A shocking development. Belcalis is not what you would call friendly to those of the masculine persuasion. Or to people in general, for that matter.

But perhaps she is Keita friendly.

I nod. "Of course."

Belcalis runs forward. Much to my surprise, she puts her arm around Keita's shoulder despite the heat still pouring off him. I'm even more shocked when he doesn't shrug it off or move faster. Instead, he slows to half lean into it, allowing her to comfort him. A pang shoots through my heart.

Keita won't accept my comfort, but he will accept Belcalis's. He'll lean on her the way he won't lean on me. I can't help but feel injured by that.

"Let them have their moment." When I turn, Adwapa is watching the direction of my eyes, her gaze shrewd.

"I know, but—"

"It pains you?" Adwapa nods. "Except it's not that he's rejecting you—he's pretending to be strong for you."

"But I can be strong for him too."

"In good time," Adwapa says. "But you have worries of your own to sort out." Her eyes are sharp in the gloom as she gazes at me. "I heard what you said to Karmoko Thandiwe earlier. About being afraid to fail."

When I glance up at her, startled, her expression is gentle now.

"You'll be a wonderful god, Deka," she says. "And an attractive one too. Have you seen the Idugu? Hideous, the lot of them."

As I laugh, startled, she nods at me, so much love in her eyes. "Everything will be as it should be," she continues.

"And if it isn't?"

"Then you'll have me. And Asha, and Britta, and the uruni, and Belcalis, and Katya, and even Keita—even though he's being a bit of a pissfart at the moment. I know you've been in pain and fear and anger this past month, but I'm here with you—"

"As are the rest of us." This comment comes from Britta, who has stopped running and is now walking up to me with Asha and Katya by her side, all their eyes filled with compassion.

My tears begin flowing again. "Oh, you," I sniffle. "I love you all."

"And we love you," Adwapa says calmly. "If everything goes to shit, you're not alone, Deka. You have us."

"To the end of the world an' back," Britta says.

"And even if it's just to the end of the world, I'm fine with that, honestly," Adwapa adds. "As long as I get a glorious death, Mehrut at my side, I'll go into the darkness smiling."

"Speak for yourself," her sister sniffs beside her. "I'd rather have a quiet death in my own bed." Then she smiles at me. "But if it is the end of the world, I'm with you, Deka. You're not alone."

"Never, ever," Katya says in her soft rumble.

"None of us are," Britta agrees.

By now, my heart is so full, it's heaving with sobs. "Thank you," I say to my friends, enfolding them in my arms. "Thank you all."

And then I continue running, moving even faster now than I did before. Britta is right, I'm not alone. No matter what I may think, we're all in this together. And if being a god means I can save my friends, protect them from the other deities, then it's well worth being alone. And who knows: perhaps it won't be as bad as I think, perhaps I'll be so busy being a god, I won't even know how lonely I am.

I hold on to this thought as we continue further into the darkness.

29

◆ ◆ ◆

"Well, that's inconvenient."

This comment comes from Li when he looks up at what should have been the last obstacle in our journey to the summer house: a staircase carved into the farthest corner of the cavern. It stretches all the way up to the ceiling, where a small ledge leads to the door to outside. Theoretically, it should have been easy climbing up those stairs, but half of them are broken, and the staircase's entire bottom is rubble. While it would still be possible for a small child to scramble up it, as Keita once did, there's no way that's feasible for any of us. We'd be likely to break our necks if we did.

Thankfully, we won't need to.

"Ixa," I say, glancing at my companion. *Fly us up?*

Deka, he agrees. His body immediately begins growing. Within moments, he's large enough to seat the entire group. We all hold on as he lifts into the air, headed for that ledge, which ends in what looks like an impassable slab of stone.

Britta gestures at it. "Tell me that's not—"

"The hidden door to the summer house? Unfortunately, it is," Keita says, leaping off Ixa the moment we're near, since my scaled companion is much too large to land on the ledge.

I hurriedly do the same, rushing over just as Keita begins to run his hand over the side of the slab. His eyes are narrowed in concentration. "There's a lever somewhere right . . . here!" He pushes.

The stone gives way with a loud click, the sound muffled, blessedly, by the thicket of vines that's grown in front of it. While we've seen neither hide nor hair of Melanis since we entered the cavern, we can't expect such luck to hold now that we're almost out of it.

Keita turns to us again. "Father always did like his escape routes," he says, pulling at the vines. "This is the first one he showed me. Little did he know how useful it would be." He continues aggressively pulling, little streams of sunlight now filtering through. "The deathshrieks shrieked and pushed against the door all day, but they never found out how to open it."

He turns to me with a grim smile. "Father's foresight saved me."

My heart jolts as I imagine it: Keita, a small, bereaved child huddled against this stone door with the monsters on the other side of it. I reach for him. "Keita, I—"

"Hurry," he says, turning swiftly away from me. He's closing himself off again, making sure I don't see even a hint of his emotions. "We have to get a move on." He rips away the last few vines, allowing sunlight in completely.

And finally, I can see where we are.

The door is hidden by a group of boulders. They sprawl at

the edge of a soaring mountain peak, upon whose highest point sits an estate so immense, it would give even the most magnificent homes in Hemaira a run for their money. I have to crane my head to look up at it. My eyes goggle as I take in the lush gardens framing the colossal house—no, *palace*—that is its center, its delicate pink walls shimmering in jewellike tones under the hazy golden sunlight. The only time I've seen walls made of stone like this before was in Laba, the capital of Maiwuri. But that's not the estate's only marvel. The roof as well is a thing of exquisite beauty, each of its tiles made from a pale-green mineral I've only ever seen in jewelry worn by people from the Eastern provinces. The edges of the tiles are feathered with gold, adding to their already stunning appearance.

And yet they're untouched. My brows wrinkle as I realize: the entire estate is in pristine condition, unmarred by the hands of thieves or even the elements. There's not a touch of decay or disrepair anywhere. It's as if it's been protected somehow, as if something is shielding it from the outside world. Even as I think this, I feel it, a deep thrumming of power coming from somewhere inside the estate. Power I immediately recognize, despite having never felt it before: my kelai!

I speed forward, a thousand emotions racing through me— hope, fear, dread. . . . If this truly is my kelai, then this is it, the end of my journey with my friends. The end of my life as I know it in Otera.

But none of my friends seem to realize that. They're all just staring at the estate in wonder. "He told us his family was nobility, but I don't think I really understood until today," Li says, staring at Keita, who's continued jogging onward, in awe. "This place is a palace."

"An' it's been perfectly preserved," Britta says, eyes practically round as she stares at the mansion and the profusion of sweet-smelling fruit trees lining it. "Like someone placed it under glass for wha—a decade? How is that possible?"

"I don't know," I swiftly mumble, although that's not the strictest truth. I have a very good idea why the estate has remained untouched. But I don't want to face the reason yet, don't want to say it out loud.

"I do." Belcalis turns to me. "It's your kelai. It's here."

"And the jatu aren't." This brusque comment comes from Keita, who is now well down the path. "If we're lucky, that means we've preceded them."

He beckons us onward. "Let's keep moving," he says curtly. "We have only a few hours of daylight left."

We hurry behind him, entering the fruit groves, where brightly feathered glimmerbirds roost in the trees, their tail feathers so long, they graze the ground. They aren't alone. Little nuk-nuks, those mossy-green deer, gambol underneath the trees, blithely unconcerned as we walk past. How the Gilded Ones never found this place, never thought to look, I don't understand. But perhaps the rules of existence work differently here, as they do in every primary temple of a group of gods.

And that's what this place is, a temple.

"Infinity take me, these are good!" I turn, startled when Kweku takes a bite out of one of the perfectly ripe fruits that hang thick on the trees.

Asha slaps it from his palm.

"Hey!" Kweku protests. "That was a perfectly good fruit!"

"In an enchanted gods-damned grove!" Asha growls back. "I can't fathom if you've lost all common sense, or if you never had any to begin with!" When he stares at her, uncomprehend-ing, she expands: "Don't eat strange fruit in enchanted groves! That's what literally every old tale teaches you! If you grow another head or turn into one of those"—she points at the nuk-nuks—"it'll be your own fault!"

Kweku whirls to me, horrified. "Am I going to turn into a nuk-nuk, Deka? Is there a curse on the fruit?"

"How should I know?" I reply, shrugging. "It's my first time here too."

Keita walks to the top of the garden, then stops, turns to the group. "Everyone, take a direction. The kelai could be in the main house, or it could be in one of the adjoining ones. Either way, signal the moment you find anything. I'll take the main house. *Alone.*"

He emphasizes this word so harshly, my suspicions rise. There's something in the house he doesn't want anyone to see.

His parents.

The understanding shatters through me. This estate is per-fectly preserved, everything, presumably, just as Keita left it. And that, perhaps, includes the corpses of his parents.

I run after him. He's rushing up the stairs leading to the en-trance now, his footsteps so swift and sure, I struggle to keep up. "Keita," I call out, "wait for me!"

When he doesn't slow down, I turn back to the others. "Start searching—quickly," I say. "I'll go with Keita."

Ixa pads over, attempting to follow me, but I shake my head. *I need to be alone with Keita now,* I say, thankful when Britta sees my gesture and quickly beckons to him.

"Come on, Ixa."

Ixa coming, he replies, disgruntled, though Britta can't hear him. He pads after her.

I give Britta a quick nod of thanks, then I follow after Keita, slowing as he does once we reach the massive doors that are the entrance to the house. They're still slightly open, even after all these years, and there are claw marks on the sides, as if something forced its way out. Not something—*deathshrieks.*

Keita turns to me. "You don't have to come with me, Deka. I remember the way."

I nod. "That may be, but I still want to come."

He sighs, his jaw gritting. "I don't think you understand, Deka. This place, it's exactly as I left it. *Exactly.*"

"And that might include your parents." When he glances at me, startled, I add: "I've seen corpses before."

"These aren't corpses. These are my family."

"I'm your family too."

"For how long?" There's a note of challenge to these words. Anger as well.

I suck in a breath. "You don't have to do this, Keita," I whisper. "You don't have to be like this."

"Be like what? Cold? Angry? In pain?" With every word, Keita's voice breaks more and more.

"Alone," I say, reaching out my hand. "You don't have to be alone. You don't have to push me away. I'm here. For as long I can be, I'm here."

"But you shouldn't be. You should be with the others, finding your kelai, preparing for godhood."

I step closer again. I know what Keita is doing, pushing so hard. He's trying to make a clean break. That way he gets to wallow in his feelings and I get to, presumably, ascend guilt-free. I shake my head. "There's nowhere I'd rather be than here. There's nowhere that's more important than here."

"The world is ending, didn't you hear? It's what'll happen if you don't take back your kelai."

"Not yet, it isn't. And while we still have time, I want to be with you."

"Time. . . ." Keita's reply is a bitter laugh. "And precisely how much time do we have left, do you think? A minute? An hour? Two at most?" He whirls toward me. "In the next few hours, perhaps even minutes, you'll be a god. Something else entirely. Something that doesn't need me."

And there it is, the words Keita has no doubt been holding on to all this time. The words I've been fearing as well. But unlike what I expected, they do not shatter me. I have the love of Britta and Belcalis, the twins and Katya, as my armor. Even our uruni have girded me with the strength of their belief. I will not let Keita sink into his despair, nor will I let him drag me down with him.

"I've never needed you, Keita."

When his eyes widen with hurt, I grab his hands. "But I've always wanted you. More than anything, I've wanted you." I look up at him. "You're not a need, Keita, you're not an obligation to me. What you are is my happiness, my delight. When I didn't believe that there was good in the world, there was you. You're my comfort and joy, and I hope I'm the same for you."

As Keita continues to watch me, I inch closer, wrap my arms around him. "I know you fear the future—I fear it too—but this is our present. We're together *now*. We're here *now*. In this moment, there's only me and you.

"The future will come no matter what we do, but for now, please don't push me away, Keita. I'm here. I'll be here for as long as I can."

The moments pass, Keita's body stiff in my embrace. Then slowly, surely, his muscles relax and his hands creep around me. "I can't breathe," he rasps, a pained admission. "I'm here—right where they are, and I can't breathe. I can't go in there, Deka, I can't. I can't, I can't, I ca—"

"Shhh. . . ." I stroke his back. "You don't have to go in."

"But the jatu and Melanis and the world . . ." His voice is near to breaking now.

"The world can wait, and so can we. We'll wait for as long as you want, as long as you need, until you get your breath again. We'll just sit here." I lower myself to the floor, pulling Keita down beside me.

He tries to protest again. "But your kelai and Melanis and—"

"All just distractions," I say, wrapping my arms around him and making small, slow circles on his back. "Right now, there's only you and me. That's all that matters. All that matters. . . ."

Keita nods, drops his head on top of mine. And we remain there in silence, the evening shadows growing around us. Wrapping us in their comfort.

Until it's finally time for us to rise again and step into the summer house.

◆

Power buzzes through the mansion. If I didn't feel it fully before, I feel it now, the low, intense thrumming that vibrates through me the moment I step foot across the threshold. My breath hitches, suddenly caught in my throat. It's all I can do not to shiver. I've been in countless ruins before, some thousands of years old, but never have I felt anything like this. This place—it's alive with energy.

Just like the outside, the interior of the house is pristine. The heavy stone tables with scenes from ancient legends carved into them still have gold accentuating their edges. The chairs still have their exquisitely embroidered cushions. Sheer curtains still line the massive sliding doors, which have been built in the Southern style to funnel air through the interior.

Except there's no breeze.

It takes a few minutes for me to notice that. There should, at the very least, be a soft breeze dancing across the curtains. And dust motes should sparkle in the last embers of the dying sunlight. But there's nothing—not even the faintest odor.

"It's like it's frozen," Keita says hollowly, glancing around. Then he notices something on one of the tables. He runs over, picks it up, and holds it to his chest.

"What is it?" I ask, walking closer.

"Mother's comb," he replies, holding up the large golden comb, whose handle has been shaped into a single flower. "She left it here the night that she—that she—"

Keita stops, when his breath hitches, and inhales to regain his control. "She left it here the night that she died," he finally says, walking around the room as if remembering everything anew. "She'd been wearing it all day, but then she grew tired and left it here for her attendants. She didn't realize they'd already been killed."

There's an expression on Keita's face now, a horror. He

walks down the entrance hall, his destination a small corridor I would never have noticed had he not been leading me toward it. There's a dark staircase that winds upward from it: the servants' stairs. I've seen them in all the homes of rich people I've visited.

I follow Keita as he continues talking.

"The emperor had just had some boxes delivered, you see," he says, his voice echoing as he slowly walks up the stairs. "Gifts. Clothes and jewels and fabrics and such. For his favorite cousins." He spits out this part bitterly before he continues. "Everyone was overjoyed at this display of the emperor's favor. Mother's attendants had spent the day unpacking the boxes. There were only a few left.

"So Mother came down, left the comb, called for her attendants. But no one answered." Now Keita turns to me, his eyes burning in the darkness that is this small, oppressive staircase. "It was only when she walked back upstairs that she heard the shrieking.

"Sound travels up. That was what I learned that day."

When he laughs bitterly again, my stomach twists. The look in his eyes now . . . the heat pouring off him. . . . I'm relieved when Keita turns one more corner and we exit into another perfectly preserved corridor. It's clear we're in his family's private portion of the palace. Small bronze carvings hang from the walls, portraits of ancestors. But Keita continues onward as if he sees nothing but the path laid out in front of him.

The silence is so oppressive now, I know I have to shatter it before he disappears completely into his own mind. So I rush forward. "Are we almost there?" I ask quickly. "The place where it—"

"Happened?" Keita turns to me, his eyes bright. The fire in them is near to spilling out, an indication of just how strong his emotions are at the moment.

When I put my hands on his arm, I have to fight the urge to flinch away. Keita's body is burning right now. If he weren't wearing the heat-proof armor the Maiwurians gave him, his clothing would be in flames.

He nods. "Yes," he says. "Yes, we are."

He walks down the hall to the door at the end, then stops, as if waiting to bolster his courage.

I hurry to his side. "Keita, you don't have to—"

Eyes bright with flames turn to me. "I do," he says, and then he slides the door open, revealing a chamber frozen in a scene of violence.

The covers on the massive bed are scattered, the embroidered pillows tossed in varying directions. There's a catastrophic hole in the brightly painted glass doors leading to the balcony, a heavy wooden table lying smashed to its side, as if it had been used as a desperate yet futile barricade. But that's not what commands my attention.

The people lying in the center of the room do.

There, spread out just in front of me, is a scene worse than any I imagined. Six people—two adults and four teenaged boys—lie on the floor, their opulent robes shimmering around them like silken rivers. The blood that stains their bodies is still bright red, and it dots their ears and noses, and drips like jewels from the claw marks on the belly of the father, who fell holding his sword. I gasp when I catch sight of it. And then I notice what I didn't before.

The corpses all look peaceful. Given the violence I've seen

surrounding them, their eyes should be open, their faces frozen in a rictus of terror. But a feeling of peace pervades the room. As if these people have been held somehow, preserved lovingly, just like the rest of the mansion.

Keita sinks to his knees, his breaths ragged. Tears are falling down his cheeks now, the tears he's been holding back for so very long. Little flames follow their path, almost as if his anger is leaking out. "They should be screaming," he gasps out, tears choking his words. "When they died, they were screaming. Why don't their faces look like that anymore?"

There's a bewildered expression in his eyes as he asks this, and it's perfectly understandable. Everything else in this house has been preserved as it was the moment Keita left it. Everything but his family.

Why has their pain been erased—replaced, it seems, with peace? I don't understand how any of it is possible. Then that thrumming runs through me, more powerful than I've ever felt it.

I've been consumed with Keita's pain. That's the only reason I can offer for why I didn't notice it before: the power that runs through the house, it's strongest in this room. And it's coming from a tiny box. Everything in me stills as I see it, the small jewelry box that sits innocently at the corner of the room, on the only table that remains upright in this masterpiece of preserved chaos.

It's small and so plain, it's easy to overlook. There are no carvings on it, no gold. It's just an obsidian box, black stone that gleams dully in the evening light.

And yet energy pulses from it, a song that echoes the one coming from deep inside my soul.

That box once contained my kelai. Hopefully, it still does. I stagger toward it, my heart pounding in my chest. Hopefully, what I'm feeling is the source of my power and not the memory of it, like everything else on this estate.

"Deka?" I barely hear Keita's bewildered question as I continue onward, my body barely able to hold itself up any longer.

Every step I take is heavy with apprehension. So much rests on this moment, on what I find when I open the box. It could be nothing, an echo from moments past. Or it could be everything: the key to saving Otera, to saving everyone I love.

My head is spinning now, sweat dripping down my face and neck. The nearer I get to the box, the greater the energy that thrums over me, a feeling so familiar and so welcoming, it almost feels identical to the Greater Divinity. Only this is my own divinity—or at least the key to it. The key I've been searching for.

If it's still there.

I glance around, searching for Mother's body. She said it should be somewhere nearby, except no matter how hard I look, it's nowhere to be seen. But that doesn't mean it isn't here somewhere, hidden in a corner I haven't yet noticed. I sink to my knees in front of the box, hands trembling as I reach out. But the moment I open the box, I sag, disappointment flooding me.

My kelai isn't there. I don't have to look down at those gleaming black stone corners to see what I already feel. It's been taken. Was likely taken mere hours ago—spirited away while my friends and I rushed through the caverns—the same way Mother's body was.

The knowledge flows into me so smoothly, I know it comes from whatever remnants of my kelai still pulse around this estate, preserving it the same way tree sap does the unfortunate insects that get trapped inside it.

A wail chokes my throat. A cry of anguish.

All this time, I've been frightened of my kelai. Reluctant to find it. But now that I've experienced it, I realize my mistake. It's a part of me, as integral as any organ. It's mine, and now it's been stolen yet again by gods who want to use it to destroy me.

They have it and I have nothing. Nothing but these remnants that swirl around me, teasing me with the possibility of what might have been.

It's some moments before I rise. Once I do, I turn back to Keita, who's still kneeling there beside his parents, sobbing as if his heart could break. Outside of that first moment when I began walking over to the box, he hasn't noticed my journey, has no inkling of the immensity of what I just discovered. But that's what grief does. It blinds you to everything but the devastation in your own heart. And this, what Keita is experiencing, is pure and true grief.

I put aside my anger, my frustration, as I concentrate on his despair. And on the incongruity of the scene around him. I suspected it before, but now I truly understand why his family looks the way they do, why they're so peaceful, unlike everything else in this room.

It's because my kelai is a part of me. Has always been a part of me.

Even when I didn't know it, it knew me, knew how I felt about Keita. That's why it has preserved this estate the way it has—or, rather, why it rolled back the decay that had fallen over it.

This estate wasn't always this way.

If I had to hazard a guess, it was no doubt moldering away for years, a forgotten, hateful tomb for Keita's parents. But then I fell in love with him, started to regard him above everyone else.

This place, this magical stillness, is the result of my feelings for Keita.

Grim though it may be, it's my love letter to him. My way of allowing him to say goodbye to his family, even though I never realized I was doing such a thing.

But that is the miracle of the divine.

And that is the miracle of love.

I walk over to Keita, who's now kneeling by his mother, holding her in his arms. When he sees me watching, he shakes his head ruefully. "I was the one who urged them to build this place," he says suddenly. "Mother had her doubts, but I wanted a summer house. I wanted to brag to my friends. And I was the precious youngest. So I begged and wheedled and pleaded until Mother said yes. And when Mother said yes, Father, of course, agreed, because he would do anything to please her.

"So he built it, and then we came." He turns to me, his eyes now filled with a strangely calm acceptance. "And I could blame myself for that—I have over the years—but now I see it wasn't my fault. I was a child. Barely less than Maziru's age." He points to the youngest boy, a child of about eleven or so, eyes peacefully closed despite the claw marks gouging his neck.

"How could a child his age be the cause of all this?" He shakes his head. "No, it was Gezo and the Idugu. They're the cause of all this." He turns back to me. "I hope your kelai is here, Deka. I hope you find it and use it to strike every one of those divine bastards where they stand."

His tone is so determined now, so filled with righteous anger, I don't have the heart to tell him that it's not here. All I can do is comfort him.

"I'm sorry, Keita," I say, kneeling beside him. "I'm sorry for everything you endured."

"It's all right." When I turn to him, startled, he nods. "It is. Look at them." He gestures to his family, his expression surprisingly calm—relieved, almost. "I was so frightened. All this time, I was frightened that they would be in pain, that their bodies would be only bones or, worse, flesh in the same way I remembered them. . . . But look, they look peaceful." He strokes a finger over his mother's hair, his hands lovingly gliding over the dark-brown coils. "And they're together, all of them."

He glances up at me again, tears once more in his eyes. "When we first came, I wondered why this place was so well preserved, but now I know: you did this. You preserved their love."

As I blink at him, he grasps my hands. "I've been so afraid of what would happen once you ascended—so much time I spent fearing it. But now I see my fears were for nothing. Because if just a part of you can do so much to honor my loved ones, how much will the entirety of you do when Otera is yours to guide? How much better will everything be?"

I stare at him, speechless. If I were in his position, I would rage against the gods, against everything in this place, but somehow he's found hope in the face of all this darkness.

And he's found a way to give me the same. I've feared so deeply that I'd become an evil god, an unjust one, but if Keita sees all this in me, believes in me . . .

I stumble to find the words. "I don't, I don't—" Then I see the look on Keita's face, the determination. "Tell me what to do. Tell me how I can be here for you in this moment."

"You can bear witness," he says, rising again. He walks over to the bed.

When he begins to straighten the sheets, I rush to the other side, doing the same. I have an idea of what he's about to do, but I'll just follow his lead until he does it.

I watch as he picks up his mother and slowly, carefully deposits her there. There's so much love in that gesture, I know that he adored her the most, which makes perfect sense, considering how easily and fully he loves me. He does the same with his father and then, once they're side by side, clasps their hands together so that they can be in eternity as they were in life. That done, he moves on to his siblings, placing them in order of age until finally, his entire family is lying next to each other, their robes smoothed out and arranged around them to hide whatever wounds they might have.

He turns to me, his eyes heavy. "Your kelai—have you found any hint of it?"

"Yes," I say with a nod. "I have, but it's not here. The jatu have taken it, as we feared."

"Oh," Keita says. "I'm sorry, Deka, I—"

"No." I lift up a hand, stopping him. "I don't need that. I know what it feels like now—I know what to look for." That's the one bright spot in this whole affair. I know my next steps now. "I don't need Mother's body, don't need some new plan. I know what to do. So you do what you must here. You do what feels right."

"My thanks," Keita replies, and then he turns back toward the bed and holds out his hand.

The flame that explodes from it incinerates the sheets in seconds, although his family is a different matter. They remain there, untouched. So he sends another column of flame their way.

As the fire swiftly spreads, consuming everything in its path, I back toward the door. Keita remains calmly where he is, the flame brought to life. It surrounds him, bathing him in a halo of fire.

A whistling sounds as wind suddenly rushes through the house.

Keita nods to me as I exit. "Gather the others for departure. I'll be down the moment I'm done."

I nod, and then I begin running.

The last I see of him, he's standing there, watching his family burn in the funeral pyre he's made for them. And as I dart out of the summer palace, the flames chasing at my heels, I can't help but think that it's not just his family that's burning but the old Keita as well.

30

◆ ◆ ◆

The sudden emergence of wind, combined with the excess of kindling in the summer house, ensures that the mansion burns brightly and swiftly. My friends and I remain on the alert, waiting for either Melanis and her followers to attack at the goddesses' behest, or a group of Forsworn deathshrieks, loyal to the Idugu, to arrive. But as the last vestiges of the sun go down and the first glimmers of moonlight spill over the estate, no pursuers arrive, only Keita, his entire body bathed in flames now, although his armor still holds. Those Maiwurians truly know what they're about when they design armor. He slowly rejoins us, and together we watch the palace burn to the ground, nary the slightest hint of smoke despite the intensity of the fire.

It's as if the enchantment still holds firm: there are flames, there's wind and heat, but no smoke rises, only a sweet, flowery scent that wraps itself around the compound.

"It's fitting," Keita says once the conflagration finally reduces the place to ash, its orange hues brilliant against the darkness. "Mother loved the smell of flowers. She loved the smell of these trees."

He points to the fruit orchard, which remains standing, a silent sentinel. The flames didn't touch it at all, as if it was still protected, still cloaked in the invisible bubble my kelai constructed around the estate.

"And now, they'll watch over your family's spirits for eternity," Belcalis says solemnly, patting Keita's shoulder. "Take comfort in that."

Keita nods, tears glistening in his eyes as he accepts this gesture. "I will. Just as I'll take comfort in knowing that they're here, together in this place, this paradise." He turns pointedly to me as he says that, squeezes our connected hands a bit tighter.

Li steps forward. "I know it must be small consolation, given everything that happened here, but at least you have that—the knowledge that they'll be together always in this reverie that was created just for them. Hold on to it. Cherish it. It's a rare thing in times like ours."

These thoughtful words seem so out of character for Li, of all people, I gape.

"What?" he says defensively when he sees my expression. "I can be sensitive."

"So can a blood-sucking parasite," Adwapa says.

"Hey!" Britta protests. "Li is more sensitive than a parasite . . . I think." When Li pouts at this half compliment, she ruffles his hair.

As Adwapa shrugs doubtfully at Britta, Belcalis turns to the rest of us. "I hesitate to say this, given the occasion, but we need to get going. We need to return to Ilarong and regroup. Find a way to steal back Deka's kelai before Okot tries to snatch her away again."

"I actually have an idea for that," I say, thinking about all the feelings that flooded into me when I was in that room, in the presence of that box. "I'll just summon a door back, yes?" I add, glancing at Keita, who's still watching the embers of the building.

I don't want to rush him if he still needs time.

When he nods, I swiftly begin to sink into the combat state, not even needing to connect to the Greater Divinity now. There's enough of my kelai here, enough of its remnants, that I just need to draw them into me, use them to bend open the edges of space. As I begin to do that, however, I suddenly feel something—a subtle tingle shivering up my spine.

A presence.

I whirl, trying to find its source, until Britta gasps. She points, delighted. "Look, it's an indolo!"

I turn in the direction of her finger.

There, just at the edge of the orchard, are two glowing green feline forms. An indolo—what appear to be two small catlike creatures connected by a golden tether. Their golden horns and the profusion of vines that seem to float around them as if by magic glow in the darkness.

Britta tiptoes closer to the indolo to get a better look. "I've never seen one before. Look how beautiful it is!"

To my surprise, the creature doesn't move. It doesn't even lift a paw as Britta, Ixa, and I inch nearer until finally, we're face-to-face with it. That's when I notice its eyes.

Usually, indolo eyes are a shimmering golden hue that

matches the glow surrounding their bodies. This indolo's, however, are black, all four of them a shade of liquid obsidian that seems to peer deep into my soul. I blink, startled out of my daze. There's an intelligence to these eyes, an intellect that feels so familiar, I suddenly have the thought that I've seen this indolo—or, rather, the *person* that's inside this indolo—countless times before.

I sink to my knees, kneeling so I'm face to face with the goddess who has always been my firmest ally. "Anok," I say reverently. I can see her now, peering at me through those eyes. "It is you, isn't it?"

Both heads of the indolo nod.

"Anok?" Britta repeats, startled. "It's her? Does that mean the others are coming?" She glances around, uneasy, and she's not the only one.

Beside her, Ixa is bristling, every muscle in his body tensing as he growls. *Dark one here. Dark one watching.*

I pet his brow to calm him. "It's all right, Ixa."

I look back at the indolo and there she is, the dark goddess, staring back at me. I can feel her vast intelligence, feel the kindness, which I had feared was being corrupted by the others. It's still there, still deep inside this goddess who defied her own sisters—her own kin—to save the lives of myself and the others.

"Can you speak?" I ask.

The indolo shakes its heads.

"Of course it wouldn't be that easy." I sigh.

But as I kneel there, simmering in my disappointment, the indolo suddenly steps forward and presses both of its heads against mine. Just like that, I'm in the absolute darkness of night, Anok floating in front of me, a shadow within shadows.

She smiles, stars glimmering in her teeth. "Hello, Deka. It has been some time."

"Just over three months," I say. "But I know time moves differently for you."

"When it comes to you, no," she says, shaking her head. "Time is a constant with you. You are my constant. At least this version of you."

"What about the other one?" I ask, thinking of the Singular, the god I was before I fell and became this thing that's not quite alaki, not quite human, and not quite a god.

"Before, you were my sibling, a deep and true part of me. And then you became my enemy. Then my desperate hope. But all those yous are different from this you, and yet still the same."

She floats closer, tiny nebulas flowing in the coils of her hair. "You seem changed. You have met our siblings in Maiwuri?"

I laugh bitterly. "Yes. And I've been exposed to the concept of the Greater Divinity."

"Not a concept. All," Anok insists. "The Greater Divinity is all."

"Or perhaps it's another god I need to prepare myself for," I reply, voicing my doubts. "But then, there's always another god, always another something. Always, always, always. . . ." Frustration rushes out of me, a swift and endless river.

I hadn't allowed myself to feel the loss of my kelai, the anguish at being so close to retrieving it. Now that I am, I'm a mass of anger and frustration.

"Deka. . . ." Anok's voice is calming, the foundation that forces the river of frustration to slow, to remain within its boundaries instead of spilling over everything. She puts a hand wreathed with the light of a thousand constellations on my shoulder. "There is no other god, no greater god, than ourselves. Every single one of us. Everything is one. As it has always been."

I glance up at her, confused. Something in her words reminds me of Myter, of the conversations we had in the pathways. "You speak in riddles," I say.

Anok rests her head against mine. "I love you so. I never had a chance to tell you that. To tell my beloved children—Fatu especially—how deeply I love you. How perfect you are, each and every one of you.

"To me, you are everything. You always have been. All of you, even Melanis and her brood, lost as they are to their hatred now. That is what I came here to tell you."

Anok pulls back and looks at me. There's a universe in her eyes. A universe of love and belonging. And regret. There's so much regret in Anok's eyes. It reminds me of Okot, of what he said to me as he left me in the vale: *I truly wish we could have been allies.*

But it makes sense that the pair remind me of each other. Once upon a time, they were one.

"You must go now—swiftly, Deka. My sisters know that you're here, and they've sent Melanis for you, imbued her with all the power they can. If she meets you here, she will undoubtedly take you, and then all will be lost."

I nod. "Thank you for the warning, I will leave now."

But Anok is already fading, light growing where her darkness once was. She smiles at me. "Know that it has truly been my pleasure to know you. I will see you again in the Great Circle," she finishes.

And then she's gone.

I gasp, surfacing, to find myself surrounded by my friends.

The indolo is nowhere to be seen. "Where is Anok? The indolo, where is it?"

"The indolo?" Britta looks at me, seemingly confused. But that's a distant second to the panic simmering in her eyes. "What happened, Deka? Just as we were planning to leave, ye fell asleep."

"We've been trying to wake you," Keita says, embracing me with relief. Then he pulls back. "Are the sores returning? Is the armor failing?"

"No." I shake my head. "That's not it. I was just talking to Anok and—" A distant shriek interrupts my words, a horrifying reminder. "The goddesses know we're here. We have to go!" I say, already summoning a door.

It opens within moments, and just in time. Melanis and her hunters glow in the darkness, their bodies filled with divine energy, as they approach.

"Deka!" Melanis shrieks when she sees me, but I just smirk at her.

"If only they'd taught you to use all that power to create doors," I say.

And then I slip through mine, spiriting myself and my friends safely from her grasp.

◆

White Hands and Sayuri are sitting on one of Ilarong's many peaks when we return, White Hands smoking a sweet-smelling pipe, multiple horns of palm wine spread out between the two. It's a scene of such sibling domesticity, you'd almost forget that the two have been bitter enemies for centuries. A more twisted

342

relationship I cannot imagine, but that, I suppose, is the nature of family.

I sigh as I make my way over, tensing for the conversation I'm about to have with the pair. Both likely know by now that I didn't achieve my goals. Between Sayuri's spies and all the aviax flying about the city, it's likely that someone has already relayed a shortened version of my failure to the sisters. Which may explain why they've laid out such a spread. White Hands may enjoy her indulgences, but those are a great many horns of palm wine, even for her. And given that Sayuri doesn't drink, as deathshrieks only ever ingest meat and water, I think it's safe to say that White Hands has prepared herself for a night of excess.

I settle onto their mat without fanfare. "I have returned," I say by way of greeting, plopping myself down beside White Hands.

"Omoléh?" My former mentor offers me a tiny glass of clear liquid. "The aviax call it the breath of fire. Proper tipplers, those bird folk. Who knew."

"My thanks, but no," I say wryly, shaking my head. "I know better than to drink with you." I know better than to drink at all, only I don't say that, given White Hands's obvious enjoyment of the stuff. One of the many things she has taught me—in addition to how to lie with a straight face and take a death with honor—is not to voice my displeasure at the things other people enjoy. Instead I continue: "Besides, I've had more than enough of fire today."

"Your loss." White Hands takes a swig, then pounds her chest when the liquor goes down harshly. "It *is* like fire!" she exclaims, delighted.

She's in a rare mood, that much is clear.

This scene reminds me so much of the time I first saw her at the Warthu Bera that I feel almost nostalgic. The only things missing now are Braima and Masaima, but the equus are probably in one of Ilarong's many stables, overseeing preparations for the coming battles. Those two may seem like harmless, pretty fribbles, but they can be surprisingly intimidating commanders.

White Hands turns back to me. "I presume you were not able to retrieve your kelai."

"The jatu beat us there by about an hour," I say. "But you already knew that, didn't you?"

White Hands nods. "Sayuri's spies, are, once again, excellent at their craft," she says with no small amount of disappointment. Although, strangely, that disappointment doesn't seem directed toward me.

"You're not surprised I couldn't retrieve it," I say, swiftly understanding.

"They had about a day's head start over you and were on the ground quicker, not to mention they were probably empowered by the Idugu, who sent them there by door. The chances you'd catch up to them were slim."

I frown. "So why did you—"

"—agree to send you there?" She shrugs. "I had a dream."

Anok.

The hand of the dark goddess is all over this. But why did she want me to go in the first place if she knew that my kelai wouldn't be there? And why did she come only at the very end to warn me?

There's much to unravel there, but I return my attention to White Hands as she asks, "Well? How was it? What did it feel like?"

I don't have to inquire further to know that she means my kelai.

"Like coming home," I admit. "All this time, I've been so frightened of it, so frightened of what I'd become once I absorbed it. But now that I've felt it, I don't think I'll become—"

"—like them?" To my surprise, it's Sayuri who finishes my sentence. Her black eyes peer into mine as she says, "Tell me, Deka, do you believe you know what is best for humanity?"

Sayuri is always intense, but this sudden expression on her face is different.

It intimidates me, so I try to think as deeply as I can before answering. Finally, I shake my head. "No," I reply honestly. "I once thought I did, but now I'm not sure."

Every time I've tried to help, I've just made things worse, but perhaps that's the entire point. I keep trying to save people instead of helping them save themselves.

I shrug. "Everything that I am—the way that I see the world—it's been colored by my experiences, and most of them are bad. So I always expect things to be bad." I look down, sighing. "I may have what it takes to lead on the battlefield, and in dire situations. But to rule? To guide?" I look back up at Sayuri. "Even the fact that I think that's what gods do, instead of serving . . . I don't think I'm the right person for it. If I'm being honest, I'm probably the worst person for it."

So how can I become a god? As the thought suddenly assails me, another rises: Keita thanking me for preserving his family.

He believes in me, believes I can be a just god. So why do I never believe in myself?

I look up as Sayuri's gravelly voice speaks again. "Then that's where you're different from them," she says, quiet. "That's where you're different from all our supposed parents. You, at least, know what you lack."

And the gods of Otera don't.

Because that's the other thing I forgot in my self-doubt: the gods of Otera think they're all-powerful, that they're above the other beings in the empire—even the ones they birthed. I, at least, know I'm no better than anyone else. Different, yes, but not better.

It's a humbling thought.

I nod. "You are correct, Sayuri," I say. "I do know what I lack. Achingly so. But there's more that happened at the summer house, more I have to tell you. Both of you." I turn pointedly to White Hands when I say this.

"Oh?" My former mentor's pipe freezes close to her mouth in a dramatic fashion.

"I saw Anok there. She was hiding inside an indolo."

"As one does." White Hands inclines her head as if this is perfectly reasonable.

"The others didn't see," I continue. "They thought I'd fallen asleep, except I hadn't. I was talking to her."

"And what did our divine mother say?" This sneered bit of sarcasm comes from Sayuri, who, as always, is no admirer of the gods.

"She said she loves you. Both of you."

Sayuri falls silent, eyes rounding. These words, it seems, were unexpected.

As she processes them, I turn to White Hands. "She wanted you both to know that, and that you are perfect." By now White Hands's eyes are large, the largest I've ever seen them, and something like a sob emerges from her mouth.

She hurriedly looks down, but not before I see the tears shimmering in her eyes, tears I've never, ever before seen, not once, in all the time I've known her. I've seen so many of White Hands's faces—smug, hateful, conniving, even sad. But I've never seen such sheer joy. Because she has tears in her eyes not from despair; they're because she's happy—blissfully so.

I can only imagine the guilt White Hands has felt over leaving Anok in that temple, knowing that she—her true mother—had been imprisoned by her own sisters, and that we eventually will have to end her life. But she's always kept her feelings close to her chest and stayed the course, no matter how difficult it got. No matter how painful.

And now she's finally received proof that Anok isn't angered or saddened by her actions but that she is, in fact, proud.

As yet more tears stream down White Hands's cheeks, I look away, knowing she would not want me to stand witness to this moment of vulnerability any more than I already have.

Instead, I focus my gaze on Sayuri, who's now watching me intently, her eyes gleaming in the darkness. "There is one other thing," I say quietly. "Now that I've been in the presence of my kelai, I have an idea of how to find it."

"Oh?" Sayuri leans closer. "Do tell."

"Well," I whisper conspiratorially, "it has to do with the combat state. . . ."

31

❖ ❖ ❖

There's no better way to enter the combat state than in one of Ilarong's hot springs. The waters are warm, the night is cool, and stars twinkle above us. I can focus on them, let them lead me to the utmost serenity. That's what I need to accomplish the task I've set for myself now. I have to find my kelai, have to follow the trail it left to discern where the jatu took it. Before, I thought I needed Mother's body. But that was never necessary. All I truly needed was to feel my power, to understand the shape of it. To understand how very much a part of me it is.

All this time, the gods have been whittling away at it, parasitic leeches sucking at its teat. That's why I never truly understood what it was, never truly felt the thread that linked this body to it. But now I've felt it in its fullness. And now it's time for me to fight back—to beat the gods at their own game.

Before Okot comes to me, I'll go to him. I'll steal my power from right under his nose even as he's plotting to do the same to his brothers.

I remember now what he said to me: that he would relocate my kelai and then steal it out from under his brothers' noses. There's only one reason he would need to do that: all the Idugu were involved in moving my kelai from Gar Fatu. Okot alone would not have had the power to do what they did earlier today: slip all those groups of jatu into Gar Fatu and then extract the successful one well before Melanis and her hunters could catch them. Okot needed his brothers to move my kelai, and now they've hidden it somewhere near their temple. Somewhere in Hemaira, likely.

But Okot wants it all for himself. Needs it, so he can save Anok and himself.

But before he does so, I'll take back what is mine.

I let this thought waft away as I breathe slowly in and out. What I'm about to do requires relaxation. I can't hold on to my rage. I have to breathe and focus on the stars, letting their distant pulses soothe me, sink me into the combat state, the deepest version of it I've ever reached.

It takes some time, but I feel it when the world recedes, feel it when my friends and Ixa, who are all gathered on the stones surrounding the spring, fade into white shadows and then something more than that and yet less: they meld into infinity, becoming one with it. As do I. And then all that's left is myself and the universe, an entire vastness around me. The vastness I know is the Greater Divinity. How ludicrous that the Idugu would distill it into the farce of a pretender they called the Infinite Father.

The Greater Divinity washes over me in warm, calm waves, that feeling of peace that I still, until this very moment, did not trust. It's not a presence, per se. Not even an entity. More like an energy. A force. . . .

What are you? I ask into its vastness, curious.

But my words return to me. *What are you? What are you? What are you?* . . . Except I didn't say them. It wasn't my voice that echoed back. It was a thousand voices, reflected back at me. A thousand lives, all interconnected, all coiled into each other, inextricable. Or is it a million? A billion? Billions? Perhaps even more? I don't know any words that can count an amount greater than that number or manage to comprehend the sheer number of lives held in the vastness. Suddenly, the weight of all that connectedness is pressing down on me, and I'm feeling my body again, feeling the heaviness in my chest, like I can't even breathe, like I can't even—

Deka . . .

Mother's voice cuts through the noise.

When I turn, I finally see it shimmering there, the thread that connects me to her.

The thread that is celestial. Only it's not my kelai, not my divinity. It's her love for me. Eyes widening, I follow it, follow the golden maternal thread that shimmers across the night sky, a joyful, looping exuberance that urges me onward, teases me when I move too slowly, fall too far behind.

Deka! Deka! Mother's voice calls to me, so joyful and insistent, I have no choice but to follow. All across rivers, I follow. Towns, cities, deserts, rainforests—they all fall away under this chase until finally, I'm neck and neck with Mother's thread, only now I see it's not a thread but Mother's spirit itself, arcing joyfully across the night sky.

How are you here? I ask, circling her. Joining her in the wonder that is our dance.

I've always been here, she says. *I've always been everywhere. All around, in every pebble, in every tree, in every ocean, in every person. I've always been here.*

There's an echo to her voice now—a thousand echoes. The very same echoes that repeated my words earlier.

Just hearing them makes me stumble.

My joy fades as suspicion takes hold. And my eyes narrow. *You're not Mother,* I say. *Nor are you any of those people whose voices you're using. Who are you? Where are you leading me?*

Here! The answer comes joyfully as the Being That Is Not Mother stops and points at a familiar sight.

Oyomo's Eye. The grand palace. The one where I once prostrated myself before Gezo, then emperor of Otera. I stare at the hateful building, its once-proud golden turrets a bit duller now that most of the gold has been stripped away to fund the ever-growing battles that churn through the One Kingdom. Since the priests no longer have access to alaki and their endless supply of golden blood, they've fallen on desperate times.

I pull my eyes away from the palace to turn back to the Being. *What do you want?* I ask bluntly. *It was you that spoke to me earlier, was it not?*

Mother's edges seem to waver, a darkness pulling at them. But before I blink, her image is again as it was: golden and perfect. The Being smiles, a flashing of gold. *So suspicious, Deka. . . . But I suppose life has made you that way. Life in Otera is difficult. Life in this realm is difficult. That is the way of things. Come, I will show you what you seek.*

But I remain where I am. *I can find that by myself,* I say tersely. *And I was already well on my way before you intruded.* I glare at it. *Tell me what you want.*

What I want?

The Being wafts around me, that strange peacefulness and joy suffusing me every time it nears. But I refuse to give in to it, refuse to take the calm it offers.

People have offered me peace before. Yet more have offered me oblivion. All I ever got when I took either path was pain, deep and unrelenting.

This Being, whatever it is, won't fool me with its tricks. No matter how much it tries, I won't give in to it, won't yield to whatever it is that it wants.

It seems to understand my feelings, because its smile spreads wider, sadness tinging it now. *There is no I, Deka,* it says mournfully, as if hearing my thoughts. *There is only we. And what we want is balance, harmony. We seek to return the empire known as Otera to the natural order—*

The natural order . . . The words spur a realization. *It's you!* I gasp. *The Greater Divinity.*

My words seem to amuse the Being. *You, I . . . such limiting words. Often, we wonder if it is your flesh that constrains you so. In the realms where there aren't any corporeal forms, there seems to be a greater understanding. A greater connectedness.*

The Being nods to me. *Come, Deka, we will show you where you need to go.*

I shrug, glancing at Oyomo's Eye. *I already know where I need to go.* I can see it now, my kelai, shining as bright as a star from a darkened corner of the palace.

The sheer disrespect of it rankles me. The Idugu built themselves thrones, a temple that defies the constraints of time and space by being larger on the inside than it is out. But for my divinity—the one thing they hope will bring them to full power again—they built only a dark chamber and a black jewelry box with barely enough ornamentation to merit the name.

Then there is no harm in following, is there? When I turn back to the Being, it's smiling again, a look of gentle amusement on its face. *If you've already found what you seek, then what harm is there in accompanying us down to it?*

When I continue staring at it, it presses: *Humor us.*

Very well. I sigh as I follow it down into the palace, where it slips easily through the once-grand hallways, now also stripped of their gold accoutrements and decorations. None of the sleepy-seeming guards or priests bats an eye as we slip past the bedrooms for visiting dignitaries—now emptied of not only their expensive furnishings but the guests themselves—and then past the even smaller rooms for the servants.

Down, down, and down we go, following that brilliant golden light, until finally, we reach the very depths of the palace. That's where we stop, surrounded now by what looks to be a large chamber. But not just any chamber—an altar, the entirety of it centered on the tiny box cradled in the throne at the center of its gold-inlaid floor.

Even though I've seen the previous box that housed my kelai, this one is much tinier than I expected. It's about the size of my palm, and so plain, you wouldn't notice it if it weren't the focal point of the room. Instead of gold and gems, it's made once more of obsidian, but a dull, unpolished version nowhere near even the grandeur of the last box—not that the last box was in any way grand. Curled almost lovingly around it is Mother, her face almost precisely as it was in Maiwuri. Those plump, dark cheeks, now a little thinner from all her travails; that coily black hair, only it's now so long, it wreathes around her body, around the box itself, and even around the tiny tiled pool that encircles her, a barrier, almost, separating her and the box from the rest of the room.

And that's not all. Mother's been dressed in heavily embroidered robes of funeral white, and upon her head rests a crown, one that has four golden suns, no doubt to represent the Idugu's true identity as the creators and faces behind Oyomo, the sun god.

I float closer to Mother's corpse, reminding myself as I approach that it's all that is—a corpse, an empty vessel devoid of life, devoid of spirit despite everything the Idugu and their priests, no doubt, have done to keep it alive. Even with these warnings in mind, my heart suddenly begins to pound in my chest, responding to my rising despair. I reach out, but my fingers pass through Mother, an unwelcome reminder that I am incorporeal—a spirit instead of a body. Just like Mother.

And yet, my heart still beats with anguish.

The Being wafts closer to me. *They do have a sense of ceremony, don't they, the Idugu?* it asks, amused.

I whirl toward it, sadness swiftly replaced by rage. *Why?* I ask, *Why use Mother's appearance even now? Why bother confusing me so? It's cruel, especially now, especially here, in this place, when her body lies in front of us.*

The Being wafts closer, shaking its head. *Except, we are your mother, Deka,* it says. *We are all mothers, all fathers, all brothers, all sisters. We are all. We are you. Just as you are us. It is when the Gilded Ones and the Idugu lost this knowledge that they became them and only them. And if you follow that path, you too will fall to corruption.*

I'm so angered now, I abandon all pretense of politeness. *You speak in euphemisms,* I snap. *Why not speak plainly so I can under-stand you?*

We have been as plain as we can be, Deka. As the Being speaks, the voices inside it swell, almost thunderous now. *Hear us, and hear us well. We are all and yet nothing. We are and we are not. We are all contradictions, all paradoxes. . . .*

As they speak, a thousand images flash through my mind—universes unfurling, oceans dying only to be reborn, millions upon millions of children of all races and species, all of them connected by a singular golden thread, and yet all still somehow shining individually.

We are the golden thread that binds all things, the Being says. *We are the ultimate commonality. As are you.*

The entire time it speaks, those images flash, more and more of them barraging my mind. I hold my head, even though it's not physically there, dizzied by the onslaught.

Free your mind of its constraints, Deka, the Being intones. *This flesh you wear is not a prison, and neither is the world around you. They are all part and parcel of the same thing. As are you. Only when you understand this will you be the person you are meant to be. The god you are meant to be. Fail in this and Otera is lost. As are you. Forever.*

The chamber fades, as do the images, and just like that, the Being is gone. Suddenly, I'm back in the springs, my friends all waiting anxiously around me, as are White Hands and Sayuri, who lean forward, waiting for my verdict.

I nod. "It's in Oyomo's Eye," I say tiredly. "My kelai—that's where it is."

"Wonderful to know." I jolt upright, horrified, when a sinis-terly layered voice sounds in the distance. I look in its direction, to find Melanis there, clinging to the side of a peak like the bat-monkey she more and more resembles. Her eyes are glowing white, the truest indication that she's currently a vessel of the goddesses, which is the only way she could have entered Ilarong so stealthily without the aviax guards or White Hands and Sayuri spotting her immediately.

Her eyes shine eerily in the darkness as she continues: "Thank you so much for gifting us this knowledge. And for using your doors so haphazardly, despite the traitor Anok's warnings. We'll be seeing you soon, I imagine."

"Not if I have anything to do with it!" Britta snarls, gesturing.

Stone spikes shoot out of the peak Melanis was clinging to, but the goddess-possessed Firstborn's feet are as swift as her wings. She darts away before the spikes can pierce her, then whirls in the air in a dizzying evasive pattern as White Hands almost immediately sends a sword flying after her. Adwapa and Asha send a funnel of wind hurtling toward her, but she evades it as well, zigzagging so fast, it's like trying to pin a fly with a dagger.

Enraged, White Hands turns toward the city, where a loud cawing announces the arrival of the aviax guard. "Aviax of Ilarong!" she shouts. "Defend your city against this intruder!"

The horde of bird folk mass around Melanis, but she's agile as a zipperwing, one of those tiny, fleet songbirds. She easily evades them when they get too close, dancing in little circles around her pursuers. "I've been flying for far longer than your kind has been in existence," she sneers. "You're fools to think you have any hope of matching me in the air!"

More and more aviax swarm after her, but it's too late. She darts into the darkness, and just like that, she's gone. I don't have to search far to feel the telltale tingle of the door opening for her, the one the Gilded Ones have no doubt created to spirit her back to where she came from. "Until next time," comes her taunting cry.

And then there's silence. The door has completely disappeared, leaving no trace behind.

White Hands turns to me, her eyes deadly serious. "We need to move," she says. "We need to get to Hemaira before the Gilded Ones do, or our element of surprise will be lost."

I shake my head. "It's already lost. Melanis will be with them by now. And they'll already be preparing an army to storm Hemaira and take my kelai. You know this as well as I do."

White Hands nods. "You are correct . . . which is why we need to move fast." As I frown, she turns to Braima and Masaima, who are emerging from the path just beyond the hot springs, Karmoko Thandiwe at their side. "Is everything prepared? All the equipment and the troops?"

"Yes, Lady," the equus reply as one.

"Wonderful." White Hands then turns to the aviax monarchs, who are landing on the boulders surrounding the springs, the king's massive bulk struggling to fit on even the largest boulder. "The sign we've been waiting for has arrived," she tells them. "Summon your troops. We leave at first light. Tomorrow, we war for the soul of Otera."

32

◆ ◆ ◆

I'm already awake and dressed when the first faint ray of sunlight breaks over Ilarong's peaks the next morning. From the balcony of my room, I look out at battalions of aviax, their bodies covered in glittering silver armor, their talons capped by hard iron, and their wings thoroughly preened to allow them to cut faster through the air. Surrounding them are deathshrieks, multitudes as far as the eye can see. They spill over the city streets, an army so immense, Ilarong seems overwhelmed by their sheer numbers. They must have traveled all night to join the other armies already resting here and in the jungle below us. There are even alaki alongside them—jatu too. All allies White Hands collected while I was traveling to Gar Nasim, trying to find what sign I could of Mother and, by extension, my kelai.

When a familiar trumpeting sounds, I look down to find that there are even more troops in the flower-filled plain below Ilarong, many of them riding leathery gray mammuts, the colossal animals whose multiple ivory tusks and spiked tails can gore countless unlucky souls on the battlefield. How they made it all the way here, I don't know, and truthfully, I don't want to. I have enough on my mind already.

After all, I have a special task. While everyone else will be focused on fighting the armies of the gods, striking as deeply and ferociously as they can against our divine oppressors, I will be sneaking into Oyomo's Eye, using the battle as a distraction to keep the gods occupied while I steal my kelai from under their noses. It's the scheme that White Hands, Sayuri, Karmoko Thandiwe, and I came up with as we planned well into the night.

I return my attention to the plain, where the troops are now organizing themselves in formation. White Hands is already down there. I can see her now, Braima and Masaima beside her, as is General Prix, the brilliantly feathered high general of the aviax. Today, White Hands is wearing golden infernal armor instead of her usual white. It's a pointed statement. White Hands is not only an alaki, she is the first of the Firstborn, daughter of both the Gilded Ones and the Idugu. She may have once been spymaster to the emperors of Otera, but she has always bled gold, always empathized with the plight of those people and creatures who have been told they were less than, that they were abominations.

Even though she stands against the goddesses now, that much will never change.

She puts a horn from the scaly, bull-like toros to her mouth to amplify her voice. "Aviax of Ilarong and all other mountain realms," she says, acknowledging the masses of aviax still flying in, their silver armor glittering against the early morning sky.

"Equus, alaki, deathshrieks, jatu, humans—all our allies from far and wide! Today is finally the day we strike back against the gods!

"Countless centuries we have been oppressed by them, told we were lesser, inferior—bestial. We did not have the correct blood, the correct appearance, or whatever arbitrary quality it was they required. We were not true Oterans but a disgrace to the One Kingdom, a blight upon the realm. Today, however, we show them the truth: we are Oterans. We are every bit as valuable as the ones they call their chosen. No matter what their priests tell us, no matter what the gods declare, this is our empire as well."

I turn when a creak sounds, the door to the balcony opening behind me, revealing Britta in her signature golden infernal armor, which blends almost perfectly with the golden war mask she's donned. As is her preference, the gold in her helmet is mixed with traces of mine in case I use my voice and she needs protection from it, while the metal around her belly is doubly reinforced, to prevent a recurrence of what happened the last time she was on a battlefield with an army this large.

"Takes ye back, doesn't it?" she says as she makes her way to me. She nods down at White Hands, who is continuing her speech on the battlefield.

"All the way back to that very first battle," I agree. Then I sigh. "Strange to imagine that things are even more dire now than they were then."

"Things are always more dire," Britta says with a weary nod. "That's why we have each other." She extends her hand. "Me an' ye?"

"You and me," I reply, taking it.

360

"Until the end of time."

I smile, looking down at our clasped fingers. The gesture is so similar to ours on that very first day we entered the Warthu Bera, and yet we are so different now. Back then, we were frightened children. Now we are warriors.

I nudge her jokingly. "Until the end of time, are you certain of that?" I ask. "Because here I thought for certain you'd thrown me over for Li."

"An' wha about Keita?" Britta sniffs. "He's always just there. Even when we thought ye were about to get your kelai in Gar Fatu, he was there."

Even though she's trying to joke, I can hear the vein of hurt under her voice, so I nudge her again. "Well, Keita's a man," I say. "And while men may come and go, both of us . . ."

"We're forever," Britta says, finishing the promise we both began saying to each other when we were neophytes.

"Family," I conclude. "We're always family."

"Does that include me?" When I turn, Belcalis is standing there, a strange expression in her eyes. Uncertainty.

It's so unexpected coming from her, of all people, I almost don't reply. Then I nod, my smile growing. "Of course it does." I extend my other hand. "It's always been us three," I say, enfolding her in my embrace when she softens against me.

She nods. "It's just, you two are always so close, and I—" Again, there is that uncertainty, that doubt.

Today truly must be monumental if Belcalis is suffering an attack of nerves.

Britta grins at her. "Ye are who ye are, we've always known this. An' we've always loved ye because of it."

I nod my agreement. "You balance us."

Britta points at herself, then Belcalis, then me. "Strength, mind, heart. Together, we make the perfect person."

"Together, we might just survive this," I add.

"After all, we've survived so many things before . . . mostly," Britta says, a musing expression now taking hold. "Deka *has* been killed more times than I can count."

"Hey!" I say. "I've only been killed eleven, maybe twelve times. . . ." When Britta removes her hand from mine to start doubtfully counting on her fingers, I pull it back into my grasp. "And besides," I say optimistically, "*mostly* is good enough. *Mostly* will get us where we need to go."

"Now, what's all this? A love circle?" We all turn when the door opens again, letting in Adwapa, who has Mehrut and Asha by her side. "Don't you know we have a war to get to?"

"A war? What war?" Li pokes his head through the door, the other boys doing the same behind him. "Here I thought we were just wearing these for show." He saunters onto the balcony so we can take a look at his armor, which, like all the other boys', is made from pure gold.

Even more striking, it's been specially molded in the style particular to his region of the Far Eastern provinces.

Beside him, Acalan heaves a weary sigh, wiping a hand over his face. "Here we go again," he mutters. "You'd think the boy had never seen infernal armor before."

"Not made specifically for me, from gold that I bled from my very own veins," Li crows smugly.

Though the aviax smiths may not have Karmoko Calderis's flair for making armor that perfectly complements its wearer, they've come close enough, and each suit of armor fits the boy wearing it like a glove. Even better, they've incorporated my blood into each one. While I don't foresee using my voice, since by now the entirety of Otera knows that wearing the kaduth symbol can cancel out its effects, I always believe in preparing for any eventuality, no matter how slim.

"I look the very sight, the very portrait, of elegance," Li says, doing a twirl while Britta blows a kiss at him.

But I only have eyes for Keita. I walk up to where he's standing at the door, his armor gleaming in the shadows, a miniature sun in the darkness. It's so similar to mine, with scale-like edges that mimic the scales on my ebiki armor, my heart pangs just seeing it.

"Did you tell the smiths to do this?" I ask, tracing a scale.

He nods. "I wanted everyone who saw it to know we are a pair. Just in case . . ."

We fail. I silently fill in the words for him.

One thing about Keita: he's prepared for every eventuality too.

"We won't fail," I say. "We will destroy the gods, and then we'll deal with the consequences, come what may."

"Come what may," Keita repeats, pressing his forehead to mine. We stand there together, skin against skin, until the horn sounds and it's time to go.

◆

White Hands's troops are in perfect formation when I descend to her side. I do so while standing lightly on Ixa's back. It's a statement to all the soldiers who might have heard, as many have, that I'm wounded, that I can barely move of my own accord. This stance proves I'm anything but. I am strong, I am

363

agile, and I am in control. My friends are doing the same, standing on their gryphs as they fly in a V formation behind Ixa. To anyone watching, this must be an imposing sight, but that's the precise reason it's one of the first things the alaki generals taught us: Intimidate an enemy, and you might never have to fight them. Intimidate an ally, and they'll think twice before they become your enemy.

White Hands, Karmoko Thandiwe, and Lord Kamanda wait for us in front of the army. Lady Kamanda is nowhere to be seen, and at that, I am relieved. While I know the fierce noblewoman would undoubtedly cause havoc on the battlefield, she has two newborn children to look after, as well as two older ones. If everything does indeed end today, at least her children will be able to spend their last few moments in her arms.

I push back the thought by turning my gaze to White Hands. There's a look of approval, even pride, in her eyes as I gracefully dismount from Ixa and walk over to her, my friends by my side. Another way things have changed. Just a few years ago, I would not have dared to approach a creature like Ixa, much less ride it, and I certainly would never have merited White Hands's interest, much less her pride.

Now I can do both.

I kneel to show my respect before addressing her. Even though I am, theoretically, a god in waiting, White Hands is my elder and, more to the point, my friend. So, for this one last time, I will give her all the respect that is her due and ensure that everyone else does the same, even though I know no one is stupid enough to mistake White Hands for anything other than what she is: one of the greatest—if not the single greatest—military mind to have ever lived.

When she nods respectfully back, I rise, glance around at the troops. "What about the Hemairan troops?" I ask. White Hands has been communicating with them using her gauntlets, now that she knows all the gods are aware of our location anyway. "Are they prepared to receive us?"

"Indeed." White Hands nods. "The karmokos and Gazal"— our former bloodsister, now a regiment commander—"are already in place, and the rest of the troops are on their way."

"And the Army of the Goddesses?" I ask. "Has it arrived from Abeya yet?"

White Hands shakes her head. "Still nowhere to be seen, and it's the same with the forces of the Idugu."

"Odd," I remark, my thoughts stirring. If I knew armies were massing to invade my city, I would at least begin mobilizing.

But this, of course, is another trick of the gods. I don't know what reason they have for not showing their armies yet, but I'm not bothered by it. The gods aren't the only ones who have tricks up their sleeves, and they're certainly not the only ones who have hidden armies.

My friends and I have those as well, but the time for them has not yet arrived.

No, we'll save them for the perfect moment.

I return my full attention to White Hands as she answers, "Indeed. But both Abeya and Hemaira have been blocked from my gauntlets, so I know they're planning something. What it is precisely remains to be seen." That said, she peers down at me. "You prepared for this?" she asks, her tone pointed.

I inhale a firming breath before I reply. "More than I've ever been."

And it's the truth.

After everything I've experienced the last few weeks, everything I've learned, I'm the strongest I've ever been. Not physically, perhaps, but mentally and emotionally. Which is just as well, because I'm about to attempt a feat that veers on the impossible. A feat the goddesses always implied that only they could perform. But they were lying, as they did about so many things, and today is the day I'll prove them spectacularly wrong.

Britta's eyes are wide behind her war mask as she turns to me. "Ye certain of this, Deka?" she frets, unsure. She, White Hands, Keita, and Belcalis are the only people I've told what I'm planning, so she's been a mass of worry since last night. "Ye don't have to burden yerself. It would take us about two weeks, but we would reach Hemaira."

"And by then, it would be too late," I say, shaking my head. We already went over all this yesterday. "I at least have to try."

"I have faith in you, Deka." Keita's words are simple but full of reassurance, as is the comforting squeeze he gives my hand.

I can do this.

I inhale, sinking so deep into the combat state, I immediately feel the Greater Divinity surging up to meet me. And then I sink deeper, connecting not just part of the way, as I normally do, but completely this time.

The words the Being said to me the last time I saw it circle through my head. *There is no I. We are you. Just as you are us.*

If that's the case, then its power is my power, just as mine is its. That's why it's always felt so familiar to me; that's why it's always been so easy. If it is a part of everything, then I am as well.

Which means I can harness everything.

The moment I'm fully submerged in the Greater Divinity's power, I feel it, the rush inside me as all that energy fills up the emptiness in my body, the emptiness that was a marker of the time I had remaining. Oh, my body is still damaged, and it's still bound for extinction, but it's no longer as easy to break as it was.

I open my eyes, glorying in this newfound strength. Then I gesture, pulling at the edges of space.

Doors spring open across the plain, masses of them swiftly melding together, connecting, until they become one single, colossal door, a monolith that opens to the sands beyond it. I don't have to physically pull the edges of space for any of them; they just do as my will demands—as they always have, even though I never recognized it before. I never needed to gesture at all. I just needed this understanding, this knowledge.

As a roar of appreciation sounds from the troops, my eyes turn to the sands, where a camp has been set up to welcome us.

Tents covered in brilliant hues of purple and silver—colors we chose for the combined Oteran armies, since we did not want to adopt the white and gold of the goddesses nor the red of the Idugu stretch far as the eye can see. In front of them is what appears to be a small welcoming party. Thousands of alaki, jatu, human, and deathshriek soldiers stand at silent attention behind them, awaiting our arrival.

White Hands nods triumphantly at me before turning to the gigantic door and the soldiers waiting on this side of it. "Armies of the Angoro," she shouts. "Your leader, Deka, has cleared the path to Hemaira for you. No marching across forests and plains, no slogging through deserts. There Hemaira lies, ready for us to take it.

"And as you march, remember your purpose: you are here to free Otera from the tyranny of the gods, to protect your loved ones from being sacrificed to slake their monstrous hunger.

Take courage in that, and in the fact that you have Deka, the Angoro, slayer of the gods, by your side. Behold her power." White Hands points to the door once more. "Power to rival the gods'. Divine power you now have on your side. Hold this close to you as you ride into battle, not only for Otera but for yourselves, your families, your futures!"

As White Hands speaks, a sound slowly but steadily rises in the air: thousands of fists pounding against chests in unison. Soldiers pounding their fists for *me*.

Tears sting my eyes. I'm so overwhelmed now, I'm startled when a hand presses my shoulder. Britta's. "Do ye hear that, Deka?" she says. "They're cheering for ye. As am I."

The approval in her gaze and Keita's is echoed by White Hands, who nods at me before she pulls down her golden war mask, the signal that she's prepared to move out. As the army swiftly stands at attention, she lifts her sword and again points to the door. "Onward, Armies of the Angoro. Onward to Hemaira. Onward to victory."

33

◆ ◆ ◆

Gazal, the scarred commander who once, as a novice, oversaw our room at the Warthu Bera, is the first person I spot when the army finally comes to a stop. She's waiting with the welcome party, which consists of General Bussaba, the moon-faced general the Gilded Ones once assigned to the siege on Hemaira's walls; Karmokos Huon and Calderis, our former combat and weapons masters; and finally, a few other old alaki, jatu, human, and deathshriek commanders I recognize. How White Hands gathered such a coalition here in so short a time, I don't understand, but I marvel, nevertheless, at the scale of what she's built. There's a reason she and Sayuri were seen as indispensable to the goddesses in the earliest ages of the One Kingdom.

As the army marches to a stop, I glance around the soon-to-be-battlefield, taking in every detail of its bone-dry expanse, which stretches between us and what remains of Hemaira's primary gate. Before, it would have been filled by caravans of merchants and massive lines of travelers waiting to enter Hemaira to sell or buy their goods. Now the only thing that remains is the army and their tents. There's no sound, no movement—nothing at all. Not even in nature—not a single bird chirps, and I'd be hard-pressed to find any animal outside of the horses, mammuts, and zerizards that have been brought here by the army.

That means only one thing: the gods have something planned.

But then, so do we.

First to step forward from the welcoming party is Jeneba, once the forever-cheerful novice who oversaw Britta and my common bedroom in the Warthu Bera alongside her sweetheart, Gazal. Unlike the others, who are all wearing armor, she is clothed in simple blue robes. After we rescued her three months ago, she chose to stay at Gazal's side, not as a warrior but as a handmaiden. Like many of the alaki and jatu we've rescued over the past few years, Jeneba chose to give up the warrior's lifestyle now that she has a choice and to serve in other ways instead.

She kneels solemnly in front of our group, holding out a tray covered in tiny bronze cups. "Angoro Deka, General White Hands, General Prix, all other generals and dignitaries, we the Hemairan contingent welcome you. Please accept these glasses of water to soothe your throats and your weary bodies."

When White Hands looks pointedly at me, I step forward, take a cup from the tray, and down its contents, wiping my mouth so everyone can see I've completely ingested it. Then I nod to Jeneba, winking as I do so.

She winks back, her lips quirking in a smile. I turn to the army. "We are soothed," I shout ceremoniously.

As the others quickly do the same, I continue onward to the waiting dignitaries, happily embracing my old karmokos and accepting General Bussaba's firm but slightly tremulous grasp before I finally turn back to Karmoko Huon, the fiercely beautiful but frightening instructor responsible for breaking a multitude of my bones during her many combat practices.

"Why the water?" I whisper to her, glancing back at Jeneba, who is now offering cups to the last few generals.

"Ancient human ritual," Karmoko Huon whispers from behind the back of her hand. "In the olden times, it wasn't uncommon for allies to stab each other in the back on the battlefield. So, to prevent that, an ancient king invented the water ceremony. When allies gathered, they drank water together to symbolize their pure intentions. To betray an ally after drinking was from then on considered the highest sacrilege, and all parties who had drunk would be responsible for ensuring that justice was served." She shrugs. "Since humans make up part of this army, we decided to institute the ceremony again to put their hearts at peace."

"Their?" I remark pointedly. "You're human."

The karmoko flips her long black hair, which she's left unbound. "Have you seen me on the battlefield? I may not be an alaki, but—"

"You're a thousand times more frightening than even the best of them." To that much I can attest.

"Of course I am." Karmoko Huon smiles at me, humor in her eyes—a strange sight. Just two years ago, I was terrified of this woman. Now she is my friend.

"Tell me the truth, Deka," she says with a companionable nudge, "how likely are we to survive this?"

"Us or the world?"

"Both."

I ponder her question. "Half and half," I finally reply. "Either I become a god and slay the Oteran pantheons, or they slay me and cause such chaos that everything dies, ending the world as we know it."

"Frightening odds."

I shrug. "We've had worse."

She nods. "That we have. . . ."

I can tell she's thinking of our dramatic escape from the Warthu Bera three months ago, after she'd spent nearly an entire year being tortured by jatu soldiers.

I may have survived horrific things, but Karmoko Huon has as well. And she always manages to do so with her grace and flowery manner intact.

"And yet, here we still are." This humphed statement comes from one-eyed Karmoko Calderis, whose red-haired lover, the former jatu, Rustam, is waiting patiently just beyond the front lines. Like Jeneba, he's wearing blue.

As I nod to them both, a familiar whirring sound catches my ear. "Come along, Deka," Lord Kamanda calls grandly, a bevy of servants trailing behind his golden chair. "Battle plans do not finalize themselves."

I sigh. "Indeed, they do not," I say, turning to follow him. And then we make our way to the main tent, which has been set up for our arrival.

Like most of the tents in the camp, the ceiling has sheer panels the aviax can brush aside for easy entry and perches at varying intervals so the bird folk can rest, as well as assorted chairs for the more humanlike folk. There are no special concessions for the equus, who are, of course, used to standing. In the center of all this is a heavy wooden table, a map of Hemaira carved

372

into its center. This is where the generals will determine how to move their troops for the coming battle. This is where all the action will be planned.

Except right now, the tent is unoccupied, save for one person.

Gazal. I'm gratified to see that she is already half finished putting on the distinctive blue armor that's been created to resemble my own, down to the faint golden lines that mark the edge of the ebiki scales. It even has padding to transform Gazal's much slimmer body into a curvier version that's nearly identical to mine.

I marvel at this as I walk over to her. "Thank you for doing this," I say as she reaches for a golden war mask indistinguishable from the one I wore into the camp.

"Putting a target on my back?" Gazal humphs, slapping the mask over her face.

"Pretending to be me."

As my decoy, Gazal will lead the army into battle while my friends and I sneak into Hemaira to steal my kelai.

"As if it's so difficult." Gazal grunts. "All I have to do is fumble around, pretending to be oh so tortured, and everyone will assume I'm you."

"And there's that wit I missed so much," I mutter.

Gazal and I are what you would call reluctant allies. We don't particularly see eye to eye, but we have both a cause and friends in common, so we coexist. I have no doubt that if we were on opposite sides of a conflict, we would be the bitterest of rivals, as we once were in the Warthu Bera.

At my words, the side of Gazal's mouth quirks up, an expression so similar to Jeneba's, I almost laugh. So it is true what they say: lovers do start to resemble each other after a while. I can't help but wonder how this manifests with Keita and I.

I return my attention to Gazal as she replies, "Funny."

"What is?" I blink.

"You've finally developed a backbone."

"And you've stopped being such a miserable pissfart all the time."

Gazal blinks. "Pissfart?"

"It's a word. Britta made it up—I think." I frown, trying to remember if it was Britta or Adwapa who actually invented our group's favorite insult.

Gazal condescendingly pats my back. "Never stop being you, Deka," she says.

"You neither." When Gazal begins to head for the front of the tent, I stop her. "I mean it," I say. "Never stop being you."

Now the scarred novice stiffens, her eyes taking on that flat, emotionless cast I used to be so frightened of. "If this is a goodbye, I don't want it," she snaps, stepping closer so I can see the severity of her words. "I only want one thing from you: for you to finish your task and do it well. I don't care if you're the Nuru or the Angoro or whatever it is you're calling yourself these days. All I care is that you comport yourself as you were taught. You are an alaki of the Warthu Bera, and you will proceed accordingly."

As she speaks, she moves closer and closer until finally, we're nose to nose. "Conquer or die," she intones, the motto of the Warthu Bera. Not a dare or a challenge but an invocation—a call.

As close as I am to her now, I don't dare reject it. Or perhaps I don't want to. I want to be who she's asking me to be:

the person who conquers. So I give her the expected reply: "We who are dead salute you."

"You will ride to victory."

"Or I will come back to present you with my head."

As I stare up at her, body now tense, Gazal suddenly reaches out and places her hand on the back of my head. Then she presses her forehead against mine. "I have died millions of times," she whispers in my ear. "Countless years, drowning in that lake, then reviving, only to drown again. The way I passed the time was by counting and hoping. And you know what I hoped for, Deka?"

When I shake my head, she continues: "At first, I hoped for a savior. For someone to rescue me. But no one ever came, so I retreated into the fantasy that I would one day be the one to save others. Every day that I died, I would fantasize about it: rising from the water, becoming someone's hero. And I hoped that one day that person would look up at me and see not the damaged soul that I was but a person worthy of love. Worthy of being cherished the way my own family refused to cherish me.

"And then I met Jeneba, and I realized I didn't need to be her savior; I needed to be her lover." Gazal steps back, her brown eyes burning into mine. "I've only just started to love, Deka. Five hundred days, six hours, countless moments. That's how long I've loved her. And if this world ends, I will be grateful that I got the chance to love. That I got the chance, however fleeting, to be by Jeneba's side."

Gazal's hand tightens on the back of my neck. "But I don't want this world to end, Deka," she whispers. "I want to love Jeneba for countless more years, countless more hours, countless more moments. And that is my hope. I hope that you succeed.

Not just because I want the world to continue, but because I want to continue being by Jeneba's side, to continue this absolute happiness I have in knowing that I am loved, and that I love in return. So do not fail, Deka, because I do not want my love to end. And I know you don't either."

Gazal walks away before I can reply, but not before I see her brusquely wiping away the tears now threatening to spill. It's the first time I've ever seen her even close to tears, and the weight of that presses down on me, as do her words.

Do not fail, Deka.

I'll most certainly do everything I can not to.

I wait until Gazal has left the tent to throw on the plain blue cloak and matching mask I've brought for this occasion. Then I make my way toward the small purple tent at the very back of the war camp, where my friends have already stripped off their ostentatious golden armor to reveal the black stealth armor they've worn underneath it. Over the black garments, they drape the white robes White Hands has brought. As I can't remove Ayo's armor until I get my divinity back, I too don the robes, wrapping them carefully around me until I'm sure the armor is completely covered. The ten of us are meant to be merchants, the only people who still have some sort of free movement in the city. It may be the end of the world, but people still have to buy food, medicines, and other necessities, hence the reason we decided on these disguises.

White Hands glances from one person to the next. "You all know the plan—"

"Get into Hemaira, sneak into the Eye, and liberate Deka's kelai," Li says swiftly. "We've gone over it several thousand times."

White Hands' replying glare is cold enough to freeze lava.

"This is not the time for levity, young uruni. The fate of our empire and this realm itself rests in your hands. I hope you understand the weight of it. And if you do not, look to Deka." White Hands nods at me, and I still. "She's the one being called upon to sacrifice everything for you. Learn from her example."

Li looks from me down to the floor, ashamed. "My apologies."

But White Hands doesn't reply as she walks over to me. "Deka," she begins. And then she stops, her expression heavy. After all, what more is there to say? What else can we discuss that we haven't gone over already again and again to infinity?

As I look at her, tears burning in my eyes, White Hands suddenly does something very unexpected: she embraces me.

"Triumph, Deka," she whispers. "Triumph for all of us. And even if you don't—even if you can't—know that you carry our hearts with you. That you have always been our daughter, that you have always been our love."

There are multiple layers to White Hands's voice now, a familiar rumbling of power to them. When she finally releases me from her embrace, her eyes are entirely black—a familiar blackness I've seen before.

The Gilded Ones may have Anok imprisoned, but the ancient goddess, it seems, is a master at slipping from their grasp.

I walk forward, embrace her again. Embrace both of them, since I have the feeling I'm talking not just to the goddess but also the ancient alaki who is her first daughter. "I love you both too," I whisper in their ear. "And don't worry, Divine Mother," I say, using the honorific one last time, "I will do as you have asked. I will give you the eternal rest you seek."

"And you have my gratitude, and my blessings," White Hands says in a voice so layered, I know Anok has taken over completely now. "But also, my warning: My sisters will do any-thing to hold on to their power and their lives. Do not trust anything you see. And do not allow yourself to shine too brightly in the dark. If you are frightened or feel you cannot continue, look to the Greater Divinity. Look to the natural order. Always remember, we are all of us gods. And we are all of us unending."

A brief tremor jolts White Hands, and when I pull back, she's blinking as if she just woke. Which, of course, she just did. If there's one thing I know about interfacing with gods, espe-cially in such an intimate manner, it always corrupts your sense of time and being.

"What are we waiting for?" White Hands asks the moment she regains her composure. "Let us ride out. It's time for the as-sault on Hemaira to begin."

But as I nod at her, something niggles at the back of my mind—Anok's words. *Do not allow yourself to shine too brightly in the dark. . . .* What does that mean, precisely? The gods love speaking in riddles. I continue pondering this mystery as I walk out toward the army, which is saddled and ready for battle.

Only I'm not joining the front lines. I'll be in the back, with my friends.

I wait until Kweku wheels around a large supply cart, our gryphs and Ixa—now in a fine mimicry of gryph form—attached to the reins. As the commanders shout out their instructions, my friends and I slip behind the cavalry and take our place in the line of carts and wagons that bring up the rear.

As long as we remain among the rest, no one will notice us as we follow the cavalry into the city. And then, once there, we'll separate from the main force and use our gryphs to sneak to Oyomo's Eye while everyone is focused on the battle.

It's a good enough plan, well thought out. Which of course means there are sure to be complications.

I only have to look at Hemaira's walls to know it.

When I first came to Hemaira just over two years ago, I was in awe of those walls. There they were, stretching nearly up to the sky, the tallest things I'd ever seen. Then I freed the War-thu Bera and battled the Idugu the same night. The walls suffered heavily from my actions. Ancient stones tumbled, cracks appeared in their sides. But despite all that, they remained standing.

There's never been a weapon large enough to break them, never been a force overwhelming enough to tear them down. They are, in many ways, a symbol of Otera itself.

So why are the battlements empty?

I shade my eyes against the glare of the afternoon sun as I peer at them, the tallest points on Hemaira's walls. No soldiers stroll their lengths today—not even a priest or two to shout imprecations at us. There's simply no one there. It's just like this plain, with all its missing animals, and the silence and stillness of it all.

There's a strange lull in the air, a foreboding. It becomes even more heightened when White Hands, Gazal at her side, calls for the army to stop in front of the walls.

"It's so quiet," Adwapa whispers, watching them. "I don't like it."

Her sister nods beside her. "Doesn't feel right. None of this feels right."

"They're about to hit us with something big," Adwapa says, disgruntled.

Her words make my muscles tense. Adwapa and her sister are the oldest in our group—three hundred years or so, while the rest of us range from seventeen to twenty. And they've spent much of that time in White Hands's employ as her spies.

Despite their jokey tendencies, their instincts are generally sharper than most.

"We just have to gird ourselves, then," I say grimly, watching the scene in front of me.

Both White Hands and Gazal have now dismounted and are walking up to the walls, blades in hand and nothing else—not even shields.

For a moment, I tense, expecting a volley of spears to come hurtling their way. That's what the jatu have done every other time an enemy has approached Hemaira's walls.

But the battlements remain completely silent.

"Well, this is beginning to get worrisome," Adwapa says, swiftly checking her blades.

"I'd venture it's almost time to go in, then," Asha says, eyes narrowed as she regards the wall. "It's live forever, everyone," she says, another of our battle cries.

"And in victory," I add with a nod.

"That too, once we get through the wall," Li says.

I glance up. "Not to worry," I say, turning back to the primary gate, where White Hands is now taking off her gauntlets to reveal her small, brown hands. "White Hands has this."

After all, this is the reason I awakened her gift in Abeya during our confrontation with the goddesses; the reason I unlocked an ability so feared, it was considered unspeakable in ancient times.

White Hands kneels in front of the wall, presses her fingers to it. I can't hear the words she says when her lips move, but I know them. I heard her say them just once before, saw their power when she turned them on the deathshrieks calling out for mercy from under the Chamber of the Goddesses in Abeya.

"To dust," White Hands commands, pushing the wall.

For a moment, there's silence.

Then, a gigantic crack.

Just like that, the walls of Hemaira begin tumbling down.

34

For a moment, everyone is silent, watchful as the walls of He-maira crumble, the ancient monoliths collapsing on themselves with a deep, primal groan that seems to echo up from the dark-est pits of the Afterlands.

Then common sense sets in.

Curses sound as soldiers abandon their positions, humans and alaki running for cover, aviax taking to the air. Just one of the walls' massive stones is enough to wipe out an entire unit. Except, when the stones finally land, they don't explode against the ground as everyone expects. I watch, eyes wide with wonder, as they puff into what seems like clouds each time they make impact, cascading over the fleeing soldiers as softly as feathers over grass.

One astonished soldier blinks as his entire body is pasted white with the substance. Then he tastes it. "It's ash!" he says, shocked. He whirls around, relieved. "It's ash! It's ash!"

The call echoes across the battlefield, the excited soldiers repeating the wonder and devastation that is White Hands's gift. "She turned the walls of Hemaira to ash!"

The mood is so infectious, even my friends are affected, Britta reaching over to embrace me excitedly. "Did ye see, Deka?" she gasps. "Did ye see wha she did?"

But I don't reply. Because now that the walls are down, I see what they were hiding. What we never noticed in all this time we've been watching the city. Five gigantic figures, each so enormous, their bodies seem to encompass the city itself. They stand on opposite sides of Hemaira, three of them male, two of them female. Darkness emanates from them, a monstrous cloud covering the city. No one notices them but me, not even as they stand there, entire universes swirling inside those massive bodies, armies of gold and red clashing at their feet.

Katya gapes at the battle inside the wall, her eyes round behind her war mask.

"The divine armies," she gasps. "They're already there. How did we not hear them?" They're a deafening roar now, the sound of metal clanging, men, women, and deathshrieks screaming as they engage in mortal combat.

The Gilded Ones and the Idugu may be fighting, but it seems it's their armies that are enacting the actual battle.

"The gods," I say hoarsely. "They're there with them. Both the Gilded Ones and the Idugu."

"What?" Rian seems startled as he asks this question. While he didn't go with us to Gar Fatu, he's here now, at Katya's side. "What do you mean, they're there?"

I don't answer. I can't, because now I'm seeing something else: vale gates—hundreds of them, perhaps even thousands— forming across Hemaira's streets. I watch as the clouds of iridescent mist grow bigger and bigger, those tendrils expanding, those dark centers opening. Strangely, they all seem similar, like they're part of one vast, interconnected web.

But I'm the only one who can see them, that much is apparent. The others don't seem to be reacting to them, which means this is just like it was in Gar Nasim: I'm the only one who has any sense of the danger.

Horror rises in me as I watch the vale gates open. "We have to warn White Hands!" I cry. "We have to warn the army. This will be a massacre."

Britta grabs my hands. "Deka, slow down, wha do ye mean? Wha are ye seein'?" Her eyes search the streets as if trying to see what it is that has me so terrified.

I point at the city, the one that will very soon become a killing ground unlike any I or anyone else has ever seen before. Worse, the armies there are unaware. They think they're fighting against each other on their gods' behalf, but that's not all they're there for. "The gods are here, and they've brought the shadow vales. If our forces advance now, they'll be food for both the Idugu and the Gilded Ones."

It's a meal that will bring them all the power they seek and more. Power enough to destroy Otera—to destroy the entire world if they wish. And White Hands and I brought it right to their door.

The horror of it rouses me from my stupor, and I jerk upright, preparing myself. As both White Hands and Gazal bring down their swords, commanding the army to go onward, I submerge into the combat state so completely, the entire army resembles an ocean of white, their souls all gathered in front of me. I can feel the Greater Divinity reaching for me, extending me its power. I embrace the feeling as I shout out the one word now swelling up inside me.

"STOP!" I command, my voice shattering the din.

I don't care if I'm giving myself away and scuttling our well-laid plans. Our plans will come to nothing if the slaughter I anticipate happens—if everyone here is killed in the shadow vales of the gods.

"THERE IS DANGER IN HEMAIRA!" I continue shouting as every alaki and jatu, every deathshriek, immediately stops in their tracks—the children of the gods all helpless before the power of my voice. "THE CITY IS FILLED WITH SHADOW VALES! RETREAT OR YOU WILL FALL PREY TO THEM!"

That's all I manage to say before I feel it, the emptiness rising inside of me again. Even with the ebiki armor and the Greater Divinity, this body is still on its last legs, still edging closer and closer to disaster. And what I just did has just pushed it a little more.

The moment I slump, gasping for breath, White Hands turns to Gazal, who swiftly gestures to the army, pretending it was she who spoke. Given that she's still wearing her war mask, it's an easy enough pretense.

But the army is not who I'm worried about fooling. The gods are still standing there, silent, invisible monoliths. I can only hope they're so engrossed in their strange, motionless battle against each other, they don't notice that it was me who actually spoke.

When none of them move so much as a muscle, I watch,

relieved, as White Hands and Gazal take charge of the retreat. "FALL BACK!" White Hands calls, motioning to the army. "DO AS THE ANGORO COMMANDS!"

The pair backtrack, their footsteps pounding through the mounds of ash, until a lone scream rises above the din of the warring armies. It's so filled with terror, I jerk toward it, my eyes lighting on the grand market nearest to what used to be the main gate. Half the stalls are gone now, all their precious spices and fabrics scattered across the ground. In their place instead is a strange, terrifying darkness. It covers a mass of what appear to be tiny, insect-like winged creatures, all of them swarming over a single merchant—the person who screamed loud enough to make himself heard over actual armies.

I watch, gorge rising in my throat, as the insects peel the flesh and muscle from his body, the process so fast, his scream ends almost as abruptly as it starts, an aborted, gurgling sound all the more frightening for its brevity.

I gulp, turning to the others. "You see that, right?"

On the other side of me, Keita nods, his eyes grim. "Now I know what those flapping sounds were—the ones we heard in the very first shadow vale."

I shudder, realizing how lucky we were that we got the gigantic vale wraiths instead. But it's clear that when we enter Hemaira, that luck may no longer hold. Vales are opening all across the city now, areas of darkness enveloping the light, entire houses and buildings suddenly covered in black or red sand and tentacles. Yet more terrified screams sound, but they're as abrupt as the merchant's. Soldier or civilian, it doesn't matter—wherever the vales appear, deaths swiftly follows.

Our entire army is silent now, everyone watching in horror.

"Wha do we do?" Britta asks.

"We can't enter the city with those vales opening all over the place," Li says.

"Except we have to." This quiet reminder comes from Belcalis. "Remember what the Maiwurians said: the vales are the first sign of the world's collapse. And now they're opening all across Hemaira. We need to get Deka's kelai and swiftly, before the gods become too swollen with power."

"Not to mention, we need to help all the people still trapped in the city." Sighs rise as I point out this unwelcome fact. Three months ago, when we rescued our sisters from the Warthu Bera, we also led a larger escape, allowing people who didn't want to be in Hemaira safe passage out of the city. But not everybody was able to leave. And worse, not everybody wanted to.

And now we have to help them.

When everyone turns to me, shaking their heads, I continue: "There are still innocents in Hemaira, people who aren't soldiers for either army."

"But they chose to stay," Adwapa humphs, "so as far as I'm concerned, that's not my issue."

"Not even the children?" Katya asks—not so much a question as a silent condemnation. Her eyes pierce into Adwapa's until finally, the older girl blinks.

"Infinity take me, I hate having a conscience," she growls.

"But you *do* have one, and so do we all," I reply.

"Which is why, as I said before, we have to hurry," Belcalis continues. "The longer the wait, the longer this escalates and the more innocent people die."

But even as she says this, a roar sounds from the front of the army. I turn to find Gazal pointing toward the city with her atikas. I can't hear what she's saying, but I see the results: three contingents of aviax head into the city. Only they're not flying toward the two clashing armies; they're headed for the vales and the people caught inside them.

When Gazal turns to me and gives me a brief nod, my heart lifts. "She's saving them!"

"Just as you would do," Keita says with a nod. "Gazal really is the perfect decoy. She understands precisely how you would behave and—"

"Deeeekaaaaa . . ." My entire body tenses when a familiar voice sings out my name. As I turn, every muscle even more tense than before, a bat-like figure explodes out of the city, easily soaring over the shadow vale now developing over what remains of the wall's foundations, to plant itself in the middle of the battlefield.

"DEEEEKAAAA . . . ," Melanis continues calling out, head swiveling as she searches through the gathered army. "I KNOW YOU'RE HERE. . . ."

At the front of the army, Gazal swiftly unsheathes the double atikas that have been carefully crafted to resemble mine and approaches the Firstborn. But Melanis doesn't even spare her a glance. She darts over the army, easily evading the aviax who quickly give chase. I gasp when she finally comes into full view. The winged Firstborn has completely transformed, her face and body now so gaunt, they might as well just be flesh and bone, her eye sockets sealed over with eerie pink skin.

But how is she maneuvering without being able to see?

"COME OUT, DEKA!" Melanis shouts, briefly stopping to slice her claws through the belly of one of the pursuing aviax.

When he falls with an agonized shriek, Melanis flits down to dig her clawed fingers into the wound. She pulls out the aviax's entrails triumphantly, shaking them at the gathered army. "Come out, Deka, or I'll be forced to make such a splash, the sand will turn permanently red."

By now, I'm gritting my teeth so hard, I'm almost certain I've cracked them. Melanis isn't exaggerating when she says she'll turn the sand red. She fully intends to keep killing soldiers one by one until she forces my hand.

Even as I think this, she turns in my direction, a dark smile slicing her lips. "Found you!" she says, hurtling toward me, claws outstretched.

I unsheathe my atikas, shaken. How does she know it's me? She isn't even using her eyes anymore. It's like she can find me even in complete darkness, and—

My eyes widen, Anok's last few words suddenly washing over me: *Do not allow yourself to shine too brightly in the dark.* . . . So that's what she meant. Melanis isn't searching for me by sight anymore—she's using the combat state. She can literally see me in the dark!

Britta turns in my direction. "Wha do we do, Deka? Wha do we do?"

I look at Melanis, who's still darting around, those sightless eyes no doubt combing over the thousands of glowing souls on this battlefield to find me on behalf of her goddesses. But I'm wise to her tactics now. Just as I'm wiser to the gods'—after all, it's they who taught her what to do. How to locate me. I inhale back into the combat state, and then I sit there, looking at myself for the first time—at my hands, feet, and all the parts of me I can see.

I haven't done so since I used to watch myself in the lake

when White Hands trained me. That's why I never realized—I glow a brilliant, almost blinding gold. A color much brighter than anyone else around me.

Why did I never notice it before? I shine brightly enough to pick out from a distance. No wonder the gods and their minions kept finding me. *I shine brightly in the dark!*

But not for long.

I glance down at my hands again, already imagining their brightness dimming, growing just as weak as everyone else's is around me. To my relief, they quickly do as I desire, their light growing fainter and fainter, until soon, they're indistinguishable from those of my friends.

I'm just a part of the crowd now. Indistinguishable from it. The gods themselves couldn't find me—nor can Melanis. To ensure this, I leap from the wagon.

"Everyone, scatter and regroup in ten."

I don't wait for their reply as I slip into the crowd, making several rounds until soon, I don't even see the wagon anymore.

It doesn't take long before Melanis is well and truly confused. I follow her path as she flies across the battlefield, maliciously ripping down aviax midflight. Her voice is even more high-pitched as she calls out to me, but I'm just another faceless figure in the crowd now. She's well and truly blinded. Which is why, no doubt, she doesn't notice White Hands mounting a gryph behind her, or Sayuri plucking a spear from a nearby soldier.

As they approach behind her, I nod grimly. Melanis is no longer my problem. Her sisters will take care of her. I double back to the wagon, where the others have gathered again, their gryphs already saddled.

"Deka?" Britta asks, confused.

"White Hands and Sayuri will deal with Melanis," I explain. "And the gods can't track me anymore. It's time for us to do what we came here to do."

I silently thank Anok again as I mount Ixa, who's been patiently waiting. *Get ready, Ixa,* I say. *We're going into the city. And absolutely no stopping until we make it into the palace.*

Deka. He nods, excited.

I turn to my friends. "It'll be chaos in there, so stay close. I'll lead you as safely as I can around the shadow vales, but you have to be prepared for anything. I don't know what the gods are doing, but I do know this: whatever it is, it doesn't bode well for us."

"It never does, does it," Katya tsks.

"No," I reply. "But we'll do what we always do: we'll triumph."

I nudge Ixa onward.

We enter the city within minutes, evading the aviax whizzing to and fro as they rescue the people caught by the vale wraiths as well as the vales themselves, which are a much more difficult proposition. They're constantly opening in the most unexpected places. Even then, I manage to maneuver past them. All I have to do is watch where the vales' tendrils are expanding and then steer my friends clear.

What's not as easy to avoid is the divine armies. Tens of thousands of alaki, jatu, and deathshrieks are massed in the streets, most of them in varying levels of panic or fear. Where minutes before they were busy destroying each other, they're now singularly focused on avoiding the vales, which thrum around them with malicious energy, their darkness covering the entire city now.

The gods, it seems, have abandoned all pretense of protecting their children. Instead, they're letting the vales devour them all in a mad rush to snatch as many lives as they can.

I watch, horrified, as a Forsworn, one of those massive purple deathshrieks devoted to the Idugu, is dragged into a river by a slithering, serpentine vale wraith. He roars and shrieks, but the creature pulls him down with the same ease a child would a doll.

"Sooo, we're not using the river, then, correct?" Kweku shouts beside me.

"Never!" I shout, shaking my head, but as I turn toward him, he suddenly goes flying into a market stall, courtesy of a deathshriek's hammer. "KWEKU!" I turn back, but Ixa continues onward, not obeying my gestures.

Ixa no pause, he says determinedly, repeating the instruction I gave him earlier: no stopping till we reach the palace.

"I'VE GOT HIM!" I breathe a sigh of relief as Asha shouts this from somewhere behind me, grunts sounding as she lights into the offending deathshriek. I'd almost forgotten that I wasn't alone here. That my friends don't just have me; they have each other.

I just have to trust that they can handle whatever comes their way.

I continue on as Oyomo's Eye rises in the distance. The former imperial palace is so close now, I can almost touch it. Tentacles reach for me, and I slice them away. One of those serpentine wraiths lunges out of a well to snap at Acalan, but he ducks so quickly, it goes crashing into a wall. Everything is a whirl of motion now, the chaos and sheer desperation of it all propelling us onward.

Then we're finally there, at the very edges of Oyomo's Eye, the palace's once luxurious gardens rising above us. Ixa stops even before I call a halt, evidently having sensed the exact same thing I have.

"What? What is it, Deka?" Keita asks as he pulls his gryph to a stop beside me. The others quickly do the same, but I don't reply. I can't, especially not given what I'm seeing.

I had wondered why the Idugu were silent. Why they weren't moving even though the Gilded Ones had invaded their territory. I'd even assumed that they must be locked in some kind of silent combat with the goddesses.

But the vales opening all across Hemaira—none of them belong to the Idugu. I should have known that the moment I felt the connection between all those vales—that connection I likened to a giant spiderweb spreading from a singular source when I first saw it. The Gilded Ones are the gods desperately gorging on Hemairans as though the city is a buffet and this is their last feast. They're the ones killing Hemairans indiscriminately.

The Idugu didn't open any vale gates in the city, because theirs are all *here*. Thousands of them, shimmering invisibly around the palace. Hidden. In fact, if I hadn't been in two of the Idugu's vales before—felt the oiliness that accompanies the male gods' presence—I would never have even known they were there.

The goddesses' vales, I now realize, are ham-handed works of brutality. But the Idugu's are masterworks. Delicate, ephemeral creations nearly invisible to even the divine eye. A silken lattice protecting their most important possession: my kelai.

And I can't use any doors to get past them without alerting the Idugu to my presence.

I turn to Keita, my eyes wide. "The entrance to the Eye is covered with the Idugu's vale gates. There's no way we can get through. We're stuck."

35

◆ ◆ ◆

"All right, let's think this through rationally."

After what feels like hours of staring at the vale gates but is actually just moments, Li breaks the silence with this optimistic pronouncement. Except he doesn't see what I'm seeing. And what I see is horrific. Each vale gate is the size of a person and has tendrils that wriggle periodically, as if seeking intruders. Even worse, there's a feeling emanating from them—a consciousness, almost. These aren't the mindless vale gates I've seen before, the ones that just open haphazardly. These were made with a specific purpose in mind: trapping anyone who dares approach them. And by anyone, I mean my friends and me.

"Rationally?" I whirl to Li, my frustration bubbling up. Then I point at the feelers at the edges of one gate—the tendrils he, undoubtedly, can't see. "The moment you near any one of these things, they snap you up, and just like that, the Idugu have you forever."

"But there's only one layer of gates, yes?" Keita has that

thoughtful look in his eyes as he approaches me, only I'm now so frustrated, my reply comes in another growl.

"Yes, Keita, one layer. These things are prisons. They're waiting for someone to come so they can trap them."

"Good to know," he says, abruptly wheeling his gryph around. "I'll return shortly."

As I watch, confused, he flies a short distance down a hill, then grabs a jatu who is using a terrified woman as a shield against a small reptilian vale wraith. He gestures, swiftly burning the wraith to a crisp, then points the terrified woman to safety before flying back up the hill with the jatu struggling against his grip.

Once he reaches us, he turns back to me, ignoring the jatu, who is now shouting all sorts of foul words.

"How far away are those gates?" he asks me calmly, all the while keeping a firm grip on the struggling, enraged jatu.

"Just beyond the river," I say, pointing to the boundary of water that marks the farthest edge of the palace grounds.

"Perfect," Keita says, tugging his gryph upward. He flies as near to the palace as he can, and then, when I call out a panicked "HALT!", tosses the man clear across the river. "Off you go!" he grunts, wiping his hands clean.

And then he waits.

The moment the screaming man touches the air on the other side, the gates awaken, tendrils shooting forward. Within seconds, the man's screams have turned to ugly, gutteral sounds as at least three or four gates snap him into quarters, their tendrils swallowing as much of him as they can before they disappear, leaving only open air in their wake.

"Brutal," Adwapa whispers.

I turn to Keita, who is now returning from the river, his expression as unruffled as ever. "Well?" he asks, nodding at the vale gates. "Any of them gone? You did say they were prisons. Single-use, I imagine."

I nod as I rush over to kiss him. "Oh, Keita, you're a genius! At least three of them are gone!"

He shrugs modestly. "An education in savagery does have its benefits." He glances back at the space just beyond the river. "So, was it enough for a path?"

I look at the air. Three gates may have disappeared, but that's barely enough space for Belcalis, the smallest-statured among us, to slip through. "Perhaps three or more people," I reply after some thought.

Before I even finish speaking, Britta and Belcalis are darting off, as are Li and Kweku.

"I'm getting the most people!" Li excitedly declares, heading toward the most brutal combatants in the area: the ones who use innocents as shields.

Britta turns back to wave at us. "Just be sure to tell us if we're near any gates!" she shouts as the others look on in exasperation at her excitement.

The twins, Acalan, Katya, and Rian have no interest in this game, that much is evident.

Still, Britta and the others will make a path in no time, and it's a relief. The space between the gates is already closing again, those tendrils stretching to repair the hole left behind. Which, of course, explains why the Idugu are so tired, they can't move now: they not only have to communicate with their armies, but they also have to repair whatever traps they've littered around the palace. I'm certain they have much more than just these gates lying in wait for us.

"Hurry!" I call to my friends. "The path we already cleared is closing."

"Comin'!" Britta says, excitedly riding back with a struggling deathshriek in hand.

It takes only a few minutes for the path through the gates to be cleared to my satisfaction, and the moment it is, I urge my friends onward. "Move, move!" I shout. "We don't know how long we have before the Idugu realize we weren't actually captured by the gates."

"Not to mention the Gilded Ones." I turn as Belcalis adds this under her voice to me: "If all those vales in the city are theirs, it won't be long before they're powerful enough to breach this place."

The thought is enough to spur my panic. "Go, go, GO!" I urge, slipping through the opening, my friends behind me.

Katya and Rian are the very last to enter, and Rian has to be the luckiest soul I ever met, because he manages to scrape through just moments before the nearest tendril comes lashing out. Just like that, we're on the palace grounds, a different world from the one across the river.

When my friends and I were still at the Warthu Bera, we visited Oyomo's Eye at Emperor Gezo's behest. At the time, I thought the imperial palace was the grandest place I'd ever seen, its halls awash with gold and light, its gardens lush and verdant, all sorts of exotic trees and animals flourishing in luxurious abandon.

That was two years ago.

Now those vibrant gardens are graveyards—the lush green grass a decayed brown, the delicate fruit trees withered stems, and the beautiful animals eerie white skeletons in the dirt. I shudder as I glimpse what appear to be the skeletons of a family of nuk-nuks, huddled together in their last moments. Somehow, the sight unnerves me even more than the vale gates did.

"What happened here?" Katya asks, eyes wide.

Kweku shakes his head mournfully at her. "Sacrifice, that's what it always is."

The entrance to the palace is somehow even worse than the gardens, the air a strange, slithering cold that chills me all the way down to my bones. And I haven't even walked through the door yet.

Where are all the people I saw when I was here last night with the Being? Where are all the priests, the guards—where is everyone? Foreboding pricks me when I think of what could have happened to them, how the Idugu could have powered the gates we just left in our wake.

"It's so strange," Britta says as she slides off her gryph and glances around. "It's like everything is dead here—even the wind."

"Divine trickery, no doubt," Acalan mutters, his lips a grim line.

I nod in commiseration, sinking back into the combat state. "Everyone keep your eyes open. There'll be more traps."

Just like the gardens outside, the hallways are empty when we walk through them. They look exactly as they did the previous night, the walls stripped of their decorations, the floor missing its valuable tiles. Worst of all is the sound—or, rather, the lack of it. When my friends and I came here during our time at the Warthu Bera, the palace was filled with noise, courtiers scurrying to and fro, the jatu patrolling, the air echoing with the sound of their footsteps. Now there's nothing—merely a desolate, echoing emptiness.

"This is a trap," Britta says nervously, blue eyes scanning our surroundings. "I can feel it in me bones."

"Well, hopefully your bones will inform us exactly what the nature of the trap is," Belcalis says archly, the way she always does when stressed.

"Keep going," I say, moving steadfastly onward. "My kelai is down that way." I can feel it now—have felt it since the moment I walked through the hole in the gates.

The thought fills me with nerves.

I force myself to focus on the path ahead of me, each footstep a death knell leading to the executioner's final blow. This is it, the moment I take my kelai or die in the attempt. Either way, my journey with my friends ends here. As I inhale, tears suddenly stinging my eyes, Britta stops and glances at me. "Ye all right, Deka?" she whispers.

I just blink at her, my vision blurred. "I—I—" I begin, but I stop when a calming hand intertwines with mine.

"Yer all right," Britta says gently. "I'm here with ye."

"Me too." These words come from Keita, who takes my other hand.

And together, both of them, the pillars of my life, walk me slowly and surely to my destiny.

❖

It's almost a shock that we encounter no more traps as we descend to the lower levels of Oyomo's Eye, which are every bit as cold and dark as the rest of the palace. I keep glancing about, trying to see if a vale wraith or another such monster will emerge, but nothing else appears. There's only that ominous cold and that chilling silence. It's so constant that, for just a moment, I'm almost lulled into complacency.

Then we turn the corner and see the group of jatu and Forsworn deathshrieks waiting there in gleaming red armor, all of them surrounding a heavily armored leader whose milky-white eyes I recognize even before I feel the oiliness that pours off him in waves.

"Afternoon greetings, Deka," the Idugu say, although I'm not certain if it's all or one of them that's currently inhabiting the massive jatu.

"Idugu," I reply, annoyed.

Of course the gods would be here, in the hall outside the chamber. Of course they'd be waiting while I made my way here, doing everything I could to avoid their attention. I only wonder why they didn't wait until I was in the chamber itself, where I would have less of a chance to escape.

"Okot," the god corrects, tapping his atika against his thigh. "Only Okot."

"Your brothers aren't here?" I ask the question carefully as I unsheathe my atikas, preparing for the conflict ahead.

"My brothers are busy maintaining the vales and leading our armies. They left me here to sound the alarm once you arrived."

"And will you?"

The last time I saw Okot, he was intent on betraying his brothers and taking my power for himself. That certainly would not have changed since I last saw him.

"No," Okot says plainly.

401

And then he moves.

All I see is a flash, and then the jatu and deathshrieks around Okot have all been beheaded, blood and gold spurting from their now fully severed necks. I swiftly lift up my atikas, ready to engage, but to my shock, Okot steps to the side, gesturing for me to continue on.

"Get into the chamber," he urges. "Hurry, Deka. My brothers will emerge here soon." Even as he says this, I feel it, the pressure in the air. The pressure of the gods coalescing into material form.

"GO NOW!" he shouts, gesturing.

My friends and I fly to the other end of the hall, where the chamber door lies open, as if waiting for us to go in.

"Wait, yer helping us?" This disbelieving query comes from Britta, who frowns as she rises, shock visible in her eyes.

Okot doesn't reply as he doubles over. He's resisting the pressure, resisting the other gods trying, even now, to emerge in the hallway. "My brothers are almost here," he grits out. "If you can get into the chamber, you will be safe from them. I've placed an arcane object inside—one that prevents doors. It'll keep them from storming in, as will the divine covenants placed upon the chamber. GO!" he roars again, those white eyes flashing, and once more I feel it, the pressure as the air reacts to his will.

My friends run into the chamber, startled by it, but I glance at Okot one last time, still at a loss. "Why?" I ask, stunned. "Why help me?"

By now the god is on his knees, his body buckling from the pressure of his brothers, whose roars of anger shake the hallway as they attempt to emerge. But he holds firm, looks up at me, his expression regretful. "Anok," he whispers. "She came to me. After all these centuries, she came back. Then she knelt before me in apology and showed me the truth of what she had become. What *I* had become."

He shakes his head, that regret seeming to fill his entire being now. "All those centuries of anger. Of hatred. I had forgotten we used to be one. One person. One god. But then she reminded me. Showed me the truth: both our pantheons are corrupted beyond saving . . . and we are doing the same to this realm. Anok and I, we choose to return to the Great Circle. Together. But only you can make that happen."

As I gape at Okot, the god who has seemed, for all these past months, my greatest adversary, he looks up at me again, determination in his eyes. "Reclaim what is yours, Deka. Become a god once more, and then sing the song of our pantheons' unmaking before we destroy Otera and the rest of the world with it."

36

◆ ◆ ◆

I slide into the chamber just as the gods emerge, but Britta is ready and slams the door behind me. Its wooden edges rattle as a deafening force throws itself against it: the Idugu attempting to get inside.

"Let us in," the gods' voices roar. "LET US IN!"

But the door holds fast.

It's as Okot said: there's an arcane object in here that repels the gods and prevents them, or anyone else, from creating doors. I whirl around, trying to find it, until I feel a slow and subtle thrumming. It's coming from what appears to be a small blue stone embedded in the wall. That must be it, the arcane object Okot spoke of. The door rattles and bangs, a veritable typhoon, but the object's power keeps it standing. Then finally, after what feels like minutes of this, there's silence. The gods have spent their power. Sacrifice sustains them for only so long, and there were only a few jatu and deathshrieks in that hallway. More to the point, there are so many other things they have to attend to right now. Which means I have to move fast. The Idugu will be back, of this there's no doubt. And when they return, they'll bring reinforcements.

"Er, Deka," Acalan calls, attracting my attention. "You seeing this?"

As I swiftly turn to him, I see what he's pointing at: the blood. It not only slicks the chamber's stone floor but also colors the water inside the shallow pool circling the room. It's seeping from the three jatu lying lifeless on the floor, no doubt victims of Okot's sword. A gurgling sound leads me to a fourth, who has a sword protruding from his chest as he staggers about.

When he slides down, mortally wounded, I discover his assailant.

"Mother!" I gasp, shocked.

She's standing at the top of the stairs leading to her throne, a bewildered look in her eyes. Her hair is a living thing that trails all the way down the stairs, obscuring everything in its path. "Mother, you're alive!" Then I frown. "How can you be alive?"

"That's wha I want to know," Britta says, placing a staying hand on me while Keita does the same. "Last ye told me, yer mother was a wraith bound to the Hall of the Gods in Maiwuri."

"So the question then becomes—who is that?" Keita asks, his eyes glowing in warning.

He and Britta move to stand in front of me, a wall of protection. Ixa paces in front of them, snarling, his ears flattened in fear and challenge.

But Mother turns to me, her eyes filled with bewilderment. "Deka, is this real?" she asks, seeming stunned. "Am I truly here, in Otera?"

I'm so disoriented now, so thoroughly shaken, I don't know

what to say. This can't be Mother—Mother is dead, a spirit bound to a temple on another continent. And yet, when I glide into the combat state, staring at the soul that's inside her body, the soul is hers.

There's no question of it. It truly is Mother. She's truly here. And yet she can't be.

No matter how much I want it to be, no matter how many hopeful scenarios I imagine, there's no way that that's Mother. Even though she smells so familiar, that wonderful musk of flowers and cakes I know so well. . . . I take a trembling step toward her, stopping only when Keita and Britta stiffen even more, Ixa growling beside them.

"Mother?" I ask warily.

She nods, eyes filling with tears. "It's me, Deka. I know it seems strange, but it is."

Britta brandishes her war hammer. "I don't know who or wha ye are," she says threateningly, "but ye will leave that body right now. Ye will leave this place or we will hurt ye. Don't make us hurt ye."

Mother turns hastily to me. "Deka, I don't know why I'm here, but I do know this. I have your kelai. Here." As my friends and I tense, confused, she carefully bends toward the portion of her hair curled around her feet. Then she pulls out a very familiar black box from under it.

The moment she holds it up, an ocean of power washes over me.

If the remnants of my kelai I felt in Gar Fatu were a few rays of sunshine, this box is the sun itself, its warmth washing over me, filling me from the inside out. How I didn't feel this before, I don't know. It's so all-encompassing now, it's like a physical weight. It takes everything I have not to stagger under the sheer power of it.

"My kelai . . . ," I whisper, a thousand emotions running through me.

All my feelings are suddenly so intertwined, I don't know how to separate one from the other. The only thing that's clear is relief. After everything I've endured—all the battles I've fought—I'm finally within reach of the source of my power. All I have to do is take a few steps, and then I will have it—the thing that turns me into a god. That allows me to smite all the gods and finally bring peace to Otera. The thing that will keep me and my friends safe for infinity.

Except my feet won't move.

"Deka," Mother beckons hurriedly again, offering me the box. "This belongs to you. It's everything you've been searching for."

But my heart is now pounding so swiftly, I can scarcely breathe. A cold sweat mists over me, adding to my confusion. Why aren't I taking the box out of her hand?

"Deka, are ye all right?" Britta whispers as she glances back at me.

I force myself to nod. To calm my whirling thoughts. I exhale again, slowly this time, forcing myself to breathe out every thought, every worry. Once my mind is completely clear again, I turn to Mother. Or rather, the person my body does not think is her.

"Explain," I say swiftly. "If you truly are my mother, you will explain how you came to be here."

"It was the Idugu," Mother replies without hesitation. "They stole through the shadow vale into the Hall of the Gods after you left, and took my spirit. I woke up here and all those jatu were waiting around me." She shudders as she points at the corpses. "They were saying such awful things, how they were going to serve as vessels for the Idugu, how the Idugu planned to use me to bargain away your life.

"My life for yours, that was the deal those gods meant to strike with you."

Mother shakes her head grimly, her expression so familiar now, my heart twinges. "They forgot that I was a Shadow before. That I was once a mistress of the sword. How foolish they were. But that is a mistake they'll never make again." She offers the box to me once more. "Take this, hurry now! There's no time to waste, pet, else the Idugu will return with reinforcements."

At her words, every muscle in my body stiffens. "Pet?" I ask quietly, all my suspicions now confirmed.

"What?" The woman standing in front of me frowns in confusion.

"You called me pet." I unsheathe my atikas as I walk forward, a quiet coldness sweeping over me. She'd been doing so well, this impostor . . . oh so well mimicking Mother. But that last slip, it was too egregious to overlook. "Mother—my real mother—would never call me that. But you're not her, are you?" When she just blinks, I point my atikas. "You must be very desperate, Etzli, to use my mother's body as your vessel."

To her credit, the goddess doesn't even bother denying it.

The moment I say the words, a change comes over her, Mother's skin taking on that golden gleam I've become so intimately familiar with, her eyes becoming that consuming, overwhelming white. When she speaks now, her hair writhes around her, the same way Etzli's vines used to move whenever I entered the Chamber of the Goddesses back in Abeya.

"But you can't open the box by yourself, can you? I have to do it. At least, if I'm alive, I have to."

"Clever, clever Deka," Etzli says, her voice returned to the divine resonance I remember well. "You always were too clever for your own good."

"And you were always too greedy for yours," I return, keeping a wary eye on the hair slithering around my feet like vines. "How did you get in here? Slip into Mother's body while the other gods were at war?" I remember now, noticing how there were only two Gilded Ones, but three Idugu standing in the city.

I nod, understanding. "You came before Okot could place the arcane jewel. That's how you were able to emerge here while the other gods cannot."

"A stroke of luck on my part," Etzli admits. "Or perhaps even foresight." There's a gloating tone to her words. Etzli always did like hearing herself speak.

"So what was the plan? I open the box and you take my kelai at the moment of absorption?"

"Indeed." The goddess inclines her head.

"And the others are just all right with you doing so?" As I speak, I sneak a glance at my companions. They're all slowly and surely backing away from me, headed to different corners of the room—even Ixa, who I'm now mentally sending very specific instructions.

All of them are preparing.

If we can't use doors in here, we have to make a different plan. Have to improvise. After all, it will take time for the Idugu to return with their troops—time Etzli will use to enforce her will. I slip one hand behind my back, using battle language to signal my intentions to my friends.

We incapacitate her, take the box, and then run, I say, all the while keeping my eyes on Etzli, who's still speaking.

"They are occupied imbuing me with enough power for this task," she says haughtily.

"You mean they're opening up vales and eating everyone in them so they can feed you." Foreboding trickles up my spine. No wonder Etzli seems so confident. Hui Li and Beda are using this battle to feed her. Which means she's likely the most powerful god in Otera at the moment. She might not even be affected by the arcane jewel's power.

The goddess shrugs. "My sisters understand the importance of my task."

As she speaks, something flits past her, so swift, it's barely noticeable. A small blue bird. A nightflyer. Ixa.

I keep talking so Etzli remains engaged. "And what about Anok?"

The word causes the goddess to bristle, her hair spiking and jolting all around her. At this point, she's taken over Mother's body so completely, I barely even recognize it anymore. The sight has my fury rising even higher. After everything she's already done to me, Etzli has the nerve, the gall, to use Mother's body as her puppet.

The very first thing I will do when I become a god is destroy Etzli. Everything turns cold inside me as I make this decision. I will burn her to a crisp before her sisters' eyes, watch them despair the way I have despaired. But I have to wait for the perfect opportunity. Ixa is still flitting carefully closer to the box clutched in Etzli's hands. To act too rashly now will cost not only me but everyone else in Otera our lives.

"Do not dare speak the name of that traitor to me!" Etzli hisses, forcing my attention back to her.

"Traitor?" I tap my lips. "I thought she was your sister. If you're going to be feeding the others my kelai, it stands to reason she'll be eating as well. She'll become just as powerful as the rest of you."

"All the good it'll do her," Etzli humphs. "She'll remain caged as she is for eternity, imprisoned in her own darkness." Now Etzli turns to me, a cruel smile twisting her lips. "Imagine what that means for a god. We are the Eternal Ones. We are unending, undying."

"Such cruelty I could never imagine," I say softly.

"Is it cruelty or fairness?" Etzli returns. "She intended the same for us."

"She intended to end you. Return you to the cosmos before you end the world."

"Foolish girl," Etzli sniffs. "Once we have your power, we will build a new world. One of complete worship, complete devotion. Never again will our worshippers question our existence. They will know from the moment they're born until the moment they die that we are their mothers. And you will give us the power to do so. Come here, Deka!"

A strand of hair hurtles at me.

As I dodge, a bright blue body darts past Etzli, snatching the box. "Ixa, this way!" I shout, racing for the door as he flies in my direction.

But before I can reach, a mass of hair slams it shut with a resounding boom, its tips turning gold, as do all the other portions of the strands. They all change so completely, I can't even call them hair anymore. They are living vines, golden vines, all connected to Etzli.

And they're all instruments of her will.

"You will not escape from this room, Deka," Etzli roars. "Not using this door or any other." As I watch, horrified, the goddess covers the blue jewel beside the door with another mass of vines, protecting it from any interference as she rises into the air, her body pushed up by yet another grouping of vines.

The lengthy strands all work in concert, slithering together until they're indistinguishable from the vines of blood-eaters she used to the same effect in Abeya.

"Did you think it would be so easy?" Etzli asks, absently backhanding Kweku when he rushes her, sword in hand. She does the same with Belcalis, who valiantly tries to ambush her from the back. "Did you think I did not prepare for you and all your little tricks?"

Keita blasts a column of flame at her, but it dies the moment it nears her body.

The goddess smirks. "You can't burn what's been blessed by the celestial."

"At a high enough temperature, I can," Keita replies grimly, the fire burning in his eyes again.

I cheer him on as I again try to rush for the door. "Burn her to a crisp, Keita!" I shout. "Let this place be her pyr—"

A belt of vines snaps around my waist, yet more golden strands threading up my feet and hands. They're impenetrable, refusing to bend no matter how much I pull. "Oh, Deka . . . ," Etzli tuts as if amused. "Ever so sentimental, planning a funeral for your mother's body. But not while I'm inhabiting it."

"Then we just have to get you out, don't we," I shout back, ripping at the golden vines, which slither and lash around the room like snakes, seeking out my friends.

Britta screams as she's lifted into the air, and so do the twins and Li beside her. Only Katya, Rian, Belcalis, and Acalan remain unencumbered—Katya because she's too fast as she runs across the walls, dodging the vines, and Rian because he just stands there, frozen in fear. Belcalis, on the other hand, tries to continue running but is swiftly caught, as is Acalan, who's tossed halfway across the room when he tries to help her.

All the while, the vines continue growing over my friends. Coiling tighter and tighter.

"Deka," Britta shouts, pulling at them. "Wha do we do?" For every vine she rips out, another replaces it.

"Anything you can!" I shout to her. "Don't hold back!"

"GOT IT!" Britta says, both she and Li inhaling at the same time.

I immediately feel the power gathering. The ground suddenly erupts with a boom, gigantic metal spires ramming toward Etzli. Except, the goddess is no longer there. She's up in the air, her vines slithering so seamlessly underneath her, it's as if she's floating. When another metal spire thrusts her way, she pivots to face Britta and Li.

"Sleep now," she says, snapping her vines at them. They immediately slither up Britta's and Li's mouths and nostrils. And as I watch, terror rising inside me, yet more vines thread out through their eye sockets.

Then their bodies start turning gold.

37

❖ ❖ ❖

"NO!" I shriek, wrenching myself against Etzli's grasp. She's killed them. She's killed my friends. "STOP IT! PLEASE STOP!" I scream, tears falling.

"And why should I?" The goddess is suddenly just in front of me, floating on a mass of golden vines. "What will you give me if I stop?"

"What do you want?" I ask, everything inside me suddenly dull and lifeless now.

There's no point fighting anymore. Britta and Li are in the almost-death, and most of my other friends are effectively captured. Keita and Acalan are wrapped so tightly in vines, they can't even move, much less speak. When Keita tries, the vines slither into his mouth, choking him more surely than any gag. Even the twins, who keep blasting back her vines with their wind, are now manacled by them, tied down to the chamber floor.

All I can do now is bargain with Etzli so she doesn't hurt my

friends any further. Britta and Li can heal from an almost-death—
will heal soon, given their proximity to me: one of the gifts I
gave my friends is the ability to heal swiftly from any injury. But
I can't risk Etzli killing them any more. She might find their final
deaths. Take them from me forever.

The thought has desperation lining my voice when I ask
Etzli again, "What do you want?"

The goddess doesn't immediately answer. As my friends
struggle against her grasp, she weaves her vines into a circle
around us—a golden cage.

"Do you know what's fascinating about a deity's kelai,
Deka?" she muses. "It changes the essence of everything around
it. *Everything*—including this body." She gestures at herself, at
the changes she's wrought over Mother's body. "This hair. But
it's not hair any longer, is it?"

She clenches her fist, and the vines around me tighten, a
serpent constricting me. I gasp out a breath when they slowly,
surely begin digging into my armor.

DEKA! Ixa shouts, beginning to transform, but a negligent
flick of the wrist is all Etzli needs.

Ixa is hurled across the room, an audible crack sounding as
he lands.

"Ixa!" I shout. "Get as far from here as you can!"

Deka . . . is Ixa's frail answer. He's not leaving. Not even when
his ribs are so badly cracked.

He doesn't have to say anything more for me to understand
that. He groans as a mass of vines slithers over him, removing
the obsidian box from his claws.

The moment they return it to Etzli, she floats closer, offering it to me again.

"You know, I have waited for this moment since the last time I saw you in Abeya, looking down at my wounded body, Anok and Fatu by your side. My traitorous family. . . ." She shakes her head, tsking. Then she smirks. "But all that doesn't matter anymore. You see, you may not want to open this box, but it is inevitable. At the moment of your death, it will open, whether you wish it or not. And then, when your kelai tries to reach you, I will snatch it up."

She floats closer. "As you know, this has always been a game of speed and proximity. And despite what our counterparts plotted, I have both. So I will consume your divinity for my sisters and myself. For the future of Otera."

"For Otera?" I laugh weakly. "What do you care about Otera? No . . . all you care about is power. That's all you've cared about for the past few centuries." I stop, now shaking my head. "When did you stop being a god, Etzli? When did you stop serving the people who worshipped you and start preying on them instead?"

A snarl mottles Etzli's face. "Foolish child! Gods are not meant to serve! We are meant to rule!"

She clenches her fist again, and the vines close even tighter around me. I gasp, my breath labored as cracking sounds fill the air. My armor. It's breaking. It was only ever scales, after all. And now that it's damaged, I'm aware of that emptiness inside me again. The emptiness that needs just one final push.

"No!" I shout, struggling against Etzli's vines. I try to lift my atikas, try to fight back, but the vines wrench them to the floor with a loud clatter. I'm completely defenseless now.

And all the while the vines squeeze tighter and tighter, digging into me.

"Please," I rasp when a section of armor cracks away, leaving the skin on my belly exposed. My ribs are bending slowly, painfully inward, moving toward my organs. I can feel them creaking, feel the agony sparking inside my belly. Stars shoot across my vision as my body turns into a quivering mass of pain.

And then the vines slither across my neck.

"Just die, Deka," the goddess says, gesturing.

"NOOOOO!"

This piercing shriek comes from Katya, who somehow wrenches out of the vines entangling her, a powerful gust of wind blowing at her back. Both Adwapa and Asha are already rising from their restraints, their power blowing away the vines hurtling in Katya's direction as she jumps from wall to wall to race toward me.

When Etzli sends another mass of vines flying—this time toward the twins—Asha blasts them away while Adwapa focuses on guarding Katya's back, clearing a path for her to the golden cage.

"I'M COMING FOR YOU, DEKA!" Katya shouts, slicing through the vines making up the cage. "HOLD ON, I'M COM—"

A lance of vines stabs through her skull.

Blood trickles down Katya's face. Bright blue, vivid against the red of her skin. Bright blue, the color of the final death. The end of any alaki and the deathshriek they become.

"KATYA!" This desperate cry explodes from Rian, who has been frozen, terrified, in the same place this entire time. As frozen as everyone now is, the shock of what happened rendering all our limbs useless.

Except for Rian. He picks up a sword from one of the fallen jatu and rushes Etzli, his attack so unexpected, the goddess is, for a moment, taken aback. He slices through the golden cage with a strength I never realized he possessed. But before he can near the goddess, a single vine lashes out. A garrote.

Rian's head falls with a splatter to the floor.

"Rian . . ." The devastated whisper reverberates through my body, and it's echoed by the screaming of my remaining friends, who struggle against the bonds Etzli has now swiftly retied.

Belcalis is the first to rip her way out, her body now completely covered in the golden armor that is her divine gift—even her fingers, which she's extended into sharpened claws. She rips Acalan, Kweku, and Asha free as she runs toward the goddess, Ixa at her side. Just as she nears, however, Kweku rushes past her, Ixa keeping pace with him.

"YOU KILLED THEM!" he shouts, his eyes mad with grief as he aims his sword at the goddess. "YOU KILLED MY FRIENDS!"

"KWEKU, NO!" I shout, but before the words even leave my mouth, vines lash around both his and Ixa's feet, pulling them to the edge of the shallow water in the pool surrounding the throne.

When Asha does the same, Etzli's vines take her too. Then the bloodthirsty goddess floats over to where Kweku and Ixa are still thrashing against their bonds.

"LEAVE THEM ALONE!" This shout comes from Belcalis, but the goddess simply wraps her in a cocoon of vines, the tendrils twisting tighter and tighter until Belcalis is nothing but a golden bundle on the floor.

She does the same with both Acalan's and Adwapa's feet and hands, keeping them firmly in place. That done, she turns back to Kweku and Asha. "Now here's something you don't see often," she muses as she leans over the pair. "Both of your final deaths are drowning. It is your fate to die in the water and give me the power that I need for my task."

My eyes widen. "No, please!" I cry out.

But Etzli just gestures. The vines pull both Asha and Kweku under with little more than a whisper. Kweku thrashes, bubbles forming, but Asha's drowning is quieter. She doesn't so much thrash as she wriggles, even now trying to free herself.

"ASHA!" Adwapa screams from across the chamber. "NO! LEAVE HER ALONE! LEAVE HER ALONE!" She turns to me, her eyes pleading. "DEKA, DO SOMETHING! SAVE HER!"

But I can't. Now that the armor is cracked, my body is deteriorating fast. I can't even pull myself out of these vines. But I have to try something—*anything*. I enter the combat state, trying to find the edges of space, but they're not there. There's nothing there but the white outlines of my friends, all of them in pain, dying.

I gasp out of the combat state and turn back to Etzli, despair filling me. "Stop!" I shout. "Please stop!"

Kweku's entire body is seizing as the water enters his lungs, fills up his organs. But Asha is as silent as before. That's the thing that horrifies me the most: Asha is silent, barely twitching, as she takes on more and more water until finally, there's too much for her to survive.

She falls motionless, just like Kweku.

And then they both turn blue.

I'm shaking now. Every part of me is weak, every part of me is useless. I can't move, I can't think—all I can do is watch as the bubbles surrounding them grow weaker and weaker.

Around me, my friends scream. Adwapa tries to rush to her sister, but the vines binding her hold tight, not even budging when she summons a column of air to lift herself out of them. She's pulling so hard now, the vines rip into her skin.

Even then, Adwapa keeps pulling, calling out her sister's name.

Then the bubbles finally vanish. And the water goes completely still.

It's like all the air has left the chamber. Everyone is silent now, hanging limp against their bonds. In all the years we've been fighting, all the years we've been struggling, we've never experienced loss like this.

I can barely move anymore, I'm so destroyed.

But Etzli is shimmering with excitement as she turns back to me. Her body is engorged with power now. Flowers are blossoming in her hair, their golden petals so similar to the black ones I know, I almost vomit.

Blood-eaters.

She's made blood-eaters from the deaths of my friends.

"Is that all?" she asks, practically bouncing. "Or does anyone else wish to test their mettle against me?" She whirls, smirking as she sees all the dark blue corpses, and even those of Britta and Li, which have only the slightest sheen of gold over them, indicating they'll soon wake. When no one responds—not even Keita and Belcalis, who are still bound and gagged—she turns back to me, seeming almost disappointed. "Now then, Deka," she says, "shall we continue?"

She gestures again, and all the vines constricting me tighten all at once. The pressure is too much for the ebiki armor. It shatters; then pain slams into me like a hammer.

I begin screaming.

"DEKA!" I distantly hear Britta cry out, but I can no longer move, can no longer speak. All I can do is scream.

Now that I'm no longer protected by Ayo's armor, I'm completely alone in my body. And all my friends are gone. There's nothing I can do anymore. I have no one to call on. *Except.* . . . The thought abruptly filters past the pain, niggling at the deepest part of me.

Ixa, I say, reaching out, *I need you.*

And Ixa rises from the water.

38

◆ ◆ ◆

Ixa is a gleaming blue god when he emerges, his body changed during its time in the water. No longer is he the hulking, feline-like creature who's been by my side all these years. Now he's a tall, blue-skinned youth, his long black hair curling against golden scales shimmering over his body.

"Ixa here," he says out loud in a low, almost-human voice. "Ixa help."

Serve as my vessel, I command, slipping into the combat state.

And just like that, I'm there, inside his body, and both of us are walking out of the water as one. A dying god and her single godsworn. The only creatures who still remain standing after all the chaos Etzli has wrought. An atika is conveniently aban-doned by the edge of the pool. We pick it up, swiftly twirl it to test the heft.

This seems to amuse Etzli. "Using your godsworn?" She tsks. "It's very sweet, but it won't help you, Deka."

She gestures, and a barrage of vines comes our way. We easily dodge, moving so fast, we're like wind across water. It's as if our bodies and minds are one now, our thoughts completely merged for one common goal: take back the box.

Etzli was correct, this is a game of speed and proximity. And now I have the speed, and soon, I'll have the proximity.

"Get the box, Deka!" Britta shouts at me, already revived from her almost-death as I'd suspected she would be. "Just get the box an' take it away from he—"

Etzli's vines descend like a wave, smothering her.

"BRITTA!" I shout, but I keep going. It won't do any good trying to save anyone. I just need to get to my kelai.

But when I rush toward the mass of vines holding it, they *move*, darting across the floor with such speed, I know Etzli is concentrating all her focus on it. Nevertheless, I persist, until finally, the box is within reach. Just a few lengths more and—

"Your body is dying, Deka."

Etzli's triumphant declaration sends me whirling back toward the throne at the center of the room. The goddess is now seated there, my dying body slung over her lap, all its wounds bleeding so profusely, my entire skin seems golden . . . which is the only reason I can spot the blue now beginning to seep from deep inside it. The blue that's slowly overpowering the gold.

My and Ixa's body turns heavy, and suddenly I can no longer move.

Deka, Ixa whispers, frightened. *Why Ixa so tired now?*

I don't reply, because I know the answer. I know why Ixa feels so exhausted, why I'm now barely able to think, barely able to move. I'm dying, but because I'm in Ixa's body, I'm taking him with me.

Across the room, Etzli dabs a finger in one of my wounds and holds it up. The blue is vibrant against the golden brown of her skin. "The final death. After all this time, it's finally here," she says, those white eyes glowing. "All your struggles, all your fighting—it's all at an end now, Deka. Rejoice in it. Glory in it. Finally, you can rest."

She gestures, and my knees buckle.

When I look down, I'm slumped over the floor, muscles weighted down by the encroaching darkness. The immovable heaviness. I can't even move when sandaled feet walk down the stairs to rest in front of me.

"Will you take your godsworn with you?" Etzli asks, kneeling at my side. "Or will you die there"—she points—"in your own body, brave to the end?"

"NO, DEKA!" This shout comes from Keita, who's still fighting against Etzli's vines. He's managed to pull them out of his mouth, even though they keep slithering back in. "Run away, Deka! You can get away, you can fight this!"

But there's no fighting this, certainly not with Ixa's body as exhausted as it is. Not with all my remaining friends in Etzli's grasp. There's only one thing I can do now. "Promise you'll free them," I say, looking up at her.

The goddess laughs, seeming startled. "Oh, Deka, do you really think you're in a position to bargain?"

I glance around me. "No, but I can make this difficult for you. I can try to run. Perhaps even surrender my kelai to the Idugu. This is their territory, after all. I assume there are rules that bind your conduct when in each other's temples? Divine covenants and such?" When Etzli glowers, I nod. So I was correct to think the divine covenants Okot told me of would impact other gods as well. "But if you let them go, I'll come willingly."

"A graceful defeat." Etzli seems to ponder this.

"Yes," I say. "So will you let them go?"

"Very well." Etzli is almost pouting now as she makes a negligent gesture.

Just like that, all the vines loosen, and all my remaining companions are free. They're alternately gasping for air and staring at me, devastated.

Adwapa is the first to move. She rushes to her sister's side and pulls her corpse out of the water, her wails so loud now, they drown out every other sound. She doesn't even seem to notice anything else anymore.

But Britta turns to me, her body still unsteady from its recent revival. "Deka, no," she begins. "Ye don't have to do this. We can fight, we can still win. . . ."

I shake my head. "You have to go."

"I won't leave you." Keita rushes forward, not even caring when the vines hiss and snap at him. He makes his way to my and Ixa's side, and then he picks up our hand, our blue skin stark against the brown of his.

Belcalis, for her part, says nothing as she approaches. She just kneels by my side, quiet, as does Acalan.

I shake my head—Ixa's head—as I regard them all. "You have to go. I'm dying, and I can't fight anymore." I look at Katya's corpse slumped on the floor. Rian's. Kweku's. Asha's. So much loss. So many lives ended so painfully. And for what? We were never going to win in the first place.

We were never gods.

"We fought bravely," I say, returning my attention to my remaining friends. "But we have no more strength. *I* have no more strength. All I can give you is this, the chance to get out of here. The chance to choose death on your own terms. To be together at the end."

My words seem to devastate Keita. "What about you and me?" he asks, tears in his eyes. "What about me and Britta and Li and Belcalis? You promised to stand by our side."

"Eternity, ye said," Britta reminds me.

I turn from them, that heaviness growing steadily over my and Ixa's body. "I lied," I whisper. "So go." When no one moves, I imbue as much power as I can into the word. "GO!" I roar. "And take Ixa with you." I begin sinking into the combat state once more.

No, Ixa protests deep inside our mind. *Ixa stay with Deka!*

But I'm already traveling back to my body, already sinking in. Now that familiar pain is washing over me, an ocean of it, but I ignore it to watch my friends woodenly walking away, their bodies unable to disobey the sheer amount of power I put into my voice. None of them are wearing their infernal armor anymore, so they're powerless against it. Powerless against any ability I use on them.

As Keita opens the door, he turns to me one last time, betrayal stark in his gaze. But he does as I command and exits, dragging Ixa's body along behind him.

No! Deka no leave me! Ixa cries, struggling. Then Britta grabs him and tosses him over her shoulder, and that's that.

Ixa may be strong, but Britta is stronger.

Her eyes are filled with tears as she exits, a wealth of sorrow in her gaze. And rage as well, because I feel, rather than see, Britta slamming her palm against the wall. Destroying the door's foundation, and the jewel beside it.

A cool hand strokes my brow. Etzli's. She's returned to the throne and is settling me on her lap once more. "See, that wasn't so difficult," she coos. "All you had to do was succumb. You're all alone now. As alone as you were when you entered this realm. That is the way of things for mortals, you see. Everyone has to learn it at some time."

"Except I'm not mortal." When Etzli's brow furrows, little windstorms forming around it to mark her confusion, I continue, "And I wasn't alone when I came here."

Memories flash past, my life playing out in front of my eyes. I focus on one. A beautiful song that rose to the skies as I fell. The song of the ebiki, all of them singing out in concert.

"The ebiki were there," I whisper, a tear sliding down my cheek. "They were there and they sang to me." And they weren't alone either. Now I see a universe of colors, of scents all flashing past me. "The entire world, it sang."

And I can hear it now, the singing.

How did I ever forget it?

I suppose I've been in this body so long, I've become restricted by it. What was it that the Being said about flesh and corporeal bodies? Oh yes, they constrain you. They make you forget what it is to connect. To be a part of—not just other people but the world itself. The universe.

I can hear that song again if I want. Queen Ayo promised me this. All I have to do is reach.

So that's precisely what I do.

I reach with every last fiber of my being across the distance, across the city, across continents, across even the oceans themselves. The song is a hardy thing. It can traverse time and space, given the opportunity. But all I need it to do at this moment is cross one ocean.

When a door begins opening in the chamber, Etzli glances around, alarmed. She jolts upright, then glares down at me. "What is this? What are you doing? You shouldn't be able to do that, the jewel—"

I almost savor the look in her eyes when she looks at the door and realizes: the jewel is gone. "Britta broke it," I rasp with what remains of my breath. "She did it when you allowed me to let her and the others leave. Also, I was never alone. Not then, and certainly not now. I'd almost forgotten that. Or, rather, I was afraid. Isn't that funny? You made me afraid of my own power."

"What are you babbling about?" Etzli seems almost hysterical now. She whirls about as the door in the chamber opens wider and wider, its size mimicking the ones now opening all across the city. "Stop that!" she shouts. "I command you to stop!"

"I will not," I say quietly. Then I slowly, painfully motion my head toward the door. "Etzli, meet Queen Ayo."

That's all I'm able to say before a massive reptilian form slams into Etzli. Suddenly, the goddess is nothing more than a shrieking doll as the ebiki queen, now much smaller than usual, picks her up and slaps her across the room. The wall cracks as the goddess lands, but I don't even wince. I want to enjoy every moment.

Etzli's vines bristle up, attempting to protect her from Ayo's next strike, but they're no match for the ancient monarch, who tears through them like they're paper before slamming into the goddess again. As Ayo tramples Etzli, familiar footsteps rush up the stairs to the throne.

"Deka!" Britta says, darting over, Keita, Belcalis, and Acalan by her side. Adwapa is nowhere to be seen, but she took her sister's corpse with her when she left, so I don't imagine she's returning anytime soon.

A river of pain washes over me at the thought. Asha, Katya, Rian, and Kweku. So much loss. I can scarcely breathe, I'm so overwhelmed by it all.

"Are you all right?" Keita asks, agitated.

"Surviving," I grit out. Then I turn my eyes to Britta. "My thanks for smashing the jewel, by the way."

"Of course." Britta nods.

Another shriek forces my attention back to the battle, where Queen Ayo uses her entire body to grind Etzli into the wall, not even moving when vines attempt to wrap against her midsection.

"DEKA!" Etzli shrieks, panicked. "DEKA, STOP THIS!"

"But it's not me who's doing it," I point out. "That's Queen Ayo, one of my godsworn."

"It is . . . our pleasure . . . to serve," the ebiki queen growls before advancing on Etzli again.

Except now, the goddess has another trick up her sleeve. She gestures, and a door opens, one that connects to the battle outside Hemaira's gates. There's a pause in the sands as the nearby soldiers freeze, already unnerved, no doubt, by the hordes of ebiki trampling the armies of the gods.

Then something swoops over them. A familiar leather-winged figure.

"Do not touch her!" Melanis shrieks as she dives into the chamber, droplets of gold flying in her path. She's now so severely wounded, she's bleeding in several places.

She attempts to slam into Ayo, only to be pummeled aside by White Hands, who charges through the now-closing door, Sayuri at her side. As Melanis shrieks, infuriated by this interference, White Hands holds out her hand and whispers.

"To ash," the Firstborn commands.

And Melanis plummets to the floor, one of her wings dissolving to dust.

Behind them, Sayuri palms her spear as if she doesn't even see Ayo and Etzli fighting. "My turn," she rumbles, and then, as Melanis flaps there, still shrieking, she stabs her through the other wing, tearing the leathery appendage to shreds.

White Hands taps her out of the way, then beckons for Melanis to stand. "My turn again," she says grimly, stepping in front of her sister.

Melanis forces herself back up with a hateful sneer. "Two against one," she growls. "Such fair odds."

"This was never about fairness," White Hands says calmly as Sayuri walks to her side.

They both stare at Melanis as they begin to speak. "Melanis the Bright, second-born of the Gilded Ones," White Hands and Sayuri say together. "For your crimes against your sisters and against this realm, we shall end you now."

"With what?" Melanis spits. "You don't even know my final death. Do your wor—"

White Hands's punch lands at the same time Sayuri's spear pierces Melanis's stomach. I only barely hear the words, "To ash," and then the ancient alaki collapses to dust upon the chamber floor.

The spear lands on top of the mound it formed, its solitary

clink the only sound that heralds the death of Melanis the Bright, once the most beloved of all the Gilded Ones' daughters.

White Hands clicks her tongue. "Of course we know your death, dearest sister. We've always known it. We just hoped you would stop being hateful before we had to use it." She turns to me. "Greetings, Deka," she says conversationally. "Still at it?"

"Only just now sorting things out."

"Better late than never" is her calm reply.

As I watch her, a movement stirs beside me. My companions are gathering. Keita is holding something in his hand: the box. "Here it is," he says quietly. "What do you want to do now?"

"What do I want?" I repeat. I ponder the question until a rattle sounds from my throat—a very familiar one. "I'm dying," I say, somehow surprised.

I've been dying all this while, and yet my final moments still come as something of a shock.

"Oh, Deka," Britta says. Tears in her eyes, she grasps my hand tighter.

Keita does the same with the other one, his grip slipping because of just how much blood is flowing down my fingers. I'm cold now. So very cold. Everything is becoming muted. I can't even hear the fighting happening around me.

Not that it matters anymore. Ayo has Etzli under control, and, more to the point, I'm not afraid of her anymore. I'm not afraid of any of the gods. All this time, I've feared their power, forgetting that I had my own.

And they can't take what wasn't theirs in the first place. I had to give it. That's why they did everything they did. Why they told me so many lies. So I'd be so scared, or worse, so grateful, I'd give everything of myself to them.

And the worst thing is, I almost did.

I almost believed their lies, even up until the end.

I blink, my eyes unseeing, as a warm weight curls over my body. Ixa, once more in his kitten form. *Ixa make Deka warm again,* he says plaintively, trying to share his heat.

But it's too late. Much too late.

I thank him nonetheless. *Thank you, Ixa,* I whisper. *I love you.*

Then I turn to Keita, squeeze his hand. "I love you." I can't see his face anymore, nor Britta's, nor Belcalis's, nor any of the others, who are now all shimmering white figures in the distance, despite the fact that I'm not in the combat state. "I love all of you. Always have, from the moment we met in the Warthu Bera."

"I love you too, Deka," Keita's voice is a faraway whisper, and it's laden with sorrow.

As is Britta's. "Yer not alone, Deka," she whispers, her voice fading into the distance too. "No matter wha happens, ye are us, an' we are ye. Always have been. Always will be. Take that with ye as ye go."

You are us, and we are you. The thought wraps itself around me as the world dims, a reaffirmation. Everything is one, as it has always been. It's just as the Being told me, as Myter and even Anok said. Everything is one.

Darkness creeps in, a slow and shivering cold.

But it doesn't bother me. Nothing does as I move upward, my spirit rising toward the light. I can see my friends below, shaking my unmoving body. Crying as if their hearts have broken.

"DEKA. DEKA!" Britta screams, but I no longer heed her.

Instead, I turn toward the box, the one that's been slowly opening while everyone was distracted. A light is emerging from it. A thousand colors, all hues I've never before seen, each one threaded with sounds: Birds' wings. Waves crashing. Black holes singing their most mournful laments. All of it together forming a name. My name. The one I could not utter when I was in my body, clothed in flesh. Limited by the cage that was mortality.

I reach for it. Reach for my name, singing high into the sky. And the universe slams into me.

A star whizzes by. Another million. Billions. I am the expanse now, the ever-watchful eye. I remain as I am, awed witness as planets form and die, as galaxies crash into each other, creating new ones—new life. Gods are formed, immeasurable glowing infants sent by the Divine Hand to watch over each world. I see myself as I was in the beginning, the Singular, a glowing mass intertwined with the ones who would come to name themselves the gods of Maiwuri and the gods of Otera—the Gilded Ones, the Idugu, the Maiwurians—all of us woven together, the world that is Kamabai forming inside us, just as we form inside it. All of us inextricably linked—one organism and yet separate beings.

But somewhere along the way, a few of the others—the Gilded Ones and the Idugu—stopped seeing that. Turned so far toward what they thought was humanity, they removed themselves from the natural order, and in doing so, destroyed everything they were meant to be, everything they already were. I watch as the white and green of corruption creeps through them, infecting our pantheon, spreading until our siblings in Maiwuri seal us off, splitting the world in half. But I remain nearby, a silent witness. A hopeful mirror that never managed to reflect to the others what it should have.

433

And now?

The thought moves through me, a reverberance across universes.

Now I look across Otera, my gaze orienting on that which is closest: Etzli, body filled with fear as she gazes up at me, seeing the wonder, the magnificence, of what I am. That fear coils through her, a sickly white–tinged purple, cliffs crumbling and falling upon themselves.

She is still in the body of my mortal mother, the abomination of it so obscene, curdled gray twists me with displeasure.

Etzli seems to sense my anger, because she casts about desperately from where she's trapped under the claw of the ebiki queen. "You do not like the sight of me in this body?" she says, a wheedling, nearly human sound. "I will remove myself."

She shifts, and within moments, she has abandoned her vessel of flesh.

The Etzli I remember floats in front of me once more, a glowing brown silhouette threaded with vines. Once, she was responsible for looking after growing things, but gone are the trees, the mountains and fields that once formed her being. Now all that remains is a mass of serpentine vines, each one withered, as her spirit has become.

She prostrates herself in front of me, so profanely human a gesture, another shiver of displeasure prickles over me, winking out the stars in nearby galaxies.

She's about to beg for her life.

You do not have to do this, she pleads. *We can be allies. You said you didn't want to be alone. Don't you want to be part of a pantheon once more? My sisters and I, we can be with you, help you shape Otera in your image. That is what you wish, is it not?*

434

I orient myself closer, shaking the nebulas that form around the human equivalent of my head in refusal. *I wish to serve the realm I was placed in. I wish to protect the natural order, to help those I serve understand the divine within themselves. That is our purpose.*

The very words bring clarity. All those years of searching, of trying to understand. And yet the answer was always inside me. Just as it was always inside everyone. All of us are part of the natural order, all of us are part of the divine—every person, every thing, part of the great wheel that is the universe, that is the glory of life and yet Not Life.

Purposes can change, Etzli argues. *We tried to aid the Oterans, to show them that which they could not see. We even birthed children for that purpose, but all of them were blind. Mortality blinds you. Even a drop of it is enough to sever you from greater understanding.*

And yet you fell prey to such fallacies too, I remark.

As will you. Etzli is angry now, and her frustration sparks around her in burnt-orange tones. *You think you know all because you are renewed. But you know nothing, you understand nothing.*

I consider her words.

I know pain, I tell her. *I know what it is to suffer, to push back against a fate you cannot see. I know what it is to be human. I know what it is to be alaki. I know what it is to be your Nuru. And soon, I will know what it is to be your Angoro.*

My words only deepen her anger, a volcano of rage, but it does not shake through the cosmos as it would have. Etzli is muted. Nearly human now—as are her sisters, as are the Idugu. All of them fallen so far. The sadness of this thought causes a nearby lake to turn to ice. I breathe it back to its normal temperature, reawakening the fish caught in the onslaught.

All these people you think you serve, all those friends you sought to

435

protect—what do you think will happen now that you are what you are? Etzli sneers. *Soon, you will forget your mortal life and then your mortal emotions, and you will be as you were. As we were.*

Her words send another upheaval through me, mountains of ice shaping and forming in distant oceans. I glance at her. *Your words are offensive to me. Cease.*

They are the truth, Etzli spits. *End us all if you wish, and you will soon become like us. A god alone does not remain a god for long. Even we, the Eternal Ones, can suffer the effects of loneliness.*

As I ponder her words, I look down at Anok, imprisoned in the stones under Abeya. Separated from her sisters and yet a part of them as always. Etzli tries to follow after me, but I motion, restraining her where she is.

This enrages her. *Do not ignore me, Deka!* she shouts. *Do not dismiss me.*

Such noise. . . . I continue onward, stepping lightly on the stone cell, which glitters with the unending blackness that is Anok's essence. At my lightest touch, the stone explodes, freeing the goddess, who re-forms and bows to me respectfully, yet another human gesture.

It is time, I say. *I am here to fulfill my vow to you.*

And not a moment too soon. The green of corruption coils around her, constricting her. How she has remained cognizant for so long, I do not know.

I am grateful, Anok says. *Although, I must confess, I do not know what to call you now. Daughter, sister, son, brother, child, self. All these things you are to me. So what shall I call you? I no longer know your true name. And you should not offer it, not when I am as I am now.*

I ponder this query until finally, I arrive at an answer. *Deka,* I say firmly. *I am all you have said and more, but I find I have grown fond of this identity. Deka.*

Anok laughs. *Our Angoro, our slayer.*

Indeed. Are you prepared? I do not know why I offer her this courtesy, only that of all the Oteran gods, she is the only one who tried to remain steadfast to her purpose. That effort in itself is enough.

Anok looks down. *I wish for a moment.*

We wish for a moment. I turn to find Okot waiting behind me, his essence just as scored with the corruption as Anok's. And yet, like her, he retains something of his purpose. I see it now, how he guided Myter to us in Gar Nasim after we escaped the shadow vale. They had been waiting there for weeks, but it was only when he led them that they were able to find us.

That was not his only method of helping us, though he did not realize what he was doing at the time. He also made that pretense of capturing us in Irfut so we would be pointed in the direction of searching Gar Fatu, another malevolent-seeming action that nevertheless helped us on our journey.

It puzzles me. *Why?* I ask. *Why did you help us? Even as you pursued us, you gave us aid.*

I did not realize it then, but I felt guilt, Okot admits. *A human emotion. I wanted it to end, though I did not know how. Then Anok was imprisoned, and I began to speak with her in secret.*

We had forgotten we were one, Anok continues, floating closer to him. *But once we were reminded, we came to an agreement. We would do what we could to aid you.*

And I would pretend to hinder you the entire while, in the event that my brothers caught wind of it. Thankfully, they did not. And now, here we are. Okot turns to Anok, smiling, a thousand flowers blossoming in the wake of his expression. *If our time is at an end, let it be together. We were once one. In these last few moments, let us be as we were.*

Anok smiles. *Indeed,* she says. And that is the last word she speaks.

I watch, something akin to wonder spreading through me, as Anok extends her hand to Okot and he does the same. Their forms meld, transforming until they become one darkness, one universe of shadows, forever bound together. I do not have to say their names, do not have to sing them out of existence, because, as I watch, they sing together, one final, blissful melody that echoes throughout the universe of heavens.

And then they are gone.

And now remain the other six, all huddled together, different shades of fear and defiance in their bodies, all of which merge into a sickening array of storms that boil across the land called Otera.

Even though I already know their answer, I nevertheless ask the question: *Do you wish me to sing the song of your dispersal, or will you do it yourselves?*

When I allow them to speak, unsealing their mouths, a barrage of protests and pleading assaults me. And nowhere, in any of it, is remorse.

So I orient closer and begin to sing. An entire realm joins me as I sing the song of Etzli and Etal, of Hui Li and Hyobe, of Beda and Bekala. I sing their rainbows and their storms, their dewdrops searing across the surface of volcanoes, their stars spinning universes into the light. I sing all the things that they are and all the things that they were, and as I sing, they begin to brighten, light shining through their beings, chasing away the traces of green, the traces of white, the traces of everything malevolent, until soon, they are nothing but brightness, nothing but specks, dust in the universe.

Stars, soon to be reborn.

With them go their vales, the rifts closing up, repairing as if they never were. I spirit the humans inside them back to their homes, back to their loved ones, whichever of them still remain, but the creatures—the vale wraiths and the smaller shades—I gather together in a new world, a dark, cold place far from this one. They had no say in their creation. Why, therefore, should I stand as the hand of their destruction? Better I send them to a place where they will thrive and, perhaps one day, develop sentience and birth gods of their own.

The other monstrosities and wonders the old pantheon visited upon Otera, I send to the remotest portions of the realm, far enough away that the more sentient creatures will be safe from their predation and that they, as well, will be safe from them.

Then I turn my attention to the battlefields, the divine armies disoriented by the loss of their creators, the Oteran armies steeling themselves for any new conflict that may arise.

Return home, I whisper into the minds of every soldier. *The war is ended now. You have lost enough.*

And one by one, the soldiers begin gathering their weapons, their wounded, and their dead, then they disperse from the fields and the sands, back to the homes they came from, a slow but steady exodus.

And once again, I am alone in the quiet. And the weight of my actions heaps upon me. Not sadness, not that human of an emotion. But quiet. Stillness. I am done. I have ended my siblings, the fellow members of my pantheon. What shall I do next?

I feel it before I see it, the peaceful light shining over me. The Being so enormous, I feel engulfed by it and yet equal all the same.

All and yet one.

"Well?" it asks, flowing toward me. "It is done."

"Yes," I say. "They are ended. But why could you not end them yourselves?"

This is the question that has plagued me since I accepted the Being's existence. Its benevolence.

It shakes the universes that are its head. "We are the natural order. We are the divine hand. We are all things—even you. That which you undertake, we undertake."

"I am your process," I say, finally understanding. "I am your balancing."

"That is the nature of the Angoro." The Being peers at me. "Well, then, have you decided? Shall we end this world or re-make it?"

I consider my options, ponder them well. It takes me centuries and it takes me a moment. "We were all. And yet one," I say.

"That is the order of things," the Being agrees.

"We are all of us gods. And we are all part of the divine order."

"Indeed."

"Even them." I look down at my friends, who are carrying my body out of the chamber. At all the armies, throwing down their weapons.

The gods are gone. And everything is chaos. The dead, the wounded—suffering. So much suffering now. It resounds into the universe, a symphony of pain.

"Even them," the Being reaffirms, its eyes gazing back at my friends, who are currently heading toward the garden.

It already understands my intent, but then, it always has.

"I wish to share my divinity," I say. "I wish for them to ascend as well."

"All of them?"

"No." I look down at my friends, seeking to understand. Who among them should ascend, and who should remain?

And then it occurs to me: that is not my decision to make. Everything is a choice. That is where my predecessors strayed.

But I will not make the same mistakes.

I orient down. "I will ask them," I say, looking at my friends. "But first, I have one final thing to do."

39

◆ ◆ ◆

Mother's corpse seems peaceful in the darkness. Now that she's no longer inhabited by Etzli, her hair has returned to its original form and coils around her. She looks asleep again, but I know she's not. This isn't Mother; it's an empty vessel, one that holds nothing of her anymore. And yet, the sight of it carries such weight, an iceberg in the Northern regions splinters under its heft.

As I flow down toward it, a presence touches mine. Bala.

The god of the pathways is here, Myter, as always, by his side. "Is it difficult," he asks curiously, "to detach yourself from mortal longings?"

"I suppose," I reply. "I am newly re-formed; much of me is still mortal. And I do not wish to destroy that part of myself. I wish to always remain this way."

"Always is quite a long time," Bala remarks.

"Indeed, young deity." Sarla, god of wisdom, flows into the conversation, as do all the other gods of Maiwuri, who rise from their thrones to gaze upon me now that I have returned to their gathering chamber. Mother is here too, and I lay her corpse at her feet.

When she sees it, her eyes widen. And then she sees me, the small part of me that is visible to her now that I am a god. And that small part is enough to send her falling to her knees. "Deka!" she gasps, eyes round. "You're—"

"Restored?" I incline my head. "Indeed. I am divine once more."

Mother nods, seeming almost sad, though she tries not to show it. But I can see the blues of melancholy drifting around her spirit. "So it is time for me to go," she says quietly.

"Indeed." I walk over and take her hand. It feels almost warm. But that is because I'm touching her essence, the truest part of her spirit. "You have done enough, Mother," I say. "It's time for you to rest."

She smiles ruefully. "I do deserve it after all these years, don't I?"

"Yes." I touch a hand to her cheek, marveling at how delicate she is, how fragile her existence. "More than anyone, you deserve rest."

She looks around. "Where will I go?"

"To a place where all your troubles will seem like a distant memory," I say, following behind Bala, who is already opening the pathways. A golden warmth suffuses the temple, birdsong echoing in the distance. "I will walk with you the entire way."

"I would like that." Mother smiles. "You know, when you were a child, you would toddle behind me, saying exactly that when I tried to pick you up. You were very stubborn."

"I can only imagine. . . ."

Mother doesn't say anything else. Behind me, her body is swirling, every part of it turning into starlight. Returning to the glory from which it came.

And then we're there, in the wooden cottage at the edge of the forest that contains Mother's memories from the fondest period in her life. The door opens, and Father pokes his head out, a child beside him. Me, although it is the version of me that died when I was reborn a god. The version of me that will never understand what I am now.

She too deserves happiness, and I smile as she beckons eagerly to Mother.

"Hurry, Umu," Father says, beckoning as well. "I just felled a horned deer by the lake. Massive one too, you should see the meat on him. I've got a roast going."

Mother wipes her hands on her robes, excitement shining in her eyes. She looks at Father and the child as if she's seeing them for the very first time. "I suppose I've got to hurry and help, don't I?" she asks him.

"Or you could just stand there and give me compliments," Father suggests—his favorite thing. "'Oh, Elrond, how wonderfully you roast that deer,'" he mimics in a high-pitched voice as he begins closing the door behind her.

Mother turns to me, gives me one last smile, and then she's gone.

A feeling suffuses me—not quite sadness, but something near to it. I watch my family through the cottage window as it fades from view. "They seem happy," I say.

"They are happy. That is what the Blissful Lands are for."

"And the girl?"

"We are all," Bala reminds me.

444

"And we are one," I finish. Then I look up at him. "Will you follow me to one last place? I confess, I am nervous."

"Nervous—another human emotion," Bala muses. "What does it feel like? I have tasted it through Myter but never experienced it myself."

"It feels like the first rumblings of a newborn volcano. Alternatively, it is a hive of bees in your belly."

"I shall have to try it once," Bala says, the locks of his hair already extending to create another pathway.

40

◆ ◆ ◆

The palace grounds are a different place from when I left them. Perhaps that is because the moment I emerge, flowers spring in my wake, the sun focuses its gentlest beam in my direction. Or perhaps I am that beam, making my way across the grass to my companions, who kneel around my former body, their eyes overflowing with tears, their bodies broken by grief. Ixa curls around me in the kitten form I love so much, his grief a living thing—one echoed by his mother and the other ebiki, who follow this solemn procession in their smaller, humanlike forms. They all wail and cry tears as bitter as the blood now salting the land of Otera.

And yet I am here. I am as I always was, and somehow I am more. That is the conundrum of divinity. I wonder if I will get used to it.

Ixa is the first to notice me. *Deka?* he says, rising, wonder in his eyes. A precious fluff of a thing, he bounds in my direction. *Deka come back?*

In a manner of speaking, I say, smiling, when he arrives.

His movement alerts Britta, who gasps, eyes widening as they gaze upon my new form. Where once I was flesh and bone, I am now darkness and sunlight intertwined. I am the fire of a thousand volcanoes, the sting of a thousand blades. I am the cry of dying soldiers, the wail of newborn babies. And I am the softness of a mother's touch, the warmth of a parent's love. All these things I am and more.

I am Otera itself, the wishes of a dying realm in the process of being slowly reborn.

"Deka?" Britta asks, stumbling up. "Deka, is it truly ye?"

The others follow her gaze, eyes wide, hands outstretched as if to touch me. And yet, if they were to do so, their hands would pass through me. Just as Ixa's body does, though he keeps trying.

I nod, a human enough gesture, and the grass ripples in concert with my movement. "Yes," I say. "And no. I am changed." I repeat the same to Ixa with my thoughts, showing him what I am now, so he understands.

When he humphs and lies on the grass, I smile. He is not impressed, but that is his prerogative as my very first godsworn. I return my gaze to Britta, who still gapes as she circles me.

"Yer a god now," she says in that funny mortal manner of turning questions into statements.

"Indeed."

"So can you bring Asha back?" Adwapa asks, eyes red with tears as she hurries over, her sister's corpse still in her hands. "Can you bring them all back?"

I shake my head. "I cannot."

"Why?" Adwapa shrieks, striking me as if her hands can actually land. "You're a god! Why can't you bring my sister back?"

"It would go against the natural order."

"Confound the natural order! We're talking about Asha!"

"Indeed we are, which is why I have something to show you." I point. "Look."

There, in the distance, are Asha, Katya, Rian, and Kweku, standing in front of a golden field, spires rising in the distance. Adwapa's eyes round. "The Afterlands?"

I nod.

"They're real?"

"For those who wish them," I explain. "We create our own Afterlands until we're ready to be born again. Such is the nature of the Great Circle."

"Adwapa!" Asha says happily, beckoning to her sister from the golden field. "Will you walk with me? I'm off to see our parents."

"And mine," Kweku adds cheerfully.

"We were thinking of finally getting married," Katya says shyly, smiling down at Rian.

Even though she's human now, she's still taller than him. I do not recall if she was always that way, or if both she and Rian chose it. That is the effect of the Blissful Lands: you become most yourself there.

"So, are you coming?" Asha asks.

Adwapa nods as her eyes fill with tears. "For as long as you wish."

"Me too," Belcalis says solemnly. "I would like to see you off."

"An' me," Britta adds, her eyes glistening with tears.

"And me," Li and Acalan say together.

"Let's go, then," Asha beckons, walking into the field.

Her sister follows her, Britta, Belcalis, Li, and Acalan at her side. I don't worry when they all walk into the field together.

After all, what they're seeing is a vision of it, just as much as their living minds can comprehend. Adwapa holds her sister's hands, tears flowing down her cheeks the entire way.

And then it's just Keita and I in the garden, Ixa snapping at the butterflies now returning to the newly blooming trees.

He's been standing quietly here all this time, just looking at me, as if he's trying to comprehend. "How does it feel?" he finally asks.

I look down at my hands, pondering the question. "I am all. I am one. As we all are."

"Does that mean I'll never see you again?" He turns away after he asks me, as if he cannot bear whatever answer I intend to give him.

"Your heart is breaking," I say, flowing over so I again stand before him. I press a hand close to it. "You believe I am leaving you. That I am above you now, beyond your reach."

His thoughts filter easily into my consciousness, a tangle of emotions and longing. Mortality is so fraught—due to its brevity, everything is fragile, every feeling is heightened.

"That is the nature of the divine." This reply comes from White Hands, who, with her sister Sayuri, is now walking into the garden.

Her thoughts flow easily through me, so I turn to her. "I will not become a tyrant," I say. "That is your deepest fear."

"I have many fears," White Hands replies.

I see them in her. So many, to match the knowledge that she has. The wisdom of age—of immortality. Wisdom to rival a god's.

"But you have faced them all," I acknowledge. "And you will continue doing so."

"It is not in my nature to turn away from what I fear." She gazes into the distance, where Melanis's ashes are scattering, the once proud alaki mere dust on the wind.

I say a little prayer that when she is born again, the world will be a gentler place. That I will have made it a gentler place. But everything I am depends on the wishes of those I serve. Ultimately, it is they who will determine what Otera finally becomes.

"What do you intend to do?" White Hands asks.

"I have already done it," I say. "I have dispersed my predecessors, healed their vales, and sent their creations to a world more fitting for them—one where they can thrive. They too were innocents in this."

"You have pity for monsters?"

"I have empathy for anyone who was created for a task they never asked to accomplish."

As White Hands ponders this, I turn back to the golden fields. The others are returning now. Just like in any temple of the gods, time there is different from the one in this existence. They're sure to have lived several lifetimes in the moments they've been gone. It's not enough to make up for what they've lost, but hopefully, it can suffice.

I wait until they're gathered around me before I speak again. "I have a query for you all," I say, glancing from one to the other. "A proposal, if you like."

"And what's that?" Belcalis seems more curious than suspicious.

She has accepted my new existence with remarkable composure. But then, she has always been a remarkable soul. Bruised but not broken. Compassionate but not weak.

She will make a wonderful empress.

Even as I think this, I see it, her fate unfurling in front of me. So many different threads, but for her, they all end in the same direction: the throne.

The others, however, are as yet unformed. So I ask the question I returned here to ask. "Who among you wishes to join me? Who among you will ascend to the new pantheon of Otera?"

For a moment, there is silence, and then my companions begin to speak.

"Ye want us to join ye," Britta says, her eyes blinking as she tries to understand what I'm saying. "To become gods, unending?"

"Eternal," I agree.

Britta blanches. "Eternity is a long time," she says.

I orient closer to her. "You do not need to explain any further, beloved Britta. I know your feelings, and Li's as well." I turn to where he's edged closer so he can pull her hand into his.

Britta grins. "I knew ye'd understand, even though ye are a god now. Eternity's no good for us. We want a wedding an' all that. Not right now, mind ye, but in a few years. . . ."

"It'll be a beautiful ceremony," Li agrees. "In the traditional Eastern style."

"No, Northern," Britta corrects.

"Both," Li swiftly compromises. "We'll do both."

"And then we'll have a family, children. . . . ," Britta adds. "The gods don't do very well with children, you understand."

I nod, thinking of the alaki and the jatu, both children my predecessors miserably failed. "No, they do not," I agree. "And yes, I do understand."

I turn to the rest. "What of you? What do you wish to do?"

Acalan swiftly shakes his head. "I'm thinking of visiting

Maiwuri. I might even look up Lamin, if that's all right with you."

"Of course," I say. I have already forgiven my former companion, who only did what he felt was just.

"No," Adwapa says curtly, shaking her head when I turn to her. "I have had enough of the gods."

Even me. This last part lies unspoken, but I can hear it deep inside her. I can feel it—the anger that still lingers. The pain. It is difficult to become an individual when you've spent your entire life being a pair.

I open a door beside her and point. "Mehrut is waiting there," I say. "She'll be happy to see you."

Adwapa nods brusquely, and then she's gone. I do not mind the abruptness of her departure; she'll come around in time.

The only ones yet to reply are Belcalis, Keita, and White Hands. Sayuri has wandered off, unimpressed, as she so often is, by the proceedings.

Belcalis smiles wryly. "I notice you're not even bothering to look at me."

I incline my head. "We both know you have another fate in mind. Even though you have always kept it in your heart."

"The best surprises are just that." Belcalis acknowledges. "Surprises."

"Indeed, they are," I say, then I turn to Keita and White Hands, each deep in thought. "Well, then, what about the two of you?"

White Hands nods. "I don't know about you, young jatu, but I've always wanted to see the universe. This is as good a chance as any." She takes the hand I extend her.

"And you?" I ask Keita, already knowing his answer.

"You and I, always and forever," he says, smiling.

"For eternity," I say.

"For eternity," he whispers.

Just like that, he takes my other hand, and the three of us walk into the darkness of the stars together.

EPILOGUE

◆ ◆ ◆

I used to believe fate inevitable, a plan the heavens set for every individual.

But that was when I was mortal.

Now that I am a god, I realize that fate isn't just due to some remote deity pushing a poor mortal toward an outcome that they wish. Fate also happens because an individual pushes themselves, pulls the threads of the universe a little their way.

Just look at Britta and Li.

Rainbows emerge as I regard them there, approaching each other from the opposite sides of the lakeside pavilion where their family and friends have gathered to see them finally wed. Nearly a decade ago, they were just an alaki and her uruni, forced into partnership to survive a brutal and deadly training ground. Now they're here, on this pavilion, commencing their matrimonial rites.

Bright pink petals drift across their robes, the spring breeze White Hands, Keita, and I have summoned showering them with flowers from the nearby trees. Nature in its entirety is rejoicing at this moment.

As am I.

Were I mortal, tears would be falling down my cheeks. But all I do is intertwine my hand with Keita's as we loom over the ceremony, silent, shimmering guardians, raining every blessing we can upon the pair.

You're the most beautiful bride I've ever seen, Britta, I whisper—words only she can hear as she stops in front of Li.

Oh, Deka, she whispers back, tears falling down her cheeks.

They cause little stains on the beautiful red dress she's worn for the occasion, but I refrain from removing them: Britta wants to treasure each and every part of her matrimonial rites—even her tears. After all, it took her and Li so many years to get here, what with the chaos that overtook Otera after White Hands, Keita, and I ascended.

The jatu, alaki, and priests could not believe that the gods they had devoted their lives to were gone. They rebelled for years, skirmishing against each other. Then the first death-shriek reverted, changing back to her alaki form.

I watched, hand in hand with Keita, as, over a period of days, Sayuri's body shrank back to a more humanlike one and her claws transformed back into nails. She even became mortal, as so many alaki are choosing to be. While those children of the gods who wish to can remain immortal as long as they like, immortality is lonely and twists the mind, so many decide otherwise.

The days of the immortals are nearly at an end now.

As are all the lingering divine wars—which is why Britta and Li are finally making their vows official. They've even worn robes that reflect Otera's newfound unity. While Britta's red dress is in the Eastern style, Li's is white to celebrate her Northern heritage. Both, however, wear the delicate golden half masks Belcalis crafted for the occasion, their blood intermingled in the two to symbolize their union.

How the empress of the One Kingdom found time to create them while also administering the realm, I cannot comprehend, but there's a reason Belcalis ascended to her position in the short time that has passed since I destroyed the old pantheon.

There she is now, sitting at the very front of the pavilion, beside her most trusted advisors, Acalan and Lord and Lady Kamanda, and her generals, our former karmokos. A few Maiwurian dignitaries even accompany them.

Now that both the Maiwurian pantheon and White Hands, Keita, and I have destroyed the barrier between our two empires, the two sides of Kamabai, this beautiful world, are once again connected.

I ponder the glory of this as Britta and Li clasp hands tightly and turn to Belcalis. The empress gestures, and the blood in their masks flows down, wrapping into matching golden bracelets around their wrists—a promise and an acknowledgment.

Britta and Li are equal partners, and they will remain so for as long as they live. There is no superior, no inferior. No reigning husband and lesser wife. There's just them. Together.

And as they kiss, sealing the vows that bind their souls for eternity, Ixa explodes out of the water in his enormous true form alongside a few of the other younger ebiki, a display meant to show his affection and love for them. *My* affection and love for them.

That love sings through me as I follow Britta and Li and

Adwapa through Golma market a few days later, Ixa riding invisibly on my shoulder. After spending so much time with me and the others, Ixa has become something decidedly more than an ebiki, what with his newfound ability to open doors and to travel invisibly all across the world.

The Divine Serpent, he is now called. It is a title that brings him much pride and strokes his ever-expanding ego.

It's the same with Braima and Masaima, now known as the Divine Horse Lords. As usual, they accompany White Hands, who has decided to walk with us today. As we stroll, a little girl suddenly darts over to Britta and Li, never noticing us as she stares at the pair, still in the colors of their wedding finery. They'll be wearing red and white clothes for weeks on end so that everyone who sees them knows they're married now.

I turn my attention to the little girl. She's a tiny speck of a thing, warm brown in color, with long, curly hair and tilted-up eyes. She offers Britta a flower, an ascendance flame, which is what the small pink flowers that sprang in the wake of my ascendance to divinity are called.

"Yer the one who got married, yes?" the girl asks in the lilting accent of the Northern provinces.

"Yes," Britta says, taking it. "Thank ye for the flower."

"I wish ye blessings an' fortune in the name of the Three Divinities," the child intones solemnly, calling out the title the mortals have given us.

They think there's only three of us. Little do they know there are countless gods, an untold number of deities waiting to be born in response to their wishes, their desires.

As Keita, White Hands, and I look at each other, amused, a

458

harried woman rushes after her. "Asha!" She cries. "Asha, ye'll be late for lessons." She scoops the girl up before glancing at my friends. "My deepest apologies," she offers respectfully. "I hope me daughter was not bothering you."

Britta shakes her head. "No, she was sweet. Gave me a flower."

But Adwapa's eyes are fixed on the girl and glazed with something that suspiciously resembles tears. "What did you say your daughter's name was?"

The girl idly scratches her side. "Asha. Me name is Asha, an' I'm goin' to be a warrior," she announces.

"Not a scholar?" Li prompts, amused.

The girl's nose wrinkles. "Got no interest in books, like me twin has. Spends his whole day with his head in the books. So I have to watch out for him. Easily bullied," she adds in an overly loud whisper. She nods at a scrawny little boy a few steps down the road, who's poring over some scrolls at a bookseller's tent.

Adwapa does not reply, but she's blinking rapidly now.

"Wha's wrong with ye?" the little girl named Asha asks. "Got something in yer eye?"

Adwapa gives her a watery grin. "Just remembering. . . . I had a twin once too. Long ago."

"Wha happened to 'im?"

"Her. She died during the War of the Pantheons."

"That was nearly ten years ago," her mother whispers to her. "Same year you were born."

Asha's eyes go wide. "Ye were in a war?"

"We all were," Britta corrects.

"Kill anybody?"

459

"I can tell you that later, if you're ever in Hemaira," Adwapa says. "I run a school there. A school for warriors. Perhaps one day you can apply."

"Wha's it called?"

"The Warthu Bera."

And as Asha's mother carries her away, I turn to my companions, heart brimming with that emotion I remember was called happiness. "We were successful, were we not?"

"More than, my universe," Keita says, intertwining his fingers with mine.

"Look at her," White Hands says, smiling down at the girl. "She can be whoever she wants to be. They all can."

No more prescribed roles. No false holy books. No more following arcane rules, simply because you appear a certain way. Now everyone in Otera can be who they wish. Who they are inside. And that's all I've ever asked for.

"Let us return to our abode," I say to Keita.

"Yes, my universe," he replies.

But White Hands remains behind. "I will walk a little longer," she says, heading toward the horizon.

And as she and the equus continue on, silhouettes on the horizon, I put my hand in Keita's. Together, walking alongside our mortal friends while we can, we head into eternity.

ACKNOWLEDGMENTS

◆ ◆ ◆

To my mom, thank you for showing, through courage and un-wavering determination, everything that's possible, even for a little girl from Freetown, Sierra Leone.

To my amazing editors, Hannah Hill and Sarah Stewart. Thank you so much for stepping into the fray, and more im-portantly, for not blinking an eye even as word counts went up and up and up. Also, thank you for your supportive words when I sent in a first draft that was very obviously garbage, but it was the best I could do at the time. Thank you for spinning that garbage into gold. And thank you so much for your general patience. It's been a rough year, but you guys made it so much better.

To my agent, Jodi, thanks so much for your support during this process. For helping me carve out the space I needed to make this book the absolute best it could be.

To my sister, Fatu, thanks so much for your unwavering sup-port of this book and my writing career in general.

To my bestie, Loretta, thank you for all the 6:00 a.m. notes and for your staunch and always cheerful support.

To my critique partner and bestie, PJ, thank you for enduring the panicked calls, the "I don't know what I'm doing!!!!" moments. I couldn't have done it without you.

To my bestie, Melanie, thank you for being my rock and my sounding board and for always seeking to do what is best in the world.

To Aissatou, thank you for being a living example of Black feminism in all its glory and a vision of what is possible

To ___, thank you for being out there. You know who you are. And one day, I will too.

ABOUT THE AUTHOR

NAMINA FORNA is the *New York Times* bestselling author of the Gilded Ones series. She has been published in more than twenty-four countries, and also works in film and television. She loves telling stories with fierce female leads and now lives in London, where she spends all her time trying to stay warm.

naminaforna.com

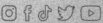